Praise for *The Killer*

"No one asked me to read Tom Wood's *The Killer*. I happened to pick it up because it looked interesting—and what a terrific discovery: *The Killer* is a nonstop, breathless, trimmed-to-the-bone thriller with action sequences that are absolutely state-of-the-art. It's the best chase novel I've read in years."

—Joseph Finder, *New York Times* bestselling author of *Paranoia* and *Vanished*

"A series of Eurozone cities provide a picturesque back-drop for the ensuing gunfights, stabbings, and explosions—not to mention sunken missiles, corrupt C.I.A. agents, and hulking Russian mobsters. The result is both a lively read and an impressively intricate thriller."

—*The New Yorker*

"A superlative fiction debut . . . Nonstop action that veers and twists from one ferocious gun battle, double cross, and betrayal to the next . . . Thriller fans will be eager to see more from this bright new talent."

—*Publishers Weekly*

"Crackles like the early work of Robert Ludlum . . . Wood bri[ng]s [his] [a]li[ve an]d en[igm]atic main character into [an intense a]nd relentless story line[.]"

—*Booklist*

"Jack Rea[ ] [ ] electrifying thriller."

—Bestselling author Simon Kernick

THE KILLER

TOM WOOD

St. Martin's Paperbacks

In loving memory of
my brother Simon, my truest believer

This is a work of fiction. All of the characters, organizations, and events portrayed in this novel are either products of the author's imagination or are used fictitiously.

THE KILLER

Copyright © 2010 by Tom Hinshelwood.
Excerpt from *War of Lies* copyright © 2011 by Tom Hinshelwood.

For information address St. Martin's Press, 175 Fifth Avenue, New York, NY 10010.

Library of Congress Catalog Card Number: 2009040295

ISBN: 978-0-312-54702-8

Printed in the United States of America

St. Martin's Press hardcover edition / April 2010
St. Martin's Paperbacks edition / August 2011

St. Martin's Paperbacks are published by St. Martin's Press, 175 Fifth Avenue, New York, NY 10010.

10 9 8 7 6 5 4 3 2 1

ACKNOWLEDGMENTS

I could not have written this book without the help of many people. First and foremost I would like to thank my brother Michael for his relentless enthusiasm, consistently excellent advice, and keen-eyed editing. *The Killer* would have been a far lesser tale without his input.

Thank you to the good people at Thomas Dunne Books for shaping this novel for the better and correcting my many mistakes. They are Bob Berkel, Angela Gibson, and my editor, Pete Wolverton. Thank you also to Elizabeth Byrne for her kind support.

I am indebted to my friends and family for their innumerable helpful comments and suggestions, in particular, to the lovely Emmalene Knowles and classy Mag Leahy for astute observations and unexpected praise. Chris Wright, Adam Bradley, Richard Graham, and Dave Thomas all deserve recognition for heroically suffering through my woeful first attempt and for being more kind than critical. Thanks also to Paul Matthews for ensuring I avoided the ultimate villain faux pas, and Simon Akrigg for helping me get past a very difficult first page.

Finally, I would like to thank my agent, Philip Patterson, for his belief, counsel, and insight.

ONE

The target looked older than in the photographs. The glow from the streetlight accentuated the deep lines in his face and pallid, almost sickly complexion. To Victor the man seemed on edge, either high on nervous energy or maybe just too much caffeine. But whatever the explanation, it wasn't going to matter thirty seconds from now.

The name on the dossier was Andris Ozols. Latvian national. Fifty-eight years old. Five-feet-nine-inches tall. One hundred and sixty pounds. He was right-handed. No noticeable scars. His graying hair was cut short and neat, as was his mustache. His eyes were blue. Ozols wore glasses for shortsightedness. He was smartly dressed, a dark suit beneath his overcoat, polished shoes. With both hands he clutched a small leather attaché case to his stomach.

At the entrance to the alleyway Ozols glanced over his shoulder, an amateurish move, too obvious to trip up a shadow, too quick to register one if he did. In Victor's experience people often paid more attention to what could be behind them, than to what lay ahead. Ozols didn't see the man standing in the shadows just a few yards away. The man who was there to kill him.

Victor waited until Ozols had passed out of the light before squeezing the trigger with smooth, even pressure.

Suppressed gunshots interrupted the early morning stillness. Ozols was hit in the sternum, twice in rapid succession. The bullets were low-powered, subsonic 5.7 mm, but larger rounds could have been no more fatal. Copper-encased lead tore through skin, bone, and heart before lodging side by side between vertebrae. Ozols collapsed backward, hitting the ground with a dull thud, arms outstretched, head rolling to one side.

Victor melted out of the darkness and took a measured step forward. He angled the FN Five-seveN and put a bullet through Ozols's temple. He was already dead, but in Victor's opinion there was no such thing as overkill.

The expended cartridge clinked on the paving stones and came to rest in a puddle shimmering with sodium-orange light. A quiet whistling from the twin bullet holes in Ozols's chest was the only other sound. Air was escaping from the still-inflated lungs—the last breath he never had a chance to release.

The morning was cold and dark, the approaching dawn only beginning to tinge the eastern sky with color. Victor was in the heart of Paris, a neighborhood of narrow avenues and twisting side streets. The alleyway was secluded—no overlooking windows—but Victor spent a moment checking that nobody had observed the killing. No one could have heard it. With subsonic ammunition and a suppressor, the noise of each shot had been muffled to a quiet *clack,* but that couldn't stop the random chance of someone deciding this particular location was a good place to relieve their bladder.

Satisfied he was alone, Victor squatted down next to the body, careful to avoid the gore draining from the quarter-inch exit wound in his victim's temple. Using his left hand, Victor unzipped the attaché case and checked inside. The item was there as he expected but otherwise the case was empty. Victor took the flash drive and slipped it into his inside jacket pocket. Small and innocuous, it barely seemed reason enough to have a man killed, but it was. One reason was as good as another, Victor reminded himself. It was all a matter of perspective. Victor liked to tell himself he did nothing more than get paid to do what the human race had been perfecting for millennia. He was simply the culmination of that evolution.

He frisked the body thoroughly to confirm there was nothing else he should know about. Just pocket litter and a wallet, which Victor opened and tilted into the light. It contained the usual: credit cards and a driver's license in the Latvian's name, cash, as well as a faded photograph of a younger Ozols with the wife and kids. A good-looking family, healthy.

Victor put the wallet back and rose to his feet, mentally re-checking how many rounds he'd fired. Two to the chest, one to the head. Seventeen left in the FN's magazine. It was simple math but protocol nonetheless. He knew the day he lost count would be the day he squeezed the trigger only to hear the dreaded dead man's *click*.

He'd heard it before when the gun had been in another's hand, and he'd promised himself then that he would never die like that.

His gaze swept the area again for signs of exposure. There were no people or cars in sight, no footsteps to be heard. Victor unscrewed the suppressor and placed it into a pocket of his overcoat. With the suppressor in place the gun was too long to be properly concealed and too slow to draw with speed. He turned on the spot, locating and retrieving the three empty cartridges from the ground before the spreading blood reached them. Two were still warm but the one from the puddle was cool.

The half moon was bright in the sky above. Somewhere beyond the stars the universe continued forever, but from where Victor stood the world was small and time all too short. He could feel his pulse, slow and steady, but maybe four whole beats per minute above his resting heart rate. He was surprised it was so high. He wanted a cigarette. These days he always did.

He left the alley, shoes virtually silent on the hard, uneven ground. He'd been in Paris for a week awaiting the go-ahead—and he was glad the job was almost over. All that remained was to stash the item tonight and contact the broker with its location. It hadn't been a difficult or even risky contract; if anything, it had been simple, boring. A standard kill and collect, beneath his skills, but if the client was willing to pay his outrageous fee for a job any amateur could have fulfilled, it wasn't Victor's place to argue. Though something in the back of his mind warned him it had been too easy.

Before he disappeared into the city he took one last look at the man he'd murdered without word or conscience. In the dim light he saw the wide, accusing eyes of his victim staring after him. The whites already black from the hemorrhaging.

TWO

08:24 CET

There were two of them.

Medium build, casually attired, nothing remarkable about either except for the fact that they were too unremarkable. The Hôtel de Ponto was on Paris's chic Rue du Faubourg Saint-Honoré, and its guests were wealthy tourists and business executives, men and women adorned with designer garments. In an everyday crowd the two would blend in. But not here.

Victor saw them the instant he was through the main entrance. They were standing in front of the elevators at the far end of the lobby, their backs to him. Both stood completely still, one with hands in pockets, the other with arms folded, waiting. If any words passed between them they did so without any change in body language.

The grand lobby was quiet, less than a dozen people occupying space. It had a high ceiling, marbled floor and pillars, an abundance of exotic potted plants set throughout, green leather armchairs grouped together in the corners and central space. Victor headed toward the front desk that ran along the wall to his right, walking at a relaxed, casual pace despite the potential danger. He kept the men in his peripheral vision at all times, ready to act should one look his way. He hadn't fully made up his mind about the duo but in Victor's business a potential threat was a definite threat until proved otherwise. In the lobby he was exposed, vulnerable, but nothing in his demeanor betrayed that. He drew no attention from the other people in the room. He acted and looked just like them.

Fellow practitioners of Victor's profession were popularly believed to dress only in black, but looking like a cliché wasn't high on Victor's priorities. Like most people he looked good in black, too good for someone whose life might depend on going unnoticed. Dressed in a charcoal suit, white cotton shirt, and monochrome silver tie, Victor looked every inch the respectable businessman. The suit was wool, off the rack, excellent quality but one size too big to give him extra room at the hips, thighs, arms, and shoulders, but without appearing too ill fitting. His Oxford shoes were black, polished but not overly so, high around the ankles and with a thick, treaded sole. His glasses were simple, his haircut boring.

He chose his attire to create a bland, neutral persona. Anyone who tried to remember Victor would find it difficult to describe him accurately. He was a man in a suit, like millions of others. Aside from the easily removable glasses, the only distinguishing feature that might be noticed, and was present only to divert attention from elsewhere, would be shaved off later. He was smart without being stylish, neat but ordinary, confident not arrogant. Forgettable.

He reached the desk and smiled politely as the raven-haired receptionist looked up from her work. She had tanned skin and large eyes, her features skillfully and subtly made up. Her returning smile was cheerfully false. She hid it well but Victor knew she would rather be anywhere else.

"Bonjour," he said, but not too loudly. "Je vous appelle de la chamber 407, je suis Mr. Bishop. Pouvez vous me dire si j'ai recu des messages?'

"Un moment s'il vous plait."

She made a curt nod and checked the log. There was a large mirror mounted on the wall behind the desk in which Victor watched the reflections of the two men. The elevator doors opened and they parted to allow a couple to exit before entering themselves, almost in unison. He saw their hands. They were wearing gloves.

Victor moved position to get an angle on the elevator interior but could see only the reflection of one of the men inside. Victor kept his head tilted to one side, his face partially shielded in case the man looked his way. The man had fair skin and a square face, clean shaven. He wore a focused expression, staring straight ahead, arms limp at his sides. His gloves were brown leather. Either he had a deformed rib cage or something handgun-shaped was concealed beneath his nylon jacket. Any doubts Victor harbored about their motives now evaporated.

Were they police? No, he decided. It was barely two hours since he'd killed Ozols and there was no way he could have been linked to the crime in such a short time frame. They weren't operatives either. Intelligence agents wouldn't need to wear gloves. That left only one occupation.

Victor guessed Eastern European—a Czech or Hungarian or maybe from the Balkans, which tended to produce particularly effective killers. He'd seen two, but there could easily be more. Two guns are better than one but a whole team would be better still for obvious reasons, especially when the target was an experienced contract killer. Only the very best can afford to work alone.

The way the men acted suggested there were others. They had no care of their surroundings, no worry about security. That said surveillance. That said a larger team. There could be as few as four or as many as ten. If there were more Victor didn't give himself much chance.

That they knew where he was staying required a considerable level of proficiency or accuracy of intelligence. Until Victor knew who he was up against he couldn't afford to underestimate them. He had to work on the assumption that they were at least his equal. Should he be proved wrong it would only be to his advantage.

The receptionist finished checking the log and shook her head. "Monsieur, il n'y a aucun message pour vous."

As he thanked her he watched the man in the elevator's focused expression disappear, replaced for a moment with pain or deep concentration. The man raised a finger to his right ear before looking quickly to his associate. His mouth opened to speak as he reached to stop the doors from shutting, but he was too late. Victor managed to read the first words on his lips before the doors closed.

He's in the lobby . . .

They were wearing radios. He'd been spotted.

Victor turned around and surveyed the area, taking a few seconds to study each person in case he'd missed other members of the kill team. The natural reaction to the imminent threat would be to act immediately. In the physiological response to danger the adrenal glands flooded his bloodstream with adrenaline to increase his heart rate, to make the body ready for action. But relying on instinct was not something he welcomed. In the wild it only ever came down to two choices—fight or flight. For Victor decisions were rarely that simple.

He swallowed down the adrenaline jolt, breathed deeply, forcing his body to calm down again. He needed to think. There was nothing to gain by acting quickly if in doing so he did the wrong thing. In Victor's line of work those who made a first mistake were rarely around long enough to make a second.

He counted ten people in the lobby. A middle-aged man and his trophy escort were heading toward the adjoining bar. A group of stiff-backed old men sat on the leather chairs laughing. The alluring receptionist was stifling a yawn. Walking toward the exit a businessman shouted into his cell phone. Near the elevator a mother struggled to control her toddler. No one who might be with the two men, but more could be entering the hotel through the tradesman's entrance at the back or maybe through the kitchen, simultaneously cutting off all avenues of retreat as they closed in on their prey. It was textbook. But no use if that prey wasn't where he was supposed to be.

For some reason their timing was off and whatever plan they'd been following had fallen apart. They would be shaken, worried they'd been compromised and that their target might escape. They'd lost sight of him and needed to reestablish that contact. Or perhaps they would just abandon any pretense of stealth and try to kill him now, while they thought him vulnerable and off guard. Victor had no intentions of being either.

He studied the display above the elevator. It flashed 4, reaching his floor. He watched it intently for a moment. A few seconds later it flashed 3. On the way back down.

Victor glanced at the main entrance. If he left now he would only have those on surveillance outside to contend with. They might not be prepared to go after him out in the street, and if he was fast he might escape without shots fired. But he couldn't leave. In his hotel room he had his passport and credit cards. All for a false identity but they already knew too much about him.

He could use the stairs but not if one of them had taken that way down to make sure he didn't. Because there was another problem. He was unarmed. The FN that killed Ozols had been stripped and each piece disposed of separately. The barrel in the Seine, slide down a storm drain, guide rod and recoil spring in a Dumpster, magazine in a trash can. Victor only ever used a gun once. Walking around with all the evidence a jury would ever need to convict him was not his style. If he could get to his backup he could at least defend himself.

There was only one functioning elevator though. An out-of-order sign dangled from the other's doors. Victor strolled across the lobby and stood in front of the working elevator the two men had used. He cracked the knuckles of his right hand one by one with his thumb.

There was a *ting* as the elevator reached the lobby. Just before the doors began to open Victor stepped to one side and pressed his back against the adjacent wall in a small recess where an elaborately decorated vase stood. He remained motionless, ignoring the bewildered gaze of a five-year-old boy. Everyone else was too preoccupied to notice him.

One of the two assassins walked out of the elevator and took a few steps into the lobby. The second didn't follow, obviously on his way down through the stairwell. The man with his back to Victor was compact, thick at the neck, ex-military by his build and gait. He was standing casually, no head movement. Even though apparently motionless Victor knew he was surveying the room, but with his head fixed, just moving his eyes, not wanting to draw unnecessary attention his way. He was good, but not so good as to look behind himself.

Victor waited until the last possible moment before

slipping between the closing elevator doors. He passed within six inches of the assassin.

A second before the doors fully closed the man noticed the young boy pointing in Victor's direction and turned. Random chance. For an instant the man looked directly at Victor.

Recognition flashed in the assassin's eyes.

The doors closed.

THREE

08:27 CET

Victor took a series of deep breaths, pulling the air into the very bottom of his lungs, holding it to the count of four before exhaling. The adrenaline in his system caused his heart rate to soar to better supply his muscles with essential oxygen. But beyond one hundred and twenty beats per minute the ability to use fine motor skills—those that require small muscle movements, such as lining up a set of gun sights—were reduced. At above one hundred and thirty those skills are almost entirely lost. To the body such abilities aren't immediately necessary to survival.

Victor would beg to differ.

By controlling his breathing Victor interrupted the normal working of the autonomic nervous system, effectively putting the brakes on his climbing heart rate.

Victor couldn't override his instincts but fortunately he could manipulate them.

He figured the guy in the lobby wouldn't waste any time in contacting the other units, informing them they had been spotted and the target was on the run, heading upstairs. Victor could get off at any floor, find a window and be gone in a matter of moments. But he needed his effects. If the kill team didn't get to them the authorities eventually would. Passports had stamps of countries and dates. Credit-card numbers could be traced. The gun would ensure they investigated him thoroughly. Every piece of documentation was for an alias, but one that he had used before. He took every precaution imaginable, but there was always a trail to follow for those who knew how to look, and at the end of that trail was the real him. He couldn't allow that to happen.

The elevator passed the first two floors without stopping. Victor kept his breathing steady. He counted off each long second until the *ting*.

Victor was out in the hallway while the doors were still opening, moving fast, heading left toward the stairwell at the end of the corridor, maybe thirty feet from the elevator. Closed.

He didn't need to press his ear against the door to hear two sets of feet leaping up the stairs. They were fit, strong, maybe twenty seconds away. He needed time to secure his things, time he didn't have. Unless he made it for himself.

A fire ax hung on the wall farther along the corridor. Victor smashed the glass with his elbow and lifted it from its perch. Returning to the stairwell he pushed the blade under the door handle, wedging the bottom of the haft on the floor. It was a good fit, sturdy.

There was a fire extinguisher beneath where he'd taken the ax. Victor hoisted it up in his left hand and moved back to the elevator. It was still on the fourth floor. He pressed the button to open the doors.

Suddenly the stairwell door shook but the handle remained rigid, the ax preventing it from turning regardless of how much strength was applied. They tried again, more forcefully, but again the handle didn't move. After that there were no more attempts.

Victor turned his attention back to the elevator. He placed the fire extinguisher between the open doors, leaned inside, and pressed the button for the lobby. They closed as far as the extinguisher before retracting and repeating the endless cycle. Victor estimated he'd bought himself at least two minutes. He needed less than one.

He reached his room without a sound and stood before the door. There could be others waiting for him inside. They'd be alert, ready. He kicked the door open and went in, immediately dropping into a low crouch, reducing his profile, head lower than where center mass would typically be. It took a split second to survey the room, another second to check the en suite bathroom.

No one.

There were the two in the stairwell, plus surveillance outside, and possibly others elsewhere in the hotel. They were good, organized. If they were really good they would have a sniper in a building across the street.

Victor didn't go anywhere near the window.

In the bathroom Victor took the lid off the toilet tank and retrieved the Ziploc bags from inside. One contained his passport, plane ticket, and credit cards. He removed the items and placed them inside his jacket. The second had another fully loaded FN Five-seveN and sound suppressor. It always paid to prepare for the worst, Victor reminded himself. He tore the bag open, took the gun, screwed the suppressor in place, and pulled the slide to put one in the chamber.

An attaché case containing a change of clothes and the rest of his possessions was already packed and sitting on the bed. Victor grabbed it with his left hand and went, keeping his gun out of sight down by his right side. He walked briskly down the corridor, alert, away from the stairs and elevator, heading for the fire escape. He would be gone long before they realized what was happening.

He stopped.

If he left he would leave knowing nothing about his would-be killers. Whoever had sent them wouldn't just call them off. He was on someone's hit list now. If they had found him once they could do so again. Next time he might not spot them so quickly, if at all.

They were a numerically superior force but they had lost the initiative. One of the first things he'd learned about combat was to never give away an advantage.

Victor turned around.

They came to his room breathless, guns in hand. One moved to the right of the door, the other stayed to the left.

The target's door was ajar, the lock broken. The taller of the two, the more senior, took a second to double-click the send button of the radio transmitter in his inside pocket. A whisper came through his wireless flesh-colored earpiece.

The assassin made a quick hand signal to his partner and they burst into the room. The first went in fast and low so the second could fire over him as he followed directly behind. The first man swept the left-hand side of the room, the other the right. Maximum speed, aggression, and surprise to make anyone inside defensive, stunned, slow to react.

The room was empty. They checked the bathroom—it was the same. While one covered the other they examined the closet, under the bed, anywhere that might conceal a man, no matter how unlikely. They had been told to be thorough, to leave nothing to chance. They checked behind the curtains, first holding out a hand across the window to give the marksman in the building opposite the signal not to fire. Their faces glistened with perspiration.

Each room was a mess. The target had obviously fled in a hurry, not hanging around long enough to take all his belongings. Clothes were strewn about the floor, the bed was unmade, toiletries left by the sink. It was sloppy, unprofessional.

Both men relaxed slightly, breathed a little easier. He was gone. They hid their guns in case anyone came their way. When the elevator had refused to appear they'd had no other choice but to run back up the stairs and break down the stairwell door. It hadn't exactly been quiet.

They left the room, pulling the door shut behind them. The more senior of the two lifted his collar and reported into the attached microphone that the target was gone. He was careful with his choice of words not to imply any mistake on his part. They weren't worried, all of the building's exits were covered, one of the other team members would spot him and move in— might even be doing so at this very moment. The target was as good as dead. Each of the team members was due a large bonus when the job was complete, and they hadn't even had to fire a single shot.

Their boss had told them to be careful, that their target was dangerous, but now the nerves they'd felt seemed misplaced. Their *dangerous* target had fled at the first chance he had and was now someone else's problem. They shared the same thought. Easy money.

Their faces changed when they learned the target hadn't left the building, that none of the others had even reported a visual. The two men looked at each other, their expressions silently echoing the same question.

Then where was he?

Victor stepped away from the spy hole of the door opposite and raised his gun. He fired, squeezing the trigger ten times in rapid succession, emptying the magazine of exactly half its ammunition. The hotel door was thick, solid pine, but the bullets in the Five-seveN were shaped like rifle rounds and cut through it with barely any loss in velocity.

Two heavy objects hit the carpet, one thud after the other.

The door creaked in front of him. He'd kept it shut with his foot, having broken the lock to gain entry. He pulled it open with his left hand and stepped into the hallway. In front of him the first man was slumped on the floor, propped up against the door frame of Victor's room, head hung forward, blood running from the mouth and collecting into a pool on the carpet. Apart from a twitching left foot he made no movement.

The other was still alive, lying face down on the floor, making a quiet gurgling noise. He'd been hit several times—in the gut, chest, and neck where the ruptured carotid artery sprayed the wall with long crimson arcs. He was trying to crawl away, his mouth open as if screaming for help but making no sound.

Victor ignored him and reached inside the dead man's jacket, searching unsuccessfully for a wallet. He went to take the man's radio receiver, but it was in pieces, a bullet having passed straight through on the way to his heart. In a shoulder holster Victor found a 9 mm Beretta 92F handgun and two spare magazines in a pocket. The Beretta was a good, reliable weapon with a fifteen-round mag, but a heavy, bulky gun that, even without the attached suppressor, was impossible to conceal completely. With subsonic ammunition the stopping power wasn't great either. For this kind of work it was a poor choice of pistol. If the guy wasn't dead Victor might have told him so.

The Beretta wouldn't normally have been his preference but at times like this there was no such thing as too many guns. Victor took the weapon and tucked it into the back of his suit pants, the grip supported by his belt, the suppressor down by his coccyx. The body jerked suddenly, perhaps from some muscle spasm, and tipped forward. The jaw fell open and a cascade of collected blood poured out, followed by half a bitten-through tongue flopping onto the carpet. Victor stepped away and turned his attention to the one who wasn't dead. Yet.

He stopped crawling when Victor's heel pressed down between his shoulder blades. Victor rolled the man onto his back and squatted down next to him, pushing the Five-seveN's suppressor hard into the man's cheek. He forced his head to one side to keep the violent arterial spray directed at the wall and away from himself. Where it hit, the pressurized blood tore at the floral paper.

The man was trying to speak but could only manage a wheezing exhale. The bullet in his neck had ripped through his larynx, and he could make only the most basic of sounds. He tugged at Victor's sleeve, tried to claw at him, not giving up the fight despite the inevitability of the wound. Victor respected his perseverance.

Like his partner he was also armed with a Beretta and equipped with a radio and earpiece. Victor unloaded the gun and checked the rest of his pockets. They were empty except for a few sticks of chewing gum, more ammo, and a crumpled receipt. He took the gum and the receipt, seeing it was for half a dozen coffees and discarded it. Victor unwrapped one of the sticks of gum and folded it into his mouth. Peppermint. He nodded his approval.

"Thanks."

He shook off the hand and moved to the stairwell to check for others. No sign of any more assassins but voices carried up from below, female, complaining about the elevator. Victor made his way back down the corridor, careful to avoid the dark stains on the carpet and moved the fire extinguisher from between the elevator doors. He stepped inside and pressed the button for the lobby. He'd left some of his belongings in the room, but he wasn't concerned. The toiletries were brand-new, the clothes hadn't been worn yet, and everything that had been handled would be free from fingerprints thanks to the silicone solution on his hands.

In the corridor the dying man had at last ceased his thrashing. Blood no longer spurted from his neck but simply oozed out onto the drenched carpet. Victor couldn't help but admire the pattern of red on the wall above the corpse. The crisscrossed lines had a certain aesthetic quality that reminded him of a Jackson Pollock.

Victor examined his reflection in the mirrored elevator walls and took a moment to straighten his appearance. In his current surroundings if he looked anything but presentable he would be noted. The elevator doors closed as a shrill scream echoed from the direction of the stairwell. Someone had just gotten something of a surprise.

Victor guessed she wasn't a great fan of Pollock's work.

FOUR

In the lobby Victor waited patiently as panic erupted around him. The hotel manager, a short slim man with a surprisingly loud voice, had to shout just to be heard above the frightened guests. Some were only half-dressed, rudely pulled from their beds by screams of a massacre. The manager was trying to explain that the police were on the way and everyone should remain calm. But it was far too late for that.

Victor sat in one of the luxurious leather armchairs in a corner of the lobby. It was very comfortable. He'd angled the chair so he could watch the main entrance in the middle of the far wall and most of the lobby without moving his head. He kept the entrance to the hotel bar and stairwell in his peripheral vision. He doubted anyone would use the elevators to his right, but if they did he was close enough to see them exiting before they noticed him.

The police would arrive soon, and the remaining members of the kill team were quickly running out of time to fulfill their contract. They would be panicking by now, having worked out that two of their men were dead. Either they would escape, which Victor didn't expect, or they would try and finish the job. In the mêlée of guests and staff members fleeing the lobby it would be too crowded to kill him on the streets outside and too risky with cops on the way.

It took about a minute, longer than Victor had anticipated, and he marked their skills down a notch for the delay. He spotted them easily, first one man trying to negotiate his way through the crowd desperately struggling to get out. A moment later the second rushed into the lobby from a ground-floor corridor. The first man had blond hair, his right hand wedged into the pocket of his black leather jacket, his left outstretched, trying to guide himself through the horde of frightened people. The other guy was tall, heavyset with a shaved head and the beginnings of a dark beard. Bulky jacket. He used both hands to shove people out of his path, no pretense of subtlety. Victor therefore deduced the blond man to be higher up the food chain and hence far more appetizing.

They reached each other in the center of the lobby and conferred briefly. They made a cursory look around the room, quickly glancing into the bar as they passed through the lobby, the blond man heading for the stairs, the big guy to the elevator. Given the mass of people between them and Victor it was an understandable mistake not to spot him, but one that was going to cost them all the same.

Victor stood, timed his movements so a family exiting the elevator shielded him from the big guy's view as they passed each other, and headed for the stairwell door. Victor was fast, coming up behind the man in the leather jacket just as he was pushing through.

The blond man saw the approaching shadow too late. He tried to pull out his gun but stopped immediately when the suppressor pushed against his ribs. Victor angled it upward, aiming at the heart. In the same instant Victor's left hand grabbed hold of the guy's testicles and squeezed with much of his considerable strength.

The man gasped and almost dropped to the floor under the sudden excruciating pain. Victor pushed him through the doorway and whispered into his ear in French.

"Right hand—take it out of your pocket. Leave the gun."

The man obeyed.

"How many of you are there?" Victor demanded.

The man struggled to remain standing, fought to keep his breathing steady enough to speak. He was terrified. Victor didn't blame him. He only managed to form a single word.

"What?"

Victor guided him up the first flight of stairs, tightening his grip on the man's balls to dismiss any thoughts of his trying something foolish. It was hardly necessary.

"This way."

They continued up the next flight and over to the door on the first floor.

"Through there. Open it."

The man reached out a shaking hand and turned the handle. The door was half open when Victor pushed him through and headed down the hallway. They passed a maid hurrying along to the stairwell. An old woman, hair pulled tightly back in a bun, barely five feet tall. Victor heard her gasp—maybe it was the man's contorted face or the hand clamped to his groin. Victor kept his own head positioned behind his prisoner's so she couldn't see his face.

By the time she'd told someone who mattered, he would be long gone. He could kill her just for extra prudence, but another corpse in a corridor would only cause him more problems, and it wasn't her fault she happened to be there.

They turned a corner into another corridor. It was quiet, every guest now congregated in the lobby or in the street outside.

"Open a door," Victor ordered.

The man was trembling, his voice labored. "Which one?"

Victor put three bullets through where the lock met the door frame. A single bullet only worked in the movies. "That one." The man hesitated, and Victor applied more pressure. "Open it. Now."

He was slow to turn the handle, and so Victor shoved him through. He gently knocked the door closed behind him with his foot as he followed.

"Throw the gun on the bed."

The man reached into his pocket and slowly pulled out his handgun, gripping it with only thumb and forefinger. He threw it onto the bed. It landed in the center. Not a bad throw considering.

Victor let go of the blond guy and hurled him forward. He stumbled and collapsed to the floor. He lay in a crumpled heap, almost fetal, clutching at his damaged testicles. His Casanova days were very over. He was younger than the other three, twenty-seven at most. His features were different, his demeanor more controlled. Victor regarded him curiously, recognizing that he didn't quite fit in with the others. An outsider. Or leader.

The man's eyes flicked toward his right foot then quickly looked away. In a black leather shin holster, barely visible where the right pants cuff had come up in the fall, was a black snub-nosed revolver. He saw that Victor had seen him look and read his thought process.

Victor shook his head just once.

He took a step forward, leveled the gun at the center of the man's forehead. "How many of you are there?"

"Seven."

"Including you?"

He nodded, grimacing, not able to speak for a moment because of the agony in his groin. Excluding the big guy in the elevator somewhere there were three more.

"How many cars did you bring?"

The blond man was quick to answer, spitting the word out as fast as he could. "One."

"Just one?"

"It's a van."

"What's the registration?"

"I . . . I don't know."

Victor put a 5.7 mm into the floor between his legs. It wasn't very economical with the remaining bullets but he didn't have time for a lengthy interrogation.

The blond man stared at the singed hole in the carpet. "*I swear.*"

"What make is it?"

"I don't know . . . it's blue. A rental."

His French was good but not fluent, not a native speaker.

Victor asked, "Do you know who I am?"

He didn't answer straightaway. Victor took another step closer and the man found his voice. "No."

"No?"

"Just an alias, we had a picture . . ."

"How did you know where I'm staying?"

"We were given the name of the hotel."

"When?"

"Three days ago."

Then his accent clicked. Victor switched to English. "You're American."

He spoke back in English. "Yes." He was from the South, Texas maybe.

"Who's in charge?" Victor asked.

"I am."

"Private sector?"

"Yes."

"Have you been following me?"

"We tried to but you always lost us."

"Why wait until now to kill me?"

The American paused for a moment before answering. "We had to wait for the green light."

"Which you received when?"

"Oh, five thirty."

Victor could tell he had decided to tell the truth, perhaps thinking he might have a chance if he answered honestly. Blissful ignorance.

"Why did you send those two guys in before I'd returned?"

The blond man grimaced again. "I lost my nerve. Thought you weren't coming back. I sent them in to check." He scowled despite the pain. "Bad timing."

"That wasn't very smart," Victor said. "What about the flash drive?"

"We had to make sure you had it, then secure it and wait for instructions."

Victor's eyes narrowed. "Who are you working for?"

The man's head slumped. Tears streamed down his cheeks. "Please . . ."

"Who are you working for?"

He looked up at Victor, saw in his eyes that there was no mercy, no pity. He sobbed.

"*How the hell would I know?*"

Victor believed him.

He shot him twice in the face.

He knelt down by the body, looking for some identification, and saw a radio in the inside jacket pocket, switched to send, the light flickering. There was a microphone attached to the underside of his collar.

A floorboard creaked.

Victor froze, looked over his shoulder.

Through the crack under the door Victor could see a shadow moving in the corridor outside. He dived to the right as the big guy with the shaved head burst into the room, submachine gun in hand, already firing before he'd acquired a target. It was a compact MP5k fitted with a long suppressor, its rapid reports reduced to a series of sustained muffled *clicks*.

The gunman shifted his aim, following Victor's path as he leaped into the adjacent bathroom, bullets blowing a line of neat holes out of the wall behind him. Ejected brass cases clinked together on the carpet around the assassin's feet.

In the bathroom, Victor came out of his roll into a crouch, letting off a quick shot, firing blind before he'd fully turned around. The bullet whizzed through the open doorway, sending up a puff of plaster as it struck the wall on the other side.

The bathroom was no more than six feet by four, a tiled box containing a bath, sink, and toilet. There were no defensible corners or objects behind which to take cover. On fully automatic the MP5k could unload its mag of thirty in just two and a quarter seconds. At this range, and with that volume of fire, the gunman literally couldn't miss.

With his left hand Victor pulled the Beretta from the back of his waistband and pointed both guns at the doorway, one in each hand. Not so good for aiming accurately but he needed the extra stopping power if he was going to drop the gunman before he could open fire. He was a big guy and neither subsonic 5.7 mm or 9 mm rounds were going to guarantee putting him down instantly unless he was shot in the head, heart, or spine. But with enough bullets it wouldn't matter where Victor hit. He held the Beretta directly below the FN so he could still line up one set of sights. Victor had seen amateurs hold two guns at arm's length, hands shoulder width apart, trying to emulate their favorite action movie stars. They always died quickly.

He heard something thud on the carpet and clink against the spent 9 mm casings on the floor. An instant later came the sound of a gun reloading and the MP5k recocked. It hadn't clicked empty but his attacker had loaded a full magazine anyway while he had the chance.

Victor stayed in a crouch, as far away from the opening as possible. If his enemy was smart enough to reload before he was empty he wouldn't be stupid enough to burst into the room when all he had to do was point the gun around the door frame and spray in some rounds. Victor sensed the gunman was creeping along the dividing wall to do exactly that. In his current position Victor knew he was a dead man. He forced himself to stay calm.

He needed to do something, and quick.

He looked around, saw a towel on a rail, a line of toiletries above the wash basin—toothpaste, shaving foam, antiperspirant, a razor, aftershave.

His eyes fixed on the can of antiperspirant.

Victor fired another round from the Five-seveN at the doorway to act as a deterrent, then another a few seconds later to buy himself some time, to make the gunman wary. He placed the Beretta down in front of him, switched the FN to his left hand, stood, and grabbed the can of antiperspirant from above the sink.

Squatting back down, he fired through the doorway with the Five-seveN, twice more so the weapon clicked dry, advertising that he was out of ammo, giving the gunman all the incentive he needed to seize his chance.

Victor dropped the empty gun, switched the antiperspirant to his left hand, and took up the Beretta in his right. Jumping to his feet, he flung the aerosol through the doorway just below the top of the frame as the submachine gun's muzzle rounded the corner.

Victor fired the Beretta three times.

The last bullet hit and the aerosol exploded in midair.

Victor was already running before he heard the scream, darting through the doorway, bent over, even as the panicking gunman opened fire.

The bullets missed, flying clear above him. The man was stumbling backward, pressed against the wall, the only thing keeping him on his feet. His gun was still raised at shoulder height, and he fired in desperation, spraying wildly.

Slim shards of glinting metal protruded from his scorched face and eyes. His hair was on fire.

The gun clicked empty, and for a moment the man's groans subsided and his breaths came quick and sharp. He blindly looked around the room, weapon still raised in some last pitiful defense. The air smelled like roasted pork.

Victor stood up straight, pointed the Beretta at the center of the gunman's chest, and put two right through his heart.

FIVE

Victor made his way through the hotel, walking quickly, keeping the Beretta in hand and hidden under his jacket. He had his empty FN in a pocket. He made his way through the corridors of the ground floor, in his head visualizing the hotel plans he'd memorized on his first night. He came to a door marked *staff only.*

He could hear policemen elsewhere on the floor, talking loudly, overwhelmed. They would be patrolmen first on the scene, responding to the emergency call. Others would be coming fast. If Victor wasn't gone soon, he knew the hotel would be sealed off and the street would follow and probably the whole block. Victor wanted to be long gone before that happened.

He drew the Beretta out from under his jacket and pushed open the door to the kitchens with his left hand, using his knuckles out of habit despite the silicone coating on his fingertips.

It was surprisingly cool inside. The back door had been wedged open, perhaps in the mass exodus of frightened guests and employees. A refreshing breeze funneled through. Victor noticed for the first time he was sweating. There were no members of the kitchen staff. Everyone had wisely fled. Victor drew the smell of cooked breakfasts into his nostrils. Eggs were burning in pans on the stove. Bread and croissants baked in ovens.

He continued breathing deeply to keep his pulse down and gripped the Beretta in both hands as he walked forward, slow, cautious of the large open space and the blind spots created by rows of appliances and storage. He kept his eyes moving as he crept toward the door, wary that there were three other gunmen very much alive. He had to assume they were still after him, leaderless or not. If they hadn't withdrawn they wouldn't have left this exit unguarded.

He moved closer, staying near to cupboards and work surfaces for cover in case someone burst through from the alleyway beyond. An approaching siren beckoned him to walk faster, but his awareness of the current danger ensured his movements were slow and controlled.

If another gunman was waiting in the alley and covering the doorway, Victor would need to have surprise on his side to stand a chance of making it out alive. Hurrying would only make an enemy's job easier. They were going to have to earn their money today.

He took another step and stopped.

Movement.

A reflection on the stainless steel cupboard door to his left. Just a blur of motion, but he understood its meaning and spun around to see a pantry door swinging open hard, a dark-haired woman charging out of the darkness, her handgun rapidly coming into line with his position.

Victor reacted faster, shooting first, two shots, hitting center mass. The impact knocked her off her feet and threw her backward into the adjoining room from where she'd emerged.

He covered the distance fast, saw her lying on her back, alive, eyes closed, two small circles of blood around the scorch marks in her blouse. She was gasping, one lung collapsed. The gun was right next to her, but she didn't try to get to it. She was too scared.

Victor's shadow fell over her and she looked up. She was surprisingly attractive, twenty-eight or -nine, pain in her delicate features, terror in her piercing eyes. She stared at him, gaze pleading, tears spilling down her cheeks, lips he would have liked to kiss, moving but making no sound, not enough air in her lungs to speak, to beg. Or to tell him anything useful. He spared a moment to consider how someone like her could have ended up in this business. But whatever her story had been, it was about to have a depressing end. Her head shook slowly from side to side.

The smoking cartridge bounced on the floor tiles.

He searched her. Like the others she had no wallet, no identification of any kind. They were clearly smart operators even if they had been dumb enough to take this contract. One of those left had to have something Victor could use. He didn't want to entertain the thought that they might not.

He discarded the Beretta and picked up the dead woman's gun. It was a good weapon, a Heckler and Koch USP, compact version, .45 caliber, with a short, stubby suppressor. He pulled out the eight-round magazine, saw the match-grade hollow-point rounds, and slammed the mag back in. Obviously a killer who took pride in the tools of her trade. Well, used to.

He grabbed a spare mag from her jacket before

rushing out the back entrance and into the alleyway, keeping low, gazing left, then right, sweeping the HK as he looked. No one. He hid the gun in his waistband and headed toward the main street, pleased that finally one of them had a decent gun for him to steal. Assassins could have such very poor taste.

With the woman dead that made five down.

Only two to go.

There was a large crowd outside the front of the hotel. Guests and employees alike, shocked, overawed and scared, seeking solace together. Only a handful of people knew what was lying in a corridor on the fourth floor, but talk of blood and bodies had spread fast. A single policeman was doing his best to try and move them back. Pedestrians were rushing to the scene to find out what was happening.

Victor exited the alleyway and walked among the crowd, his pace brisk but no quicker than anyone else's, moving laterally as much as he could, not wanting to give any possible snipers an easy target. It was unlikely that anyone would take such a shot, but he wouldn't bet his life on it. He saw the blue van parked fifty yards down the street, sitting anonymously along the curb by a phone booth. The rear doors were facing toward him. He couldn't see if anyone was behind the wheel.

If it hadn't gone yet there was a good chance that at least one more assassin was still about. As Victor approached he caught sight of exhaust gases emanating from the van. Good, there would be someone behind the wheel while the engine idled. In the commotion, Victor knew he could get right up alongside the van before any driver knew he was there. He went to cross the street, his right foot leaving the curb, but he went no farther.

On the other side of the road, directly opposite from the hotel, a stocky man was hurrying down the steps at the front of a whitewashed apartment building. Slung over his shoulder was a large black sports bag, the kind that could easily contain a tennis racket, hockey stick.

Or high-velocity rifle.

He stopped dead when he saw Victor looking straight at him. His reaction a perfect ID. Both men stood completely still as chaos swept around them. The sniper was first to break the stalemate. He glanced to his left, toward where the van was parked. He and Victor were equidistant from it.

Victor took a step forward. The sniper took one backward. He reached into his jacket. Victor did the same. A police car turned onto the street, lights flashing, siren blaring. Both men saw it and any thoughts of drawing guns vanished.

The sniper again glanced at the van, perhaps in the hope that help might be coming. When he realized it wasn't he turned around and rushed back up the steps to the apartment building.

Victor quickened his pace but to avoid drawing attention couldn't run. He reached the opposite sidewalk in time to see the door slam shut behind his prey. He took the steps two at a time. He tried the door handle but it was dead bolted. He couldn't risk kicking it in or shooting the lock through, not with more police entering the street.

Victor descended the steps and looked both ways down the street, searching for some way to get round to the back of the building. There was an alleyway twenty yards to the right. Victor hurried toward it.

As soon as he was out of sight he sprinted, coming out of the far end and into the backstreet, .45 in hand. No sign of the sniper. If he'd left the building already Victor would be able to see him now. Which meant he was staying put. Victor was surprised. The sniper had chosen to wait, to fight.

Victor wasn't about to disappoint him.

The lock on the back door was a good one and would've taken Victor almost thirty seconds to pick had the fat .45 caliber slugs not blasted it to pieces. He loaded a full magazine and stepped into a wide, sparsely furnished hallway, the floor covered in a colorful mosaic. There were three interior doors, two with numbers on them. A large staircase dominated the space.

Victor approached it, gun held out before him in a two-handed combat grip. His hotel room had been on the fourth floor and so it would be from the fifth that the sniper had been covering Victor's window. That room was familiar, safe. If the sniper had fled to anywhere, he would have gone there.

Victor took the steps one at time, slowly, quietly, always looking up, ready in case the sniper was waiting to ambush him. He reached the second floor, scanned the landing, then started his way up the next flight of stairs.

He paused for a few seconds on the third floor to listen. When he didn't hear anything he made his way up to the fourth. From the fifth floor, he heard a door open, then a woman's voice, somewhat surprised, but friendly, helpful.

"Est-ce que je peux vous aider?" Can I help you?

Then a *clack clack* followed by the thud as a body hit the floor. Victor made his move, sprinting up the flight of steps while the sniper was momentarily distracted. He saw the sniper as he was turning around from his kill, standing at the top of the stairs.

Victor fired on the move, the angle bad, and a hollow point blew a chunk out of the banister. The sniper instinctively lurched back, and two more bullets blew holes from the ceiling above him, a fourth struck the black iron lattice beneath the banister and sent off a flash of bright sparks. The sniper let off a few rounds from his own handgun, firing blind as he threw himself out of Victor's line of sight. He appeared again briefly, firing as he moved, Victor returning fire, neither man hitting.

Victor went into a crouch before he reached the top of the stairs and peered through the iron lattice. He saw the body sprawled out in the doorway of her apartment. A silver-haired woman in a raincoat lay dead, her only crime having asked politely if she could help the stranger waiting by the stairs. A good deed was its own reward.

The other of the floor's two doors was half open, the sniper nowhere to be seen. Victor crept up the last few steps. He looked over to the first half-open door. It led to the apartment overlooking the same street as the hotel. The place where the sniper had originally taken up position, the place to which he had no doubt retreated. Except Victor did doubt.

Making no noise, he carefully stepped across the landing, avoided the glistening pool of blood, and pressed himself along the wall. He edged toward the open door that led to the dead woman's apartment. Victor almost smiled. He wasn't about to fall for the oldest trick in the book.

When he reached the door frame, he looked across to the other apartment, the one where the sniper would have been stationed, judging the angle to determine where someone inside the dead woman's apartment would need to be to properly cover the other doorway.

Victor crouched down; placed his left hand on the door frame; and, using it as leverage, spun himself into the room. He saw the sniper straightaway, in a crouch, leaning around a partition wall, gun trained at the door to his old apartment. The sniper's eyes widened in surprise.

Victor fired twice, one bullet missing but the second grazing the sniper's head above the ear, sending up a small spray of blood. The sniper managed to get a shot off in response before he fell back into cover. The bullet hit the door frame inches from Victor's face, blowing a cluster of long wooden splinters into his cheek. He didn't flinch.

Victor was on his feet in an instant, quickly changing position, moving into the center of the room, knowing that he had to keep moving, that to stay in the same place only made it easier for his assailant.

The sniper ducked back round the corner and fired off two quick shots in the direction of the doorway, the bullets sailing through the open space where Victor's head had been seconds before. He moved further into the room, making the angle between him and the sniper more and more acute. If the sniper wanted to see him he was going to have to stick his head around the corner. When he did, Victor was going to blow it off. But he didn't take the bait.

Five seconds passed and Victor imagined the sniper moving through the apartment to get behind him. There were two other ways out of the lounge, too far apart to watch them both at once.

Victor dashed over to the dining-room entrance, leaned round the corner. The sniper had gone. There was an open door at the opposite end, through which Victor could see the kitchen. Silently he moved over to the kitchen and peered inside. Empty. There was only one other door. Victor hurried over to it, noting the tiny dark spots of blood on the white tiled floor.

Looking through the doorway he saw the sniper. He was crouched down in a hallway, his back pressed against a wall, gun in both hands, about to lean into the lounge and shoot Victor in the back. At least that's what he thought.

He was taking a series of deep breaths, summoning courage. He stopped mid inhale. Maybe he saw a dark shape in his peripheral vision, maybe some sixth sense warned him. He twisted to fire and Victor shot him in the chest. He slumped farther down the wall, still alive, the gun held loosely in his hand. On his face was etched an expression of amazement, as if he couldn't comprehend he'd been shot. A red mist hung in the air.

The slide was back on the .45, so Victor released the empty mag and slammed the spare in, pulled the slide to load a bullet into the chamber, and shot the sniper twice more.

Victor checked the body, took the earpiece and transmitter, but found nothing else. He headed to the floor's other apartment. Inside the hallway he found the black sports bag; unzipping it he discovered a SIG556 ER rifle with scope and what looked like a custom-made suppressor. In a side pocket, he found a dry-cleaning receipt and an electronic door key. He took both. On the receipt it said: *Le Hôtel Abrial.*

Now he had something.

He moved into the lounge and opened a window. Leaning out, he saw the blue van still parked by the curb in the street below.

A crackle of static. A voice came through the earpiece. The French was broken, strained. Another foreigner. The ones who could speak French probably used it as the common language. Maybe it had been a requirement on the application form.

"Venez dans quelqu'un, quiconque."

In the background he could hear a police siren, close to the speaker. The last man was outside. Then the voice came through again. The same plea for contact. Again the police siren in the background, then the rumble of an engine as a vehicle passed the speaker. Victor watched a police motorcycle slowly pass the blue van before stopping right in front of the hotel.

He took the rifle from the bag and extended the collapsible buttstock. With his left hand, he turned the radio's frequency dial a fraction counterclockwise, to add some static. He held the radio up and pressed send, speaking in French, his accent deliberately off, sentence construction as basic as possible to make sure the guy would understand.

"We're the only two left," he said, sounding scared. "He's killed everyone else."

He released the button, giving whoever it was a chance to respond. The voice that came back was thin, desperate.

"Where are you?"

"Inside the hotel."

"The target?"

Victor began screwing the suppressor in place.

"Heading for the front exit. He's wounded. I shot him."

He made sure the suppressor was tight and attached the telescopic sight.

"If you're quick you can get him when he comes out. He's not armed. *Hurry.*"

He checked the scope's magnification, made sure a bullet was in the chamber, and thumbed off the safety. Victor put the radio down, took up a seated position on the window sill, and held the rifle out of sight.

The driver's-side door opened and a man jumped out onto the curb. He was strongly built, well over six feet tall, short hair, wearing a loose denim jacket. He quickly

moved along the exterior of the van and leaned round
the back end, looking toward the hotel across the street.
He drew a handgun and held it out of sight under his
jacket, attention firmly fixed on the hotel entrance. He
was in good cover, between the van and a phone booth.
Victor watched him, anticipating his movements. The
man moved well, skill evident. They should have used
him inside.

For a long moment he remained perfectly still, watching, waiting. After a minute his posture stiffened and he
glanced from side to side, eyes searching the crowds.
He stepped back, out of cover, turned around, looked up.

Straight at Victor.

Through the telescopic sight Victor watched the
man's eyes go wide for an instant before a corona of
blood erupted from the back of his head. He dropped
out of sight, leaving half the contents of his skull sliding slowly down the van's rear windows.

SIX

08:45 CET

Victor left the apartment building through the front
door. In the street outside the crowd had grown considerably. He counted half a dozen police officers, but
none of them were paying him the least bit of attention.

Farther up the street Victor could see the red splash on the back of the van, but the body was hidden between the parked vehicles. Everyone was too preoccupied to notice it.

Knowing he didn't have much time, Victor hurried along the sidewalk, weaving around pedestrians who stood gawking at the commotion. The morbidity of the general public always amazed him. He closed the distance to the van, glancing down to see the corpse lain down in a heap between the van and the sedan parked behind it. No one was looking, but it wasn't worth the risk to check the body's pockets.

He opened the door against the curb and climbed into the driver's seat. It smelled musty inside—the smell of too many men in an enclosed space for an extended period. Resting on the dash was a cardboard tray with six empty coffee cups. There was nothing else in the cab, so he opened the glove compartment. Inside was a manila envelope that contained his dossier, thankfully brief. It was a single piece of paper listing his details—race: Caucasian, height: six-one/two, weight: one hundred eighty pounds, hair: black, eyes: brown—and included a short paragraph stating he was a contract killer and a dangerous target. Scrawled by hand at the top of the sheet was the name of his hotel, his room number, and his current alias, Richard Bishop.

Victor placed a hand to his stomach. More like one seventy eight.

Beneath the dossier was his face, or at least a face that could have been his. It was a digital composite, close enough to the real thing to have been composed from reasonably reliable and recent information. A verbal description here, a grainy closed-circuit camera image there—add a dash of rumor and serve.

The photo-fit was a worry, but he was relieved to find that their knowledge of him was so limited. If they knew anything else it would be here as well. Even the most amateur of assassins knows the value of a detailed dossier, and even the most cautious of clients wants his hirelings to have every advantage available. He folded the sheet up and placed it into his inside pocket. There were no postmarks on the envelope so he left it.

In the back of the van were the greasy remains of takeout breakfasts but nothing else. He wasn't surprised by this. The only thing of use he'd found had been in the dead sniper's bag. The other members of the team had been careful not to bring anything unnecessary with them.

Victor looked in both side mirrors to make sure no one was watching and climbed out onto the sidewalk. A perimeter around the hotel was being set up by the police and he joined the crowds, allowing himself to be funneled out of the street and away by a harried police officer.

At the end of the road Victor hailed a taxi and told the driver to take him to the Musée d'Orsay. The taxi driver asked him what had happened, gesturing to the adjoining street and its huge crowd.

Victor shrugged. "Ca a l'air serieux." Something bad.

It was then that someone noticed the brainless corpse lying in the gutter and more screaming started.

The man watching the taxi pull away was tall with gelled dark hair. He stood among the crowd outside the hotel, pretending to be as bewildered as the throng of Parisians around him. He shared their anxiety, but not their ignorance. His eyes tracked the taxi until it had left the street and he pulled a slim notebook from his inside jacket pocket. He flipped over a few pages and wrote down in clear handwriting the license plate of the taxi and a brief description of the passenger.

The face on the photo-fit hadn't had a beard and the hair was different, but there could be no mistaking who it was. The tall man sighed heavily. This was bad.

He negotiated his way through the ever-expanding horde of onlookers and finally came out of the crowd feeling hot despite the chill November air. The man was dressed in a suit and raincoat and looked like any other soldier of commerce. Unless absolutely necessary he wouldn't speak with anyone around him. His French was good but not fluent.

He walked away at a controlled pace, hurrying like the terrified crowd, though he wasn't scared. He would have liked to have stayed longer but there were police everywhere, and more had to be on the way. Cops were already examining the crowds, narrowing in on potential witnesses and suspects. It would not be good for him to have to answer any difficult questions.

He knew there was a pay phone farther down the

road, on a side street, which he headed toward. It was sufficiently out of the way to be used discretely but close enough to the hotel so that he could report in promptly. The report he was about to give was far from what had been expected.

He didn't know exactly what happened inside the hotel, but he could make a reasonable enough analysis. The target had escaped in such a manner as to attract a huge police presence, and there was no sign of the team that was supposed to do the job. He'd overheard people in the crowd talking about bodies. None of the team members had left the hotel. It didn't take a genius to connect the dots.

He passed a group of young women heading toward the commotion and took a left into the narrow side street, where a café released a myriad of exotic smells into the air. The phone booth was unoccupied and he stepped inside, closing the door behind him, thankful for the muffling of the exterior noise that allowed him to think more clearly.

He dialed a number, and while he waited for the line to connect he thought about how best to phrase that the job had been a spectacular failure.

His employer was not going to be pleased.

SEVEN

Less than a mile away Alvarez looked down at the corpse on the steel tray before him and sighed heavily. The wrinkled skin was pale, the eyes closed, the lips tinged with blue. A small red hole marked the skin of the left temple. Entry wound. The hole in the right temple was larger, rougher. Exit wound.

"Yeah," he breathed. "That's the poor bastard."

The French assistant mortician responded with a brief nod. He stood a few feet away, on the other side of the table, a young man in his twenties, and despite the cool temperature Alvarez could see there was sweat on his brow. The mortician shifted his weight, fidgeted. Alvarez pretended not to notice.

The American realized he wasn't helping calm the kid. Alvarez knew he had a face that seemed to be perpetually scowling and made people who didn't know him better feel uncomfortable. Even smiling didn't help, and his size only exacerbated the problem. Alvarez had a neck wider than his skull and shoulders that filled a door frame. When it came to confrontation his appearance gave him an edge, but the rest of the time it was simply a hindrance. He had to work twice as hard as anyone else just to get people to trust him.

He had the pathologist's report in hand. He glanced over the details to where it described the bullet wounds. There were two more to the chest. He gestured.

"Show me."

The mortician looked around nervously before carefully gripping the white stain-proof sheet. He folded it backward from the body's neck to reveal the torso.

Alvarez examined the two neat holes in the sternum. "They look small caliber to me. Twenty-twos?"

"No," the mortician answered. "All three wounds. Two to the chest, one to the head. 5.7 mm rounds."

"Interesting." Alvarez leaned forward for a closer look. "What kind of range are we looking at?"

"No powder burns so it wasn't point blank, other than that I can't tell you. Listen, I'm just an assistant here. I'm not a ballistics expert. I . . . I don't know very much."

No shit, Alvarez thought. He considered for a moment. That the rounds were 5.7 mm meant an FN Five-seveN, one of the world's slickest and most expensive handguns. He pictured the scene in his head. Double-tap to the heart, then, as the victim was prone, head to one side, the killer put one extra through the frontal lobe. Not taking any chances. Alvarez was no stranger to professional killings, and this execution was about as thorough as they came. He blinked the image away.

"Look," the mortician began, "my boss is going to be back soon."

Alvarez could take a hint. He opened his wallet.

Outside the hospital he buttoned up his coat against the drizzle. Where the hell was Kennard? It took a couple of minutes before the dark sedan pulled up outside.

"Sorry," Kennard said, as Alvarez climbed into the passenger seat.

Alvarez rubbed some of the rain from his buzz cut. "It's Ozols," he said. "He's dead."

"Jesus," Kennard exhaled. "The package?"

Alvarez shook his head. He summarized what he'd seen.

"What do we do?" Kennard asked.

Alvarez chewed on his thumbnail for a moment. He reached into his jacket for his cell phone. "I've got to speak to Langley."

EIGHT

09:41 CET

Le Hotel Abrial was located on the Avenue de Villiers, west of the Seine. Victor had caught a second taxi at the museum, and it was a long, slow drive through the Parisian traffic. The driver was thankfully silent, and Victor gave him a moderate tip. A generous tip or no tip at all and the driver might remember him if asked at a later date.

Victor noted that it was a nice area, glowing with all the positive things that tourists tell their friends about Paris but without the rain, the dirt, and the sour-faced Parisians. Victor made his way along the busy street, passing the hotel. He found a pharmacy a couple of blocks away where he purchased a bar of soap, disinfectant, tweezers, cotton balls, and deodorant. He then found a quiet bar where he bought a lemonade and used the bathroom to wash himself.

He then turned his attention to the wooden splinters embedded in his face. At the time adrenaline had blocked the pain, but Victor no longer enjoyed such luxury. The splinters were small but rough and snagged in his flesh. With gritted teeth he drew them from his cheek with the aid of the tweezers. He would have preferred to get it over with quickly, but he had to work slowly to avoid their breaking. When the last one was out, he held a cotton ball soaked with disinfectant against the tiny wounds for as long as he could stand it.

If the bullet had struck the door frame a few inches higher, he would've been pulling splinters from his eyeball instead of his cheek. Not a pleasant thought. He withdrew a small bottle of eyedrops from a pocket and splashed some silicone solution onto his hands and rubbed it in. It dried in seconds. He allowed himself to light a cigarette outside and smoked it leisurely as he walked along the sidewalk. The hit of nicotine was just what he needed. Being alive felt good.

He promised himself it would be the first and last one today. He'd been trying to keep up a one-a-day rate for the last week and was determined to stick with it this time, maybe even cut down further in a couple of weeks. Or maybe not. Either way, he wasn't going to ruin the post-battle elation worrying about his little addiction. Victor discarded the smoked cigarette, momentarily feeling bad for littering but eased his guilt by conscientiously disposing of the toiletries—in several different trash cans.

The hotel lobby was simple but tasteful, thankfully quiet. He caught the eye of a happy-looking receptionist behind the desk who was scratching his bleached goatee and walked over.

"Quis-je vous aider, monsieur?" the guy asked.

"Oui, avez-vous un téléphone public?"

The receptionist pointed to the far end of the lobby, toward the sign for the bathrooms. "Juste autour là."

Victor thanked him and crossed the lobby. Around a corner there were two outdated pay phones. Victor checked the inside line number for room service and called it. A cheery female voice answered.

"Hi," he said back. "I have some laundry to deliver, but I can't read the room number." He gave the reference code on the receipt.

There was a strained sigh. "I wish they'd sort that out." Victor heard fingers punching keys with rapid efficiency. "Mr. Svyatoslav." It took a couple of attempts to pronounce. "He's in room 210."

It was a pleasant room with a comfortable-looking bed, spacious en suite bathroom, and elegant decor. Victor switched on the TV and used the remote to flick to a news channel. So far nothing about the shootings. He doubted it would be long before a story about the killings aired. He turned the set off and looked around the room. The sniper hadn't been in any hurry to leave. Clothes hung on the outside of the wardrobe, toiletries still lined the sink in the bathroom. Maybe he had planned to do a little sightseeing after he'd shot Victor. A foreigner in Paris, why not take in some of the culture? Now the only sightseeing he'd be doing would be in hell.

Victor looked forward to the postcard.

He expected the other assassins would have rooms at different hotels throughout the city. Less conspicuous that way, especially for a multinational group whose members, Victor believed, didn't know one another before they had been assembled to kill him. Without any clues to where they had been staying, he would have to make the most of his current location.

There was nothing on the tables by the bed or in the drawers next to it. He ran his fingers between the mattress and the frame, finding and removing a brown leather wallet that was empty except for a few euros. No passport or plane ticket. He supposed that would have been too easy.

Victor searched the room thoroughly, first checking the toilet tank to see if the sniper used the same security methods as himself, but nothing was hidden there. A shame. It would have been nice to share a little kinship with the man he'd killed.

Every other feasible hiding location proved to be empty. The hotel safe then. That made sense. No chance of the maid or anyone else walking away with something valuable or incriminating.

The sniper had made a telling error in having personal items with him on a job. It was inexcusable, if understandable. After all he did not plan on being killed. And dead it hardly mattered anyway if someone found out who he was. That reaffirmed what Victor already knew about the team. They were independent contractors, not affiliated with any organization. If they had been, the sniper would have been more careful. So who assembled them? Someone with resources, someone with means. Hiring assassins wasn't as simple as flipping open the phone book and looking under *A*.

Victor made enemies just doing his job, but only someone who knew he was going to be in Paris could have had killers stationed in the city. As far as he knew only two people fell into that category. His client and his broker.

The person who had supplied him with the job he knew only as the broker. This was the individual who acted as the middleman between Victor and the person who actually wanted the job done. The client. Victor didn't know the identity of either. Victor likewise didn't know why the client wanted the target dead, except it had something to do with the item now in his jacket pocket.

What association the broker had with the client Victor didn't know. Sometimes brokers were individuals, free agents; other times they worked for a country's intelligence services, private security firms, organized crime, or other groups. Or they might be associated with the client through other business practices, such as a lawyer or consul, or the client may have been passed to the broker through other intermediaries.

There was always the risk a broker was in fact some member of a police or intelligence force who had somehow found out about Victor and was hiring him so they could apprehend him. One of the many dangers of the freelance trade. The broker who had passed this job to Victor had been a first-timer, at least in his dealings with Victor. He knew nothing about the broker except that the efficiency and professionalism demonstrated suggested that this broker had dealt with hired killers before.

Victor took out the flash drive and examined it closely. Just a memory stick—not very exciting, but he guessed the information it contained was to someone. He was supposed to stash the drive at a secure site of his choosing and contact the broker with the location so it could be picked up.

The broker had petitioned for a personal handover of the drive, but Victor never met anyone directly connected to his work unless he also planned to kill them. Not only did he want to avoid having anyone see his face, but a prearranged handover would always present a perfect opportunity to ambush him. Now it appeared an ambush is exactly what would have occurred had Victor gone along with the broker's request. Since he'd refused to comply, they'd been forced to try to kill him immediately after he'd killed Ozols, while they still knew where Victor was. If they had waited until he'd stashed the drive and contacted the broker, they might have lost him.

If the motive for wanting him dead was to ensure that any subsequent investigation or reprisals could not be traced back to them, then it was understandable but stupid. Aside from communiqués over the Internet there was no connection between Victor and the broker and absolutely no connection between Victor and the client. This method protected all parties. Or maybe it was simpler than that. Maybe they just didn't want to pay him the second half of his fee. Still, hiring a whole team of assassins couldn't have been cheap, even for ones he doubted charged anywhere near as much as he did.

In the lobby he gave Svyatoslav's details to the desk clerk and asked to check out before adding, "You have some of my things in the safe."

If the clerk decided to check the photograph in the passport against the man standing in front of the desk there could be no mistaking the two. He reached into his coat to flick off the .45's safety but decided against it. The clerk was young, skinny. He wouldn't put up much of a struggle.

The clerk returned a few seconds later and handed Victor a passport, plane ticket, and credit-card wallet. There was no change in the clerk's cheery expression. Victor was satisfied he hadn't bothered to make any checks. Victor had a look at the items, as might anyone concerned about leaving something behind. He noted the plane ticket was for Munich, business class. Inside the wallet were two credit cards. Both cards and plane ticket were for Mikhail Svyatoslav. Victor placed the wallet and ticket in his pocket. No keys. Too late to worry about where they might be now.

He signed out and paid the bill with the more worn looking of the sniper's credit cards after subtly checking the signature on the back. His forgery wouldn't get past a handwriting expert but it was close enough for a clerk who looked like he would have trouble reading the articles in a porn magazine.

The clerk handed him a copy of the bill, which Victor

saw included the sniper's address, and said, "We hope you had a pleasant time in Paris."

He sounded genuine. Victor considered how genuine he would have been had he known that moments before Victor had been deciding how best to kill him.

Victor raised an eyebrow.

"It's been stimulating."

NINE

13:15 CET

"What the hell is going on here?"

Alvarez and Kennard stood on the Rue du Faubourg Saint-Honoré. In front of them the crowd was three ranks deep before a police barrier. The road had been cordoned off on either side of the hotel. Alvarez could see numerous uniformed and plainclothes officers and crime-scene personnel going about their duties.

Kennard got off his phone and turned to Alvarez. "From what I can make out something crazy went down this morning. I'm hearing eight people dead—shot—and one suspect at large who may sound familiar."

"Holy crap, John." Alvarez looked at Kennard expectantly. "The same guy who capped Ozols?"

The younger man nodded. "The shooter shares the same taste for exotic projectiles. Apparently several people were shot with 5.7 mm subsonics. It's too early for them to have matched the bullets yet, but . . ."

"The chances of two separate gunmen both using that specific round in Paris on the same morning—"

"Are slim at best."

"Skeletal, even." Alvarez did his best to peer over the heads of the spectators who were eager for a glance at something juicy. "When did all this go down?"

"Sometime in the AM is the best anyone can tell me. So not long ago."

"Before Ozols got clipped?"

"Not sure, at least an hour later I think."

"We've got to get inside there."

Alvarez pushed his way through the crowd. He was a big man by anyone's reckoning. He had wrestled his way through college, strictly Greco-Roman, and at six even and two ten he still looked like a warrior, even if his black hair had developed more than a few gray friends. His size could be intimidating, and he had exploited that plenty of times before, but these days Alvarez realized it was far better for people to underestimate him than to be afraid of him. At times like this, though, he put his bulk to good use.

He met a palm the instant he reached the line. Alvarez showed his credentials. After examining them for a moment the guy gestured for his superior. The Frenchman who sauntered over was middle aged, short, meticulously groomed, looking annoyed at actually having to do something. Alvarez still had his hand up and the policeman squinted at the opened wallet for a few seconds.

"Yes?" he asked simply in English.

"Are you in charge here?"

The guy nodded. "I'm Lieutenant Lefèvre." He paused. "What can I do for you?" He added the second part almost as an afterthought.

Alvarez put his wallet away. "I'm with the United States Department of State working out of the American embassy here in Paris. I believe your suspect for this shooting may be the same individual who killed a contact of mine earlier today, a Latvian national by the name of Andris Ozols."

Alvarez could tell Lefèvre knew of the connection already, but he doubted Lefèvre knew what Ozols had been doing in Paris. "So?" he asked simply.

Alvarez wasn't exactly surprised, but he would have liked a more encouraging response. "So," he echoed, "it's in both our interests to pool our resources on this. If I can take a look around the hotel I—"

"I'm afraid that's impossible."

"Why, did you not hear what I just said?"

Lefèvre shifted the weight between his legs, which, judging by his gut, was considerable. "This is our investigation. You have no jurisdiction in this country."

Alvarez resisted taking the bait; instead, he took a breath and said evenly, "I'm not looking to steal your suspect from you or your credit, I just want to help find him. And crazy as this sounds, I thought we might help each other to achieve that."

"Thank you for the offer," Lefèvre said, with no attempt at sincerity. "If your assistance is required you can be assured we'll ask for it."

He turned around and headed back toward the hotel.

"What a dick," Alvarez muttered after he'd gone.

He pushed his way out of the crowd less politely than he had made his way in. He got out his cell phone and looked at Kennard.

"Okay, time for plan B."

TEN

Charleroi, Belgium
Monday
17:02 CET

The kid behind the counter took Victor's money without looking up from his graphic novel. With one hand he opened the register, dropped in the euros, and handed Victor a slip of paper without speaking a single word. Victor took a seat at one of the computers farthest from the entrance, selecting a position where he could still see the door without having to turn his head.

The computer monitor was a flat panel, seemingly recently purchased, but dust had collected in the grooves of the keyboard. The plastic was yellowed and shiny from overuse. Victor, typing quickly, entered the ten-digit code from the piece of paper and hit enter.

The Internet café had half a dozen other customers. They were all young. A Chinese teenager, her hair streaked with pink, entered while Victor waited for the browser to appear. An exchange student perhaps. After a cursory glance he paid her no attention.

He would have preferred a more crowded establishment to provide anonymity, but no one paid him a second of attention. The kid by the door hadn't taken his eyes from the comic since Victor had paid. The front cover was all huge breasts and curved swords. In five minutes Victor would be gone, and five minutes after that he would be forgotten entirely.

A light rain was falling. Through the window Victor could see pedestrians hurrying along the street outside, some with umbrellas, the unlucky without. No one seemed to be observing the café.

The rational part of his brain told him that no one could have followed him across the border, but there was a certain level of paranoia necessary for survival in Victor's work. He understood that he was most at risk not when he was obviously vulnerable but when he felt safe.

After leaving the sniper's hotel Victor had spent an hour on the Paris metro going back and forth between stations and changing trains at random to elude any possible shadows. It was highly unlikely that there were yet more people available to follow him, but protocol demanded caution at all times. And this was no time to abandon methods that had kept him alive for almost a decade in a profession as unforgiving as they came.

The Heckler and Koch he'd taken from the female assassin was thrown into the Seine after being wiped down thoroughly. A mile upstream his second FN Five-seveN suffered the same fate. The passport he'd been traveling under was burned and another taken from a safety-deposit box he rented under a false name. He had boxes in several European capitals and other cities around the world. In Victor's experience prevention was always better than cure, and his earlier encounter vindicated this philosophy.

He'd discarded the nonprescription glasses and taken out the blue contact lenses before having a backstreet barber cut his hair clipper short and shave him with a cutthroat razor. On a wall-mounted television Victor had watched a news item about the hotel shooting. So far the police had released few details. The dead man in the alley received no mention, probably because a mass murder was far more exciting to the viewers.

Victor had purchased a new suit from a department store and another shirt and a pair of shoes, each from a different shop. If he purchased them all from the same place the shop assistant might remember him. His other clothes were bagged and left in an alleyway to be recycled by the city's tramps. The only physical evidence that he'd ever been in Paris were the corpses he'd left behind.

Perhaps if he'd stayed he might have found more out about his attackers, but while he remained in France he had to protect himself against both his hunters and the authorities. Outside it was one on one. Much better odds.

He had been careful at the hotel to make sure the security cameras hadn't gotten a good shot of his face, but maybe the receptionist or a guest would remember his features. The beard, glasses, hair, and colored contact lenses would all help corrupt any artist's sketch, but even so he would probably need surgery to change his face. He sighed heavily. It was a necessity that over the years he'd been forced to accept, even if he would never fully get used to it. The face that stared back at him in the mirror was no longer his, altered so many times he couldn't remember what he truly looked like. Sometimes he was glad of that.

The Internet browser finally loaded up, and he entered the address for a proxy server where he had an account under a false name. Then, using the proxy server to disguise the computer's IP address, he typed in the Web address for an online role-playing game forum based out of South Korea.

The game was hugely popular, and the forum had hundreds of thousands of registered users. The forum had its own sophisticated security system to prevent hackers disrupting its service. Not so good against governments, but with the amount of traffic that passed through the forum's server it would be near impossible for anyone to intercept his communications.

Victor entered his login details and selected the instant-messaging option. He preferred it over a traditional message board, where posts can be stored almost indefinitely. With instant messaging the data passing between the computers left no trail at the forum for someone to discover. The only traces left would be at his computer and at the receiving computer his broker used.

Once he'd logged in he saw that the only name in his contact's list was online.

The broker.

Victor double-clicked the name, opening up a chat

window. He typed a message. To further hamper the odds of the NSA or GCHQ picking up on such conversation, he always avoided any of the obvious tags government supercomputers were programmed to look for. No Allahu Akbar or the like.

I had a problem.

The reply was almost instantaneous: *What's happened?*

There was another firm in on the deal.

What are you talking about?

Seven rival sales reps, well briefed on my pitch. They waited until after my morning meeting and offered me a new position. Of the permanent variety.

The response took a few seconds. *I'm sorry to hear that.*

Be sorry for those reps. I was out of their price range.

Did the deal go through?

Yes, he typed. *The customer found my offer irresistible.*

Did you collect the item?

Victor thought for a moment being typing. *I have it.*

What do you need from me?

An explanation.

I don't understand.

Then allow me to enlighten you. Besides myself, the only people who knew where I would be finalizing the deal are you and whoever you work for.

What are you getting at?

I'm not in the habit of sabotaging my own contracts. This is not what you think.

Then what is it?

Whatever happened had nothing to do with us.

Victor sat back. The use of the word *us* made him think that the broker and the client were more closely connected with each other than he had thought.

Victor didn't type anything.

The broker continued. *I know nothing about what happened except for what you've just told me. You have to trust me.*

If there was a button to simulate a loud laugh on the broker's computer, Victor would have pressed it.

I prefer to trust myself.

So how can I convince you?

You've had your chance.

What about the item?

I won't be delivering it.

There was a long pause. *Please reconsider.*

At best you were so incompetent as to allow a third party to find out about our arrangement. At worst just stupid enough to try and undercut me. Regardless, this is where we part company.

Wait.

You won't see or hear from me again, Victor typed. *But I may be seeing you.*

He logged off as the broker was still typing a reply. It felt good to end with a threat. An old friend used to tell him any victory, however small, was still a victory.

The broker had said *us.* It could have been a momentary lapse in concentration revealing the broker and client had colluded to set him up, or it could be nothing. There was no way to be certain at the moment.

A noise made him look up. The annoying novelty

ringtone of a cellular phone. The Chinese student fumbled in her pocket to retrieve it. Victor typed in another memorized Web address. There was a momentary delay before the new site appeared on the screen. He clicked one of the twenty links available and watched as the program downloaded.

It was only a few megabytes in size and it took just seconds on the café's fast Internet connection. Victor then ran the program. He watched passively as a gray box popped up and a rapid stream of numbers and file names appeared, scrolling downward. Two minutes later the program had run its course, having deleted all records of recent Internet activity from the computer's hard disk. The program had not only deleted these records but also overwritten with useless data those sectors of the hard disk where the Internet records had been stored. It had then deleted that data and overwrote it again. This process repeated itself thousands of times in rapid succession, ensuring that the original data could never be recovered.

It then repeated the process on itself. Thirty seconds later there was no trace of what sites Victor had visited or what he had done there. A skillful technician might be able to find evidence of the program, but that would be all.

Victor rose from his seat and left the café. There was a security camera watching the front door, so he kept his face angled away as he'd done on the way in.

He headed for the train station.

ELEVEN

Central Intelligence Agency, Virginia, U.S.A.
Monday
13:53 EST

Five time zones west stood the CIA's sprawling Langley headquarters. At the center of the 258-acre site, over two million square feet of glass, steel, concrete, and technology house the world's most highly funded espionage organization. Composed of the original sixties headquarters and the eighties upgrade, the CIA complex employed around twenty thousand men and women. Of these only a handful could rightly call themselves Roland Procter's superior, and of this fact he was immensely proud.

Procter sat behind his desk in his enviable top-floor office. The office was light and spacious, climate controlled, tastefully decorated, and of a noticeably large size. The best feature by far was the beautiful view Procter enjoyed of the Virginia countryside surrounding the agency's headquarters. The associate director for the National Clandestine Service placed the phone down, stood, breathed in to button up his suit jacket, and exited the office.

With long strides Procter made his way through the featureless corridors to the conference room. He was there in less than a minute and pushed open the door. Everybody else was already seated around the long oval table.

Only about half actually needed to be there, all big dogs from his department. The others were mandarins from across the hierarchy who had seats because of their status instead of their usefulness. The Ozols operation had been a big deal and plenty of people, even if they had personally contributed nothing toward it, had had a stake in its success and now its failure.

The pleasantries were kept brief as Procter took his seat. Sitting across from him was the department's deputy director. Meredith Chambers was short and slim, with a narrow face and graying black hair that she vehemently refused to dye. She was a good few years Procter's senior, but he had to admit she looked pretty good for her age, even if he usually preferred women with far more meat on the hips. Wearing a fine navy pantsuit, Chambers looked as regal as ever. She had been in charge of NCS for less than a year and was still a bit wet behind the ears in Procter's opinion. Her office was a fair chunk larger than Procter's own but he had the up on the view. He'd bet his pension she was a firecracker in the sack.

"Right," Chambers began. "I understand Alvarez is on the line. Can you hear me?"

Alvarez's voice came through the table's speakerphones "Yes, ma'am."

Procter knew Alvarez pretty well and knew that although he had all the attributes necessary for a good field agent, he was also one of the true good guys. There was a sense of duty and patriotism so ingrained in him that his blood wasn't just red but white and blue as well.

Over a long career in the CIA Procter was surprised to say that he found straight shooters like Alvarez few and far between.

Chambers said, "Okay, then. A few of us are up-to-date with what's happened today, some are not, so if you could begin by giving us a summary of the operation's background."

"This morning, Paris time," Alvarez began, "I was due to meet one Andris Ozols, a retired Latvian officer of the Russian navy and the Soviet fleet before that. Ozols claimed to know the location of a Russian frigate that had sunk in the Indian Ocean back in 2008. The Russians have never acknowledged the accident, a catastrophic engine malfunction that led to the deaths of all sailors on board, one because it came embarrassingly soon after the Russians and Chinese navies had been doing exercises in the area, and two because, according to Ozols, the ship was carrying eight Oniks antiship cruise missiles."

Chambers said, "I'd now like William to tell us about the Oniks."

William Ferguson sat on Procter's side of the table. The head of the Russian office, Ferguson was one of the company's true old boys. He was in his late sixties, and his face was deeply wrinkled, but he hadn't lost a strand of the gray hair that was combed back from his high forehead. Unless he wore his long overcoat to bulk him out, he looked thin, half-starved almost, but never weak. He had fought three tours in Vietnam and had received more major medals than Procter had fat fingers. The old guy was a staunch patriot and career spy who had done

America's much-needed dirty work for forty-odd years. His list of exploits against the Soviets during the cold war was legendary, and to those who knew of his achievements he was rightly regarded as a hero. Even though he was a decade older than Procter, Ferguson was one step down the food chain. That was, in Procter's understanding, Ferguson's choice. He had remained in the trenches of his own free will, and Procter had huge respect for that.

"The SS-NX-26 Oniks," Ferguson began in his slow baritone, "is quite simply the missile we wish we'd designed. It is the replacement for the SS-N-22 Sunburn, a missile that was described by some experts, myself included, as the most dangerous missile on the planet. The Oniks is even more lethal."

He cleared his throat before continuing. "These missiles practically come guaranteed to ruin your day. They have a range of 162 nautical miles and can cruise at an altitude as low as nine feet if necessary, flying at two and a half times the speed of sound, carrying either a 550-pound conventional warhead or a 200-kiloton nuke. For comparison purposes, our equivalents, the Harpoon and Tomahawk, have a range of less than fifty miles and fly at subsonic speeds. Think of a push bike versus an Indy car.

"But it's not just the speed or even the range that keeps our admirals awake at night, it's the accuracy of these weapons. It's extraordinary. In '03 Russian and Chinese fleets performed joint war games in the Indian Ocean, simulating attacks against aggressive American-carrier battle groups. The timing of the demonstration was not coincidental. We just happened to be flexing our own naval muscles at the same time, in that same part of the world." He showed a wry smile. "The highlight of the show was when a Chinese missile destroyer fired a Sunburn with a practice warhead. A high-speed camera recorded the missile hitting the center of a white cross painted on the hull of the target vessel over sixty nautical miles away. The Sunburn flew at just twenty-two feet above sea level. The Oniks is faster, carries a larger payload, and is even harder to detect, let alone stop.

"Do we need to be concerned about this weapon?" Ferguson looked around the room briefly. "Absolutely. They've been specifically designed to defeat the U.S. Aegis radar and Phalanx defense system that protect our ships. Phalanx's replacement, the rolling-action missile, has never been tested against these kind of weapons. Quite simply, we have no proven defense for the Oniks or even the Sunburn. They completely upset the balance of naval warfare, and a few humble destroyers armed with these missiles can take out an entire carrier group. We don't have anything that comes close to the Oniks. And we want them. Bad."

Ferguson enjoyed his little speech, Procter could tell. The old man had spent his career battling the Soviets, and since the Berlin wall had come down his experience and knowledge just wasn't as valuable. Now, everyone was more concerned with the Middle East than the Russians. If the shoe had been on the other foot Procter knew he'd be resentful of that fall from glory. If Ferguson carried any resentment though, he hid it well.

One of the mandarins decided to get his money's worth. Nathan Wyley was on Procter's side of the table. Though he was just on the sunny side of fifty, Wyley looked at least ten years younger with his ridiculous shock of floppy blond hair. For some reason Procter had yet to work out, Wyley didn't much like him, not that Procter cared how the lanky streak of piss felt.

"How the hell do the Russians have this missile and not us?" Wyley asked.

Ferguson sighed and motioned for his deputy, Sykes, to answer for him. Procter wasn't one hundred percent sure of Sykes's first name. It was Karl or Kevin or something. He had the build of someone who trained at the gym but not enough to warrant advertising the fact. Procter didn't know exactly how old he was, but Sykes looked as if he was somewhere in his midthirties. Though in the wrong light his tired eyes made him look much older. His suits were always immaculate, tailored, far more expensive than his pay grade should allow. Procter had put Sykes under investigation a couple of years back to find out if he had been supplementing his income, but it turned out he had wealthy parents and a trust fund.

Sykes was something of an unknown quantity to Procter. He had the nice clothes, the clean-cut face, good teeth, and said all the right things. He was almost the antithesis of Ferguson—young and frighteningly ambitious. Sykes was in the department to make a name for himself, and probably disliked being assigned to the unglamorous Russian office, but he was keen to impress.

Procter could see shades of his own ambition in the guy's eyes and didn't always like what he saw.

"Because," Sykes began with a smile that showed lots of bleached teeth, "believe it or not, we're not the top of the pile when it comes to missile technology. Russia may have left most of her arms development in the trash, but the budget strings are still thick in places. Russia has focused on a few key technologies and has more than kept up in areas such as fighter jets. In certain missile technologies they're the market leaders by a long way, earning billions in sales to other countries. Their antiship–cruise missile capabilities are not just a step up from our own but a whole leap. They're at least twenty-five years in advance of anything we've got."

Chambers: "If we could let Alvarez continue now."

Ferguson nodded as though his approval was actually required.

Alvarez's voice came back through the speakerphone. "In short, Ozols was going to sell the location of the sunken ship to the highest bidder. The buyer would then be free to recover the missiles at their leisure. As you can imagine, there are a lot of regimes out there who would love to get these kinds of weapons for their arsenals. Ozols claimed that he had half a dozen other potential buyers interested when he approached us. He wanted to sell the information for two hundred million euros, but I bartered him down to a little over one hundred million."

Chambers sighed. "I cannot overstate the importance of our being the ones to recover those missiles. Not only would we improve our own antiship–cruise missile technology, but, more significantly, we can prevent some less-than-desirable faction from potentially using the technology against either us or our allies. Furthermore, it would enable our own navy to improve and develop defenses against these kind of missiles." She paused before adding, "Let's not forget the Chinese and Iranians have these kinds of weapons already."

Wyley leaned toward the speakerphone. "A hundred million bucks for a grid reference seems a little steep."

Ferguson came to the rescue. "Each year we spend more than the GDP of most countries making sure we have the best toys. A hundred million to leapfrog a quarter century of arms development is the bargain of a lifetime. Especially because we've been after the Sunburn for years and Russia won't sell."

"And they'll still work after all this time underwater?" Wyley asked.

Sykes nodded. "Maybe, maybe not. They're housed in airtight casings that protect them from the elements but aren't designed for submersion in salt water. The casing may have corroded, and any that have been exposed to seawater will be useless, but the technology will still be extractable, as will the warheads carried, which could be anything. Anyone who recovered the missiles and their accompanying electronics would be able to reverse-engineer the design and create their own equivalents. Against a regime with these kinds of missiles our naval capabilities are extremely reduced. Even replicas with fifty percent of the capabilities of an Oniks can cripple or even destroy one of our aircraft carriers."

"And why deal in Paris?" Chambers asked.

Alvarez's voice again emanated through the speakerphone. "The man was paranoid as hell. He was convinced we were going to double-cross him. He would only meet on neutral soil. Somewhere he thought we would have difficulty pulling any stunts. Paris was his idea. He gave me a seven-day window, promising he'd call at some point during that period with the time and location of the meet. He phoned just before six this morning, said he wanted to meet an hour later. Obviously he didn't show."

Chambers leaned forward gracefully. "I suppose it's too much to hope that Ozols gave any clues as to where the frigate is located before you were due to meet."

"Unfortunately he did not. He was coy enough not to give me anything even remotely specific. What he did tell me was that Moscow believed the ship had sunk in deep water and so wasn't worth recovering but that in fact it had come to rest on the continental shelf in shallow water. Ozols claimed it's in international waters so anyone with a boat and its location can get to it easily. I'm sure you can appreciate that there is a lot of continental shelf out there in the Indian Ocean."

"Why didn't he just try selling the information back to the Russians anonymously?" one of the mandarins asked.

"My guess is he knew if he tried to they'd be able to work out who was doing the selling and send a nice little SVR execution team to offer him a better deal."

Chambers asked, "How was the exchange supposed to happen?"

"Ozols had agreed to supply the information on a flash drive that he was going to give me on the day he was killed. I would then check the information, and, if it appeared genuine, I would wire half the money to his bank account. I would then walk away with the drive once he had checked with his bank that the money was there. The other half would be held in an escrow account that he would get access to once we had located the ship. It was the best deal I could negotiate."

"Okay," Chambers said. "Now take us through what happened in Paris."

"We still haven't gotten even a fraction of the details yet," Alvarez began. "The French are keeping as many people out of the loop with this as possible. It's so sandwiched in crap it's taken this long just to chew through it."

"Don't tell me you're surprised at this," Ferguson interjected. "Our friends across the pond may be among the least intellectually blessed of our allies, but they're not quite as dumb as we would like to believe. They have eyes and ears. They know we're keeping them in the dark about something and they don't like it."

Procter smiled inwardly. The old man always spoke his mind without restraint, quite often without decorum as well.

Wyley cleared his throat before getting involved again. "Do you think they found out about the op?"

"Unless there's a leak or they've developed extrasensory perception, then of course they haven't," Ferguson responded. "But Gallic paranoia has probably conjured up a host of incredible explanations for events thus far. None of which will be close to the truth, so stop worrying about them. For the time being at least the French are nothing more than an annoyance."

Chambers gave Ferguson a polite but firm look. "Continue, Alvarez."

"This is what we know. The medical examiner puts Ozols's time of death at sometime between five and seven AM. He was supposed to meet me to make the exchange at seven. He was shot in an alley just off the Rue de Marne. Corpse found by a shop owner pretty quickly. No identification, but I saw his body myself at the morgue. Double-tap through the heart with holes so close they were touching, and one through the temple from close range. No witnesses. No physical evidence. The killer was definitely a pro.

"Anyway, this is where it gets interesting. At eight fifteen the Paris police were called to a hotel where they found eight dead bodies. Five inside the hotel itself, two in a building opposite, and another in the street. One of the cops I spoke to, off the record, told me that they think one man killed them all. Bullets found in several of the corpses were 5.7 mm subsonics, the same round that killed Ozols, though fired from a different but same-model gun."

"What the hell happened?" Procter asked.

"At this time I have no idea," Alvarez answered. "I need to get inside that hotel, watch the security tapes, and look at the police report if I'm going to find out. I haven't been able to do that on my own."

"I'll make sure that happens," Chambers said.

Ferguson was shaking his head. "Someone killed Ozols and then went on a rampage through a Paris hotel? Doubtful."

"That's exactly as it appears," Alvarez stated firmly.

Chambers asked, "Do we have any indication whatsoever of who this killer represents? I'll take a guess at this stage."

"Ozols never told me who else he was negotiating with but I think we can make some educated guesses. Russia and China already have them and Iran has Sunburns, so Ozols wouldn't go to them. Ozols wanted to deal in Paris so the French probably aren't involved. But all the other usual suspects would love to get their hands on the Oniks: Israel, Saudi Arabia, Great Britain, India, Pakistan, North Korea. If someone found out Ozols was selling to us and not them then it's not unreasonable to think they'd try and get the information anyway. Sending a professional killer is a hell of a lot cheaper than paying what Ozols wanted as well. And let's not forget that the Russians might have found out what Ozols was up to and tracked him down."

"So, to clarify," Ferguson began, "you're saying the killer could be working for anyone?"

The voice that came through the speakerphone was deadly serious.

"I'll still find him."

TWELVE

Southeast of Charleroi, Belgium
Monday
19:48 CET

"Les billets, si vous plait."

Victor handed the conductor his ticket and thanked him when it was stamped and returned. The conductor made his way slowly along the aisle, periodically bracing himself against the train's lateral movement. He looked eighty years old and unlikely to make eighty-one.

It was snowing outside. Flakes had collected on the window to Victor's right, matted against the corners of the glass. Outside the scenery was invisible in the night, but when Victor leaned his cheek against the cold glass he could just make out fields and hills, the occasional twinkling light in the distance.

The train was two hours from the German border, and it would take into the early hours to reach Munich via Strasbourg, but Victor didn't allow himself the luxury of sleep. He wasn't sure that he could, even if he wanted to.

He was the only person in the carriage, sitting in the last row of seats, to the right of the aisle, the wall directly behind him. Sat straight in his seat he could see the far door and anyone who might come through it.

Any assailant entering through the door to Victor's left wouldn't see him until he or she was already right next to him. Then, if they were right-handed like ninety-percent of the world's population, they would have to turn their whole body or extend their arm completely in order to shoot at him. In either case it would give him enough time to make sure they didn't get the chance.

The door opened to Victor's left and he automatically stiffened in his seat. Adrenaline surged, readying him for attack.

It was a child, a girl, four or five. He relaxed. She didn't even look at him, just ran down the aisle bumping into seats on either side as she went. When she reached the end of the carriage she turned around and ran back, smiling as she bounced off one seat to the next. She stopped when she reached Victor, seeing him for the first time.

Eyes almost impossibly wide stared at his. He stared back but the intensity of her gaze made him uncomfortable, as though she could see through his eyes, past the veneer of his humanity to glimpse the real him that lay just beneath. But then she smiled, the gaps in her teeth showing, and any notion she possessed such power dissipated.

Feigning a look of puzzlement, Victor leaned forward and reached behind her ear. Her expression mimicked his. When he withdrew his hand he held a coin. A smile took over her face again. He rolled the coin back and forth across his fingers and the smile turned into a laugh.

He switched the coin into his left palm and passed the hand over his right. When he turned his left hand palm up it was empty. She laughed and pointed to his other hand. Maybe she'd seen the trick before, but Victor hoped she was merely perceptive beyond her years. He turned the closed right hand over and opened it. No coin there either. A look of confusion replaced the girl's smile. He sat there with both hands turned palm up and shrugged.

The door opened and a woman appeared, instantly calling to the girl. The child responded by running off again. Her mother hurried after her, the volume of her voice rising with each shout. She looked flustered as if she had chased the girl down the whole train.

The mother caught the child's collar before she'd reached the next door and marched her back the way they'd come with a sour expression on her face. In German she chastised her about running off, but the girl didn't seem to care.

As she came closer Victor caught the child's eye and gave her a look that said *better luck next time.* She grinned, and he slipped her the coin as they passed. Her eyes lit up for a second before she was gone and Victor had never felt more alone in his life.

The train rounded a long bend in the track and the overhead lights flickered momentarily. Victor drew a smartphone from his pocket and powered it on. He purchased it while in Charleroi, paying with cash to the shop owner's delight. When it had loaded he took out the flash drive and plugged it into the USB port. The drive allowed him to access it, but the only file it contained asked for a password when he tried to open it.

He put the flash drive inside his jacket. He forced

himself to think when all he wanted to do was shut down. Two hours after completing his assignment Eastern European assassins led by an American tried to kill him at his hotel. He thought about the dossier he'd found in the killers' van. They may not have had many personal details, but to know his face and where he had been staying required extremely accurate intel.

Only someone who knew he would be in Paris to kill Ozols could have had assassins in place to kill him. He didn't believe some third party was involved. The broker or client, or both together, had set him up, for safety, to save money, or some other reason he didn't yet understand. At this moment the why wasn't his priority. Staying alive was paramount, killing his enemies was secondary. Everything else was immaterial. If knowing why made it easier to protect himself only then did Victor care.

He opened up a file on the smartphone into which he had copied down all the sniper's details. It was too risky to try to take the actual documents across borders. He needed to find out who had hired Svyatoslav. Maybe it had been Victor's own broker or maybe someone else entirely. Either way Victor had to know. Svyatoslav resided in Munich so Victor would start his hunt there.

He realized his eyes were closed and forced them open. His body needed the rest, but while his enemies were still out there he couldn't afford to lessen his vigilance. He had spent his whole life being invisible, yet somehow, despite all the precautions, he'd been seen. Now more than ever he had to be on guard.

And in Victor's opinion the best form of defense was to attack.

THIRTEEN

Paris, France
Monday
22:48 CET

On the computer monitor a black-and-white image flickered incessantly. The picture was grainy, in places distorted, but the quality was just about adequate. It was low-res CCTV, so Alvarez was hardly expecting crystal clarity, but it would have been nice if the footage hadn't given him a bitch of a headache.

He pinched the skin between his eyebrows and wiped the tears from his strained eyes. He felt like shit and guessed he looked no better. He stood in the basement of the U.S. Embassy along with Kennard while a young tech guy whose name he didn't have time to remember controlled the equipment.

After he'd gotten off the call with headquarters, Chambers evidently had applied pressure on the French because Alvarez had received copies of all pertinent documentation. He'd also been given copies of the security tapes from the hotel in which five people, including a woman no less, had ended up shot to bits. According to the police report one of the two corpses found in the apartment building opposite was another woman, and an elderly one at that. This was the single craziest thing he'd worked on in his time in the CIA.

Alvarez had been an operations officer in the National Clandestine Services, previously known as the Directorate of Operations, for nearly eleven years. Before that he had served in the Marine Corps after leaving college, but life as a jarhead hadn't been for him. It had felt like treading water, always waiting for something to happen, but it never had. He'd joined up as a punk kid eager to see what he was made of, and the continual training and occasional humanitarian mission hadn't shown him what he wanted to find out. It had been a different time then, now he would probably get more action than he could stomach. He had joined the forces for the wrong reasons, but he had signed up with the CIA for all the right ones. Alvarez hadn't looked back since.

On the screen two men entered the elevator.

"Who are these guys?"

While Alvarez stood straight-backed with his big arms folded in front of his bigger chest, Kennard was hunched over, sleeves rolled up, elbows resting on the desk as he peered at the monitor. Kennard was a decade or more younger than Alvarez and was technically his number two, but Kennard liked to act as if they were partners. Alvarez, always the diplomat, let it pass to keep their working relationship friendly.

Kennard had an inch or two over him, used too much junk on his hair, and seemed to be on the agency gravy train just to get the health care. He was probably looking at it as a career stepping stone. Join the CIA out of college, get a few years under the belt; get experience and training; and then move on to bigger, better, and more highly paid things in the private sector. Alvarez didn't have much time for that kind of attitude. He was in the CIA to do his duty as a patriot.

Kennard was usually all mouth and wouldn't shut up unless his life depended on it, but he hadn't been his usual cocky self all day. Perhaps the seriousness of the work had finally given the guy a much needed wake-up call. People were dead. This wasn't some game.

Alvarez flicked through the photocopy of the preliminary case report. It had some extras his original copy didn't have. He'd acquired the additional information from an agency source inside the Paris police. It had cost the U.S. taxpayer a pretty dollar, but the thick wad of euros had done what the supposed agreement to cooperate had not.

He found the section of the report that listed each of the dead bodies. Apart from the old lady killed outside her front door, none of the corpses had identification. What most did have were radios with earpieces, guns, and ammunition. The French hadn't ID'd any yet, but Alvarez had fed his copy of the fingerprints into the system and was waiting on the results. Something very big had gone down at the hotel involving some very bad people.

Watching the tapes was a mind-numbing process, but Alvarez's motivation couldn't be higher. Andris Ozols had been set to meet Alvarez when he was murdered and the intel he had been carrying stolen. Recovering that information was Alvarez's priority, but equally important to Alvarez was catching the fucker who killed the Latvian and, at the very least, nailing him to the closest available wall.

Unfortunately the hotel made use of only two CCTV cameras, one in the lobby and one at the rear entrance. Cameras on every floor would have made Alvarez's life a whole lot easier. With only two tapes of footage to go on, Alvarez had to rely on what the police report told him to piece together what had happened. That report was, however, still frustratingly brief and full of holes. It would be a while before those gaps were filled.

"Here he comes," Kennard said. "Walking to reception."

Alvarez looked at the report. "Mr. Bishop, room 407."

On the screen Alvarez watched the mystery man move from the reception desk to the elevator, where he seemingly waited for it to arrive before suddenly standing by a cigarette machine. Obviously hiding from the two men who stepped out.

Both he and Kennard had watched the relevant parts of the tapes at least twenty times, and it still amazed Alvarez what he was seeing. As the two men stood in the lobby, the killer moved right past them, coming so close it looked as if they were touching, before slipping unnoticed into the elevator.

"Smooth," Kennard whispered.

Alvarez found himself nodding. "Fast-forward a moment."

The tech worked the controls and a whizzing sound accompanied the scrambling picture for a few seconds.

"That's enough," Alvarez said.

On the screen the two men were clearly anxious, frantically stabbing at the elevator buttons before rushing to the stairwell and disappearing.

Kennard shook his head. "And a few minutes later they're both corpses."

"They came to the hotel for him, not the other way around," Alvarez said. "Okay, let's skip until the other guys come in."

Alvarez loosened his tie for perhaps the tenth time, while Kennard stared at the screen. The tech worked silently on the fast-forwarding. The room was stuffy. There were no windows and the air conditioner was on its way to machine hell. Outside it was bitterly cold, but Alvarez, Kennard, and the tech geek had been in a ten-by-ten box full of electrical equipment for several long hours. The air was practically poisonous.

"Here we go," Kennard said.

The man who had to be Ozols's killer stepped out from the elevator and headed toward the center of the lobby, where he sat down in an armchair. Infuriatingly he kept his face hidden from the camera at all times, not overtly so, but with a gentle angling or inclination of the head ensuring the camera didn't pick up his features. It was too much to be just luck.

He couldn't have known where the camera was positioned before he arrived at the hotel, but he had checked in several days before, and the hotel only kept tapes for forty-eight hours. After that they were reused. Alvarez couldn't see the point of that. The hotel might as well not have any fucking cameras at all. He'd told the manager as much.

The killer reappeared on the recording for just a few seconds, moving through the lobby to the stairwell. Then he was gone again, and that was the last time he appeared on the footage. One body had been found in the kitchen, so to Alvarez it was a reasonable guess that the killer had left that way instead of the tradesman's, where the second camera was located. Then, more people had been killed in the building opposite, and another in the street itself.

Alvarez stood without moving as the rest of the tape played on, hoping for something else that might help. He was dog tired. His eyes stung. He was sure Kennard was feeling the same. He guessed the tech geek was used to staring at screens all day and didn't have a problem with it. He probably found this kind of crap exciting. Freak.

After another thirty minutes Alvarez finally pulled out a chair and sat down.

"We're not going to get anything more from this."

Kennard nodded. "Agreed." He cracked his knuckles. "You think they do Chinese chow in this town? I don't know about you guys but I could do with some crispy duck. I'm sick of this frog-food crap."

The tech found his voice. "There's a good place a couple of blocks west with some damn fine Asian ass waiting tables. I'll show you."

"Good." Kennard slapped his stomach. "I'm starved."

Alvarez was in no mood to eat. He spoke, half to himself. "One guy murders Ozols, then two hours later he goes back to his hotel where seven shooters try and kill him, but instead he kills them all."

"Yeah," Kennard said, eyes on the door.

"We've got a description from the receptionist for a tall or average-height Caucasian with brown or black hair. But it could be dyed. Can't remember the eye color. Maybe glasses. Some age between twenty-five and forty. He's got a beard but that'll be shaved by now if it wasn't stuck on, so what we're left with implicates pretty much every other white guy out there."

"That's about the size of it," Kennard agreed. "This is bullshit. We've got nothing." He picked up his jacket.

Alvarez couldn't argue. He pushed his palm against the grain of his stubble as he thought about what to do next. He was drained but didn't want to sleep. There was still too much to do. Alvarez's cell phone rang and he was quick to answer it. When he had hung up he smiled at Kennard.

"You were saying?"

FOURTEEN

Munich, Germany
Tuesday
01:12 CET

It was raining when Victor left the train with fourteen other passengers. The station was mostly empty at that time of night and the amount of open space around Victor gave him some cause for concern. He did his best to exit quickly but without looking like he was trying to do so. Outside the station there were no taxis waiting so he set off on foot. After sitting down on the train for several hours he was glad of the chance to stretch his legs.

He found a fast-food place that was still open and took a seat by the window to eat his meal. Substandard even for junk food, but he needed the calories and there was no quicker way to get refueled. At least the milkshake wasn't too bad. Vanilla.

He hailed a taxi, telling the driver the name of the sniper's street, acting as if he didn't speak German so he wouldn't have to talk inanities during the journey. The building was a four-story apartment block in the east of Munich. The area was affluent, a nineties development of expensive river-view apartments and spacious housing.

The building's main door was dead bolted, and Victor had no key, so he spent the night sampling Munich's all-night bars, allowing himself no more than one drink an hour. He spent his time eyeing members of the opposite sex like the other single men. He stayed a maximum of two hours per bar to avoid people remembering him too easily. At six he took breakfast in a small café before heading back to the building, a takeout black coffee in hand, steam clouding in the frigid air.

He stood on the opposite side of the road to the building, shielded from the drizzle by a bus shelter. The shelter also gave him a reason for waiting on the street should anyone notice him. The sniper lived in apartment 318 according to the hotel records, but there was always the chance he wasn't really Mikhail Svyatoslav. Victor was pretty confident this wasn't the case. Svyatoslav's passport was too well used to be a random identity so it was either the sniper's genuine passport or his only cover. It contained numerous stamps for trips to countries outside the European Union, mostly old Soviet states—Estonia, Ukraine, Latvia, Lithuania, among others. He either traveled frequently for work or had been a keen tourist with limited taste in destinations. In any case, the address the identity corresponded to would be worth investigating.

Victor took a sip of the coffee. It was typical German fare. Awful. They made world-class firearms but seemingly couldn't brew a good cup of coffee if the survival of their nation depended on it. Assuming they'd run out of guns.

Victor watched four people leave the building but no one enter. They were all dressed in suits, long coats, carrying briefcases. City drones on their way to service the hive. Between sips of coffee he watched people walking in the direction of the building, trying to gauge who intended to enter.

The morning was cold, damp, the sky above invisible beyond slate-gray clouds. In summer Germany could be beautiful, but more so than any other European country Victor found it oppressive in winter. The Viking hell was an icy realm called Niflheim, and Victor imagined the Northmen had been picturing something not dissimilar to Germany in November.

He took another sip of coffee and saw a man with a woolen coat hurrying into the street, a metallic briefcase in hand. He had a long, pale face, dark hair. Victor recognized him, had seen the man leave the building ten minutes before. Better than perfect.

Victor waited until the time was right, threw the coffee cup into a trash can, and headed across the street. He controlled his pace to reach the steps at the same time as the man. He glanced Victor's way, but Victor's gaze was averted, his hands fumbling in his pockets for keys that weren't there.

Victor allowed the man to reach the door first, who opened it with his key.

"Danke," Victor said, taking the door before the man had a chance to question whether Victor lived in the building or not.

"Kein problem."

The hallway was brightly lit, clean, and spacious. Victor took the stairs, noting from the unblemished banister and spotless steps that the elevator was hardly ever out of use. The resident hurried to his apartment on the ground floor, disappeared inside. Victor hoped he got back to work in time.

Reaching the third floor, Victor opened the stairwell door and stepped out into the corridor. There were three locks on 318. Definitely the sniper's place.

It took two minutes to pick the locks, and he went inside. It looked as if the sniper had just moved in, not lived there for any length of time. There were just the bare essentials of furniture, a couple of photos, no real personal possessions to articulate his personality. It reminded Victor of his own residence. It was not a reassuring comparison.

There were two bedrooms, one of which was fitted out as a gym with a selection of free weights and an exercise bike. There was a large TV in the gym, positioned so it could be watched while the exercise bike was being used.

The master bedroom was as empty as the rest of the apartment, with just a bed, neatly made; dresser; wardrobe; and another TV fitted so the sniper could watch it in bed. There was a stack of films against one wall, console games against another. The ingredients of a sad and lonely life. The kitchen was modern, clean, almost straight out of a brochure. An old television set stood on one counter.

Victor searched every room, every drawer, every cupboard. He found nothing. No evidence of who the sniper was. He had been smart. Nothing that even hinted at the fact that he had murdered people for money.

Victor got himself a glass of water from the kitchen. He felt tired, drained. He turned on the TV, eager for some light distraction. Nothing happened when he pressed the on button. He noticed the TV was an old boxy set, out of place among the other modern goods. He pushed the on button again. Still nothing. The standby light glowed red.

Three TVs for one person in a small apartment was excessive, and an aging set in the kitchen when everything else was new just didn't feel right. Victor ran his fingers along the TVs case, finding the screws in the plastic depressions. The screw heads felt sharp on his fingertips. Recently used.

Victor searched the drawers until he found a screwdriver. He unplugged the portable TV and turned it around so he could see the screws. They were marked and grooved. It took him a minute to unscrew them all and take the back off the TV. Inside he found why it wouldn't switch on. Apart from the standby light it was hollow. A hide. Inside was a 9 mm Browning handgun, a .22 Luger, a separate suppressor for the Luger, a couple of spare magazines for each, a variety of knives, and two boxes of shells for the handguns. Just a weapon's stash. Nothing else.

He'd been hoping to find a lot more, some small clue to help him find out who hired the kill team. He'd wasted his time, likely compromised himself in the process, and was no closer to his enemies. Victor resisted hurling the TV off its perch and took a breath to compose himself. He reattached the case to the fake set and placed it back exactly as he'd found it. He then washed the glass, dried it, and returned it to where it had been on a shelf. He performed another sweep of the apartment to make sure he hadn't missed anything, and he hadn't.

Outside he headed back to the city center. There was nothing else he could do in Munich with what little information he had. But he had the flash drive. Whoever wanted it was still out there, unseen to his eyes. How long could he stay unseen to theirs? He needed to formulate a new course of action. But for the time being he had to lay low, gather his thoughts while he considered his next move, rest where he knew it was completely safe. There was only one such place where he could do that. Near the village of Saint Maurice, north of Geneva, Switzerland.

The closest thing he had to home.

Before he left there was one other place that he needed to visit. It was that time of the year again, though because of the circumstances he had been putting it off, but he could do so no longer. He changed direction.

It was a run-down building, a specter of the old in the modern area where he found it. The bricks were faded, grimy, dark in the rain. Orange streaks of rust stained the walls beneath windows protected by iron grilles. The door was unlocked, and he pushed it open. Inside it was dim, the high ceiling lost in the shadows above.

Victor's shoes clicked on the tiled floor, the only other sound his breathing. He could feel his pulse rising steadily with each step that brought his ultimate destination closer at a frightening pace. It took a lot of willpower, as it always did, not to turn around and walk straight back out.

He pulled the curtain back and stepped inside the box he likened to an upturned coffin. He pulled the curtain shut behind him and fell to his knees, head bowed, palms together.

In a quiet voice Victor spoke to the faceless silhouette on the other side of the mesh panel.

"Forgive me, Father, for I have sinned."

FIFTEEN

Procter noted the mandarins were all absent at this early hour, so it was just Chambers, Ferguson, and Sykes around the table with him. Chambers looked as presentable as ever, but both Ferguson and Sykes were looking a little rough around the edges, Ferguson especially. He was too old to still be doing 6 AM starts and only had about a year left before retiring.

Alvarez's voice came through the speakerphone. "I've spent all night liaising with the French police and their intelligence services, who have thankfully cut us some slack. I've got a copy of their crime-scene and lab work, but unfortunately it doesn't help us a whole lot. As I expected there's nothing useful from the scene where Ozols was killed. The way the cops have it the killer was waiting in the alley for Ozols and shot him from close range. He took his empty shell cases with him, not that it would have mattered as you'll understand in a minute.

"Now, at the hotel we got a second chance at getting something from this guy, but it doesn't get any better. No unidentified hairs or traceable fibers. The only fingerprints found in the killer's room belong to the maid who cleaned it. This time he didn't take his empty shells with him, but no fingerprints on them either."

"He wore gloves the whole time?" Procter asked.

"Negative," Alvarez replied. "Surveillance footage shows the killer didn't wear any. If he had wiped down everything he'd touched there wouldn't have been the maid's fingerprints left behind in the kinds of places you would expect to find them. What the lab people did find were traces of silicone. So far I haven't been able—"

"Washing your hands with silicone solution prevents fingerprints," Ferguson interrupted.

Procter looked Ferguson's way.

"It creates a waterproof barrier over the skin," Sykes continued for his boss. "The oil from your fingers can't get through it, so you don't leave prints behind on anything you touch. You can't tell if someone is wearing it either as it's completely clear. It was developed to help prevent industrial dermatitis in factory workers."

Procter nodded. You learn something every day, he thought.

"Okay," Alvarez continued. "That solves that little mystery, so thanks. We haven't got a shot of his face from the surveillance tapes as he kept it angled away from the cameras at all times. He's white though, tall, wearing a suit, he's got dark hair and blue eyes, wearing glasses. Had a beard too. If he takes the glasses off and has a shave no one's going to pick him out of a crowd though. Ballistics is a dead end like everything else. The ammunition was made in Belgium but, although not something you see every day, is too common to trace further.

"He was checked in to the hotel under the name

Richard Bishop, a British citizen. No one by that name has left the country since yesterday and from what I'm hearing no British citizen by the name Richard Bishop even entered France in the last month. It'll be bogus, I'm sure, but it would be worth just double-checking with the Brits."

"I'll get someone on it," Chambers said and scribbled herself a note. "I've personally contacted the heads of station in London, Moscow, Berlin, Riyadh, Delhi, Islamabad, and Seoul. So far no one's hearing anything suspicious about Ozols. I'm expecting callbacks throughout the day, but I'm not hopeful. Whoever organized this assassination has done a good job keeping themselves hidden."

Procter hadn't made up his mind about Chambers yet. He considered her to be just a stopgap, someone to keep the chair warm until a long-term candidate could be found. How she performed on this would answer his doubts one way or the other. On the one hand the brain on her practically poked through her skull, but on the other Procter just wasn't sure she had the balls for the role. Literally more than figuratively.

He leaned forward. "And we've had no intercepts relating to Ozols, Paris, or the missiles. No known assassins have been spotted in the region recently and we haven't got a hope of ID'ing him based on the few details we have. I've been on the phone to my equivalents in allied countries to see if anyone recognizes the MO but it's too vague to produce any leads."

It was Sykes's turn to speak. "We've been checking the Russian angle, and no matter who we speak to it's the same. Moscow believes the frigate lost in '08 and everything on board it is unrecoverable. Obviously we can't ask too many questions unless we tip them off to what we've been doing."

Alvarez continued, "Interpol likewise can't do a lot with what we have so far but we might have caught a break with this hotel incident. What the CCTV footage showed us with the way I've pieced it together is as follows. The killer murders Ozols and returns to his hotel approximately two hours later. When he gets there he spots two men and he either recognizes them or something makes him suspicious. He keeps out of sight until they're out of the lobby, but they come straight back down in the elevator. But he avoids them and gets in the elevator, but not before being spotted himself.

"A few minutes later he kills them in the corridor outside his room, shooting through a door opposite. A couple of minutes later two more men enter. He waits for them, follows one, and ends up killing them both. Disabled or tortured one with an exploding aerosol if you can believe it. All these people are armed by the way and aren't carrying ID. Next, he kills a woman in the hotel kitchen, a guy in the apartment building opposite, and from the same building shoots another outside with a rifle. An old lady gets murdered along the way, but the bullets that shot her match the gun of the sixth guy killed, so she probably just got caught in the cross fire.

"Information on the seven others our guy killed is coming through all the time. They look like hired shooters. The way they acted tells me they were in Paris to take out Ozols's killer. Obviously he took them out instead."

Ferguson's brow furrowed. "So you're telling us that one assassin kills Ozols, and a couple of hours later seven other assassins try and kill him, but he shoots them all dead?"

"That's exactly how it appears."

Ferguson raised his palms. "Someone please explain to me how this makes any sense?"

Chambers took off her glasses. "Is there any indication who sent the team?"

"At this stage no," Alvarez answered regretfully. "But I don't think it will be too long before we have them all identified. That gives us seven chances to find out who sent them. And whoever did send them obviously knows a hell of a lot about Ozols's killer. So if we can find out who hired these guys, we'll have a good shot of getting the killer, and maybe we can still get those missiles too."

Chambers and Ferguson were nodding, but Procter noticed Sykes wasn't looking so relaxed. Procter understood why. The kid was out of the loop, had nothing to say, no opinion to offer, and he didn't like it. He was still comparatively young, and Ferguson obviously thought highly of him, so he shouldn't be worried by his lack of contribution. There was no point speaking just for the sake of it. Ferguson should have taught his apprentice that much at least. If Sykes was really smart, he should be satisfied at this stage of his career just to watch and learn from the playmakers.

"The final and maybe most important thing I've

found out," Alvarez announced, "is that the killer didn't leave Paris straightaway after being attacked. Seems he hung around to investigate the guys who tried to whack him."

Ferguson spoke. "How do you know that?"

"Because one of the gunmen, found riddled with .45-caliber slugs in the building opposite the killer's hotel, checked out of his own hotel about an hour after he was killed."

There was a momentary silence in the room. Procter could hear the creak of leather.

"That's a clever trick for a dead man," Sykes offered with a smirk that showed his bright teeth. Everyone ignored him, and Procter shook his head imperceptibly.

"The clerk at the hotel described the man as quite tall, lean, with dark hair, glasses, and a beard," Alvarez explained. "The real man, Svyatoslav, doesn't match that description. He's shorter, stockier. The description of Ozols's killer, however, does match."

Procter leaned forward. "Let me guess, the assassin acquired Svyatoslav's things?"

"Yes," Alvarez agreed. "He pretended to be him and signed out. The clerk gave him Svyatoslav's passport, plane tickets, etcetera that were stored in the hotel safe. They haven't popped up on the grid, so he didn't use the passport to leave the country."

Chambers asked, "What do you think the killer would want with Svyatoslav's things?"

"I think he must be trying to learn about him," Alvarez said. "That's why he went to the hotel. He didn't flee the country; he went to where one of the guys who tried to kill him was staying."

"And if he is trying to identify his attackers, and who they were working for, what's his next logical step?" Procter asked.

"To check out Svyatoslav's address," Alvarez answered.

Chambers said, "Please tell me we know where that is."

"Munich."

Chambers placed both hands on the table. "Okay, this is what we're going to do. We're going to contact German intelligence straightaway and get them to put the address under immediate surveillance. Let them know what kind of person they're dealing with. I don't want them trying to apprehend him, just keep him in sight. I'm not having anyone else getting killed because of this. Alvarez, as soon as you've finished briefing them, I want you on the next plane to Germany to see what you can find out. Call me from Munich. If he's still there you'll have as much support as you need."

When Alvarez was off the phone it was Ferguson who spoke. His thick silver hair, normally swept neatly backward, was looking a little unruly today. "The chances of this killer still being in possession of the information are slim at best. If his job was to intercept Ozols and take the drive, then he will be delivering it to his employer—he won't be off chasing leads in Germany. That makes no sense whatsoever."

Chambers sighed. "Maybe it was his employer who

tried to have him killed. Saves paying him. Or maybe he's already done it. But until we have more indication on who sent him, this is our best approach. We're against the clock here; as soon as that information is delivered, those missiles are going to vanish in a matter of days, and the next we hear about them will be when someone uses the technology against us. If there is a slim chance the man who killed Ozols might have gone to Germany, then so must we." Ferguson didn't look convinced. "Unless you have any other ideas you'd like to share with us." The challenge in her voice was obvious.

Ferguson's expression was one of quiet contempt. He shrugged his narrow shoulders. Procter looked at Chambers. Evidently she wasn't bothered about getting the old guy's back up whatever his history.

Maybe there was a pair dangling between her legs after all.

SIXTEEN

Geneva, Switzerland
Tuesday
18:32 CET

Victor walked through Place Neuve and passed the Grand-Théâtre. The city was alive with people, tourists out for a good time and locals happy to have finished the working day. Victor cast a fleeting glance at the Grand-

Théâtre, wishing he had the chance to take in a performance, something by Puccini or Mozart perhaps. Instead he walked back and forth among the crowds to throw off any shadows.

The sun had set an hour before, and no one noticed him as he passed through the streets of the city. It was after dark where he really belonged. In the daytime he could hide within a crowd, but at night he could be invisible. In front of him walked a couple, arms entwined, stumbling slightly and laughing. They were so enraptured with each other they wouldn't have noticed him whether he'd let them or not.

From Munich he'd traveled to Berlin and then on to Prague before heading to Switzerland. It had been a long and tiring journey, but Victor never traveled in straight lines. He veered off into a side street, taking an indirect route to the train station. It was brightly lit, busy with suited commuters. Like most of Geneva's males, Victor was dressed in a thick overcoat, gloves, and hat. He was glad of the cold that forced everyone to pile on the layers, blending the crowd into a mass of conservative colors. Even a whole team of expert shadows would have their work cut out following him in such a place.

He hadn't slept in almost forty-eight hours, and he was very aware of the fact. Sleep deprivation slowed the mind as much as the body, and now more than ever Victor needed to be at 100 percent. But while on the run he couldn't rest until he knew he was safe. Every hour spent asleep gave his enemies a chance to get closer to him.

He consumed a bad sandwich and a strong coffee in a small café while he waited for his train. When it arrived he waited for the last possible moment before climbing on board and sat with the window to his right, at the rear of the carriage. From Geneva Victor traveled north, the train winding through the mountains.

He'd lived in Switzerland for several years, finding its climate, people, and lifestyle to his liking. Living at a high altitude gave his endurance a significant boost, plus the country's secretive banking systems and relaxed attitude to firearms suited him particularly well.

The train took Victor through the Valais, Switzerland's third largest region, or canton. The region contained the Rhone valley, which fed Geneva's famous lake. It was late when Victor stepped off the train in the village of Saint Maurice. Snow fell heavily, and he pulled his collar up and hunched his shoulders. He'd bought appropriate clothing for the mountains in a boutique at the train station and changed on the train.

The village itself was isolated, far away from the closest town, consisting mainly of wealthy foreigners who only spent a few weeks of the year in their expensive log chalets during the ski season. It was a place where few people knew their neighbors and where no one was surprised to see strange faces and vehicles. Victor, coming and going frequently, never appeared suspicious.

At one of the world's most expensive grocery stores he bought whole milk, free-range eggs, a selection of fresh vegetables, English cheddar, soya and linseed bread, and smoked salmon. He resented having to pay the extortionate amount of money to the woman behind the counter, but he knew it served him right for living there.

He walked through the rest of the village with the two bags and his attaché case held in his left hand. He used the side streets instead of the main road. There were few people about, and when he was finally sure he wasn't being followed, he headed off into the trees, moving in a half-circle around to where his chalet lay a mile away from the main cluster of buildings. He moved carefully through the dark forest, knowing the way without needing to see properly.

When he saw through the trees the chalet illuminated by the moon and starlight he wanted to rush inside and collapse on his own bed. He desired nothing more than to sleep, than to forget his life for eight hours straight, but discipline made him stop and squat down, looking for signs of intruders. It was almost impossible to believe that anyone would know where he lived, but after Paris he was taking no chances.

He placed the shopping down and spent an hour circling the building until he was satisfied no one was inside or nearby. The chalet was sheltered on all sides by dense pine trees, with a single narrow path only usable by rugged four-wheel-drive vehicles leading to the main road. Victor's own Land Rover was parked in a freestanding garage. It was too dark to see any recent tracks in the path or footprints in the snow around the building, but he saw and heard nothing to suggest anyone was nearby.

Inside the ornate wood and steel-reinforced front

door, he breathed a little easier but still took the time to check the interior thoroughly. The chalet was five years old, Victor the only owner, and it was built in the traditional Savoyard chalet style with slate roof, wooden beams, stone walls, and a log fire. Its two stories had four bedrooms, far more than Victor really needed, but chalets here were not built with a single occupant in mind.

It had no conventional alarm. If someone broke in Victor did not want the authorities alerted and snooping around. Instead he had custom-made motion sensors linked to high-resolution security cameras and sensitive microphones that covered every corner of the building. Each item was carefully disguised, and the cameras and microphones were programmed to only begin recording two minutes after they were tripped. In this way they should remain undetected by anyone sweeping for electronic bugs when they first entered a room.

All the windows were fitted with three-inch-thick polycarbonate and glass laminate windowpanes that would stop even high-velocity rifle rounds. The reinforced front and rear doors and frames would take more than a handheld ram to get through. Few windows opened and none fully.

Victor examined every room in a set order in a set way. Everything was in its place, and nothing was there that did not serve some purpose. There were no photographs, no items of any personal significance. Nothing to show who he was or where he had come from. If anyone ever did get into the chalet, they would leave with almost no information about him.

He was pleased to find nothing had been recorded by his security system. He opened the door to the small boiler room and checked the control box for tampering. Should he enter a certain code it would set a three-minute timer that would detonate the C-4 carefully positioned around the ground floor. One day he may have to leave in a hurry and never come back.

Once he was satisfied, he put the groceries away and was finally able to relax. He treated himself with a long shower. Outside his chalet he never took them. Back to the door, naked, unarmed, pounding water blocking all other noise—even the most skilled target was defenseless in one. Victor had killed enough people in them to know they were death traps. Here it was safe though. His body ached. He noticed he'd lost a couple of pounds too, but two days on the run tended to make an effective diet program. Plenty of decent food and rest would put him right in no time. He had no significant injuries, and, considering what had happened, he knew he was fortunate to be in one piece. Thinking of food made his stomach groan.

When he couldn't ignore the hunger any longer he dried himself, checked the house once more to satisfy his paranoia, and made himself a large cheese and salmon omelet with the groceries he'd bought. He followed it with a protein shake loaded with vitamins and minerals before taking a half-empty bottle of Finnish vodka from the freezer. He went into the lounge, sat down in front of his rosewood piano, and tore the seal from the bottle.

Victor poured himself a glass of vodka and rubbed a

smear from the piano with his sleeve. The piano was an 1881 Vose and Sons Square Grand he'd found rotting in a Venetian dealership. He'd bought it for a good price and had it couriered to Switzerland to be repaired but not restored. Victor found a certain beauty in the absence of perfection. The piano had existed for several times longer than his own life span, and it wore its battle scars proudly. He played a little Chopin until he found his eyelids drooping.

Later, he poured the last of the vodka into the glass and used the piano to help him stand. He headed upstairs slowly and lay down on his double bed, the single pillow hard beneath his head. He fell asleep with the glass on his chest.

He didn't dream.

SEVENTEEN

Munich, Germany
Tuesday
22:39 CET

Alvarez shivered as he left the building and nodded to the German police officer smoking a cigarette nearby. The officer's return nod, Alvarez noted, was somewhat halfhearted. Evidently he did not appreciate the task of questioning the building's occupants that Alvarez's presence had won him.

German intelligence had been very cooperative and had agreed to Alvarez's request on just the vague information the company have given them. News of the Paris shootings had reached across the border, and the Germans were keen to help.

As with the French authorities, he told them nothing of the missing flash drive. His priority was to recover it rather than to apprehend Ozols's killer, but it wouldn't do to tell members of another nation's intelligence service that. They would want to know what information the memory stick contained, and the best way to answer that would be to take possession of the drive themselves.

He climbed into his rental car and drove back to the hotel. It had been a long two days, and the strain was showing in the face that looked back at him in the bathroom mirror. He had another progress report to give to Langley, but he would need an hour's sleep before he started it.

His achievements were limited at best. A man matching the assassin's description had been let inside the building by a neighbor. There was no evidence Ozols's killer had been inside Svyatoslav's apartment or had found or taken anything, but that didn't surprise Alvarez. Svyatoslav's financial and phone records were being assembled, and Alvarez did not relish the thought of having to pore through them.

The neighbor, Mr. Eichberg, had provided another description and aided a sketch artist. The assassin had shaved his beard and cut his hair, but the remaining identifying features could've been anyone's. He couldn't have had the decency to have a big nose or a cleft chin, Alvarez thought bitterly.

A drawing had been issued to police forces across Germany, but Alvarez knew the killer would not have hung around. He was most likely out of the country long before Alvarez had even arrived. All CCTV footage at airports and train stations were being checked by the authorities as a matter of course.

Alvarez took the hair clippers from his suitcase and gave his head a once over with the number two attachment. He had a brief hot shower and afterward lay down on his bed to sleep but couldn't make it happen. A few years ago, when he couldn't sleep, he would have grabbed the phone and spoken to Jennifer, but there was no one to speak to these days. Alvarez kept people at arm's length without having to try, and, even when he made an effort to bend his elbows, he just found his arms were still longer than those of most people.

Some women seemed to like the challenge of getting close to him, but once they realized it wasn't going to happen they bailed. Mostly sooner, but in Jennifer's case later. He thought about calling to speak to Christopher, but it was hard talking to his son when he saw so little of him and the kid called someone else daddy.

A ringing phone woke Alvarez. He launched himself off the bed and grabbed it from the sideboard. He saw by the clock that he had been asleep for only a few minutes.

"Hello?"

"Mr. Alvarez, this is Gens Luitger of the BKA. We met earlier today."

The BKA—the Bundeskriminalamt—Germany's equivalent of the FBI. Luitger was a high-ranking and well-respected officer in the organization, and, from the short time Alvarez had spent with him, he seemed extremely competent. His English was flawless, with only the occasional trace of an accent.

"Yes," Alvarez said. "How are you?"

"I'm good," Luitger answered. "And I have some good news for you. We've been trying to clear all single men matching Mr. Eichberg's description who have entered or exited the country, but we haven't yet narrowed down the number to a usable amount. However, I've had people double-checking passports for lone-traveling men in their thirties who've exited the country, and I believe we have had some luck. Yesterday a British national by the name of Alan Flynn boarded a flight to Prague, out of Berlin. This is odd because Alan Flynn is currently residing in a secure mental-health hospital in the north of England. The man using Alan Flynn's passport also matches your target's description."

The second British one he's used, Alvarez thought. "How sure are you?"

"As sure as one can be."

Alvarez detected a slight difference in Luitger's tone, as if he had been offended or insulted by Alvarez's question. He understood why. Luitger wouldn't have phoned unless he thought the information was sufficiently reliable.

"Do you have his face on the security cameras?"

"No, unfortunately our mutual friend was lucky enough not to have been picked up by the CCTV cameras. At least his face wasn't."

Alvarez smiled to himself. "No, that's not luck, that's him alright. Thank you for calling me so promptly."

"That's no trouble. I feel it is important for our security services to aid one another whenever we can, even if our leaders would not always agree."

"Absolutely."

"How do you want to proceed? My people will continue the investigation as best we can, but I think we might have to accept the suspect is already out of Germany. If so my authority stops at the border."

Alvarez's mind was already running in fifth gear trying to sort through all the possibilities. He needed to get the new information out to Langley as soon as possible. If the killer had gone to the Czech Republic, then things were not looking good. He would need to speak to Kennard to update him and find out what, if anything, had been discovered in Paris. He realized Luitger was still on the phone.

"That's fine, my friend," Alvarez assured, despite feeling dejected. "You've done more than enough already."

They said their good-byes and Alvarez hit a speed-dial number. After a few rings Kennard answered. The guy sounded tired.

"John, get this: The killer did pay a trip to Svyatoslav's apartment," Alvarez said.

"Did he find anything?"

"That's the million-dollar question."

"What about you, you find anything?"

Alvarez shielded the phone while he sneezed. "According to the BKA the killer took a plane to the Czech Republic."

"The Czech Republic?"

"Prague to be exact, but by now he could be anywhere."

"What the hell is this guy up to?"

"That would be the billion-dollar question. You got a pen? Write this down."

Alvarez gave Kennard a list of instructions then hung up. He sneezed again and hoped he wasn't coming down with a cold. That would be just his luck. He picked up the phone and called room service for a big pot of strong coffee. It was going to be a long night.

EIGHTEEN

Paris, France
Tuesday
23:16 CET

Kennard flipped his phone closed and considered carefully for a moment. He was at the killer's hotel with the complete crime-scene report, doing a walk-through, trying to get an accurate picture of everything that had happened in case they'd missed anything. The French police were still pretty damn unhelpful, but at least they left him to it.

Now that Alvarez had briefed him about the situation in Germany, Kennard abandoned what he was doing. He hurried through the hotel and out onto the Rue du Faubourg Saint-Honoré. It had been sealed off in front of the hotel from junction to junction on the previous day, almost immediately after the killings. Kennard remembered watching the harried-looking policemen at either end of the cordon as they tried their best to divert the angry morning traffic.

Now it was as if nothing had happened. The only barriers still in place were within the hotel itself. Outside, Parisian motorists whizzed too fast down the road in their pathetically small cars, hitting their horns each and every chance they had. It seemed not to matter if there was real cause.

Kennard hated the French, hated everything about the country. The people, the language, the so-called culture. Even the food was bullshit. Sure, if he paid a month's salary he could get something half-edible, but greasy omelets, tough bread, rank cheese, and meat that smelled rotten was not his idea of fine eating. He'd take a quarter pounder with good old freedom fries any day of the week.

He continued to walk along the sidewalk, going past where his car was parked. A group of drunk executives were heading his way, failing miserably to walk in a straight line. No doubt they had been celebrating a deal of some sort. They looked the type.

As they drew closer one of them shouted something to him in French. Kennard recognized the aggression. Maybe the Frenchman had noticed the antipathy in Kennard's face, or maybe he was just looking to have some fun.

The man was just taller than Kennard and twenty pounds heavier, most of it around the gut, but beneath his suit Kennard wasn't the soft guy he looked. He would have liked to have demonstrated that he was no easy target, but instead he diverted his gaze and moved out of the group's path. He couldn't afford to get into any trouble. He heard laughter and jeers from behind him as they walked away. Lucky for them that they did.

Kennard crossed the street. His face remained blank, but he could feel the pressure of blood in his temples. Alvarez had given him a host of urgent tasks to complete, tasks that could not wait, but Kennard wasn't returning to the embassy. He had something more pressing to do first.

After another minute walking, he turned into a side street. He found the pay phone again and had to wait a difficult thirty seconds before the young woman inside had finished her call. Kennard entered the booth and took out his cell phone to check the latest number. He pushed the buttons quickly but carefully. He would wipe down the surfaces he had touched when he was finished.

The back of Kennard's collar was damp. He wasn't supposed to make phone calls that were not prearranged, but after Monday's disaster news like this couldn't wait.

The phone didn't start ringing immediately, and, when it did, it seemed to take forever before someone answered. He coded in.

There was a long silence before anyone connected. When the voice on the other end of the line spoke, it practically dripped disdain.

"This had better be important."

Kennard took a deep breath before continuing. "It's been confirmed. He did go to Svyatoslav's apartment in Munich, but he's long gone. We're pretty sure he flew to the Czech Republic. After that, we don't know yet."

There was a long pause. "Okay," the voice said. "This is what we want you to do . . ."

NINETEEN

North of Saint Maurice, Switzerland
Wednesday
08:33 CET

Victor's breathing was labored. The thin mountain air expelled from his lungs in clouds of white vapor. The first two hundred feet had been difficult, but the last fifty had been murder. He grunted and pulled the ice hammer from where it was embedded in the frozen waterfall and hacked it into the ice above his head. Ice and snow rained down over him and fell to the base of the waterfall far below.

He watched the glittering fragments fall for a moment and took in several large gulps of air. His face was red from the cold and exertion. A pair of climber's goggles shielded his eyes from the unfiltered sun above. The ice of the waterfall was bright blue and white but much darker, almost black in the depths of the cracks and fissures. A distorted reflection watched him climb.

Up here it was easy to forget about the events of the last few days. He had no choice but to focus solely on what he was doing. Nothing could invade his mind except the task at hand, because if it did those thoughts would be his last. He'd rested his body as much as he could, but now he needed to clear his head. He had no friends he could talk to, no one to share his problems with, and this was the next best thing.

Alone in the mountains he felt as though he was the only person in the world. Just him and the brutal honesty of nature. He was as far from civilization as he could hope to get, and yet up here the world seemed far more civilized.

He pulled with his arms and pushed with his legs, wrenching the crampons of his boots free from the ice before jamming them in farther up. The stress of the climb shook his body, but the inherent danger calmed his mind. He was confident in his abilities, but he had to maintain 100 percent concentration. He used no screws, carabiners, or rope—so if he didn't concentrate, he fell. If he fell, he died. It was that simple.

The only sound was that of the wind, of metal hitting ice, and of his own heavy breathing. The sense of utter freedom was prevalent. He was relaxed and at peace.

After another ten feet he paused. Leaning backward, he took one hand from an ice hammer and reached into a pocket to pull out a hard candy, pleased to find it was a green one. He threw it into his mouth. They kept his mouth moist so he didn't feel thirsty, but more than that they tasted good. Victor sucked on the candy and tilted his head to one side to enjoy the view. All he could see were mountains and trees topped with snow.

He could've stayed hanging there for hours, but he felt water strike his face. He looked up, squinting against the glare. Droplets of water glistened in the sun. The ice was melting. Not surprising with a cloudless sky. He climbed on, not hurrying, knowing he would reach the summit long before there was any danger.

The ice above groaned.

Victor stopped climbing and looked upward. Twenty feet above his head a sheet of overhanging ice broke away. Victor flattened himself against the waterfall, and chunks of ice and snow fell past him. He took back his previous judgment and quickened his pace. His muscles, craving more oxygen, filled with lactic acid, and his lungs ached from sucking in the frigid air. He climbed fast, driving the ice hammers and crampons home, pushing and pulling and repeating until he reached the summit and collapsed spread eagled onto the snow.

He arrived back at his chalet several hours later and made himself lunch, his own recipe for bruschetta con funghi to start and two large sausage sandwiches for his main course. Just what he needed. He followed it with a protein shake and swallowed a handful of supplement pills. After bathing he sat naked on his bed and drew the handgun from the holster attached to the underside. He withdrew the magazine and popped the rounds, reloading them in the order they'd come out. He put the gun back.

It was late morning, the sun streaming between the Venetian blinds on the east wall. He walked over to the window on the west wall, pulled the string sharply to raise the blinds. The valley stretched off into the distance, the village of Saint Maurice visible at the center, its triangular roofs topped with white. Pine trees covered the mountainsides. Snow-capped peaks lined the horizon.

There had been a time when Victor had almost believed he could separate his life from what he did for a living. Such a time had long passed. Now he realized he was merely just alive, that he didn't really live. Normal people didn't hide themselves away in remote mountain villages, protected by reinforced doors and three inches of armored glass. It was hard to remember when it had been any different.

He lived alone for his own protection. Here nobody knew him and he knew no one in return. He found it easier, too, to live away from cities, from people. It was hard to miss something he didn't see every day. Living alone had never been difficult for him, but total solitude was something Victor had been forced to learn to deal with. But like any skill he needed to survive, he had mastered it eventually. Staying busy was the most important element. When he wasn't working he spent hours each day keeping himself in top physical condition, hours more training and honing his skills. Weeks may go by between contracts, but his was a full-time vocation. The rest of the time he climbed, skied, read, played the piano, and took frequent trips to explore the globe.

There were some things that such distractions could not replace. Victor's idea of a relationship was a call girl he liked enough to use more than once and who was good enough an actress to pretend she didn't find his touch repellent.

Looking out over the picturesque valley it was almost possible to pretend what happened in Paris wasn't real. Here he was just another wealthy businessman enjoying an isolated mountain retreat. Maybe he wouldn't leave. He had enough money stored away to live comfortably for years if he was careful. Maybe when it had run out he could take a regular job, teach languages or even climbing. He knew only in his imagination was he good enough to teach piano to anyone other than beginners. If he wanted to teach though, he knew he was going to have to work on his people skills. Maybe in time he could actually start to live like a regular person. Assuming he could remember how to.

The first step would be to smash the flash drive into a thousand pieces, throw them into a ravine, and forget he'd ever taken the Ozols contract. He had escaped whatever enemies wanted him dead, and no one knew he was here. He could stay hidden, take no more contracts. They would never find him here. He nodded.

Yes, it was time to get out.

He started to turn away from the window when his eyes were drawn to a point high in the forested hills that lay to the west of the chalet. He saw a glint, a tiny flicker of light. The reflection of the sun on metal.

Or glass.

He understood what it meant too late, seeing the small, bright flash that appeared in the same place an instant later. He started to move to his left when a hole exploded through the window before him.

The bullet hit him in the middle of his chest and everything went quiet. He saw the cobweb of cracks in the reinforced glass, saw the tiny hole in the center of the web. No sound reached his ears except the dull echo of his heartbeat.

Victor's vision faltered. Lines blurred into one another.

The window seemed to move sharply away from him, and the ceiling came hurtling down. He didn't understand but then the back of his head smacked against the polished floorboards. He tried to breathe, gasped, struggled to suck air into his lungs.

He raised a hand, inched his fingers along his bare chest, felt sticky blood, pain as he touched the hot bullet in his flesh. He'd expected to find a gaping hole with blood pumping freely, but the end of the bullet was protruding from his skin. It hadn't penetrated the sternum.

The chalet's polycarbonate and glass-laminate windowpanes would stop even high-velocity rifle rounds . . . not quite, Victor thought.

The glass hadn't stopped the bullet but had slowed it considerably, so that, when it had struck, its kinetic energy was almost spent. Ignoring the burn, Victor pulled the bullet from his skin and tossed it aside. It exhausted him to do so. He tried to stand but couldn't remember how to tell his limbs to move. The ceiling beams melted into one another above him.

He realized what was happening but could do nothing to stop it. The bullet's impact had sent ripples of hydrostatic shock through his body, interrupting the normal rhythm of his heartbeat. His body didn't understand what had happened and so was doing the only thing it knew how to do in the face of intense shock or trauma.

It was temporarily shutting down.

The shooter would have watched the bullet hit and Victor fall but wouldn't be able to see him as he writhed on the floor, incapacitated but not dying. With no exit wound there had been no spray of blood, but maybe the assassin wouldn't notice. But all he would have to note was the thickness of the cracked window to realize that Victor was still alive. And he would come to finish the job.

Victor's eyelids closed.

TWENTY

The assassin peered through his Schmidt and Bender 3-12X scope at the thickness of the windowpane. It was made up of alternate layers of glass and plastic. He recognized it straightaway. Armored. *Shit.*

McClury silently berated himself for not noticing before. He should have spent more time studying the house's defenses, but he consoled himself with the fact this had been a rushed job from the very start. Beginning with a phone call twenty-four hours ago, he'd been told to head straight for Geneva. In the back of a car, he'd been given the name of a town, a location, a photograph.

It stank to high hell of a cleanup.

McClury folded back the rifle's bipod and stood, disturbing the light covering of snow that lay across his body. His weapon was an Accuracy International L96, a bolt-action rifle made by the Brits. In McClury's opinion one of the best all around rifles in the world for this type of work. Precise and powerful but not too big or heavy. He'd used enough of them in the past to qualify his opinion.

He wore white Gore-Tex pants, a jacket with a hood, and a white ski mask. The rifle's furniture had been wrapped in strips of white electrical tape. McClury unbuttoned and unzipped the jacket and threw it off. It was camouflage and protection against the cold but impeded movement. Underneath he wore a black thermal shirt. He felt the chill immediately, but for now he could live with it. He left the white ski mask in place.

His hide was a little under five hundred yards away, overlooking the target's chalet. McClury had been set up just under the crest of a snowy outcrop dotted with trees to hide his silhouette and to make him virtually invisible.

He'd been holed up outside for twelve hours straight, watching the house the whole time, waiting for the perfect shot, eating and drinking while lying down, urinating into a bottle, defecating into a plastic bag. On his own he couldn't watch both exits at the same time and had set up with a good view of the front of the chalet, expecting the target would at some point leave that way. The target would have been dead a second after stepping out the front door. No such luck.

Soon after first light the target had left through the back way and McClury had changed positions to shoot him when he returned. Hours later he noticed the target was back in the chalet and realized he had entered through the front. Out one way, in another. Damn, he was a slippery customer.

So there had been no more fucking around waiting for him to leave. McClury had shot the naked bastard while he stood looking out of a window—only the window's thick wooden crossbeam had denied McClury the head shot and forced him to go for the heart instead, only to have the armored glass deny him the kill. It was enough to drive a guy crazy.

McClury slung the rifle over one shoulder, hooked a

satchel over the other, clipped a small bag around his waist, and grabbed his 12-gauge Mossberg pump-action shotgun by its pistol grip. He was going to have to get up close and personal to finish this one. It had been a while since he'd done so, and he was looking forward to the change in MO.

He set off down the slope, his free arm bracing against trees to slow his descent. The slope was steep, treacherous to the unwary, but he negotiated it deftly.

His eyes locked on the chalet in the distance and his prey within.

The loud noise woke Victor with a start. He sat straight up and grunted. The pain in his chest was intense; it felt as if a massive weight strapped to his ribs compressed his chest inward. He coughed several times. His lungs felt crushed.

He groaned but forced the pain from his mind. He had to think. It had been a clear half second after the muzzle flash before he'd been hit. It would have had to have been a large-caliber, high-powered rifle to have pierced the glass, probably with a muzzle velocity of around three thousand feet per second.

That meant the assassin would have been approximately fifteen hundred feet away in the foothills. It was rough terrain in that direction and would take Victor at least ten minutes to cover the distance in a hurry. He couldn't imagine many people doing so faster.

Six hundred seconds.

Not long. He looked at the clock to see how long he had been out, to see how long before the shooter was upon him, but couldn't remember the time when he'd been shot. He was confident there was just one man. If there was a team here to kill him, they would have assaulted first, not relied on the sniper, and Victor would be already dead.

If he could only get to the village . . .

Adrenaline was pumping through him, temporarily numbing the pain, but he knew he would feel worse when it wore off. He felt weak but could still function. He had to get out. But without knowing how long he'd been out for he didn't know if he would be running into a trap. The chalet had two exits, a front door and a back, one too many for a single man to cover. The assassin wouldn't be able to take up a position and wait for Victor to leave. If he did that he would only have a fifty-fifty chance of picking the right exit. He would have to come inside to kill him.

Victor was still naked, would have to dress if he tried to run. Getting clothes on would eat time he might not have. It was painful just breathing. He didn't know how hard he would be able to run or for how long. The assassin would surely be faster. Going outside would only make his job easier.

Defending the house was his best option. Inside Victor knew every inch and how to use each blind spot to his advantage. If the assassin wanted him, he would have to come and get him. Victor, in a crouch, one hand pressed to his chest, went over to the bed, reached beneath it and drew the loaded FN Five-seveN from the holster. A floorboard creaked.

The stairs.

In medieval Japan, with the ever present threat of the deadly ninja, samurai lords had protected themselves from assassination by a simple but effective method. In their castles nightingale floorboards "sang" when someone stepped on them, alerting the occupants that they were under attack.

Victor had employed the same strategy in addition to his other security precautions. The stairs had been deliberately adjusted so that every other step creaked under the slightest pressure. Other floorboards throughout the chalet did the same, with varying pitch. A moment of silence.

Then another creak followed immediately by the sound of heavy boots rushing up the stairs, the attempt at stealth abandoned.

Victor flung open the bedroom door, leaned out, the FN leading in the direction of the stairwell. The shotgun's report was excruciating, the blast blowing a huge chunk from the door frame. Victor ducked back inside the room as another shot followed. The 12-gauge tore another hole from the pine frame. His wrist stung. A single pellet had grazed his skin. Victor slammed the door shut and locked it.

The Mossberg roared again, punching a fist-sized hole through the door to Victor's left. He heard footsteps on the landing, the racking as the assassin fed another shell into the chamber.

Victor rushed over to the other side of the room, crouched beside the bed, the Five-seveN trained at the door.

* * *

McClury stepped carefully along the landing. To his right he could see down into the living room on the floor below. He kept the Mossberg pointed at the target's door at all times.

He was aware of the sound his boots made on the wooden floor but it hardly mattered. The target knew he was coming whether he made a sound or not. There was no way out of the bedroom. The armored windows didn't open. He was going to pay for that protection now.

McClury inched closer to the door but didn't step in front of it. He stopped and reached inside the bag at his waist.

Victor heard the footsteps stop. His enemy was right on the other side of the wall, just to the right of the door. The moment he stepped in front of the door Victor would empty the FN through it.

The floorboard outside the door creaked. The handle started to turn. Victor opened fire. He had the gun held loosely in his right hand but firmly in the left, making it easier to fire faster, his right index finger squeezing rapidly, sending bullet after bullet through the wood, aiming high and low.

He stopped, his finger aching, having fired fifteen rounds in just over three seconds. There was no scream, no bang as the sniper hit the floor. Light streamed through the holes in the door.

He'd hit nothing.

McClury waited patiently for the firing to finish. He had his back to the wall and held the Mossberg by the barrel. He'd used it to press the wide floorboard directly in front of the door, figuring it would creak like the stairs. His instinct had been right. McClury had looped his belt around the door handle to pull it down without having to expose himself before the door. Evidently it had been a convincing enough trick.

He dropped the belt, reached into the bag, pulled out two grenades and ripped the pins out with his teeth. He held onto them for a quick two count before throwing them through the large splintered hole blasted in the door.

Victor was sprinting the instant he saw something appear through the hole in the door. He heard two metal objects hit the floorboards and knew exactly what they were. He reached the adjoining bathroom, saw the grenades rolling on the floor out the corner of his eye. He flung the door shut behind him, throwing his weight against it.

The grenades exploded with a dull *crack*.

The door blasted open, knocking Victor against the wall with a grunt. Smoke and dust filled the air. Sizzling pieces of shrapnel jutted from the door.

Victor rushed out of the bathroom as a single shotgun blast destroyed both the door handle and lock and took a chunk from the frame. He threw himself to the side of the door, pressing his back flat against the wall, his left arm extended at the elbow, his forearm fixed in a diagonal line before his face.

The door was kicked open and swung in Victor's direction. It smacked painfully into his arm but in doing so he stopped it smashing into his face. The assassin opened fire from the doorway, sending a shotgun blast into the bathroom. The mirror shattered above the sink. Broken glass smashed and clattered in the basin and on the floor.

The moment Victor heard the assassin step forward to get a better angle on the bathroom, Victor hurled himself forward, sending the door crashing into his enemy and knocking him back through the doorway. Spinning around, Victor raised the Five-seveN and fired twice. Two holes blew through the door, chest height. There was a grunt, followed by a stumble from outside the room. He hesitated, unsure whether his opponent was dead. A shotgun blast tore through the door.

The exclamation of a foe still very much alive.

McClury grimaced, feeling warm blood trickling down his chest. He'd been shot just beneath the collar bone on the left side, but the bullet hadn't come out so there was no huge exit wound leaking blood. No organs pierced, no bones broken, no arteries severed. Tissue damage mostly. It hurt like fuck but there was no immediate risk.

He was low on ammunition, and the target was alive and fighting. If anything, McClury was now the more wounded of the two. It wasn't supposed to happen like this. He thought all he'd have to do was finish him off, not have a room-to-room gun battle. This wasn't working out.

He wasn't an assaulter; he was a sniper.

So snipe, he told himself.

TWENTY-ONE

Victor waited, crouched in the far right corner from the door—diving distance from the bathroom if the assassin tried any more grenades. Victor had the FN reloaded, sights lined up to put bullets through his enemy's skull the moment he showed himself. But nothing was happening. Victor watched the minutes tick by, glad of the chance to rest. The small wound in his chest had stopped bleeding. It hadn't stopped hurting.

He was hoping the assassin's wound was worse, but he couldn't rely on it. He knew his enemy was doing exactly the same as he was, waiting, gun trained on the door, ready to fire the instant Victor revealed himself. If the assassin was playing a waiting game, Victor knew he could wait longer, but with each passing second the prospect of the assassin charging into the room seemed more unlikely.

The sound of an engine, coming from outside.

Victor sidestepped to the window, making no noise, gaze never leaving the door. He peered briefly through the glass, seeing two big SUVs with police markings heading up the steep track to his chalet. Smart, Victor thought.

He rushed over to the door, hooked his big toe under the bottom to pull it open. There was no shotgun blast. He stood shoulder to the frame and peered around quickly. No assassin. As he expected. A pair of boots sat unlaced on the floor, removed to aid a stealthy withdrawal.

Victor ran back into his bedroom, dressed quickly into khaki pants, fleece, winter jacket, waterproof hiking boots. He zipped the flash drive into a jacket pocket, opened the drawer by his bed, took the remaining magazines for the FN.

Downstairs, in the boiler room, he severed the pipe to the 250-gallon propane tank. Escaping gas hissed, quickly filling the room and drifting through the chalet. Victor entered the code for the high explosives. The timer began the three-minute countdown.

He saw through the front windows the police vehicles nearing. Possibly four officers in each, armed. The assassin must have notified them, told them some enticing story, trying to flush Victor out of the chalet. And it was going to work. But he couldn't use the front door now. Eight against one and they had vehicles. If he started shooting it would only bring more cops. He moved to the opposite end of the chalet. The back door was hanging off its hinges, blown open by a shaped breaching charge. The noise that woke him. Somewhere on the other side the assassin would be lurking, crosshairs hovering over the back entrance, an easy shot when Victor was forced to rush out. Not a bad trap. Credit where it was due.

He couldn't leave through the front. He couldn't leave through the back.

He couldn't stay.

The smell of propane was strong, urging him to move,

reminding him if he hesitated too long there would be nothing left of him to need identifying. That was due to happen in all of two minutes.

The bright sun that found its way through the blinds made him squint. He looked into the light, blinking. He pictured the assassin, poised, waiting, oblivious to distractions, concentration absolute, one eye closed, one eye staring into the scope's eyepiece, gaze fixed on the back doorway. Close to the rear of the chalet were dense pines that impeded line of sight. If the assassin was positioned to snipe him he could only do it from one place.

Victor turned around on the spot, catching his reflection in the mirror that hung near the back door. He approached it. Roughly two feet square, smooth, clean. Perfect. He lifted the mirror from its hooks.

McClury kept his breathing steady and regular despite the pain in his chest and his thumping heartbeat. He was in a crouch a hundred yards from the chalet, among the trees halfway up a gentle slope, the L96's bipod resting on a fallen tree trunk. It was the only location that allowed a clear line of sight to the chalet's back door. The sun was directly behind McClury so wouldn't reflect off his scope and give away his position. The distance was good. The concealment was good. The trap was good.

He ignored the cold, the pain, everything but the image the scope provided. He had the door centered in his scope, the Schmidt and Bender calibrated for the distance, windage, and shallow downward angle. He couldn't keep the reticule still—the pain in his shoulder caused his arm to tremble. But at this distance it wouldn't matter. A bullet just above the eye has the same effect as one between them. When the door opened and the target came running out, it would be over.

The rumble of the approaching police vehicles was close, almost outside the chalet. McClury's prey would have to make a dash for it now.

He did. The wrecked door swung open and McClury held his breath, waiting for his prey to emerge from the shadows of the doorway. McClury saw something move but stopped himself squeezing the trigger too early. It wasn't him. It was shiny, moving erratically. Reflective. A mirror.

The target was still in cover but holding a large mirror through the doorway. McClury could see his arms but not his head, torso, or legs. McClury waited, staying calm, watching the mirror, wondering what the hell was going on. Was he trying to signal someone? It made no sense. McClury considered blowing off one of the target's arms, but then he'd never come out, and the police would only keep him alive. Then the sun caught the mirror's surface at just the right angle and the reflected light shone right into McClury's eye, magnified by his scope to ten times intensity. He winced, dazzled, large opaque spots appearing in his vision. He instinctively pulled away from the scope and fired.

The bullet shattered the mirror into a thousand glittering shards.

McClury could barely see but he managed to make

out the target sprinting away from the doorway. He was heading for the trees, head down, weaving from side to side. McClury cursed, wrenched up the rifle, put his left eye to the scope. He swung the rifle to the side, trying to track the target through the blinding spots, crosshairs hovering a little way in front of him to compensate for his speed.

He fired, the bullet kicking up snow near the target's feet. The recoil from the unsupported rifle made McClury's arms rise sharply. He worked the bolt action quickly, loading another bullet into the chamber, and fired again. This time blowing a chunk out of a tree. *Goddamn.*

McClury loaded another round, swept across with the scope, went to fire, but the target was in the trees.

Gone.

Victor ran, his chest burning. Each beat of his heart sent jolts of pain through him. The snow was ankle deep and slowed him down, but he was in the trees now, and the mass of pines would hamper the assassin's line of sight. Hitting a moving target was hard enough without a forest in the way. He had cuts on his arms and hands from the shattered mirror. He ignored them.

It would only take a few seconds for the assassin to recover from any blindness, and Victor wanted to be well out of sight by that time. The only logical sniping position to snipe on the back door was the small rise one hundred yards to the rear of the house. On the near side it was just a gentle slope, but at the far side the hill was a small cliff face, a stream at its base. Victor headed toward it. This was his home, his territory, and no one knew it better.

No more shots were fired. Good.

Now Victor had become the hunter.

In the boiler room the gas tank continued expelling propane, spreading it farther throughout the ground floor of the chalet. Near to it the electronic timer reached two, then one. Zero.

The shaped C-4 charges detonated, destroying structurally essential areas of the chalet's load-bearing walls. The gas exploded an instant later, blowing out the front door and ground-floor windows, spewing huge clouds of flame through the openings. The concussion raced outward, knocking snow from the surrounding trees.

At the front of the building the door sailed through the air, hitting the first police SUV, smashing the windshield. Shards of exploded armored glass peppered the bodywork. Swiss police officers taking cover behind their vehicles in response to the gunshots, dived to the ground while debris struck the snow around them.

Instinctively McClury dropped to the ground when he heard the explosion behind him. He looked back, saw the obliterated chalet burning fiercely as if it were made from nothing more than matchsticks. It collapsed in on itself. Fire and smoke mushroomed skyward. *Cool.*

He scrambled to his feet, slinging the L96 over his shoulders. He reloaded another five shells into the shotgun and gripped it tightly with both hands. The fact that he had failed to kill his prey three separate times burned more than the hole in his chest.

The target had been running to the south before Mc-Clury lost sight of him, so McClury set off in that direction. He'd taken his boots off to sneak out of the house without the target hearing, and his feet were cold in the snow despite the thick socks he wore. He moved quickly, eyes fixed forward, pausing at intervals to listen, pressing against trees for cover.

He wasn't worried about the police. They would have their eyes glued to the burning chalet for the time being, all thoughts of gunshots forgotten. But if they did choose to stick their noses where they didn't belong, Mc-Clury had no compunctions about blowing those noses off. Two years working Europe had made him hate the Continent and its self-important inhabitants with a passion. He welcomed the chance to pay back some of that hatred on idiot Swiss cops.

Tracks up ahead. He hurried over to them. Deep footprints a yard apart that continued south. The target was fleeing, trying to cover as much distance as possible. Mc-Clury followed them, moving fast. They led deeper into the trees, the ground sloping as they did. *Idiot.* The target was heading away from the higher ground. He evidently knew little about tactics in the field.

McClury started to breathe heavily, feeling the strain of the run. That he was shot was never far from his thoughts, but there would be time to get it looked at later. He'd been killing people professionally for as long as he could remember, and he hadn't let a target escape before and he wasn't about to start now.

The tracks veered off to the right, following the base of the hill until McClury found himself on its north side, where it was steep and rocky, the crest of the hill some thirty feet above him. He rushed across a narrow stream, continued to follow the tracks as they stuck to the contours of the hill. Again he considered his prey to be a fool. He should have used the stream to disguise his tracks. He was looking less good and more lucky by the second.

The tracks continued to follow around the small hill, and it seemed like the target was looping back in the direction of the house. That didn't make any sense unless he was a coward and had decided giving himself up to the police was going to keep him alive. McClury smiled. Let him think that.

He heard the tumble of loose stones, saw from the corner of his eye small rocks land in the snow at the base of the cliff face. Something had disturbed them. McClury spun around, dropping to one knee. He looked up to the crest of the small cliff. A dark shape loomed at the top.

A shot rang out, echoing through the trees.

It felt like someone had whacked McClury on the arm with a baseball bat. He was bringing the Mossberg up to fire when a second bullet hit him in the shoulder and his right arm went limp. Blood splashed on the snow.

The shotgun landed at his feet. He felt himself wavering and reached his good arm out, pressing his palm flat against a tree trunk to prop himself up. He'd never been shot before today, and now he was shot three times. He almost laughed. McClury heard more stones clattering behind him, realized the target was scaling down the rocky face. Bastard had led him down here to the low ground so he could loop back to exploit the high ground.

Snow crunched underfoot.

A voice behind him said, "I'm going to ask you some questions."

McClury's reply was curt. "Fuck you."

"Now, that isn't very polite."

"I won't talk."

The voice continued, "I'm going to ask them all the same, and you will answer."

The Mossberg was right before McClury, no more than a couple of feet from his free hand. The hand he couldn't move.

"You're going to die anyway," the voice continued. "If you answer me freely you won't have to die screaming."

McClury believed him. He knew through experience that under torture everyone talked. The shotgun, so close, yet it might as well be a mile away. If he tried to get to it with his other hand, he would just fall over into the snow with the gun trapped beneath him. He might be able to roll over, but not before the target had finished him off. His outstretched arm was already shaking. He didn't know how much longer he could keep himself supported.

"I was only doing my job," he wheezed.

"Then you should have done it better."

McClury nodded for a moment. Fucker had a point. He released the arm that was supporting him and fell forward, straight on top of the shotgun.

For a second McClury's hand fumbled underneath his chest.

The shotgun's blast blew half the American's skull off, spreading a triangle of gore across the snow. Steam rose from the blood. Victor shook his head. Snow was falling. Victor searched the body, finding nothing useful. But he saw the assassin's tracks clearly in the snow and followed them first back toward his burning chalet. He kept low, mindful of the police officers that were still around. He followed the tracks to the small rise where the assassin had been covering the back door. He found brass shell casings in the snow.

The footprints then split off, toward his former residence and also farther north. Victor followed them away from the chalet. The footprints were sharper, deeper, the assassin having moved swiftly through the snow. Before he had removed his boots.

They took a more or less straight line, veering off only for trees in the way. After ten minutes Victor stood at the base of a rocky outcrop. There were no more footprints, but he could see the fallen snow at the bottom of the steep slope, disturbed rocks, exposed earth. Victor made his way upward, using the trees for support. He noticed he was wheezing, the coarse sound of his breathing getting louder as he climbed. He'd already pushed himself more than he should. He was injured; he needed to rest, for a few days at least, to give his body time to heal. Soon, he told himself.

Just before the top of the hillock, Victor found the assassin's hide. It looked like he had been there overnight. There was a discarded winter coat, a backpack, a two-liter bottle half-filled with urine, and a plastic bag full of excrement. The jacket was empty. Victor took the backpack, and slung it over one shoulder, his own bag over the other. He began following a second set of tracks, ones that came from the west, deeper into the forest. It had snowed in the last twelve hours, but no more than an inch. There still remained shallow depressions in the snow, more than deep enough for Victor to follow with ease.

He came upon the assassin's vehicle after forty minutes. A Toyota SUV, parked off-road. Victor searched through the side pockets of the backpack, found the keys, and unlocked it.

He stopped suddenly, hand clutching his chest. He retched, tasting iron, coughing up blood. He stayed leaned over for a minute until the pain had subsided. He used a handful of snow to wash the blood from his mouth and used some more snow to hide the blood on the ground.

There was nothing in the vehicle to identify the man who'd tried to kill him. The Toyota had a rental sticker fixed to both front and rear windows and rental documents in the glove box. It would have been rented in a false name, Victor was sure. He threw the two bags onto the backseat and started the engine. He gave the vehicle a few minutes to warm up before he carefully reversed out onto the road.

He sighed heavily. Whoever wanted him dead had found out where he'd lived. An impossibility had it not just been dramatically proved. In the rearview mirror Victor saw smoke from his burning chalet rising above the tree line. If whoever wanted him dead had found him here, they could find him anywhere.

Whatever semblance of a life he'd made for himself was over.

TWENTY-TWO

Paris, France
Thursday
15:16 CET

Alvarez took a big slurp of his three-sugar French-excuse-for-a coffee and typed clumsily on the keyboard resting on his thighs. He sat with his feet up on the desk, shoes on the floor. A mostly empty plastic ballpoint was wedged between his teeth, slowly being chewed. He was in his temporary office of the CIA's Paris station on the second floor of the U.S. Embassy.

The office was barely big enough for him and his desk and was so small he liked to refer to it as his shoe box. It was quiet, though, and Alvarez could do without distractions. Near to his feet sat a photograph of Christopher from the school nativity play. He'd been a shepherd. The little trooper had nailed it perfectly, even if the kids playing sheep couldn't *bah* worth a damn.

Tracking down Ozols's killer was going nowhere fast. If he was traveling under Alan Flynn's passport, then, according to the Czechs, he hadn't left the country, but Alvarez thought it more likely he'd just switched passports and gone who knows where? Alvarez didn't have the time or the manpower for a Europe-wide manhunt, so he had focused his efforts on investigating the seven dead shooters. If he could find out who hired them, maybe that would reveal enough about Ozols's killer to lead to who hired him. Then maybe there would be a shot at getting the missiles or at least stopping the technology from ending up in the hands of America's enemies.

He'd discovered a lot over a couple of days. Mikhail Svyatoslav, who the killer had impersonated, had been a former member of the Spetsnaz. He served in Afghanistan during the eighties before doing a brief stint with the KGB. He got shown the door when the Cold War ended and went freelance, mainly working the Eastern bloc, taking out the trash for crime lords and other scum.

With him had been a few Hungarians, ex-mob by the looks of it, and some Serb irregulars, including a woman. Alvarez had to shake his head at that. In short, he had compiled a list of the world's worst assholes from every cesspit from the Balkans to the Urals.

Hired guns, ex-soldiers, mercenaries, killers. Two of the bastards were wanted for war crimes in Kosovo. It's good that they're dead, Alvarez thought. Only dead they couldn't be questioned. They were a bunch of typical Eurotrash hitmen. Alvarez had expected nothing less.

What he didn't expect was to find out that one of the hitters was an American, James Stevenson, and a former U.S. Army Ranger. Stevenson had even tried out for Delta but hadn't made the grade—not only that, but he applied to get into the CIA after he dropped out of his unit, but once again didn't make the cut. He had an aptitude for fieldwork, but he was a discipline problem waiting to happen, too much of a risk to go on the agency payroll. He got into the private sector through an old army buddy and was based out of Belgium. Stevenson did a lot of protection work and other unspecified jobs for a security firm in Brussels.

On the computer screen Alvarez had bank records, phone records, e-mails, memos, even utility bills. They belonged to the recently-shot-twice-in-the-face James Stevenson, former soldier, former mercenary, former fucking scumbag. The guy had deposited a huge amount of euros in cash into an account at a not-prone-to-asking-difficult-questions type of bank. This had happened two weeks before he'd become closely acquainted with a pair of 5.7s.

A quarter of that money had then been wired to seven separate bank accounts belonging to the other members of the team. Alvarez assumed they would each have received the same amount again after the job, with Stevenson pocketing half the total for himself. Now the money was sitting gathering interest in the name of dead guys.

Who the hell had given Stevenson the cash in the first place? was what Alvarez wanted to know. Stevenson hadn't been the shrewdest operator in the history of contract killings and had left several clues on the hard drive of his personal computer, a portable copy of which was now plugged into Alvarez's laptop.

Stevenson liked to keep things organized, and he had details of each of the other members of the team in a spreadsheet, complete with e-mail addresses and phone numbers where appropriate. This information helped identify a couple of the more elusive corpses but didn't help track down who had hired Stevenson.

He referred to the job itself as ParisJob, a rather unimaginative title in Alvarez's opinion, but Alvarez supposed it hardly mattered what it was called. The private security firm in Brussels, through which Stevenson had done several protection jobs, had already been grilled and claimed they had nothing to do with Paris. Alvarez believed them. They made too much money hiring out mercenaries legitimately to have had a hand in a risky contract killing.

It wasn't beyond the realm of possibility, though, to think that whoever had hired Stevenson had been a previous client for the security firm. The list of potential suspects was huge and spread worldwide: private businessmen, multinational corporations, Saudi oil barons,

African governments. Stevenson himself had worked with all sorts of clients, any one of whom could be the person Alvarez was after, or maybe the individual had nothing to do with the firm. If so, the list of suspects had risen exponentially.

His gut told him that whoever had hired Ozols's killer had also hired Stevenson and his crew to kill him after the job's completion. Maybe he'd fucked up, maybe it was to tie off loose ends—it hardly mattered. But if Alvarez was right, and the killer had figured out that it was his own employer who'd tried to have him killed, there was a chance he still had the information. That meant, the missiles were still out there and still attainable.

The phone rang and he answered with a blunt, "Yeah."

It was Noakes, one of the CIA officers who worked out of the embassy. Noakes worked in the basement along with all the other technophiles. He was an okay guy, if a little too hyperactive on caffeine and sugar for Alvarez to have much patience for.

"I've got something you might be interested in," Noakes said with his usual hundred-mile-per-hour speak. "Stevenson tried to be sneaky with his hard drive and used a piece of software for deleting files securely. It's the kind of thing my dad would use. I mean, for Christ—"

Alvarez jumped in. "Let me guess, it doesn't do what it's supposed to."

"Not quite," Noakes said. "Or at least it doesn't do it as well as it's supposed to. I've managed to extract some of the more recently deleted files, but the older ones are going to take longer, if they're still there somewhere, which I don't know. They could be. Or they might truly be gone for good."

Alvarez held the phone a fraction farther away from his ear. "What did you find?"

"Oh yeah." Noakes laughed. "Almost forgot to tell you. I've dug up some deleted e-mails between Stevenson and an unidentified person. We've only got the last few in what appears to be an ongoing conversation. They're discussing payment for something called ParisJob."

"Good," Alvarez said. "Get those e-mails to me as soon as possible."

"On it now."

Alvarez put the phone down, pleased to be making some progress but aware of how little he really knew. He stood and walked to the window. Alvarez stared outward through the glass, through Paris, to the person out there who'd started this whole mess.

"Where are you?" he whispered.

TWENTY-THREE

Central Intelligence Agency, Virginia, U.S.A.
Wednesday
16:56 EST

He looked like a kindly old gentleman, face craggy but tanned, thin but still strong, hair gray but thick. Kevin Sykes watched Ferguson pour himself a cup of coffee from the brushed steel pot and take a sip. It was bitter, tasteless crap, but the caffeine content should at least meet with Ferguson's approval.

"Has the room been swept?" Ferguson asked. He looked at Sykes through the reflection in the office window.

Sykes nodded. "Just before you got here."

Ferguson turned around and said, "Then please explain to me what the fucking hell has just happened."

Sykes tensed visibly. "Tesseract showed up in Switzerland."

"And?"

Sykes shook his head. "Swiss police found a body in the woods north of the village of Saint Maurice. My man."

Ferguson sighed heavily and sat down. "What about Tesseract?"

"We don't know for sure. The house was burned to the ground. I guess there's a chance he was in it."

"That sounds to me like a fool's hope, Mr. Sykes. If

he killed your man I doubt he would have managed to get himself cooked afterward."

"I'm afraid I'm inclined to agree with you, sir."

"So he's gone then, with the flash drive?"

Sykes nodded.

"Unless it was lost in the explosion. Which would take this from disastrous to catastrophic," Ferguson added. "When did all this happen?"

"A few hours ago," Sykes replied, half to himself. "Look, this isn't over yet. We have leads. We—"

"So why did you not inform me of this earlier?"

"This is my show, and I've been handling it. Telling you before I knew the facts would have achieved nothing except to inflame the situation. There isn't anything you could have put in motion that I have not already done."

Ferguson frowned. "And whom did you use this time?"

"Carl McClury. He was ex–Special Activities Division with a solid record in wet work, before that Special Forces. He wasn't prone to asking questions either. He was freelance, did contract work for the company. His cover was as a security guard at the Zürich embassy, so he was the perfect choice for a cleanup op."

"You have got to be joking." Ferguson stepped forward angrily. "You used a CIA employee? Are you out of your fucking mind?"

"A *former* employee. He's not on the books."

"Don't get cute with me, Mr. Sykes. It amounts to the same thing. What do you think will happen when they find that out?"

"Nothing," Sykes answered confidently. "McClury was an agency contract shooter, and everyone knows it's not unheard of for our contractors to do work for other people. Who knows who McClury may also have been doing jobs for? Europe's a hell of a big place. Lots of potential clients. His death will go down as an occupational hazard. Plus," Sykes added, "there is nothing that connects McClury to Tesseract. There'll be no evidence that the man who killed him was the same guy who shot up Paris. And let's not forget that nothing connects us to McClury or Stevenson and his crew. We're so clean we're practically virgins."

Ferguson ran slim fingers through his hair. "I'm afraid I don't share your confidence."

"There are at least two people between us and McClury, and neither knows where their orders came from. McClury was payment on delivery, and he didn't deliver. Before him, Stevenson was paid in advance in cash. Alvarez won't be able to identify the man who paid him. And that money was shipped through the usual methods—intermediaries, offshore accounts, etcetera. No trail. We let Stevenson gather his own team, remember? We've got nothing to worry about."

"That remains to be seen."

"Yes, McClury's death makes things awkward, but he was a shrewd operator. Meticulous. He won't have left any tracks to follow like Stevenson. Besides, he was totally deniable alive, and he's even more deniable dead."

"You forgot to add incompetent to his list of qualities."

"He had an impressive track record."

"Right up until the point he got himself killed."

"Be that as it may, he was the only choice for the op given its unique criteria. We needed someone fast, and disposable hitmen aren't exactly easy to find."

It was a good retort but Ferguson waved a hand to dismiss the point, and Sykes swallowed down the anger that flared up inside him. He reminded himself who he was speaking to and didn't press the issue further. Ferguson wasn't just his boss, he was the architect of their scheme, and he demanded obedience at all times, even when he was blatantly wrong.

"What are you going to do about McClury?"

Sykes already had everything planned out in his mind. "It'll be a day before he's identified by the Swiss police, another day at the very least before anyone that matters realizes he's former agency. That's more than enough time for me to sour McClury's reputation. I'll make it seem as if he'd been taking contracts for some very objectionable people. The kind of people who don't mind killing the hired help when they're no longer useful. That'll be sufficient to muddy any trail. No one will think to connect his death with what's been happening elsewhere."

Ferguson seemed to take a long time placing his cup back down. He carefully wiped the corners of his mouth with the thumb and forefinger of his left hand. Somehow Sykes managed to stop himself from smiling. He knew he'd won the old bastard over. Ferguson just didn't want to give Sykes any praise.

"Things have gone bad so far, I accept that." A little

humility would go down nicely, Sykes thought. "But this thing isn't over yet. Tesseract is still out there, still with the flash drive I'm sure, so we have options. People are looking for him now, the French, Germans, Swiss, the agency. That'll help us close in on him. And when we do, I've got some more contractors on standby. I know it's risky, but we can make it look like someone else got to him first. Sure, things won't have been as clean as we would have liked, but the end result will still be the same."

"There won't be a next time."

"You don't know that. It's too early to give up."

Ferguson paused for a moment. "This is what we're going to do instead."

"The plan is still good; we can make it work."

Ferguson continued. "I'm afraid I don't share your optimistic evaluation of the circumstances. Your incompetence thus far has made it even more difficult to salvage this operation. Have you forgotten what's at stake here? Because I haven't."

"Of course I know what's at stake. You're the one who's losing sight of the objective, not me."

"You arrogant little shit," Ferguson said with a smile. "I've spent my entire career moving from one mission to the next without letting anyone get in my way. I've never lost sight of an objective. You can count on that. But I'm not going to put my freedom in jeopardy because you seem incapable of killing one man."

"I think you overestimate Tesseract's chances."

"I think you overestimate your own."

"Nothing has happened so far that cannot be fixed."

Ferguson shook his head. "Stand the contractors down immediately."

"What? No, we have to keep them ready."

"Tell me why exactly? May I remind you of the considerable efforts it took to track Tesseract down in the first place when he didn't know we were trying? Now that he knows people are after him, do you think that's going to make him easier to spot? Frankly, I'm amazed you think that's a workable course of action at this time, and I'm even more amazed that you're willing to put more people at risk after what just happened to McClury."

"What else are we going to do? Hope Tesseract dies of natural causes and leaves us the location of the missiles in his will?"

"Comments like that do nothing to reassure me, Mr. Sykes. You don't leave me any choice. I'm taking it out of your hands."

"What the hell does that mean? What are you going to do?"

"Something I should have done from the very beginning. Had I known this killer would be quite so adept at staying alive I never would have waited. I'm making a call."

"What? To who?"

"To someone who can help us. There's a man I've used before. An expert."

"An expert?"

"A killer."

"Who?"

"He's not on our files, he's SIS."

"As in the *British* Secret Intelligence Service? That's insane. What about the British government?"

"They'll never know. He's a contract agent. He'll just do some moonlighting for us."

"Moonlighting?"

"Her Majesty can't pay him what I can."

"What's the guy's name?"

"You won't have heard of him. His name, or at least the name I know him by, is simply Reed. From this point onward he takes over the hands-on part of this operation."

"This is ridiculous; we don't need an outsider. It'll only complicate matters."

"I don't care if it does complicate matters. Getting this mess buried is all I give a damn about. The only way we can proceed is by using an outsider."

"That's bullshit."

"If you can't speak like a grown-up, don't speak at all. What else are we going to do? Gather together another bunch of clueless mercenaries? Or just dispatch more former company men and hope no one joins the dots if they don't come back?"

"We can still make it work."

"You're not hearing me. Now that McClury is dead our hands are tied. You've had your chance and you've failed. Reed is our only hope of getting this situation cleaned up without bringing us into the spotlight."

"And where are you going to send this Reed? Like you said, we don't know where Tesseract is anymore."

"Tesseract can wait for the moment. Reed can be in Paris by the morning."

"Why Paris?"

"I don't think we have any time to waste. Do you?" Sykes shook his head, unsure what question he was answering. "Good," Ferguson continued. "When Reed lands in Paris I want him to meet up with your man on the ground as soon as possible. What's his name again?"

Sykes kept his face level, trying not to show he didn't have a clue what was being discussed. "John Kennard."

"That's right," Ferguson said. "Have Kennard supply Reed with a list of everyone who's had an active role in this operation. Reed will then take care of the rest."

"What do you mean? Why would he need that list?"

Ferguson didn't answer, but his eyes, peering through the steam from his cup, said it all.

"*Jesus*," Sykes gasped, finally understanding. "All of them?"

Ferguson nodded as if it was of no consequence. "And they will be missed." He didn't skip a beat. "But sacrifices must be made for the greater good."

"The greater good?"

"Alright," Ferguson admitted with a half smile that Sykes didn't appreciate. "Maybe not for the greater good, but for the good of you and me. I am still assuming that you don't want to spend the rest of your life behind bars?" Ferguson paused and Sykes didn't respond. "I didn't think so, and that is the price of failure here, Mr. Sykes. You are still aware of that?"

"Yes, sir."

"This operation of ours has failed."

"Sir, I think it's too early to—"

"Shut up and let me finish. This operation has failed. Achieving our original objective is now a secondary consideration. Getting our hands on those missiles is going to take nothing short of a small miracle, so I suggest we focus our efforts elsewhere."

"What about the list of buyers I've been working on?"

"For the time being you can forget the money, Mr. Sykes. Our priority at this moment is to make sure we come out of this with our skins intact. The only way this could've worked was to have no loose ends, but we've gone way past that now. Now, it's damage limitation. We can't have people walking around with knowledge of an illegal op that spectacularly failed."

"But none of them know the full details of what we're doing or even who they're working for. Only one is true agency anyway. And besides, we'll need to use them again if we're going to make this work, and they're good, they're trustworthy."

"Don't kid yourself. They're about as trustworthy as you are." Sykes's eyes narrowed. "Or I am for that matter. What if one of them puts the pieces together about what's been going on here, what are we going to do then? Hope they don't tell anyone?" Sykes looked away. "Alvarez is already on the scent and looking as if he might actually be getting somewhere. Or maybe that fat idiot Procter will stop worrying about his promotion prospects long enough to make the appropriate leap of faith. Do you really think that this disaster will stay buried if anyone besides ourselves knows even some of the details?"

"But two are Americans for Christ sake."

Ferguson's expression didn't alter. "It's unavoidable."

Sykes's head rose slowly. "You haven't just decided this, have you? You would have had them killed even if things had worked out perfectly."

Ferguson nodded. "Eventually yes, using Reed over an extended period of time, but this accelerates the urgency."

"And when did you plan on telling me?"

"Don't get all precious on me now, Mr. Sykes," Ferguson said. "I told you at the very beginning if we were going to pull this off it had to be completely clean. No traces back to us. What did you think I meant?" Sykes's eyes dropped a fraction. "You've been in this business long enough to know what I was talking about. You may not have admitted it to yourself, but you knew exactly what you were getting yourself into, so don't act so shocked now. There was always going to be a cleanup phase to this operation, and Reed was always going to be part of that. Experience has also taught me that you need a backup in case the unexpected occurs, and I knew Reed could be that trump card. And, as events have transpired, it's a good thing I had that foresight. Until now you didn't need to know the details."

"Evidently."

"I trust this isn't a problem for you?" He paused. "Is it?

Sykes's voice was quiet. "No, sir."

"That's settled then. Reed will need all their details straightaway, and I do mean all their details."

"I'll make sure he gets them promptly."

"That's my boy." All sympathetic smiles now, Sykes noted sourly, like a father explaining to his son the necessity of having the family dog put to sleep to avoid the veterinary bills. "It's for the best."

"Yes, sir," Sykes said, finding himself staring into space. He realized Ferguson was watching him closely and straightened up.

"I do hope you have the stomach for this, Mr. Sykes," Ferguson said.

"Of course, sir."

Ferguson's voice dropped a few decibels. "Because I would be very disappointed to find my trust in you to be misplaced."

"You don't have to worry about that, sir."

"I'm glad to hear it."

"This Reed character," Sykes said, to take the spotlight from himself, "just how good is he?"

Ferguson raised an incredulous eyebrow.

"He's killed more people than Stalin."

TWENTY-FOUR

Charles de Gaulle Airport, France
Thursday
07:30 CET

She saw him approaching, walking toward her in a perfectly straight line, relaxed, unfazed by the chaos of the
airport around him. He was about five-ten, broad shoul-
dered yet slim. Dark haired. He was wearing a fine black
suit, jacket open, top button of his white shirt undone.
No tie.

There was something almost mechanical about his
movements, each action measured, controlled. He already had his passport in hand, and she took it from him,
opened it up. Borland, James Frederick. *James*. He
looked like a James.

He hadn't shaved today, and the dark stubble disguised
his otherwise strong jaw line. His skin badly needed
some color, and his hair wasn't styled, just cut short
and fashionless. He had great bone structure but clearly
didn't make the most of himself.

"What is the purpose of your visit to France, Mr.
Borland?"

The man's reply was candid. "Business."

His British accent was cultured, refined, the voice of
a true gentleman. He had the natural class of someone
who didn't have to try. With a bit of work she could make
him into a real head turner.

His eyes were blue, incredibly intense. He was

especially handsome she decided, but it took a second look to realize. She compared the passport photo with the face before her and noted how in life he wore the same serious expression. She could tell he was a very deep person. If he blinked she didn't see it.

She remembered she had a job to do. "What kind of business are you in?"

Again a one word answer.

"Removals."

He wasn't a big talker, but that didn't matter. Nothing worse than a guy who never shut up.

"Are you from London? I love London, it's a fantastic city. I think you English are the nicest people in the world."

No reply. Not one for chitchat then. He just waited with that unwavering blank look on his face. Maybe he was just shy. Yes, that must be it. She managed to sneak a glance at his left hand. No ring. No jewelry of any sort, in fact, and his watch looked like the kind of thing a diver would wear, not a businessman. What was with this guy? It was almost as if he was trying to play down his appearance. What was the point of being a looker if no one looked? If he hadn't been walking directly toward her, she probably wouldn't have noticed him.

She smiled, touched her bottom lip with the tip of her tongue, ran a finger along her neck, fluttered her eyelashes like mad—anything to give him the signal to chat her up. He wasn't taking the bait. Yet. Maybe he liked to tease.

She checked the information on her computer. The man traveled a lot: Luxembourg, Egypt, Hong Kong.

And they were just in the last month. She added well traveled to his list of qualities. She hit a few buttons on her keyboard and handed the passport back to him. He took it from her fingers so smoothly that she had to look down at her hand to make sure he actually had it.

"Enjoy your stay in France."

She gave it one last try, tilted her head to the side, and looked at him all doe eyed with her best take-me-to-dinner-and-fuck-me look. He walked away without a word.

Arrogant prick, she thought. He was probably queer.

TWENTY-FIVE

Budapest, Hungary
Thursday
17:46 CET

The sky above the city was overcast. The rain soaked through Victor's overcoat. He shivered as he walked down a narrow street lined with puddles. The road was cobbled, the sidewalks uneven flagstones. There were no streetlights, just the glow from overlooking windows providing illumination. No one walked nearby. His footsteps echoed.

He hadn't dared stay in Switzerland, where both the police and his hunters would be looking for him. Hungary seemed like a good idea. Victor hadn't been to Budapest for a couple of years, so there had to be less chance of his being tracked here than some other cities. He didn't believe a private operation could have followed him to Saint Maurice without his knowledge. It would take multiple teams of skilled shadows, precise coordination, access to CCTV footage, aerial and probably satellite surveillance.

Only an intelligence agency would have those kinds of resources and manpower. Even then, few organizations had the reach to make such a thing possible. The assassin who'd tried to kill him in Switzerland had been an American. The leader of the kill team in Paris had been American too. Victor didn't believe in coincidences. It could only be the CIA.

The walls of Victor's world were crumbling down around him. He was on the execution list of the furthest-reaching covert service on the planet.

He was as good as dead.

His hotel was lost within the backstreets of Budapest's red-light district. The room came with a bed with a metal frame and a whole drawer full of fliers for hookers, male as well as female. The hotel was the kind of place where he could lay low for as long as he needed while he collected his thoughts and decided on the next course of action.

Victor left the alleyway and kept walking, staying to the side streets, avoiding people, watching for shadows. He walked for longer than he planned, thinking, analyzing. He thought about Paris, thought about his chalet in flames. Two attempts on his life within a week. He felt unpopular.

The sands of his life were running out with every passing second. Already the CIA would be scouring surveillance tapes, liaising with the Swiss authorities and foreign intelligence services—all the time narrowing down their search, closing in on him. He found an Internet café and took a terminal where he could watch the door. There were things he had to check if he was going to formulate a plan. And whatever plan he put into practice would require money. It was possible that if the CIA knew where he lived they had also frozen his bank accounts. There had been a time when a Swiss bank would never have revealed information about its clients, but the world had changed that day in September 2001. Now anything was possible.

He was relieved to find his money still in place at the primary bank he used. He would have to withdraw all the money as a precaution and booked an appointment at the bank. Victor had money stored in various safety-deposit boxes around the Continent, but at the moment he was only concerned with his money in Switzerland. He realized he hadn't eaten for a while and devoured three cheeseburgers at a nearby café. He finished off the milkshake on the street.

Nothing made sense to him anymore. Did the CIA want him because of Paris, or did they arrange it in the first place? Did they hire him or did they hire the guys who tried to kill him or both? Did they track him from France to Switzerland or did they already know where he lived? Any answers he could think of led to more questions. He was reduced to speculation, guesswork, and he hated it.

He thought about the broker. *This is not what you think*, whoever they are had said. Maybe he should have listened. Perhaps the CIA had found out about his job and had tried to kill him afterward; maybe Ozols was a CIA asset; maybe the flash drive belonged to the CIA; or maybe the CIA just wanted it for itself. Maybe the broker had been part of the setup; maybe the broker was the CIA; or maybe the broker was on the same hit list as he. Too many maybes, not enough certainties.

Victor hailed a taxi, deciding at the last second to walk instead. The taxi driver hurled abuse at him in Hungarian, the gist of which Victor understood to be a reference to his mother. He didn't look back. Falling snow mixed with the rain. It felt good on his skin. He walked past a group of homeless men passing around a bottle of something potent, judging by the stink in the air. He felt eyes watching him.

He put a hand to his chest for a moment. The pain was an annoyance but far from debilitating. There would be no long-term damage, but he now had a large bruise in the center of his chest. When his current predicament was over, he planned to visit the company who had supplied him with the glass and creatively demonstrate to them just how bulletproof it really was.

The broker must have known something, he was sure of that now, but he had been so convinced they'd set him up he didn't contemplate anything else. Now he was running for his life, maybe because of that bull-headedness.

He performed countersurveillance on autopilot, passing through side streets, doubling back, taking buses, changing. He'd decided to contact the broker long before he reached another Internet café, after trying unsuccessfully to come up with a course of action that didn't go against his paranoia. If he had been right the first time and the broker did have a hand in what had happened in Paris, it wouldn't matter, he would still be up against the same odds. But perhaps the broker knew something that could help him. He still had the flash drive. It could be the bargaining chip he needed.

He logged on to the game's message board. The broker wasn't logged in, but there was a personal message in his profile's in-box. From the broker, dated Monday. He opened it. A response to their last communication, a rant about honoring the arrangement, about "trust" of all things. Victor deleted it. He composed his own message:

Tell me what really happened in Paris and I may deliver the package.

He thought it short and sweet. All he had to do now was wait.

TWENTY-SIX

Paris, France
Thursday
22:22 CET

Kennard walked through the deserted street with his hands deep inside his coat pockets. Clouds of moisture billowed around his head with each step. He had a lot to do, like checking his operational e-mail, but this was the most important. He reached the public toilet and had a cursory look around. Protocol dictated that he should check out the area first, but it was too fucking cold for that by-the-manual shit.

His shoes echoed on the concrete steps as he descended beneath the ground. The stink of piss was perhaps less overpowering in Paris than it might have been in L.A., but repugnant is repugnant, whatever the strength. He slipped a coin into the slot and pushed his way through the creaking gate.

Only one of the three ceiling lights was working. A single bare bulb providing the grim illumination, casting deep shadows from the fixtures. The air was even colder than it was outside. The American saw his breath misting in the gloom. The walls were stained, the urinals cracked, taps rusted, floor wet.

What a shithole. No wonder the French were such a sour people when they had to put up with public restrooms like this. At first glance the place was empty, and Kennard checked his watch. He was exactly right on the button. He rubbed his palms together, hoping the asset wasn't going to be much longer.

He became aware there was someone in one of the stalls a second before a toilet flushed. A moment later the door opened and a figure emerged. He moved to the sink, casting Kennard a brief sideways glance.

The man was dressed in a dark suit and overcoat. There was a squeak as the man turned a faucet and began washing his hands. He did so slowly, in a methodical manner, seemingly unbothered by the cold. The reflection of the man's blue eyes stared at Kennard in the mirror above the sink. This had to be him.

"Blake?" Kennard asked.

"I'm Dawson," the man who was neither Dawson nor Blake answered.

His British accent confused Kennard, and for a moment he hesitated. But the accent didn't matter. The code had been completed. Kennard moved to the sinks and reached a hand into his coat. The other man turned violently toward him, so fast that it made Kennard freeze in place.

"It's not wise to make such moves," the man stated flatly.

Kennard believed him. Slowly finishing the action, he drew a small but thick manila envelope from his inside pocket.

"For you," he said.

The man eyed it for a few seconds, turned, and used the back of his wrist to hit the hand dryer. Kennard stood, envelope in hand, feeling like a chump, waiting for the Brit to finish. After the dryer had completed its cycle the man turned back and took the envelope from Kennard's fingers.

"You're supposed to open it now," Kennard explained.

The man looked questioningly at him for a second before he tore open the envelope and reached inside. He drew out a sleek smartphone, turned it once over in his hands, and went to slip it into his inside jacket pocket.

"You need to access the files now," Kennard said. "I was told you'd have the password."

The British guy looked at Kennard for a few seconds then turned on the smartphone and opened the files. Kennard watched his eyes absorb the information, the man's face illuminated by the glow of the screen. The smartphone contained several files that Kennard had received from his employer. He had no idea what the files contained; the phone was password protected. It was no doubt the operation plans so someone could assess who was to blame for the fuck up. The fact that Kennard's contact was British meant that it had probably been a joint black-bag op with MI6. And one with potentially severe repercussions, hence all this cloak-and-dagger bullshit. But he was only guessing, and in Kennard's experience it didn't pay to do too much thinking in his job.

The Brit stared at the smartphone for a long time before finally looking up. He gestured to the American.

"I think you should read this as well."

Kennard nodded as the phone was handed to him. Text filled the small screen. Kennard tried to absorb what the document said, but the light stung his eyes. It had details: height, weight, hair color, biographical information, what looked like a CIA record. It was someone's dossier. There was a photo, slowly coming into focus. A face. His face. Two words above it. Two horrible words.

John Kennard.

Kennard was an experienced case officer, highly trained. He didn't hesitate. He dropped the phone and immediately went for his gun. But the man was already coming forward, too fast to be believed, doing something with his hands, just a blur of movement Kennard didn't understand. The man grabbed Kennard's wrist as the gun came out of the holster.

He tried to get the gun up, angling it so he could take a shot. The man was too strong, too close, Kennard couldn't see where the gun was pointing. He fired anyway.

The bang was excruciating, the flash made him blink. He'd missed. The bullet harmlessly shattered tiles around the sink. Kennard fired again. This time the bullet hit a urinal, smashing it into pieces that fell clattering to the floor.

He grabbed desperately at the man's arm with his free hand. Kennard was at least three inches taller and far heavier, but he was outmatched by his attacker's leverage and balance. Then he realized—he didn't know where the man's other hand was.

The breath caught in Kennard's throat as the blade entered his abdomen, knife easily slicing through skin and muscle. Explosions of agony rushed through his body. His gun fell from fingers too weak to hold it. Kennard gasped as the blade was pulled free and driven back in again and again. And again. The knife plunged so deeply the tip scratched the back of his pelvis.

Kennard sank downward, eyes wide, hands still grabbing uselessly at the man who was killing him. The knife was pulled free a final time, and Kennard slumped onto his knees. He clutched at the torn shreds of his stomach, fingers warm with blood and touching slick innards no longer inside him. Kennard didn't scream. He couldn't.

He felt fingers on his head, grabbing and pulling upward. Then, on Kennard's own hair, the man carefully wiped the blood from his knife.

When the weapon was clean, the man released him. The blade didn't look like metal—matte black. Kennard watched the man fold the blade away and replace the knife in a wrist sheath hidden on his left forearm. The man moved back over to the washbasin and once again began to methodically wash his hands. Kennard watched helplessly, clutching at the slippery, ragged mess of his stinking guts. He felt so tired.

By the time the man had finished drying his hands, Kennard's head hung limply forward. He heard the click of the man's shoes on the tiled floor, saw the dull black leather as the man walked past him. Kennard heard the creak as the man pushed through the gate, and the slowly lessening sound of his ascending the stairs.

Kennard reached inside his coat for his cell phone but couldn't find it. His wallet was gone too. He hadn't even noticed. He saw it on the floor nearby, empty. To make his death look like a mugging, he realized. The smartphone had gone too.

Kennard didn't move, didn't try to crawl away. There was no point.

He knew he didn't have a chance.

TWENTY-SEVEN

Marseilles, France
Friday
05:03 CET

Rebecca Sumner adjusted her glasses and scrolled down the information displayed on her laptop's screen. An American citizen from California attached to the U.S. Embassy had been stabbed to death in Paris last night, just a few hours ago. The police believed it to be a mugging since the dead man's wallet and phone had been taken. Further in the text it stated that the man worked as a cultural attaché at the embassy, which meant he might actually have been a cultural attaché or, in typical agency style, it could have been a cover for his true position. His name was John Kennard. The name meant nothing to her.

Rebecca felt the beating of her heart begin to quicken. The timing of it seemed wrong, so close to Monday's massacre. Her orders had been to stay put and await further instructions, and she had been doing just that. But then the unexpected communiqué had arrived in her in-box and her control hadn't gotten back to her about it. And now this. It seemed like too much of a coincidence to be unrelated, or was she just being paranoid? She sat at her desk in the sparsely furnished apartment she had called home for the past few months. The glow of the monitor illuminated her face. She had no other lights on.

She didn't know the name of her control, had never met him. Their only communications had been over secure satellite phone links and the Internet. She didn't know who else was working on the operation or who had ordered it. She was on need to know, and apparently she didn't need to know very much. What she did know, but which no one had told her, was that the op was off the books, way off the books.

It had been nearly five days since everything had gone so wrong, and Tuesday had been the last day her control had contacted her with the directive to hold her position and await new orders. So she had. For four days she had lived off of whatever was in her cupboards, never venturing outside, always at her computer, always waiting. Twelve hours ago something had happened that changed everything. The killer had sent her a message. That hadn't been in the script.

So she'd disobeyed orders and contacted her control by e-mail within minutes of the killer's message arriving. It always took a few hours for the control to get back to her, but, half a day later, there was still no reply. Her actions had been a clear breach of the strict protocol by which the operation had been run, but she felt the communication had warranted it. Surely it was a chance to get back on track. She had assumed that she'd received nothing further because those in charge were working out what she should reply back with. But then this John Kennard had been killed.

On the phone her control had spoken with a West Coast accent; she'd guessed he was an LA native. She stared at the screen for another minute, searching for information. John Kennard was from California, the report said.

Maybe the reason why her control hadn't gotten back to her was because he'd been stabbed to death in Paris last night.

If this Kennard was really her control, then why had no one else contacted her after he'd been killed? It was over seven hours since his time of death. Plenty of time for her to get a phone call or e-mail. It was late here but not in the States, and no one slept for long on something like this anyway. Her control would have superiors who must know about her role in the operation. But what if no one else knew the control was dead? The op couldn't be salvaged if no one knew what was going on.

If they needed to speak, her control always phoned her, but he had given her a special number to call in case of dire emergencies, a cell phone number, and she considered this about as big an emergency as it could get. Rebecca picked up the phone.

Her wide eyes stared into the darkness when she heard the automated voice say the line was unavailable. She waited a minute and tried again. Unavailable. And again. Still unavailable. Lines like this didn't become unavailable. Rebecca felt the unnerving compulsion to look over her shoulder at the apartment door.

She slammed the phone down hard, suddenly understanding what was going on. First what happened in Paris on Monday, then an American from the embassy killed last night, now the emergency line dead. The only explanation was terrifying, but she made a determined effort to remain calm. There must be something you're missing, she told herself. She pored over all the reports, every scrap of intel she had access to. She needed to prove herself wrong or prove herself right—and quickly.

Interpol gave her the answer she was dreading. She read through a report that came out of Switzerland. A house had burned down north of Geneva, and a man found dead. Police were looking for the killer. Rebecca's eyes focused on the address. She had seen that address before. She'd helped find it. They'd tried again, but no one had told her. She was out of the loop. Which could only mean one thing.

Rebecca grabbed the files from her desk, carried them into the kitchen, and threw them into the sink. She rummaged through her cupboards and found the bottle of super strength rum she'd been saving for a rainy day. Today it was pouring outside and in. She unwrapped the top, tugged off the stopper, and splashed some into the sink. She took the lighter for the stove off its hook, put the end into the sink, and stood well back.

She clicked the button and the rum ignited. Rebecca took a swig from the bottle and watched the files burn for a moment. It didn't take her long to throw some clothes into a suitcase. She took practical items, nothing fancy. She had a wardrobe full of clothes she loved but it was no time to be sentimental. She had to get out as fast as possible.

There was a cleanup job underway; she was certain

of it now. All the signs were there. The op had gone wrong and whoever was in charge had pulled the plug, and they were cutting off the loose ends. She knew this kind of thing happened in the old days, but she never would have believed it still occurred in this age. You'd better believe it, she told herself.

Why the need to start killing people? Just what the hell was really going on? She had the sinking feeling that the op wasn't just off the books—it was out of the library entirely.

Her control was already dead: The report said that he was killed late last night. Only seven hours ago. They would be sending someone for her too; they might have sent them already. She looked at her watch. Each passing second brought her own demise hurtling closer.

Her heart was pounding as she zipped up her laptop and grabbed her personal effects. She left the comms equipment. She didn't need it, and all the files were on the computer. In the kitchen the thick smoke made her cough as she turned on the faucets to put out the fire in the sink.

She left the apartment, her throat choked with fear, and walked along the corridor expecting a man with a silenced pistol to appear at any moment. No, she reminded herself, they wouldn't do it like that. She'd have an accident, maybe take an overdose. Maybe get mugged in a restroom.

She decided against the elevator and took the stairs. She hurried down them, her face slick with perspiration. On the ground floor she didn't use the front door but found a fire exit at the back and pushed it open into an alleyway. The cold wind tossed her hair over her shoulders. Rain soaked her.

Rebecca could hear traffic nearby but could barely see. If she ran they might hear her, so she walked slowly and carefully to the end of the alley. Relief washed over her as she stepped out onto the street.

Maybe she was wrong, maybe her control had just been unfortunate, but she had spent her life analyzing the odds, and the odds told her to get the hell away. She had a car but didn't go to it. They would know about it. It was registered in her name. Maybe there was a bomb waiting underneath it or the brake cables were severed.

Rebecca walked down the street, the rain beating down on the top of her head. She felt safer to be near other people. They wouldn't do anything in public. She hailed a cab, telling the driver to take her to the airport. She had a place she knew she could go, where no one would find her. On the way she thought about what had happened and what might happen, and a plan started to formulate in her mind. By the time she got out of the taxi she knew exactly what she was going to do. It was dangerous, crazy even.

But it might just keep her alive.

TWENTY-EIGHT

Paris, France
Friday
08:12 CET

Alvarez pulled his bulky frame out from the hotel bed of nails and headed for the shower. After three efficient minutes of washing and scrubbing, he got out, dried himself, and dressed. He'd had only a handful of hours of sleep the night before, the same as every other night over the week, and he felt like pounded crap. He was running on fumes, and the fumes were running out. When he was younger he could do whatever the job required, whenever, but things had taken a downward trend somewhere along the road after taking Route 35. Route 40 was just around the corner.

Things weren't going to get any easier, with the job or with his body. Time was the worst enemy there was. The way Alvarez saw it you were smart if you knew fighting it was a losing battle, but you were a coward if you didn't fight anyway. Alvarez had allowed himself an extra half hour in bed in an effort to rejuvenate his brain and sinews. The big-ass yawn told him it hadn't been enough. The hunt for Ozols's killer had gone cold, and it felt like they were clutching at oiled straws. Alvarez's orders were to concentrate on trying to find out who hired the seven shooters to kill the assassin. Things hadn't gone too bad on that front. With bodies, fingerprints, and DNA a lot could be achieved.

Seven out of the seven dead shooters had been identified, and of those the American, Stevenson, was the
best lead so far. Noakes had found a series of photographs on Stevenson's hard drive of some kind of meeting between Stevenson and an unidentified man, dated
a couple weeks before the Paris massacre. A third individual had taken the shots secretly, mainly of the mystery man, an overweight guy in his fifties carrying a
briefcase. There were pictures of him arriving at a café
in Brussels and taking a seat at one of the tables outside where Stevenson waited; of the two conversing for
a while, drinking coffee, and eating pastries; and of the
fat guy standing to go, leaving the briefcase beneath
the table.

The photographer had then followed him to his car
and taken a few pictures of him driving away. For some
reason the guy with the camera had failed to get a shot
of the license plate, but Noakes was doing his best trying
to get it from reflected surfaces. So far without luck.

Stevenson's bank records showed that he had deposited one hundred thousand euros in cash a day later. No
one at the bank had questioned the deposit or notified
the authorities about it. The bank manager had since
been fired. Alvarez was determined to identify the guy
with the briefcase and was working toward that goal
with his typical composed efficiency.

Alvarez's ability to remain calm in a crisis was one of
his most highly prized traits. It took a lot for him to get
emotional and even more for him to act on that emotion.
In his time in the military he'd been on the receiving
end of some hairy situations, and as an operative of the

Central Intelligence Agency more than one gun had been pushed in his face. Only once had he genuinely feared for his life, and at that moment he found that fear focused him and made him deadly.

If anything it was easier for him to deal with danger than it was the more mundane varieties of stress. People not answering the fucking phone pissed him off far more than staring down the barrel of a .45.

Kennard had disappeared off the radar, his phone taunting Alvarez with his all-too-perfectly-well-rehearsed voice-mail message each time Alvarez hit speed dial. The previous evening Alvarez and Kennard had shared a drink in a shitty little Parisian apology of a bar. Alcohol was something Alvarez usually saved for special occasions, but Kennard had been wearing a face like he'd been sucking jalapeños for a couple of days, and Alvarez understood the importance of morale.

It felt good letting his hair down. The week had been an ungodly bitch, and he was feeling the effects. A few beers had chilled him out, but Kennard had been a bundle of nervous energy. Something was definitely under the younger guy's skin, but Kennard was keeping his lips well and truly locked. Woman trouble, Alvarez guessed. Some slutty French piece of ass not returning his messages or some other bullshit. After draining the last of his beer, Alvarez had suggested finding a burger joint but Kennard shook his head.

"I would," Kennard had said. "But I've got something I need to do."

Alvarez's eyes widened a fraction. "Something, or someone?"

"I wish."

Alvarez was firing up his laptop and onto his second cup of black coffee when his phone rang. Less than sixty seconds later he was heading out the door.

It was a short hop on the metro to the embassy, and he made his way to his office hoping that someone had made a terrible error. They hadn't. The police report was waiting for him, including photos. Alvarez sat down, unhooked his office phone, switched off his cell, and carefully read through the information.

Kennard was dead. Murdered. Stabbed multiple times in the gut, ultimately dying from loss of blood. Signs of a struggle. His phone was taken and his wallet emptied. No witnesses. Paris's finest had it down as a robbery. Poor schmuck.

Alvarez had lost people before, albeit rarely, only two in his whole career with the company. They were assets though, not true CIA. He accepted it as an inherent risk of the operational side of the business, but it wasn't something he'd ever become used to. Alvarez leaned back in his chair and exhaled heavily.

He'd never particularly liked Kennard and wasn't about to pretend to grieve for his passing, but he was genuinely sorry the guy had been murdered by some fucking snail-eating piece of shit. Probably some homeless junkie so he could score some crack. It was no way for an officer of the Central Intelligence Agency to die. Far better to have been killed on duty than while going for a piss.

The way the cops had it and the way it looked in Alvarez's head too was that the perp had surprised

Kennard with a knife and demanded his things. Kennard had tried to draw his gun and had been stabbed repeatedly. Kennard was full of himself enough to have tried something stupid like that. He should have handed over the wallet and waited for the guy to go and then put three in his spinal column.

Alvarez thought for a moment. Kennard, though hardly a lethal weapon, was a fully trained operative. It was hard to see how some lowlife could've gotten the drop on him. Alvarez scratched the back of his thick neck. He sighed and shook his head. He was reading far too much into it. The guy had been killed. It happened, even to the best. And Kennard certainly wasn't the best.

Alvarez was going to have a shitload of extra work to do now that Kennard was out of the picture. The guy gets himself killed when they're up to the eyeballs on the hunt for a professional contract killer. Perfect timing.

Alvarez put the file down and turned on his phone. He had three missed calls and a voice mail. He listened to the message. It was Noakes telling him about the photographs on Stevenson's hard drive. He called him back.

"What have you got?"

"I've found something in a couple of the photos from Stevenson's meeting."

"Such as?"

"In the ones showing the mystery man leaving, we've got some shots of his car—"

"But none of the license plate, I know."

"Yeah, well, that's right, but on two we get a look at a windshield sticker, once I'd enhanced the image. It's from the rental-car company."

"Who are they?"

"They're based out of Brussels. We didn't have a clear shot of the sticker, just the first half of the name and phone number, but that was enough to narrow down the list of suspects until I found out who it was. There aren't that many rental-car companies in Brussels with similar names. I've e-mailed you the pertinent details."

Alvarez hung up a minute later and opened up Noakes's e-mail expectantly. He pushed the police report to one side. It was a damn shame about Kennard, but he would deal with the bureaucracy of his death later on.

Right now he had more pressing matters.

TWENTY-NINE

Debrecen, Hungary
Friday
20:12 CET

Victor had spent the morning in Zürich emptying his primary bank account before burying the money minus twenty thousand euros. The cash would be his only source of funds for some time. He couldn't carry any more across borders without attracting suspicion and putting the rest in another bank was not an option.

Going back to Switzerland had been a risk, but if he was going to continue living he would need the money. He had then flown back to Budapest and from there taken the train out to Debrecen as an extra precaution. It was important to keep moving, to avoid staying in one place for too long. The CIA was after him, and he had to do everything possible to hinder its efforts to track him down.

The CIA was extremely well funded and far-reaching, but it was not all-powerful. If he stayed mobile and did nothing to attract its attention, he was confident he could keep out of its crosshairs for now. How long that would remain true, though, he didn't know.

The temperature was in the low thirties. Victor spent an hour at a coffee shop until he was sure he wasn't being watched. He then moved on to another similar establishment, where he spent a second hour making doubly sure. A week ago he would have been satisfied that he wasn't under surveillance, but now he didn't fully trust his own abilities, especially when they were going up against an organization with twenty thousand full-time employees and many tens of thousands more foreign agents and assets.

Victor took a taxi into Debrecen's city center, passing through the clean streets with his eyes constantly watching the mirrors for potential tails. He knew his fixation with the mirrors unnerved the taxi driver, and Victor helped relax him by keeping the driver in conversation. They talked about soccer, women, politics, work.

"What do you do for a living?" the driver asked Victor.

They were driving past the grand building of an insurance firm, so Victor said, "I sell life insurance."

The driver smirked. "Everybody dies, right?"

Victor kept his gaze on the wing mirror. "I seem to have that effect on people."

Out of the taxi he spent some time walking with the crowds, stopping occasionally, doubling back often. He browsed through a number of stores, not buying anything but watching who came in after him and who was standing outside with a view of the door. When he was satisfied he wasn't being shadowed he caught another taxi and sat in the back.

Victor climbed out fifteen minutes later in downtown Debrecen. Here the streets were quieter, and although it would be easier for a team to shadow him, it would also be easier for him to spot them. No one set off his threat radar. Another taxi took him back into the city center and to his true destination.

The Internet café was of a fair size and pleasingly full of customers, some of whom smoked. Victor didn't, but only because he was passively smoking more than enough nicotine to satisfy his craving. He was sure there would be a reply to his e-mail from the broker; he just wasn't sure what the reply would contain.

Victor sat down at the most-sheltered terminal in front of an old PC. The flickering screen immediately made his eyes start to water. He could hear its noisy hard drive, half-humming, half-gurgling. Victor logged on to the message board. He noticed his heart rate was slightly up.

There was a message waiting for him.

He almost expected the computer to explode into pieces when he clicked to open it, but nothing out of the ordinary happened. A part of him almost wished it had.

You won't want to call, but we need to speak. I can help you.

He hadn't known what to expect, but it certainly hadn't been that. He stared at the screen for a long time. It didn't sound like the broker. There was no pretense of subtlety in the message. It was blunt, to the point, appealing for further communication. There was a phone number.

Had someone other than the broker sent the message? If the CIA had found him, maybe it had found the broker too and the message was a lure to trap him. Or if he'd been set up from the start, was this just another setup in the making? Perhaps the change in tone was genuinely because of the unusual situation. He noticed he was getting a headache.

Victor had no true friends, no real allies, barely a handful of acquaintances. It had been one of the things that had kept him alive so long. The less contact he had with the world around him, the fewer potential points of compromise. Now that kind of protection had left him isolated, vulnerable. He was alone, on the run, with no clear idea why his hunters were after him. Regardless of the whys, he knew his chances of survival were diminishing with each passing hour.

Something had to change.

Victor was in no doubt about his own skill, but, though he hated to admit it, he was out of his depth. If things stayed the same he just wasn't going to make it. He had been discovered twice, despite all his precautions, and he would be again. It might take weeks, even years. But how many times could he escape his enemies? Sooner or later he wouldn't be fast enough.

His only lead had taken him nowhere. On his own he had no option other than waiting for the next attempt on his life. He needed help. And the only person offering it was the first person he'd thought had set him up. So far there was no proof to the contrary.

But he was out of options.

He memorized the number and left the café. He found a secluded pay phone, dialed. The twenty seconds it took for someone to answer the phone seemed like the longest moment of his life.

"Hello?"

The voice was female and that threw him for a second. He hadn't considered who might have answered, but he wouldn't have expected a woman. An American woman.

Eventually he found his voice. "It's me."

The response was instantaneous, the surprise obvious, seemingly genuine. "My God, it is, isn't it?"

"Yes."

"I wasn't sure you'd call."

Victor kept his gaze on the street, checking people, cars. "What's going on?"

"Not over the phone."

Ten seconds.

Victor said, "I haven't broken protocol in half a decade, so we're going to do this my way or not at all. Understood?"

"Yes."

"Then tell me what you know."

"Not yet."

"Good-bye."

It wasn't a bluff.

"No, wait."

Twenty seconds.

The broker spoke quickly. "I know who they are, who's been trying to kill you. I can help."

"Tell me."

"I'll tell you when we meet. Not before."

"If you won't tell me now, I'm gone."

"You won't make it on your own."

"I beg to differ."

"If you really believed that," the voice said quietly, "you wouldn't have called."

Thirty seconds.

Victor stared at his reflection in the glass of the phone booth. It was hard to look himself in the eye. He took a breath. "If we meet, where?"

"Paris."

"When?"

"Tonight."

"Why so soon?"

"Because I might not be alive tomorrow."

Forty seconds.

"Give me the details."

"Call this number when you arrive. I have to go now."

The phone went dead.

She'd ended the conversation first. It was a good sign, despite the anger it caused him. He'd been trying to drag it out to a minute to test her. If she'd have let it go over sixty seconds he would have known he couldn't trust her. Still, ending it early could just as easily have been a trick to convince him she was genuine. If it was, she was in for a big surprise. He didn't trust anybody.

But there had been a desperation in her voice that made him think she was the real thing, that she wasn't trying to set him up, that she was in as much danger as he. Though he rationalized that a good actress or a gun in the face would add that sense of desperation particularly well.

This whole thing had started in Paris, and now he was being asked to return. His enemies had tried to kill him there already, and going back seemed like a great idea if he fancied suicide. If his enemy knew he was arriving today, the airport and train stations could be put under surveillance. Kill teams could be set in place. He'd be easy to spot. If he made it out onto the streets he could get himself a weapon from his safety-deposit box, but that too might be compromised. He couldn't risk it so that meant no gun. He would be going straight to his foe's doorstep, unarmed, making their job easier. It was the last thing he should be doing.

But if there was even the slightest chance the broker knew something useful, then he needed to hear it, whatever the risks. It was either that or start running and never stop. In his gut it felt like a setup, and no matter how much he thought about it he couldn't shake the feeling that he was walking into a trap. And walking into it of his own free will.

By going back to Paris he would find out one way or another what was going on. If she was telling the truth, so be it; he could use whatever information she had to work out what to do next. If it was a trap, then at least he'd know for sure he was on his own. That or he'd be dead and it wouldn't matter.

Two choices.

Go to Paris or disappear for good.

Neither prospect was enticing, but spending the rest of his life as a target of the CIA held the least appeal.

THIRTY

Paris, France
Saturday
00:09 CET

Named after someone whose life had been filled with such complexity, Charles de Gaulle Airport's stark simplicity always seemed to Victor like a deliberate irony. Even in the best of moods, passing through it could feel like a long walk to nowhere. The terminal was especially uncrowded, even for midnight, with only a few people anxiously checking the departure boards for news of their delayed flights. There had been particularly bad weather over much of western Europe. Either that, Victor thought, or the French air-traffic controllers were on strike again.

He'd seen no one at the airport whom he thought was a shadow, but he couldn't be sure. At the airport he was safe from being killed if not arrested. There were armed and wary guards who would shoot anyone without a second's hesitation who even looked as if they might pull a gun. Without a weapon he was safe from them, at least. As soon as he was in the city, everything would change, if he hadn't been taken into police custody by then. In a city where murders occur daily, his own would barely warrant attention. He wouldn't die easily though. If he was walking into a trap, then, for his enemies' sakes, there had better be nothing short of a platoon waiting for him.

Making it through passport control had given him the confidence that the French authorities weren't expecting him. It was one less thing to worry about. He would still be careful of the police and security services, but it was the CIA that was currently sitting at the top of his threat radar. He made straight for the exit, not bothering to do any countersurveillance. If there were people watching him, he wasn't going to shake them all, and the more time he spent confined, the easier he was making their job. His best chance was to get into Paris as quickly as possible. In the city he could blend into the scenery, disappear.

He reached the exit without incident and went through the automated doors fully expecting to be gunned down the second he stepped foot outside. The sky above was black, the clouds angry, roiling. The bitter wind bit at his flesh, an almost visceral assault. The rain came down straight and hard. Victor saw the raindrops pelting the ground as a hail of bullets.

There were fewer than a dozen people outside, but any number of them could be a killer just like him. He'd come too far to turn back now. He'd made his choice, good or bad, and he was going to see it through. But no one shot at him, no one so much as made eye contact. If he was to die, it wasn't going to be here in the rain.

It had been five days since the attack in Paris, and he would never have believed then that he would be back before the week was out. But a lot had happened in that time. The scratches on his cheek were as good as gone, but his chest still ached, and there were scabs on his hands and wrists. Victor wasn't sure how many lives he had left. He climbed into a taxi and told the driver to take him to Paris and the closest pawnshop.

"None will be open."

Victor reached for the seat belt. "Just find one."

They drove into the city, Victor silent despite the driver's attempts to draw him into conversation.

"Do you mind if I smoke?" Victor asked.

The driver shook his head.

It seemed a long time until the car pulled up alongside a curb. The shop had a barred and meshed window, a reinforced door. Two of the letters in its yellow neon sign were black.

Victor told the driver to wait and went inside. He came out five minutes later, a few hundred euros lighter, but heavy with one Benchmade Nimravus knife with a four-and-a-half-inch black tanto blade, two unlocked prepayed cell phones, and a car charger. He'd examined the knife in the store, checking its sharpness and balance before the scrawny owner's staring eyes. Victor climbed into the back of the taxi and had the driver plug in the first phone, telling him to swap them over after five minutes.

"Are we close to a bar?"

The driver smiled into the rearview mirror. "Like that, is it?"

"Yes," Victor replied. "It is."

The driver took him to a nearby bar. It sat near an intersection. The road outside was busy with people and cars.

"Take me to another one."

The driver gave him a look, but Victor said nothing. The next two bars he likewise dismissed. The fourth was on a quiet street, no nearby intersections.

"Better?" the driver asked.

Victor reached for his wallet.

In the bar he bought a vodka and told a confused bartender he needed to borrow some tape. In a toilet stall he taped the knife, point up, onto the skin of his lower back. He tucked only the front of his shirt back in. It felt better to be armed. Now, at the very least, he could take some of them down with him.

He used the bar's pay phone. The line connected after just a few rings.

"Are you at De Gaulle?" were the broker's first words.

"I'm in the city."

"Write this down," the broker said. "I'll meet you there."

"No, you come and meet me." Victor told her the bar's address. "If you're not here in thirty minutes all you'll find is an empty glass."

"Hold on a second; this isn't how this works. You come to me."

"We play by my rules or I'm on the next plane out. Decide."

A pause. Then, "Okay."

"Wear something red."

He hung up.

The bar was half-empty, just the serious drinkers who looked like they spent a lot of time there. He knew he'd been noted as an outsider, but it wasn't important, no one here was going to go out of their way to volunteer information to the authorities. Most were too busy pickling their brains to even remember him.

Victor paid for his drink and stepped out into the cold. He looked both ways down the street. To the left, the road led into an industrial neighborhood; to the right, it headed toward the freeway intersection. He couldn't see a sign for the metro and didn't think she would come on foot. There were sirens in the distance, but the rain seemed louder.

He crossed the road and found an alley where he could watch the entrance to the bar. At a time like this he would normally have taken out his gun, chambered a round, and flicked off the safety before putting it in the front of his waistband, to the left of his belt buckle, where he could get to the gun quickly. But he had no gun, only a knife. It wouldn't be enough if they sent a kill team, but it was better than nothing.

He had some shelter from the wind and the incessant downpour, but the rain still found him, and the chill still pricked his skin. Victor didn't care. It felt great.

Cold, wet, but still alive.

He had been standing for exactly twenty minutes and smoked one delicious cigarette by the time a white taxi pulled up outside the bar and left a tall woman standing on the curb, a cloud of exhaust fumes disappearing into the air around her. She was dressed in an ankle-length gray coat. Dark hair tied back in a ponytail protruded from underneath a woolen hat. A burgundy scarf was wrapped around her neck.

The broker.

She took a moment to compose herself and went inside the bar. He was surprised the taxi had dropped her off right at her destination, even more surprised that she went in without even checking her surroundings. Either she had no idea what she was doing or was playing the part of someone who didn't.

There was no evidence of a kill team on the street, the road clear, sounds of cars only in the distance. A man was walking down the street with a dog, but Victor discounted him. Too much insulation around the midriff. The dog was a Doberman, and the man strained to keep it in check. A kill team wouldn't use a dog, even as a distraction.

Victor exited the alleyway quickly, head down, col-

lar up, just a man who'd taken a short cut and was eager
to be on his way. He stroked the Doberman before crossing the road. On the other side, he stood to the right of the
bar's entrance, his back against the wall. He kept his
hands in front of him, outside of his jacket despite the
cold. He lit a cigarette and smoked it slowly. He watched
the roads.

The door opened five minutes later. She stepped out
into the night. Before she knew what was happening he
took hold of her arm.

"This way."

He heard the breath catch in her throat, but she didn't
resist. Victor took her west, further along the street, and
turned into the first alley they came across. He pushed
her against the wall and searched her. She took in big
gulps of air.

"I don't have a gun."

It only took a few seconds for him to know she was
unarmed. He'd wanted to find a gun so he could use it
himself. He led her out of the alleyway.

"Where are we going?"

He didn't answer her, just kept walking, his fingers
tight on her arm, her legs working fast to keep up with
him. He could see her looking at him out of the corner
of his eye, but he didn't look back. He kept his own
gaze on his surroundings.

Victor led her to the end of the street and into the industrial area. The roads were wide, clear. Fences lined
the sidewalks, beyond which factories stood. Some with
lights on, others without. A car appeared, heading toward
them. Victor's hand moved to his back. At ten yards, if it

looked as if it was going to stop, he'd slit the broker's throat and throw her into the road in front of the car before he started running. Down an alley, he'd find a hiding place, ambush the last man, drive the knife through his spine, take his gun, kill the others or die shooting.

The car didn't stop.

The broker said, "Tell me where you're taking me."

He didn't respond, but she got her answer five minutes later, after they had circled through the deserted streets. The bar was farther along the road.

"Why are we back here?"

He took her inside, ordered a drink for both of them, and took the table farthest from the door, near to the entrance to the restrooms. Earlier, on the other side, he'd seen a door marked *staff only*. There would be a back entrance somewhere on the other side should he need to use it.

It had thrown him before to find out the broker was a woman, and it threw him again now as he looked at her. She was younger than he would have thought. Thirty, maybe as young as twenty-eight. That meant she was good at what she did or they were using her to confuse him. He didn't let his surprise show.

The broker was as wet as him now and didn't look as if she liked it one bit. Not a field operative, then. She had a slim face, dark eyes. She sat with her fingers cupping her glass. She didn't look at him much.

"I didn't bring anyone."

Victor almost believed her. His natural suspicion didn't sit well with the person opposite him. She was too young, too scared, and too stupid to be setting him up. Maybe she was just involved in something way out of her depth and was desperate for his help. He had no plans to do so unless it also helped him. Or maybe he was wrong. Either way her chances of survival were not looking good. He rested his hands on the table.

"Why did you have me come back to Paris?"

"Someone is trying to kill us both."

It was tempting to be sarcastic but he resisted. "Because of Monday."

She shook her head. "The Paris job isn't what you think." She looked around the bar. "We shouldn't talk here."

She was so nervous she couldn't keep still, checking the door every few seconds as though she'd seen the move in a film. She was drawing too much attention.

"Okay," he said. "Where?"

"I have an apartment in the east of the city. It's safe."

Victor raised a skeptical eyebrow.

"I've been staying there since yesterday," she explained. "No one knows I'm there or I would have been killed already."

It was a well-delivered point. He believed her.

Victor downed his drink. "Take me there."

THIRTY-ONE

"Here we are."

The broker glanced at him before she turned the key and opened the door. She couldn't have known it, but her next action would determine whether or not he would kill her right now. She stepped inside. If she'd have said or even gestured for Victor to go inside first he would have snapped her neck, knowing it was a trap. But she hadn't. For the moment at least she stayed alive.

Her building was prewar, seven stories of no character and in need of some maintenance. It might have looked good once, but those days were long gone. The apartment was little more than an empty shell, only the most basic of furniture and fixtures, simply decorated. A typical low-cost, inner-city rental. The broker flicked the light switch and walked into the center of the room.

Victor flicked the light back off and closed the door behind him. She pivoted on the spot. In the gloom he could see the fear that spread across her features as she mistook the action. Victor ignored her, walked over to a table that stood by the wall, and flicked on a lamp, angling it so it wouldn't cast their silhouettes onto the thin curtains.

He kept his back to her for a moment longer than he needed, giving her a seemingly good opportunity to try something. He listened for movement, for the change of footing that would give her away. She didn't do anything. He almost wanted her to just so he would know for sure. Victor faced her.

"My name's Rebecca," she said.

"I don't care." The broker started to speak again, but he cut her off. "Be quiet."

Victor looked around the room, examining light fixtures, plug sockets, under tables—checking for bugs. He searched the rest of the apartment. There was a meager kitchen, bathroom, a double bedroom. A tiny balcony was accessible from the kitchen. He had to be quick just in case time was an issue. He didn't find anything.

She was standing in exactly the same place when he reentered the lounge. There was a two-seater sofa and an armchair she could have chosen to sit in, but she hadn't, her nerves plainly evident. It was a good sign.

"I'm going to search you," he said.

"What? You already have—"

"Take off your coat."

"You think I'm wearing a wire? Why would I?"

"Take off your coat."

Victor's tone didn't change, but his gaze demanded obedience. Her mouth was open as if she was going to protest but she didn't speak. She unbuttoned the long coat and slipped it off her shoulders. She looked at Victor.

"Stand over there and hold out your arms."

She moved toward the table, into the desk lamp's arc of light. She raised her arms so they were level with her shoulders. Her silhouette was cross-shaped on the wall.

Victor stood in front of her. She was a tall woman,

in modest heels only a couple of inches shorter than he. She had olive skin, dark eyes, the Mediterranean somewhere in her blood. He could see the hint of training in the way she was standing, the way she carried herself. Maybe military, but he guessed intelligence. There was fear in her eyes, but that fear was controlled. He could see the tiny, rapid flexing of the skin on her neck. Fast, but not overly so.

She was wearing dark jeans, not tight but not loose either, a dark cardigan over a cream blouse. Smart-casual, playing down her looks but still allowing for shoes that were more stylish than practical.

He ran his palms along the outside and underside of her arms, down her back, down the sides of her torso and center of her chest, not caring that she flinched when he touched her breasts as part of the search. He squatted down to check around her waist and her legs before standing again.

"Take off your shoes and jeans."

She kicked off her shoes. "No, forget it. I'm not doing that."

"You will if you don't want me to put my hand into your underwear."

She was stunned, glared at him, her eyes full of disgust. He held her gaze, showing no emotion. There was nothing to negotiate. She would do what he told her. After a moment he watched the fight drain out of her, and she nodded slowly. She took her shoes off first, then turned her head away so she didn't have to look at him, unbuttoned her jeans, and slipped them off her hips. They fell to her feet.

"Step out of them."

She did.

"Stand with your legs a little farther apart."

Again she did as instructed.

Victor looked at her closely for a moment. "Turn around."

She pivoted slowly on the spot.

"Okay," he said, satisfied. "Get dressed."

Victor stepped away and stood to the side of the lounge window, his back to the wall. The broker pulled up her jeans and put her shoes back on. He was embarrassed to find himself watching her as she dressed. He looked away before she noticed.

"Are you happy now?" she asked when she was clothed.

"Not exactly," Victor answered quietly. "I've broken more rules than I can count by coming here so what you have to tell me had better be worth it."

"Otherwise what?" the broker challenged. "You'll kill me?"

"Yes."

It wasn't just a threat, and Victor saw that she understood this. There was an immediate shift in her posture, a drop in her shoulders, the shifting of weight, the instinctive change in body language that told an enemy there was no threat, no challenge, no need for violence. He saw that though she may have convinced herself beforehand she could deal with him, she was fast finding out just how wrong she had been.

The broker asked, "What's your name?"

The question caught Victor off balance. "Excuse me?"

"I said, what do I call you? You were always referred to as Tesseract in our—"

"Why Tesseract?"

"I don't know, it's just a code name," she answered. "So, what shall I call you?"

"You don't need to call me anything," Victor said.

"Okay."

"Tell me what you know."

"It's the company that wants you dead."

She delivered the information as if it were a huge revelation. There was no change in his expression.

"You already know," she stated, surprised.

He nodded.

"But how?"

"If you expected me to be shocked, I'm sorry to disappoint you. I haven't been standing idle since this thing started."

"What else do you know?"

"I'm not here to answer your questions. For now let's stick to what you know."

The broker nodded and folded her arms in front of her chest. "This has to work both ways."

"I don't remember agreeing to anything to that effect."

She stared at him for a moment as if she was considering a particularly choice retort. But he'd broken her will and instead she said simply, "It's the CIA who wants you dead because it was the CIA who hired you."

Victor's face showed nothing, but his mind was a mess with questions. So it was a CIA setup from the beginning. "How do you know that?" He found he disliked having to ask her questions immensely.

"Because I used to work for them," she answered.

"Used to?"

"They want me dead too."

"Explain."

"They killed my control and cut me loose. They want me dead just as much they want you."

"What about the flash drive?"

"There's something on it they want. Information, obviously."

"Information on what?"

"I don't know."

"Then what good are you?"

"Ask me something else and find out."

"Who was the man I killed?"

"Andris Ozols."

"I didn't ask for his name. Who was he?"

"A former officer in the Russian navy."

"That wasn't in the dossier."

"You didn't need to know."

The muscles in his jaw flexed momentarily. "What was he doing in Paris?"

"Selling the drive to someone."

"Who?"

"I don't know."

"You didn't need to know?"

"I guess not."

"What about the flash drive? Can you decrypt it?"

"Do you have it?"

"No," he said.

"But you have it somewhere?"

"Yes. Can you decrypt it?"

"Maybe. But I won't know until I try. I have friends at the agency who—"

"Not an option," he said and immediately had an idea. Something he hadn't considered until now.

She saw him thinking. "What is it?"

"Nothing," he said. He changed the subject. "So they wanted me to get the drive before the buyer got hold of it?"

"Yes."

"I assume at that point it would be considerably harder to obtain. The buyer must be too well protected or someone they didn't dare kill."

"Who are you thinking?"

Victor kept his thoughts to himself. "Why didn't the CIA just do it, why use me? And why try and kill me afterward?"

"Those two questions share the same answer." The broker took a step forward. "But I can't be sure."

"Then why am I listening to you?"

"Because you don't have a choice."

Victor was surprised by her words and more surprised by the strength of her tone. He reassessed his opinion on her will.

"And neither do I," she continued. "But what I do know is that they tried to have you killed to cover up the operation. They don't want Ozols's death ever coming back to haunt them."

Victor listened, face showing nothing.

The broker continued, "If the plan had worked all anyone would have to go on is the body of a killer in a Paris hotel room with no clue as to who hired you. At best they would have realized that you were a hired gun with no affiliation to anyone. Any connection between you and those who ordered Ozols's death would have been neatly severed."

"And that's it? They want me dead to cover up a job that I actually did? It's not as though I'm going to advertise what I'd done. If nothing else it's not the best way to generate new clients."

Victor realized there was more emotion in his voice than he would have liked to have revealed.

"True," she said. "But they couldn't risk your being captured, interrogated."

"I couldn't have told anyone anything because I don't know anything."

"Be that as it may, if you're dead they don't have to worry. The link to those who ordered the hit dies when you do."

"But why use me? Why not some punk? Any amateur could have killed Ozols. The CIA didn't need me to do it."

"Because some punk wouldn't have taken a fraction of your precautions. Someone else would have left a trail to follow. At the time I wasn't told why, but we needed a killer who had no record, someone who was capable but to all intents and purposes didn't exist. They needed someone who was invisible, and you fit the criteria. I suppose you can take that as a compliment."

"I'm flattered."

"There's no need to be sarcastic."

Victor ignored the comment. "And how do you fit into all this? Why do they want you dead too?"

"I'm part of the chain. The operation failed. You lived; they didn't get the drive; and now they need to cut all the links to make it clean."

"Guilty by association?"

"Something like that."

"But they haven't gotten to you yet."

"I didn't give them the chance."

"Why exactly did you bring me here?"

The broker moved from where she had been standing, a couple of steps to the left. Nervous release maybe. Victor watched her. Light from the lamp accentuated her cheekbones, danced on her full lips.

"Because we can help each other," she said.

"Help each other to do what?"

"Remain breathing."

"I hope you're not suggesting we try and give them the drive and pray they leave us alone."

"Of course not."

"Then what?"

"We take out our enemies."

He wanted to say, *to where?* Some people just didn't like to say *kill*. Ridiculous euphemisms, however, were fine to say. He supposed it helped them sleep at night.

"And how are we going to do that? I can't kill the entire CIA. I don't have that many bullets."

"The hit on Ozols wasn't officially sanctioned," the broker said. "It was strictly off the books, old-school black bag. Someone ordered it, people implemented it, but the wider organization doesn't know about it."

"Why do you think that?"

"There are lots of different reasons," she explained. "Starting with the way I was approached for the job. I had anonymous phone calls and meetings. I wasn't told who I was working for or with or what exactly I was working toward. It went way beyond need to know. Plus the fact that they needed you, a contract killer, one with no prior agency links. If it was a white job they wouldn't have needed to kill you afterward or me or my control when it went wrong. They would have just used their own people or known contractors in the first place. Whoever is behind this *really* doesn't want the rest of the CIA to know what they're up to."

"The shooters who ambushed me in Paris," Victor said. "They were private sector. They didn't know who they were working for."

"Exactly."

"And I had a run in with an American killer at my house."

He didn't say where that had been. To some extent it didn't matter; he wouldn't be moving back, but revealing personal information unnecessarily was one habit he wasn't about to start.

"In Switzerland, I know," she said. The fact she knew stung him, but he hid it. "It would've been a contractor, not an operative."

Her voice carried weight, even if she didn't explain herself. He believed her. No need to tell her he'd originally thought the opposite.

"You'd already iced their shooters in Paris," she said, adding to the ridiculous euphemism count. "So they didn't have much choice but to risk using someone closer to home to get the job done. They wouldn't have been able to take the chance you might disappear while they assembled another unaffiliated execution team."

Victor nodded, accepting the assessment. "This means that the wider agency isn't looking for us at least."

"Yes, for the time being. But at any time something could happen to bring this out into the open. That blood-bath at your hotel attracted a lot of attention. I'm sure the legitimate CIA has people looking into it. Plus the French and the Swiss are now in on the party. Things are getting pretty crowded, even without the people who want us dead."

"So we'll get to them before they get to us."

"Precisely."

"But how?"

She looked at him closely. "So you're on board?"

"I'm thinking about it."

THIRTY-TWO

01:50 CET

Victor stood so he could see the front door and the entrance to the kitchen without moving his head. The broker was getting herself a glass of water. He heard her open a cupboard, then four seconds later the faucet began running. The sound of water hitting the metal sink. If the sound didn't change within another four seconds he would go into the kitchen to find out what she was really doing. After three seconds he heard the glass filling.

There was a part of Victor that told him any time he spent with her only compromised him further. She had set him up before. He could never be sure she wouldn't do so again. He knew he should just kill her now and be done with it. He spent his whole existence managing risk, and the survivalist part of him screamed that this was too much of a risk to take.

But the flip side of the coin had considerable weight to it. In one conversation he had learned more from her than he had in several days on his own. And there were still things he did not know or understand. He would listen to what she had to say and then decide whether or not to kill her. Not for revenge—which meant nothing to him—but for his own protection. The broker knew too much about him. She couldn't know it, but she was interviewing for her life.

The broker reappeared. She took a sip of water and placed the glass down on a table. "Where did I get to?"

"Black bag."

She said, "At first I thought the operation was simply unsanctioned. I didn't know that it was completely illegal or I would never have signed to it. Now, that helps us because it means we're against only a few people. As long as it stays the way it is we can do something about it."

"Like what?"

"If they want us dead to kill the connection between them and Ozols's assassination, the reverse must also be true. We go after those who ordered it, everyone who knows about it. Maybe two or three people. Cut off the head and the body dies."

"When you say we, you mean me, right?"

"But I'll help you find them," the broker said. "At the moment we don't know who our enemy is. I only had contact with one person, my control, and they've already had him killed. But I can find out who's behind this."

"How?" he asked.

"We follow the money. That's how we do it."

"Explain."

"Where there's money, there's a trail. The money from the Paris job was deposited into your Swiss bank account from another numbered account that I had control over. It was transferred into my account from, you guessed it, yet another numbered account."

"How does that help us? The account could have been set up purely for the Ozols killing."

"That's not the case."

"How can you be sure?"

"I used to work for them, remember?"

"I haven't forgotten. What's your point?"

"My point is that you used to work for them too."

"No I haven't." He wanted to throttle the truth out of her. "I'm freelance. I work for private clients. And I don't like games. Just tell me."

"I'm telling you that the Ozols job wasn't the first one

you've done for them. Over the last six months you've done three other contracts, through me, for the CIA."

"You can't be serious."

"You think I'm lying. Why would I?" He couldn't answer. "I've been your broker three times, each time pretending to be a different person, acting out a different character. The job before this one, in Sweden, you killed an arms dealer. The time before that a Saudi. Do I have to go on?"

Victor looked away.

"That's how you people found out where I lived," he said, half to himself, now understanding. "The other jobs were dummies just to track me down."

"Not exactly. They were legitimate targets. Very nasty people, but yes, the jobs were covers for the surveillance. And it took three intensive ops just to get one shitty photo-fit put together. But we got where you lived." There was a measure of pride in her voice that made his teeth grind. "No one thought it would take so long. You were better than anyone thought."

He shook his head. "You people."

"Don't you dare." She actually looked angry. "You're a hired murderer, remember? You have no right to judge anything anyone else does."

He had to admit she had a good point.

She continued. "Don't think I want to be here. It makes me fucking sick just being this close to someone like you."

"Don't swear."

"What?"

"I said don't swear."

She glared at him. "Don't swear? Why the hell not?

A line appeared between Victor's eyebrows. "That includes blasphemy."

It took her a few seconds to see that he was being serious. She widened her stance. "Let's get this straight. You don't tell me what I can or can't say."

"I just did. Get used to it."

She scowled. "I think you're forgetting I'm not working for you on this. We're working together. That means you don't tell me what to do or say and vice versa. *You understand me?*"

Victor checked his watch. "Have you finished?"

The broker took a series of calming breaths. She wanted to say more, he could tell, a lot more. He could imagine her practicing being strong in front of a mirror.

"You were saying something about a money trail," he said calmly.

She took another breath and swallowed. The look in her eyes told him she was telling herself to drop it, that he wasn't worth the effort. It was a minute before she finally spoke, a measure of time he guessed would reassure her pride that she hadn't back downed too easily.

She spoke. "The money that was paid into your account came from me, which came to me from someone else's account, who probably got it from someone else's, and so on. So we track backward, account to account until we find who started the first account."

"And you know how to do that?"

"Yes."

He nodded, almost believing she knew what she was talking about. "How?"

She was sitting down now, perched on the arm of the sofa. He heard wood creak when she moved. She spoke with her hands a lot, gesturing, emphasizing, illustrating. Victor remained standing, his back to the wall next to the window so he could watch her and the door at the same time.

"We find out who or what that first account belongs to," she said.

There was a commotion outside. Some pimp yelling at his property. Victor had the window open so he could listen for people arriving.

"You've said that already. How do we find that out?"

"From the bank."

"Bankers don't hand out information on their customers."

"You just have to know how to ask."

"And you do?"

She nodded.

"And what's my role in this?"

"You don't have one. At least not yet. After I have the information you'll use it."

"Sounds simple."

She shrugged.

"And are you confident this will work, what you've proposed?"

It was the end of the interview.

Yes, she lived.

No, she died.

Victor saw her thinking carefully about her response.

He watched her closely. Her lips pursed momentarily and she swallowed before answering.

"Yes," she said, voice strong, assured.

"Good answer."

She smiled slightly, misunderstanding.

He reached into his pocket and withdrew the flash drive. He flicked his wrist, threw it to her, impressed when she deftly snatched it out of the air in one hand. Good reflexes and dexterity. She looked it over for a moment before looking up at him questioningly. He saw her wanting to ask why he'd lied but she didn't say anything. She moved over to her computer and plugged it into the side. Victor stepped forward to watch. She sighed when she was asked to input a password.

"They didn't give it to you then?" he asked.

She shook her head. "I was never supposed to come this close to it. I know a little about cryptography, but I can't tell what level of encryption it is. If it's low end I could probably break it myself in a few days with the software on my computer. Simple brute-force attack. But if I was transporting something people would kill over, I'd make sure it was high-end encryption, the best I could get. My laptop doesn't have the processing power to even scratch the surface of those kinds of ciphers."

"I have an acquaintance," Victor said. "Someone who may be able to help decrypt it. I stress *may*. I'll try them while you collect the information on the account."

"If anyone can hack this, my contact at Langley could."

"No. It puts it too close to our enemies."

"Does it matter? If they intercept it maybe they won't come after us."

"Given their efforts to kill me so far I can't see them giving up quite so easily. And if they did get their hands on it they'll know I gave the drive to you. I've compromised myself by meeting you. I don't want them to know that."

"I'll try and decrypt it myself then."

"I prefer my way."

"We can do both," the broker said.

"As we can't do both simultaneously, I'll try mine first."

"Who says we can't do both at the same time?"

"The laws of physics. We only have one drive."

She didn't speak. Her fingers worked the keyboard for a few seconds. Victor watched the file copying across from the drive to her computer. It took seconds.

"I never thought to try," he found himself saying.

"The file carries the encryption, not the drive itself. It's just a commercial memory stick, a carrier, nothing special, no hardware-based security. Now you can try your way and I can try mine."

"And double our chances."

She smiled at him. "See, we've made a good team already."

He found himself looking at her lips. "Stop right there," he said, as he raised his eyes back to hers. "We are not a team."

"Then what are we?"

He struggled for a second thinking about how to describe them, but without success, then said, "Nothing."

The broker looked away. "Okay."

"Neither of us should be under any illusion about why we're both doing this. You're only helping me because you need me. I'm only helping you because for the moment you can help me, too." He avoided saying he needed her. "That's the end of it."

"And what's going to happen when I can't help you anymore?"

It took guts to say it. Victor respected that.

"At that point we'll part ways," he said. "And you'll never see me again."

THIRTY-THREE

Marseilles, France
Saturday
01:59 CET

Reed held his palm over the sink. He felt no heat, but the air smelled faintly of burned paper and alcohol. He moved around the kitchen slowly, then into the lounge area. The communications equipment looked state-of-the-art and was cool to his touch. He stood in the darkness, seeing with the dim light of the city filtering into the apartment and his own natural night vision. He made his way to the bedroom, noting the open wardrobe and drawer, the discarded garments on the bed.

He found an all-night café where he ordered a black tea and composed an e-mail on his smartphone, explaining with an economy of words that the target had left recently, and in a hurry. He asked what he should do next.

The waitress who brought him his tea wanted to flirt, but Reed pretended not to be able to speak French. She still tried despite the perceived language barrier, and he politely ignored her. Not for the first time, he mused, that life would be far easier as an ugly man. He finished his tea with a minimum of fuss and went on his way. He had a room booked at a fine hotel on the seafront and set off on foot, the ground wet from the rain but the air pleasant and cool.

He enjoyed the walk, listening to the sounds of talking, laughter, and music drifting out of bars and clubs. Reed was neither disappointed nor annoyed that the target was not where the dossier claimed she would be. It was not in his nature to become emotional when working. There was a secondary–potential strike point listed where he could try if his anonymous client wished.

There were five targets in total that his client wanted removed, the first of which Reed had left dying in one of Paris's less-than-hygienic abodes. Aside from the Marseilles disappearing act, that left three more, one in Milan, one in London, the last in a yet-to-be-established location.

As yet there were no stipulations on how the remaining targets were to be eliminated, but Reed prided himself on killing efficiently, subtly, and reliably. These were the reasons he had been hired and were the reasons he was able to charge such a pretty penny for his services. Suicides and accidents were his specialty, and when there wasn't the opportunity for such a demonstration of his talents, he would select another means of death that didn't spell out assassination.

At times in Reed's line of work a more direct approach was needed. Some targets were too well protected, skilled, or just too careful to be removed discreetly. In such cases, Reed opted for more appropriate methods of removal than those he usually employed. He found the nine millimeter variety was usually quite sufficient but he preferred sharpened ceramic for a more personal touch.

The last of the listed targets held particular interest to Reed. There was no name, just a code name, and that alone told Reed much. This nameless man was a contract killer, and by all accounts a good one at that. If the information he had been given was correct this Tesseract had killed seven gunmen who tried to ambush him at a hotel, as well as avoiding another assassination attempt in Switzerland. Reed had to admire such performances, even if the results had been achieved with rather less finesse than he liked to enact himself.

Reed looked forward to the killing of this target. Other professionals were always the most difficult to execute cleanly, but Reed enjoyed a challenge. Like Reed himself, the experienced ones were almost obsessively paranoid in how they conducted themselves, and the precautions they took were more often than not especially extensive—not forgetting the little fact that they tended to be more than capable of fighting back. Which was exactly why they were such good fun to murder.

The fact that this quarry was in possession of skill appealed to Reed, who judged his own achievements in relation to the quality of his victims. He killed for money, whether it was the Firm's or some private client's banknote, but he still took pride in his craft. Participating in a sporting kill gave Reed considerable personal satisfaction, even if, by the very nature of his own abilities, such contests were so heavily stacked in his favor. But it was only in performing against the very best opposition that one's true aptitude could be measured.

Reed walked across the vacant parking lot behind a fast-food restaurant. The smell of heart disease ruined the otherwise pleasant evening air. He just hoped this Tesseract was good enough not to get himself apprehended by the authorities before Reed caught up with him. That would be most unsatisfying.

Footsteps.

Boots, trainers. Multiple feet on the asphalt behind him, making no effort to conceal their noise. Not professionals.

Reed knew what he was going to see before he turned around. A gang of adolescent toughs and degenerate twentysomethings approached him. They were a mix of races, almost all with heads shaved, clothes a mix of baggy sportswear and knock-off designer labels, cheap jewelry abundant and gaudy.

They spread out, and he allowed himself to be

surrounded so the braver ones would naturally face him. Cowards at his back did not bother him. Some struck bizarre poses, and if Reed didn't know better he would assume they had spinal deformities. He counted twelve, six or seven of which he could tell by their physiques were capable of handling themselves and by their demeanors were more than willing to. The others didn't carry the same capabilities or confidence.

"You're passing through my kingdom," one said in French, the largest and most brashly dressed. "So you have to pay the tax."

Reed held his gaze. "Trust me when I say that you do not want to do this."

The large youth stared at Reed with something approaching disbelief, obviously unused to facing anything but dread. The complete absence of fear in Reed's unblinking eyes caused his expression to falter. He looked at the others. Reed knew the kid had come too far to back down now.

He drew a gun from his jacket and held it loosely in his hand. A nickel-plated Beretta. It looked like it was polished regularly, but Reed doubted the working parts would be cleaned with the same diligence. The guy raised the gun to Reed's face, a poor grip, holding it horizontally to complete his perception of cool.

"Wallet, phone, watch," the leader demanded.

Two of the others showed their own weapons. One held his revolver loosely by his side, the other lifted his shirt and rested his fingers on the automatic tucked into his waistband. Reed said nothing, merely stared unblinking at the person before him, the kid who knew he was out of his depth.

"*Fucking hand them over.*"

Reed's expression remained blank. "Why?"

"Say what?"

In that moment when confusion combined with anxiety, Reed grabbed the outstretched arm before him, wrapping his left hand around the wrist and pulling the kid forward sharply, directing the gun away and to the side. He took hold of the kid's lower triceps with his free hand and twisted the wrist in his grip, locking the arm. He wrenched it downward, hard—against the joint— snapping the arm at the elbow and into an inverted V.

The gun clattered on the asphalt and the awful wail momentarily stunned the others. Reed released the wrist and the kid collapsed. Among the screams he managed to find his voice.

"*FUCKING KILL HIM.*"

Reed sprang forward toward the other drawn gun, knocked the weapon aside as it was raised to fire, using his forward impetus to multiply the force of the elbow he sent into his enemy's face. His head snapped backward, blood splashing from his mouth, and the kid went down heavy, out cold, jaw broken.

The other youth armed with a gun backed off, palms showing, eyes wide, head shaking. Reed ignored him, heard the click of a switchblade opening, turned, side-stepped as his attacker lunged and overextended himself into empty air, stumbling, completely off balance, arms flailing.

The next came from behind, his feet scraping on the ground. Reed whipped round, threw the edge of his hand into the guy's throat. He fell down convulsing.

Two more came forward at the same time, one wielding a hunting knife with a four-inch drop-point blade, the other a crowbar. The crowbar swung at him first, from the left, aiming for his head. Reed caught it and the attacker's hand together, redirected it downward, using the kid's momentum against him to twist the bar from his fingers and into Reed's own.

He smashed an elbow into the youth's side, knocking him backward, gasping, ribs cracked. Reed followed through with the crowbar, backhanding it into the side of his attacker's skull. Blood splashed on faces in the crowd.

The hunting knife passed within inches of Reed's face, a wild swing, clumsy. Reed dodged backward, waited for the next attack, used his forearm as a shield to turn the blade aside and the crowbar to sweep his attacker's feet out from under him. Reed drove the bar down into the kid's face, exploding his nose across his cheeks.

The small youth with the switchblade recovered and yelled as he attacked again, a frenzied stab. Reed dodged, invited another thrust, and brought the crowbar down hard onto the youth's exposed arm, shattering bones. He screamed and dropped the knife, wrist and hand hanging limply from midforearm. Reed reversed his grip on the crowbar, swung it upward, cracking the youth under the jaw, the force lifting him off his feet and dropping him back to the ground in a silent heap.

It was all over in less than seven seconds. Six lay on the wet ground, some completely still, others moaning and writhing. They would all live, but not as they used to. The others stood paralyzed in a mix of awe and terror. Reed looked at them for a moment. He knew he could pick up the Beretta and execute every one of them within a matter of seconds, but they were just idiot kids, and twelve gunshots would bring police officers. Half a beaten-up gang was attention enough without creating corpses. Besides, as things stood, even the ones he had not crippled would take the time to rethink their lives, and Reed felt almost proud of that public service.

He twirled the crowbar around his hand before handing it to a reluctant recipient. The youth took it, grimacing, feeling the wet blood and skin of his gang mates matted to the metal. Reed straightened down his jacket and eyed those who were lucky enough to still be vertical.

"Move."

They parted reverently to let him pass.

THIRTY-FOUR

Central Intelligence Agency, Virginia, U.S.A.
Saturday
10:49 EST

Chambers was acting like a big shot on the Hill, and so
Procter chaired the briefing. Both Sykes and his old bastard mentor Ferguson were looking like they'd had long
weeks—Sykes especially, though he'd found the time
to visit a tanning booth since the last meeting, judging by
the renewed shade of his face.

Alvarez was on the speakerphone going through what
he'd found out about Stevenson and his mystery employer. "Stevenson made some blunders when it came to
covering his tracks," Alvarez was saying. "He didn't do
a very good job of deleting sensitive information from
his computer, and we managed to extract certain e-mails
from his hard disk. These e-mails are communications
between him and his client, who was never referred to by
name. This is the person who gave Stevenson the suitcase
full of cash he deposited at his bank.

"In the e-mails they were arranging a meeting to hand
over the money. The location of this meeting and the
time and date were in code, but we've discovered Stevenson met his client in Brussels just under three weeks
ago."

The lines in Ferguson's forehead deepened. "You
cracked the code?"

"No, we didn't need to," Alvarez replied. "Stevenson

did the hard work for us. Elsewhere on his hard drive we found photographs of the meeting that showed Stevenson and another man, his client, outside a café in central Brussels."

Procter leaned forward. "What kind of photographs?"

"Surveillance photos. Seems Stevenson was an untrusting kind of guy and had someone else along with him without his client's knowledge. Probably one of the other seven dead guys, but we don't know for sure. The photographs show the name of the café and are dated and timed. I would guess Stevenson had the photos taken as some kind of insurance policy in case anything went wrong."

"Do we know anything about the man he was there to meet?" Procter asked.

"We had several clear shots of him arriving and leaving so we put him through facial recognition but didn't get lucky. We did get some luck after enhancing other photos. We established the name of the rental-car company Stevenson's employer used. I contacted the company and only one car of that particular make, model, and color was out when the meeting took place."

"So who is he?" Procter asked.

"Sebastian Hoyt," Alvarez said through the table's speakerphone, "is a Dutch businessman and CEO of a small financial-consultancy firm located in Milan. I checked flights in and out of Brussels that day, and Hoyt arrived and returned the same day."

"Great work," Procter said. "What do we know about this Hoyt?"

"Not that much," Alvarez answered. "But it's early

days. He's a private businessman, that much is obvious. I've already spoken briefly to our people in Italy and asked them to start digging."

"I'll liaise with the Italians too," Procter added. "I want to know everything there is to know about this individual, and I want to know fast."

"He used to be one of our assets, back in the eighties," Ferguson said matter-of-factly.

Procter and Sykes looked at him.

"You're sure?" Procter asked.

"I should hope so," Ferguson replied. "He used to be one of my assets."

"Tell me more."

Ferguson nodded. "He's a trained lawyer from a wealthy family, but he deals with some very unpleasant people. He was doing business with a corrupt Soviet army officer when I knew him. He supplied me information on the Red Army from this general—training techniques, armaments, that kind of thing. In return I let him get away with the arms brokering he was doing for the officer. Mainly shipping AKs and RPGs to Africa."

"So what's he been up to since?" Procter asked.

Ferguson shrugged. "I don't know. After the Wall came down we didn't have much use for him, not that I could've continued paying him with what was left of my budgets. I expect he'll still be doing what he's best at, trading in illicit commodities, arms, people, information. If he has his own firm, he's come a long way; and if he's still operating, then he's either gone legitimate or

has been clever enough not to get caught or tread on anyone's toes."

"Until now," Procter added coldly. "Do we have a
file on this clown?"

Ferguson nodded.

"What about your own personal files?"

"I'll get them out for you."

"And Alvarez," Procter said.

"Yes, sir."

"I heard about John Kennard. I'm sorry."

"Me too."

"I didn't meet him, but I'm told he was a good man.
What happened to him?"

"Wrong place at the wrong time. He was just unlucky."

Ferguson and Sykes sat perfectly still.

In the corridor outside the briefing room, Sykes waited
for Ferguson to come out. Sykes's pulse was racing,
and he was finding it difficult not to look like he was
crapping himself. Ferguson had stayed behind to have
a word with Procter. Sykes needed to consult with him
immediately. Alvarez was only a step away from Hoyt.
Things were going from bad to shit at warp ten.

It was about five minutes before Ferguson finally
appeared a moment after the big guy, but to Sykes it
could've been five hours. He'd wiped perspiration from
his face at least three times.

When Procter was out of earshot Sykes moved closer
to Ferguson.

"Before you say anything," Ferguson began, "take a breath and compose yourself."

Sykes took a breath, but even if he took a hundred more he didn't think he would miraculously calm down. "We're fucked," he said.

"Is that your professional opinion?"

Sykes had never seen Ferguson truly rattled, and he didn't look rattled now. "How can you remain calm at a time like this?"

"Because, unlike you, this isn't my first extracurricular activity," Ferguson said. "And I also have a pair of these." He put a hand to his testicles.

"What the fuck happened in there?" Sykes whispered. "Since when do you have a relationship with Hoyt?"

"Since always."

"Why in God's name didn't you tell me?"

"There was no need."

"Bullshit. What happened to all that crap about making sure we weren't connected with anyone else involved in this op?"

"We didn't have a choice but to use Hoyt. We needed hitters who weren't on CIA files, and I don't know about you, but I'm not acquainted with too many of those. Hoyt, however, is connected in such circles. He was necessary to the success of our objectives. The fact that he was a previous asset of mine had no relevance to that."

"Except that Alvarez is now onto him. And therefore onto us."

"We couldn't have known Hoyt would have delivered the money to Stevenson personally. I would have thought he'd have been more careful than that."

Sykes stared at Ferguson. "Greed tends to make people forget to be careful."

Ferguson ignored Sykes's tone. "And we couldn't have known that Stevenson would be so paranoid as to have their meeting photographed. It's what in this business us grown-ups call bad luck."

"Chance favors the prepared mind," Sykes said with another hint of sarcasm.

"Indeed," Ferguson said, and Sykes was unsure whether he didn't notice the tone or was just ignoring it. "Which is why we have Reed. Have him get the next possible flight to Milan and deal with Hoyt."

"He's probably going after Rebecca Sumner again."

"Hoyt is far more urgent."

"But what about Alvarez?"

"He won't move on Hoyt until he knows everything about him there is to know. There will be plenty of time for Reed to work his magic."

"Okay, but why the hell did you have to tell them all that shit about Hoyt in there anyway? Surely you could have waited instead of putting them one step closer to unraveling this thing."

"Listen to me carefully and learn. I told them about Hoyt because by tomorrow or the next day they would have found out he'd been an asset of mine regardless. The kind of asset one doesn't forget in a hurry. How would it have looked if I had neglected to mention that? Mildly suspicious doesn't quite cover it."

"What if the girl doesn't hang around? Reed missed her once in Marseilles already."

"I'm well aware of that. After Reed has taken care

of Hoyt he can deal with Sumner. You have another potential strike point?" Sykes nodded. "So don't worry about it. Even if she doesn't stay put, she's not a field operative, she won't stay alive for long."

"I hope not."

Sykes leaned against the wall and sighed heavily. He scratched the back of his neck.

"Pressure getting to you, Mr. Sykes?" Ferguson asked.

"As a matter of fact, yes," Sykes replied. "I didn't count on all of this bullshit."

"Welcome to the CIA," Ferguson said bitterly.

THIRTY-FIVE

St. Petersburg, Russia
Saturday
16:23 MSK

It was minus fourteen degrees Fahrenheit when Victor landed, and the short wait for a taxi outside the airport was an excruciating one. He asked the driver to take him to the best hotel the driver knew and to turn the heater up. The driver mumbled it was hot enough, but Victor held out twenty dollars for him to see in the rearview and he flicked the switch up to maximum.

Some years had passed since Victor had last been to Russia. Though Russia and its neighbors were a huge marketplace for professional killings, Victor preferred not to travel to the region if he could help it. He had fulfilled several contracts in the region in his early years and had a reputation in that part of the world. Once that infamy had served him well, now it was a permanent crosshairs.

The taxi took him deeper into the city. He saw St. Petersburg as a city of contrasts. The new modern skyscrapers of capitalism stood alongside the decrepit structures of the Soviet era and between them, somewhat out of place, stood the grand buildings of historic Russia that had survived the war. The weather was no different. At the height of summer it could be as hot as in Madrid, but in the dead of winter it was difficult to find a colder place on the planet.

The hotel was expensive compared with the St. Petersburg norm, which made it quite reasonable to Victor. He booked a room for a week but only intended to stay for a few days at the most. He always found it best if hotel employees knew as little about his plans as possible. Another taxi took him east, where he gave the driver directions to a bar lost in one of the city's industrial districts. The name of the bar had changed since he'd last visited, but he hoped its patronage remained the same.

He ordered a vodka and sat at the end of the long bar sipping it quietly. When he had finished he waved the bartender over for a second drink. Victor spoke to him in fluent Russian with a hint of a Ukrainian accent.

"I'm looking for Aleksandr Norimov."

He asked as though he was just curious, as if it didn't matter what the answer was, but the young man behind the bar visibly tensed up. "I used to know him," Victor added, pretending he didn't notice the bartender's reaction.

He shook his head. "I don't know who you mean."

"He still owns this bar, doesn't he?"

The barkeep shrugged. "I don't know."

He gave Victor his drink and moved to the other end of the bar. He took out a rag and started wiping it down, his eyes occasionally twitching in Victor's direction. Two minutes later the barkeeper walked over to the pay phone and inserted some coins. Victor couldn't hear what he was saying, and he couldn't see his lips to read them. The call took no more than forty-five seconds, and the bartender then went back to cleaning the bar. This time he didn't look Victor's way once.

Good. He didn't expect he'd have long to wait.

By the time Victor had finished savoring his third vodka two men entered the bar. Both were well over six feet and had the build of serious weightlifters. They had typically Russian pale skin, cheeks ruddy from the cold. Victor noticed their long overcoats did more than just protect them from St. Petersburg's freezing weather.

Victor watched them out of the corner of his eye while he ate his potato chips. They walked over to the bar and exchanged a few whispered words with the bartender. He didn't give them any drinks but gestured Victor's way. The two men approached slowly, no trepidation, just an arrogance gained from both size and status. Clearly they had no idea who they were dealing with.

Their shadows fell over Victor as he turned in his seat, head tilting back to look at them.

"Who are you?" one asked.

There was a deep resonance to his voice and he spoke with a thick Siberian accent. In Victor's experience Siberians were an especially tough breed even among the already-tough Russians.

"I'm a friend of Aleksandr Norimov."

The Siberian paused a second before responding. "Who?"

"The owner of this bar."

"He's not the owner anymore."

"So you do know who I'm talking about?"

The big muscles in the Siberian's jaw flexed. "Norimov died last year."

Victor let out a long breath. "Then I appreciate your coming all the way over here just to let me know that. You're really too kind."

The Siberian paused, mouth slightly open, unsure whether Victor was being serious or sarcastic.

"What do you want with Norimov?"

"What does it matter if he's dead?"

The Siberian shook his head in disbelief, but there was menace in his eyes. "Who the fuck do you think you are?"

"I'm a friend of Aleksandr Norimov."

"Are you deaf? I told you he's dead. So you're wasting your time here."

"I'm finishing my drink." Victor gestured to the empty glass of vodka.

"You've finished," the Siberian said.

"I'm afraid we disagree on that."

He moved surprisingly fast for a big guy, knocking the glass hard with the back of his hand. It shattered against the wall behind the bar. All other conversations immediately halted.

The Siberian wore a smug grin. "Now you've finished."

"Are you going to take me to see Norimov or not?"

The Siberian laughed.

Victor sighed. "Shall I take that as a no?"

"If you like."

"I suppose I'll be leaving then."

He stood. The Siberian was in front of him, the other man behind. The Siberian gave Victor a hard stare, from which Victor was quick to lower his eyes, causing the Siberian to exhale loudly, half-grinning, buying the sign of submission. He stepped aside to allow Victor past. The Siberian looked at his associate and raised his eyebrows. The other man nodded in agreement.

At that moment neither was watching Victor.

As he stepped past the Siberian, he brought his left arm up and threw it backward, slamming his elbow into the Siberian's face. He felt the nose give way. The Siberian grunted, blood splashing from his nostrils. His eyes filled with water. He slumped backward against the bar, sensibilities knocked from him.

Continuing his motion, Victor spun around to see the second guy pull a heavy Baikal handgun from the pocket of his overcoat. The big Russian would have been more effective grabbing Victor from behind, but he hadn't, electing to go for his gun instead. His mistake.

Victor stepped forward inside the man's reach, negating the gun's threat, knocked the weapon to one side, and punched the Russian with the heel of his right palm, in the side of the chest where there was little muscle for protection. Ribs cracked. The Russian fell, gasping. The Baikal clattered on the hard floor. Victor turned his attention back to the Siberian, who was struggling back to his feet. Even with his nose smashed he was quick, pulling a switchblade from a coat pocket.

The blade appeared and he lunged at Victor, who grabbed the Siberian's wrist and elbow, locking the arm and twisting it. The Siberian screamed, knife falling from his fingers. Victor let go of the arm and punched him in the gut. He barely flinched.

Hands grabbed Victor by the jacket, lifted him from his feet and hurled him. He landed hard but rolled to absorb the impact. He sprang to his feet to see the Siberian already coming at him. Victor slipped the punch, and another, dodging sideways, clear of one of the big guy's fists, letting the Siberian's momentum put him off balance. Victor kicked him in the back of the knee, and he stumbled forward. Victor grabbed the Baikal from the floor just as the Siberian recovered and turned.

The two pounds of hard steel in Victor's grip connected under the guy's jaw and dropped him to his knees. A second blow to the temple made sure he stayed there.

Victor reached inside the Siberian's overcoat and pulled the gun from an underarm holster. It was a Baikal as well. He dropped it on the other side of the bar and looked around. The rest of the bar's patrons were dumb-struck, all silent, completely passive. He didn't need to tell them not to cause any trouble.

Victor pushed the barrel of the Baikal into the Sibe-rian's face. "Get up."

The Siberian spat out teeth and managed to pull him-self to his feet, one hand under his nose draining blood, one palm against his temple.

"Turn around," Victor ordered. "Put your face on the bar."

The Siberian hesitated. He raised his hands. Victor grabbed him by the hair, forced his face down against the bar, making sure his broken nose took the brunt of it. He cried out. Victor pressed the gun against the base of the man's skull.

"Where's Norimov?"

No answer.

He smashed the Siberian's face into the bar again, making him cry out a second time. "Where is he?"

Again no answer.

Victor ordered, "You behind the bar, get me a bottle of your strongest vodka."

The bartender looked no older than twenty, probably had never seen a gun before. This was clearly all too much for him. He was too terrified to move.

Victor pointed the Baikal at him. "Do it, or I paint the wall with your brains and get it myself."

He needed no further encouragement.

Victor pushed the Baikal harder against the Siberian's skull. "Your gun holds ten bullets, if you move I will empty every one into your face. Do you understand?"

Victor took the silence as a yes. He stepped back, glanced back at the big Russian on the floor, saw him writhing, hands clutched to his chest, each breath an exercise in agony. He wasn't in a position to try anything. Victor knelt down, never taking his eyes off the Siberian, and picked up the switchblade with his left hand. He stood back up, spun the knife around in his palm so the blade was pointing downward, and drove the point through the Siberian's ear, pinning him to the bar.

Ignoring his cries, Victor took the bottle of vodka from the barman, checked that it was strong enough, and walked to the other end of the bar. He pulled the top off the bottle with his teeth and walked back toward the Siberian, dribbling vodka along the bar's surface. When he reached him, Victor emptied the rest of the bottle over his head. The Siberian gasped but didn't move; even the slightest struggle tore more of his ear on the knife's blade.

Victor looked at the bartender. "Get a lighter."

The Siberian found his voice. "*No.*"

Victor grabbed the knife and twisted it, making the Siberian yell. "Shut up."

The bartender offered Victor a disposable lighter.

"No," Victor said. "Take it to the other end of the bar."

The bartender reluctantly moved to the far end.

"*NO*," the Siberian cried again. "*Please.*"

"You had your chance to do this the easy way." Victor kept the Baikal against the man's skull and wrapped the fingers of his left hand in the Siberian's hair, pushing him harder into the bar. "Now we do it my way."

The big Siberian grunted and struggled, his huge hands braced on the edge of the bar. Blood mixed with vodka on the bar's surface.

"You're going to tell me exactly where I can find Norimov and you'd better hope I believe you." He looked at the bartender. "Light it," then back at the Siberian. "You've got about ten seconds until you go up like a Roman candle."

From the corner of his eye the Siberian watched the bartender strike the lighter and lower the small flame to the bar. The vodka ignited, burning with a blue flame. It raced along the bar toward the Siberian's wide eye.

"Nine seconds." Victor stated flatly.

"*OKAY, OKAY,*" the Siberian screamed. "*I'll tell you.*"

"Tell me now. Seven seconds."

"*The Kalari train yard.*"

"Will you take me there? Four seconds."

"*YES.*"

Victor let go of the Siberian's hair and pulled the knife from his ear. The Siberian lurched backward, his face leaving the bar a second before the flame reached him. The big man stumbled, lost his footing, and fell into a table, breaking it under his considerable weight.

He lay stunned for a moment, breathing heavily among the wreckage. When he looked up he saw Victor standing over him.

"Well," Victor said. "What are we waiting for?"

THIRTY-SIX

Zürich, Switzerland
Saturday
13:11 CET

Rebecca found the chill invigorating as she boarded the electric streetcar. She sat at the back so she could watch who else got on, taking the precautions that her new partner or associate or whatever the hell he was had stressed. The streetcar took her into Zürich's financial district, and she kept her anxiety locked up deep inside as she passed through the clean streets of the city. Rebecca liked Zürich, liked the quiet efficient way the Swiss went about their business. It was a city bathed in history, but it hadn't yet been ruined by tourists. People came to Switzerland to work or to ski, not to sightsee.

She could have rode the quiet streetcar the whole way, but paranoia made her get off and circle back on herself, stopping to window-shop intermittently so she could watch the reflections of people passing by. Again, as he had told her to do. She didn't see anyone she'd seen before, but she was painfully aware she wasn't trained for this kind of thing. Someone could have followed her all the way from Paris with a funny hat on and she probably wouldn't have noticed. When she had taken control of her fear she caught another streetcar and took the last available seat.

She gave it up for an elderly man with a sad face who boarded on Bahnhofstrasse and she was off three stops later in downtown Zürich. Here every person seemed to be dressed like her, and she relaxed in the crowd, walking a little more easily.

Rebecca walked past boutiques and cafés that catered to the horde of bankers who called Zürich home. There were banks everywhere, and where there were no banks there were financial institutions of other sorts, some openly advertising their services, others hidden from passersby.

The chill air tightened the skin on her face as she thought about him, the killer whose name she didn't even know. She looked at her watch. It had been several hours since they'd gone their separate ways. Already she was having doubts about what she was doing. And even if she was doing the right thing, she couldn't trust him. How could she? He killed people for money. He was about as dishonorable as a person could get.

But she hoped his own desire to survive was as strong as hers. He was clearly smart too, and a smart man in his position would know that he was going to have to work with her. Neither of them could do it on their own. That was of course unless he managed to decrypt the drive for himself. Maybe then he would try something else, without her. Then she'd be on her own, defenseless.

She took a deep breath, tried to think rationally. She'd seen his face, seen the unflinching self-belief in his eyes and the absolute displeasure at needing someone else's help. He wouldn't have come to her in the first place if he'd had even the slightest confidence he could do it alone. She hoped.

Rebecca bought some chocolate shortcake from a shop on the Paradeplatz. It had a great placebo effect and helped settle her stomach before she headed off the main plaza and into a less-busy side street. She took the steps casually and smiled politely to the doorman as she pushed through the revolving entrance.

It didn't look like a typical bank and that was the point. The lobby would have seemed more at home in a grand hotel. She made for the information desk and gave her details to the meticulously groomed man behind it. He picked up the phone with a smooth, practiced action and whispered into the receiver.

"Someone will be with you momentarily, madam."

"Thank you."

She waited in one of the fine but uncomfortable chairs, her chin resting in her palm. She made sure to appear hurried but not restless. She kept her coat on even though it was warm inside the bank.

After a few minutes, Rebecca was aware of a slim man in a stone-brown suit walking toward her and stood up to greet him. They took a wood-paneled elevator to the second floor, and she followed him into another room, where Rebecca entered her ten-digit account number into a small handheld device.

The man checked the screen for verification and said, "This way please."

They passed two security guards, and, at the door to the office of a senior banker, she declined coffee and was taken inside and left to wait again. The office was classically furnished and designed to ooze wealth and power. To Rebecca it was old-fashioned and uninspiring. She was a contemporary woman through and through. Making her wait was also becoming tiresome, especially considering she had told them she was coming.

It was five minutes before a short, overweight man in glasses entered. He was finely dressed in a pin-striped suit that desperately tried, but failed, to camouflage his waistline.

"Miss Bernstein," he said to Rebecca. "How nice to see you again."

Rebecca had seen him once before, just over three months ago when the account was set up for operational funds. It seemed a lifetime ago, but the overweight guy seemed to recognize her. Or at least pretended to recognize her. She shook his hand; it was soft, warm, and slightly moist.

"Nice to see you again too."

Joel Malliat sat down in the huge red leather chair. He looked ridiculous—dwarfed by its size. Rebecca pretended not to notice just as she had during their first meeting, and she wondered how many other clients did the same.

Rebecca unbuttoned her coat and took it off, placing it over the chair slowly so that Malliat had time to study her from the front and side. She wore a tan sweater that was one size too small and clung to her like a second skin. Underneath she was wearing a padded push-up bra that made her breasts seem several cups bigger. The effect of the tight sweater sprayed to her breasts had shocked her when she'd first seen it. She hoped Malliat was similarly affected.

It may still have been a man's world, but Rebecca knew women still had a big advantage over the opposite sex. Get some blood moving south and there was less inside their brains to think with.

They exchanged pleasantries for a few minutes, Malliat ticking all the boxes on the charming-but-trustworthy banker checklist. Rebecca didn't try to interrupt the charade and allowed Malliat to come to the purpose of the visit in his own time.

"I'm sure you're a busy woman Miss Bernstein," Malliat said. "So how is it that I can assist you today?"

"I have a small problem with some transactions, which I'm hoping you can help me with."

Malliat looked alarmed. "A transaction problem?"

"Nothing that the bank has done. You see, embarrassingly, I seem to have lost one of my client's details. One of my former employees was, well, incompetent, and I believe she accidentally deleted some files from our system that we've been unable to recover."

"Most unfortunate."

"Therefore," she continued, "I've been put in a very

difficult position. I can no longer contact my client—a very important client. All I have is their account number from the funds put into my own account."

"I see," Malliat said, understanding.

"So, Mr. Malliat. Joel. I would be eternally grateful if you could give me the contact details of that account number."

"Miss Bernstein, I'm very sorry, but that information is confidential, and I would go against my banking ethics to tell you."

"I understand your position, but I'm not asking you for information that I didn't already have. Up until a few days ago that information was on my system. You would just be telling me what I already knew."

Malliat smiled sympathetically. "That's beside the point. I'm simply not allowed to tell you. I suggest you hire some computer specialist to retrieve the deleted files."

"I have already, but they were unsuccessful."

"I'm sure your client will contact you eventually."

"I expect like many of your banks customers, I do not run the kind of business where there is much communication between company and client."

She added enough emphasis to the key words that the subtext was obvious.

"I don't know what to say to that," Malliat said.

"Say you'll help me. It is imperative that I get hold of my client immediately."

"I'm very sorry, but I just can't do what you're asking."

The subtle approach had failed. Time for plan B. She stood up angrily and walked to the window, giving

Malliat a good view of her ass, legs, and three-inch heels that were killing her feet. She turned around after he'd had a chance to stare. She noticed his eyes had to move up to meet hers.

"This is outrageous," she said, hands on hips. "I'm an account holder here, and I demand to know who has put hundreds of thousands of dollars into my account. If you don't extend me this simple courtesy I will have no choice but to close my account and take my business to one of your competitors."

She saw Malliat make a quick calculation in his head. Rebecca already knew the figure. Almost two million dollars had been paid into the account in less than three months. At that rate, over a year, it would be nearly eight million dollars. Too much money to lose interest on for something as minor as a name and address.

Malliat sighed and nodded after a minute. "Okay," he began. "I'll help you, but I won't give you what you want to know."

"Then you're not helping and I won't be using your services anymore. I'd like to withdraw all my funds immediately. In one hundred euro bills."

"Wait," Malliat said quickly. "What if I give you information on the accountant who made the payments on behalf of the account holder. Will that do?"

Rebecca resisted smiling. It was as much as she'd hoped for.

"I guess it will have to."

THIRTY-SEVEN

St. Petersburg, Russia
Saturday
16:58 MSK

They'd taken the Siberian's car. Victor rode in the back, sat directly behind the passenger seat so he could watch the driver. The car was a black eighties BMW with all the trimmings. The interior stank of stale smoke, and the upholstery was dark and stained.

Victor had locked the Russian with the broken ribs in a back room at the bar, telling the bartender to let him go after an hour. If he released him before then Victor would come back to castrate him. Victor could tell by the wet patch on the guy's jeans that he'd been believed.

They drove in silence, the Siberian's eyes fixed on the road, taking Victor through parts of the city he didn't recognize: Anonymous factories lined the streets, dead areas of wasteland stretched between, and in the distance steam rose from tall towers and mixed with clouds.

After thirty minutes the car slowed. Derelict warehouses, empty for years and left to rot lined both sides of the street. The road was uneven, potholed, curbs full of litter and black water. Victor's eyes met the Siberian's in the rearview.

"We're here."

Up ahead a chain-link fence and gate bisected the road. A tall man in an astrakhan fur hat stood in front of the gate smoking a cigarette. Behind him, through the fence, Victor could see long low buildings, dark with pollution.

The Siberian brought the car to a stop five yards in front of the gate and lowered the driver's window. The tall man threw his cigarette away and walked over to the car. He leaned down and peered in, whistled when he saw the Siberian's smashed face.

"*Holy shit, Sergei,*" he said. "Another jealous husband with a crowbar?" He was about to laugh when he noticed Victor in the back. "Who the fuck is this?"

Victor spoke before the Siberian could answer. "Just tell Norimov that Vasily is here to see him."

Beneath the astrakhan the tall man's face creased in thought. He stepped back from the car and took out a cell phone that would have embarrassed any Western teenager. He turned his back on the car while he spoke. After a ten-second conversation he put the phone away. When he looked back at Victor there was fear in his eyes.

"Go on."

He pulled open the gate and the Siberian drove through onto a wide expanse of uneven blacktop with puddles of dirty water mixed with oil. The stars were lost in the dark clouds above.

The car drove slowly toward two large factory buildings. The rusted shell of a train carriage lay on its side in the distance. The car turned into the gap between the two buildings and came to a stop. A roll-up door was open to Victor's right, leading into one of the factories.

The Siberian gestured toward the door. "Through there."

Victor climbed out of the car, pretending not to have noticed the dark shape lurking on the sloping roof above or the one standing in the factory behind him. He kept his movements deliberately slow, doing nothing that might cause a nervous Russian to discharge his weapon unnecessarily.

He walked toward the opening, keeping his hands outside of his pockets despite the cold. Inside he could see the shells of old electric trains, half-built and rusted, dominating the space. Victor looked around, imagining that in the days of the Soviet Union the vehicles built here were exported thousands of miles to every friendly state and that, when the empire collapsed, the train yard had shut down, the work simply halted, never to start again.

Victor stopped, seeing two huge Russians emerge from the shadows and walk toward him. In their thick clothes and beards they looked more like apes than men. One appeared to be in his forties, his beard streaked with thin lines of gray. The other was younger, his face and neck scarred sometime in the past by fire.

He carried an assault rifle, an AK-74, a later variant of the infamous Kalashnikov. It wasn't pointed at Victor, but the way the scarred man held it meant it could be snapped into a firing position in an instant. Former armed forces.

The older man carried no weapon in his hands, but it wasn't his ribs causing the irregular shadow under his left arm. The Russian with the AK stood back while the other approached Victor.

He slowly unbuttoned his coat and held his arms out at right angles to his body. The Russian searched him roughly but with a weariness in his eyes. He frowned when he felt the Baikal in Victor's pocket. He pulled it out.

"Any others?" he asked.

Victor shook his head. The man searched him anyway. If there had been any other weapons the man would have found them.

"This way."

The man turned around and led Victor through the factory with the AK guy following a dozen steps behind. The factory was just as cold and damp as outside. There were gaping holes in the roof and Victor was careful to avoid the puddles formed beneath them. The two Russians were both wearing boots and didn't care about walking through the near-freezing water. Their heavy footsteps echoed.

When they reached the far side of the factory they stopped. A set of metal stairs led up to offices that stood overlooking the factory floor. Victor noted one of Norimov's men on the roof of one of the trains, another standing in the darkness beneath the offices. Each was armed with an assault rifle.

The man who had searched Victor told him to wait and walked up the metal steps and into the office above. He came out a minute later but didn't come down. He took up a position on the stairs, now armed with an AK just like the others.

Five men with assault rifles now covered Victor,

each positioned so that they could fire without risking hitting one of their own. As things stood, if they so wished, Victor had no chance.

He had to admit they were good at what they did.

The office door opened and Norimov came out. He hadn't had much hair when Victor last saw him and he had even less now. What was left was cut short to just a few millimeters. He was a tall man, face square, wide at the shoulders, massive arms. He looked ungainly, but Victor knew Norimov's size was deceptive. There was enough speed and agility hidden away to give most would-be aggressors an unpleasant surprise.

He wore a neutral expression, his eyes deep set, shadowed under thick eyebrows. The once-dark beard was mostly gray now, neatly trimmed. He was dressed in a black suit, looking more the respectable business-man than the ruthless entrepreneur and former govern-ment agent. A curious half smile appeared on Norimov's face as his eyes met Victor's, a mixture of disbelief and caution.

"Vasily," Norimov called. "You've taken me some-what by surprise."

He had a smooth refined voice as befitted his privi-leged upbringing.

Victor returned the half smile. "You know I like to make an entrance."

"Yes, yes I do. But when I got a phone call five min-utes ago saying you were here I didn't actually believe it was the real you. I thought the next time I'd see you would be on the far side of the River Styx."

"Do I take it then that you aren't glad to see me?"

"Now," Norimov said, smile widening. "I wouldn't say that."

"Then what would you say?"

"That your methods were perhaps somewhat excessive. You didn't have to be so rough with Sergei and Dmitri."

"I had to use a language they could understand."

"Did you try Russian?"

"I must be rusty."

Norimov grunted. "They were just looking after me, making sure I wasn't bothered unnecessarily. Like screening phone calls." He laughed. "These days I have to be more careful than ever. If it's not my many rivals after my blood it's stinking corrupt cops. I don't know which is worse."

"The price of progress," Victor said.

Norimov nodded. "Things are more cutthroat now than they ever were. You look different."

"That's the idea."

"Surgery?"

Victor nodded.

Norimov smiled. "You were prettier before."

"I know," Victor agreed. "That was the problem." He held the Russian's gaze for a moment. "Are you going to come down from there?"

Norimov put both hands on the railing. "I'm quite happy up here."

"Do you think I'm here to kill you?"

The sudden change in Norimov's face told Victor he had been thinking exactly that.

"I am unarmed." Victor said, holding open his jacket.

"I believe you," Norimov said. "But when has not having a weapon ever stopped you before?"

Victor nodded, accepting the point and backhanded compliment. "If I had wanted to kill you," he explained, "I wouldn't be standing in front of you now. I want to talk."

Norimov considered for a moment. Victor kept his eyes locked on the Russian, ready for any possibility, ready for the hand gesture that would signal the guards to fire. If it came he had no idea what he was going to do. Die would be the most likely course of action.

"Okay," Norimov said at last. "Let's talk."

THIRTY-EIGHT

17:27 MSK

They were in an office above the factory floor. It was fitted with filing cabinets and shelves like any legitimate place of business, not the nerve center of an organized criminal network. Norimov sat behind a simple polished desk, on which rested a silver-colored laptop and a stack of papers and envelopes. Victor sat opposite him. One bodyguard stood behind him, the other behind Norimov. There was another man stationed right outside the door. All were openly armed.

With so much protection Norimov seemed a virtual prisoner in his own office, and Victor wondered how long this had been the case. He also wondered if Norimov even realized he was an inmate of his own making.

"I apologize for the less-than-cordial welcoming, but you can forgive my suspicion, I'm sure," Norimov began. "But when a hitman calls on you unannounced, it is better to err on the side of caution than on the side of death."

"Don't use that word."

"What word?" Norimov asked, seemingly perplexed. "You mean hitman? I forgot you aren't fond of it."

"No, you didn't."

A wry smile formed on Norimov's face. "It's been what, three years?"

"Four."

"A long time. You've aged well."

"I take my vitamins." Victor's eyes scanned over Norimov. "You seem to be getting enough to eat."

"Yes, quite. I've filled out at the waist and thinned on top," Norimov laughed, slapping his generous stomach. "It's just protection from the cold, I swear."

"How's your shoulder?"

Norimov blew air out through his nose. "*Ha*, it still gives me problems. I went to a specialist in Moscow only last year. He told me there was a fluid buildup behind the shoulder blade. I promise you, he put a needle this big into me to drain it." Norimov gestured, his palms a good twelve inches apart. "It's no better. Some weeks I go through a whole bottle of painkillers."

"That's too bad."

"Between the pain of living and the painlessness of death, I choose the pain gladly."

"Nicely put."

"Thank you." Norimov tilted his head. "And you, Vasily, still bulletproof?"

Victor thought about the huge bruise on his chest and the tiny scab in the center. "I wouldn't like to say."

"Don't want to tempt fate?"

"Something like that."

Norimov pointed. "You used to say you make your own fate."

"I still do."

"No matter how good you are, how fast you are—"

"You can't outrun a bullet," Victor finished.

Norimov gestured to one of his bodyguards. "Get us both a drink."

The bodyguard opened a cupboard and took out a bottle of Scotch and two tumblers. He poured Norimov and Victor a generous measure each. Norimov clutched the glass tightly, hungrily. There was a red tinge to Norimov's cheeks, damaged capillaries showing under the skin. He never used to drink so much.

Norimov raised his glass. "To old allies."

"To old friends," Victor corrected.

Norimov downed his drink and grunted in approval. Victor followed suit, but without the grunt.

"This is nice," Norimov said. "To share a drink with a friend. It's not often I get to talk to someone who isn't afraid of me."

"I'm surprised anyone is afraid of you."

Norimov laughed. "Yes, well, maybe not of me but what I can have done. All these worms that work for me now, none of them know who I was ten years ago, or even five years ago. They think I'm old, slow. I doubt anyone remembers I was ever any different."

"I remember."

They held each other's gaze for a long moment. Victor opened his packet of cigarettes and took one out with his teeth. Norimov's eyes widened a small amount.

"I thought you quit."

Victor struck a match and brought it toward his mouth. "I did."

"Those things—"

"I know," Victor said. "So don't say it. I have been cutting down."

"Even Bond doesn't smoke anymore."

Victor rubbed the match out between his thumb and forefinger and drew in smoke from the cigarette. He raised an eyebrow. "Who?"

Norimov grinned for a moment. His teeth were yellow. "What score are you up to now?"

"I don't keep count."

"You used to."

Victor nodded. Once it had seemed important.

The Russian gave a caustic smile. "Still go to church to confess your sins?"

The leather of Victor's chair creaked. He glanced at his glass. "How long are you going to make me wait for another?"

Norimov motioned for his bodyguard, who promptly

refilled the glasses. They both took a sip. "So, how is the killing business?"

He thought for a moment. "I need some more reliable employers."

"I would like to be able to hire you myself. But I can keep four good men at my side for the best part of a year for what it costs me to employ you for one night's work. When you have numbers skill is not so necessary."

Victor didn't see the need to challenge the point. "I charge a lot more these days, anyway."

Norimov laughed hard. "Why am I not surprised?"

"And you, Alek, how's the aspiring empire?"

"I'm the only honest criminal left in this town. See what it gets me?"

Victor took a taste of whisky. "How's the delightful Eleanor?"

Norimov's face was hard. "Dead," he said easily.

"What happened?"

"She was sick."

"Sick?"

"The doctors didn't think it was serious. By the time anyone realized, it was too late."

"I'm sorry to hear that." He was.

"Thank you."

"She was a beautiful lady."

Norimov looked away. "Not at the end she wasn't."

The silence hung heavily for a moment. Victor didn't say anything. Though uncomfortable it would have been vulgar to speak banalities just to sit a little easier.

But it was Norimov who broke the silence. "Do you still take all that shit?"

"Not anymore."

The Russian cracked a smile then sighed, as if saddened to turn the conversation to the inevitable. "I'm assuming that this isn't a social call."

"Someone's trying to kill me."

The Russian smiled. "Shouldn't that be the other way around?"

"Quite," Victor agreed. "I have acquired some enemies."

"I imagine that's an ever-present hazard in your line of work."

"It's somewhat more complicated than that. I need your help."

There was something approaching amazement in Norimov's expression. "*You* need *my* help?" Victor nodded. "This must be serious."

"It is."

"So what can I do?"

"I want you to make some inquiries for me."

"I stopped doing work for them before you did. I—"

"But you are still connected to the organization, are you not?"

Norimov nodded absently, the action seemed almost subconscious.

"Good," Victor said.

"What do you need?"

Victor reached into his coat. He did so slowly, so the two bodyguards couldn't mistake the action for something else. Victor pulled the hand out from under his coat. In his fingers was the flash drive.

"On this is a file. I need its encryption broken."

Victor placed it onto the table, and Norimov picked it up and examined it closely.

"Where did you get this?" he asked.

"From a former business acquaintance."

Norimov raised a knowing eyebrow. "Tell me what happened."

"I did a contract in Paris on Monday, a part of which was the recovery and delivery of that memory stick. When I returned to my hotel there was a kill team waiting. I'd like to know who sent them."

Victor thought it prudent to leave out the fact that the someone appeared to be the same person who had hired him, who also happened to work for the CIA.

"Paris? I read about that, but I never would have guessed it was you. You're not one for making headlines."

"This time it was unavoidable."

Norimov leaned forward. "They said eight people were shot dead at that hotel. All you?"

"I only killed seven," Victor corrected. "Another beforehand. Another since."

"I thought you weren't counting."

Victor looked at him for a moment. "Some habits are harder to break than others."

Norimov shook his head. "Well, you haven't lost your touch anyway."

Victor ignored the remark. "Whoever tried to kill me wanted that drive. As of this moment it's all I have to go on. If the information on that thing is worth killing for, then I need to know what it is."

"And what will that achieve?"

"Maybe it will help track down my enemies. Maybe not."

"But why do you want to? You've never cared about revenge before."

"I don't care about revenge now," Victor said. "And I never will."

"Then why?"

"Because they found me."

Norimov held his gaze and nodded. "I still know people in the organization, computer people, who may be able to help."

"Thank you."

"But what you ask is highly irregular. People will be suspicious, questions will be asked."

"Then bribe them. I will cover any expenditure."

Norimov looked at him closely. "They still want your head, remember?"

"I'm not likely to forget."

"And you're willing to take that risk?"

"I'm here aren't I?"

The Russian weighed the response for a moment. "I always used to think that for a man who is so careful to stay alive you sometimes act as if you have a death wish."

Victor made sure to show nothing in his expression.

Norimov ran a hand over his beard. "They've asked me about you before, you know? An ex-SVR general, Banarov I think his name was, had died. Suicide. Shot himself in the head with his own pistol. They thought it was you, said they could place you in the country that week."

"What did you tell them?"

"That I hadn't seen you for years."

"They believed you?"

"Who knows? The investigating officer didn't like me, I can tell you that for nothing. Aniskovach his name was. I made a point of remembering that one. A rising star I think. He had that look about him, arrogant but clever. He reminded me of you actually." Norimov smiled briefly. "He brought with him a list of corpses as long as my dick, wanted to know who out of them you could've killed."

"And you said?"

"That you could've killed them all for all I knew, but I told him I'd heard you were dead, so even for you it would be a tall order. That's when he showed me a photo of you, said it was recent."

"Taken where?"

"I couldn't tell. Don't worry, it was your good side." He flashed a grin. "Aniskovach wanted you for Banarov though; the others didn't matter. He was just trying to track you down through one of your other jobs."

"He told you that?"

"He didn't have to."

Victor nodded.

"So," Norimov began, "was it you who killed Banarov?"

Victor's expression remained blank. "I don't remember."

Norimov's face was serious. "But they do, Vasily."

"Then I'll be careful to do nothing to jog their memories."

"And have you thought about me in all this? They don't like me as it is. What do you think they'll do if they find out I helped you?"

"When have I ever asked you for a favor?"

"Never." Norimov paused. He looked at Victor for a long time before speaking. "You've changed."

"I'm thinner."

"No, not that."

"I'm older." He didn't like saying it.

The Russian shook his head. "It's something else."

Victor stopped himself shifting in his seat.

"One thing I know," Norimov said, "is that people like us don't change. We adapt."

"Necessity."

"Remember when I told you about what makes you special?" He didn't wait for Victor to respond. "People like you, like me, we either take that thing inside ourselves that others don't have and make it work for us, or we stand by and let it destroy us."

"I still believe that."

"If I do this for you, then we are even for Chechnya."

"Naturally," Victor agreed without hesitation.

Norimov nodded slowly. "I'll do what I can."

"Thank you."

"Don't mention it."

"You'll need a copy of the drive."

Norimov smiled. "Why, don't you trust me?"

"No."

Norimov's smile disappeared, and he stared hard at Victor.

Victor stared back.

Norimov looked away first and plugged the flash drive into his computer. "Will it allow me to copy the contents?"

"The information on the drive is encrypted, not the flash drive itself."

It took seconds for Norimov to copy the data onto his computer. When the transfer had finished, he pulled the original out of the laptop and handed it back to Victor.

"All done. I'll copy it onto a disk and give it to my contacts. I'll delete it from my laptop afterward, don't worry."

"I don't worry," Victor said. "And it'll be safer if we don't meet here. Somewhere busy instead, somewhere public."

"There was a glow in Norimov's face. "Like the old days?"

"Exactly like the old days."

"How do you want to do it?"

"I'll call your bar, give them a time and place for you to meet me. How long will it take?"

Norimov stroked his beard for a long moment. He looked away. "If the people I know can do it, it won't take them long." He looked back. There was something in his eyes Victor couldn't read. "Forty-eight hours at the most."

Victor downed his drink and stood.

"Then I'll see you on Monday."

THIRTY-NINE

Central Intelligence Agency, Virginia, U.S.A.
Sunday
06:05 EST

Chambers's expression was dour. She was perched elegantly on her chair, leaning slightly forward, elbows on the table. "I know it's Sunday and I know it's early, but I'm sure everyone appreciates the gravity of what we're doing. Somebody we very much don't want to see better armed could be recovering those missiles as we speak. This goes beyond arms superiority; this is about global safety. If this technology gets into the wrong hands, our ability to protect our interests as well as our capacity for peacekeeping will be critically diminished. I don't think anyone around this table wants that to happen."

Procter nodded his agreement. Ferguson and Sykes gave their own solemn nods of consent.

"I know none of you need motivational speeches to pull out all the stops," Chambers continued. "We all know the clock is ticking. It's been almost a week since Ozols was killed and the information stolen. If we're going to crack this, it has to be soon." She paused and looked at Procter. "Are we any closer to finding Ozols's killer?"

Procter shook his head. "Alvarez is following a lead toward who hired Stevenson and his crew, but we're completely stalled on locating Ozols's killer, I'm afraid to say. With what little we have to go on we can't even establish whether he's government or private sector. We have some witness statements that aren't worth the paper they're printed on, some CCTV footage of a man but no face, no solid physical evidence. We missed him by a day in Germany. He probably went to the Czech Republic, but we haven't heard from him since.

"All departments have been involved in this. Every station has been briefed. We have people on the look-out all over Europe. We can't find him."

Chambers's brow wrinkled. "So he's just vanished?"

"He could be right under our noses and we wouldn't necessarily see him. We don't know who we're looking for."

"We must have suspects though," Chambers said. "Which known assassins can't be accounted for? What intelligence services are making suspicious movements?"

"Even if we assume he's not a direct operative for a foreign-intelligence service and that he was hired for this job, of which we have no proof, we're not starting from a good position. There are hundreds of these guys operating in Europe, maybe even thousands. We know about a tiny percentage of them, and of those we can only rule out another small percentile. That leaves a huge number of suspects, most of whom we have absolutely no information on. And this guy is good, let's not forget. He's a needle in a hitman haystack."

Chambers removed her glasses and rubbed her eyes. "Best guess on him?"

"We have a receptionist who says he spoke French like a native, and in Munich the neighbor said he sounded

German. Either he's from both France and Germany or he's good with languages and could be from anywhere. He has used two British passports so far, so that might suggest he's from the UK." Procter sat straighter. "We can speculate until we're blue in the face, but I think the fact we're dealing with a dead former Russian and Soviet naval officer who was trying to sell Russian missiles tells me the killer is probably SVR."

"If that's the case we'll never get that technology for ourselves," Chambers said. "Moscow would just love that."

He nodded. "It would, but it doesn't really feel like the Russians, does it?"

"How do you mean?"

"If this guy's SVR, then that explains a lot, but who then hired seven guys to kill him after completing the job? Who would know the SVR was sending him there? And gunning Ozols down in an alleyway is pretty basic. No polonium in his tea. Not even a suicide. Just painlessly executing a traitor isn't really their style."

Chambers pushed her hair back behind her ears. "I didn't realize they had any style."

Procter noted Sykes's subservient smile. He looked at Ferguson. So far the old man had barely said a word. "What do you think?"

From behind his glasses Ferguson's dark eyes met Procter's. "I'm not sure, buddy."

The old guy never used Procter's actual name. It was always buddy, pal, or friend. Procter found it annoying, bordering on insulting, as though Ferguson did so as a sign of disrespect, but Procter told himself he was reading too much into it. And even if he wasn't, he sure as dammit wasn't going to get a rep as a precious a-hole by bringing it up or insisting Ferguson call him Mr. Roland Procter.

"Russia is your territory, Will," Procter said, happy to have returned the overfamiliarity favor. Procter was quite aware Ferguson disliked his first name being shortened. "Are the SVR a likely suspect?"

Ferguson looked at him and considered for a moment. "It's more than a possibility for sure. This is Russian weapons technology we're talking about, after all. Moscow will do anything it needs to do to protect its secrets."

"You think it's their style?" Chambers asked.

"You think it isn't?"

"I'm not sure."

"Don't think the KGB aren't more than capable or willing to execute Ozols. If they'd found out what he was up to, then do you honestly think they wouldn't try to get the information back and silence the leak? And traitors are always punished, no matter where in the world they are."

Procter knew Ferguson's referral to the SVR as the KGB was heritage from his Cold War days. To him they were one and the same. Ferguson may have been something of a hero during those dark days of the twentieth century, but he had failed to upgrade and modernize his thinking. The world had moved on. East and West were no longer ideals, merely compass points.

Procter continued, "But to risk the fallout—"

"What fallout?" Ferguson actually looked angry. "Unless we had irrefutable proof they were behind it, which of course is impossible, the most we would do these days is tell them off. What could we realistically do? And let's face it, we would have a hard time doing that with a straight face. Remember, we were trying to steal their technology, hardly a sound moral basis for us to criticize their methods. Ozols was a traitor, don't forget. We would have no right to rattle our saber, and they wouldn't care if we did.

"And, may I remind you, this is technology that Moscow refused to sell to us on more than one occasion. Everyone seems to think that because of glasnost the bear has lost its claws, that fifty years of rivalry has been replaced by friendship. It's a ridiculous notion, and one I can't believe that America has lapped up so easily. *A bear is still a fucking bear.* He may be weaker now, but that only means he has to be more cunning."

An uneasy silence hung in the air for a moment. Ferguson's face was flushed. Procter was momentarily lost for words. So the old bastard did carry some resentment about the changing world order and his relegated place within it. Ferguson had obviously spent far too long fighting the communists to let it all go. It was quite pathetic, a shame really, but the sooner Ferguson retired the better.

"So," Procter said eventually, "what do you think we should do?"

Ferguson took a calming breath. "Finding out what

the hell the Russians are really up to would be a good place to start."

FORTY

Zhukovka, Russia
Saturday
21:04 MSK

Colonel Aniskovach climbed out of the SVR limousine and nodded to the driver, who closed the door behind him. Gravel crunched beneath Aniskovach's feet as he approached the front of the three-story dacha. It was built before the revolution and was a huge, resplendent building protected from prying eyes by tall pine trees that were now flecked with snow. For a building with twelve bedrooms, to Aniskovach *dacha*, which means "cottage," seemed a laughably inept description.

The town of Zhukovka was home to many such houses, owned by Russia's powerful and wealthy figures. Some people called it the Beverly Hills of Moscow. Aniskovach had never been to Beverly Hills, but he knew enough about it to know that Zhukovka was the more tasteful of the two. A manservant had the front door open for him, and Aniskovach stepped inside from the cold and into the warmth. He unbuttoned his long coat and handed it to the servant.

Inside, the dacha was even more impressive than

outside, and Aniskovach took a moment to take in the marbled floor, paneled walls, and original oil paintings that hung from picture rails. He could hear faint voices, laughter, and soft music drifting into the room from somewhere else in the residence. It sounded like a cocktail or dinner party where the usually very boring guests had been softened up by alcohol enough to finally start having a good time. He was motioned toward a doorway and stepped into a study. The room was empty of people, and he stood in the center, hands held behind his back, waiting. He tried to look unruffled by the setting and occasion, but he knew that he had been brought here to make an impression, and he would do well to act, at least in some way, as expected.

A decanter of brandy was visible on a sideboard, two glasses next to it, all on a silver tray, placed for his host and him to drink while they talked. On a whim he poured himself a glass while he waited. To pour oneself a drink without invitation could be considered particularly rude, but Aniskovach believed his host would see it as a sign of strength and be impressed with his confidence.

Most people would have been nervous if they were put in a similar position, but Aniskovach was as calm as he had ever been in his life. He checked his reflection in an oval mirror hanging above the room's fireplace. He'd nicked himself shaving, just a tiny cut on his chin that regrettably marked his looks but, he noted, gave a certain rugged manliness to his striking features. He had a jaw set like an anvil, and with his dark, absorbing eyes he knew he was easily the best-looking man in his department—and, if he wasn't being modest, the whole organization. He liked to imagine that most of the female employees at headquarters lusted after him.

Aniskovach heard the footsteps in the hallway outside, but he pretended to be taken by surprise when a voice behind him said, "Forgive my tardiness, Gennady."

Aniskovach turned around and bowed his head briefly. "It is an honor to meet you, comrade Prudnikov."

The man in the doorway was tall and heavyset and wore a well-fitting dinner jacket that shaved off at least ten pounds. He was in his late fifties but looked younger by some years. He wore a friendly smile and was by all reports very personable, but Aniskovach knew him to be quite ruthless. This was the first time he had met the head of the Sluzhba Vneshney Razyedki.

Aniskovach placed his brandy down and approached his superior. They shook hands, Aniskovach letting Prudnikov be the one to grip harder, though only marginally.

"It is to my regret that we have not had chance to meet before, Colonel Aniskovach." Prudnikov's eyes glanced at the glass of brandy and then to the decanter, and for a second Aniskovach feared he had offended him, but Prudnikov smiled. "You're a drinker, then, I see—good." He released Aniskovach's hand and moved to pour himself a large measure. "I don't trust a man who doesn't drink."

Aniskovach smiled internally at having judged the situation so aptly. "I'm inclined to agree with you."

Prudnikov tilted his head slightly in Aniskovach's

direction. "Are you saying that because you actually believe it, or just because I'm your superior?"

Aniskovach shrugged, showing nothing in his expression as he was studied. "A bit of both."

The head of the SVR turned fully and smiled. "I've been familiarizing myself with your file. Very impressive."

"Thank you, sir."

"There is no need to thank me for realizing what is as obvious as my waistline."

Aniskovach knew Prudnikov was hoping for a smile and he didn't disappoint.

"You've had a distinguished career." Prudnikov continued. "A pride to our organization and your country." He paused for a moment. "I can tell you are an ambitious man."

"Yes."

"You want my job one day."

Aniskovach nodded. "Naturally."

Prudnikov smiled. "Ambition can be a positive trait; it makes us strive to succeed, to conquer." He paused. "But it can also be a hindrance or a danger, even, if used unwisely."

"It will be ten years before I'm in a position to have a chance at running the SVR," Aniskovach said. "I'm no threat to you now."

"But how do you know I will have retired then?"

Reliable sources told Aniskovach that Prudnikov had a hole in his heart. He wouldn't be alive in ten years, let alone running the SVR at the time. "I don't, sir." Aniskovach lied. "Only that if you do indeed see me as a potential threat you would not have brought me here and made me aware of your concerns."

"And why wouldn't I?"

"It would have been more effective to sabotage my career and halt any chance of advancement without my knowing you were behind it. You are too shrewd not to do so."

Aniskovach knew he'd slipped the compliment in without it being obvious, and Prudnikov nodded slowly. "Very good. So why have I brought you here?"

"I have no idea."

"If you were to guess?"

"I don't guess as a general rule." He looked around briefly. "But judging from the fact that we are talking at your home and not at headquarters you either need my help with something you cannot trust to those close to you or you enjoy my company. So unless my invite to your party was lost in the post I think it's safe to say it isn't the second option."

"My wife's party," Prudnikov laughed. "I was right about you, I can see that already. You're quite correct, I do want you to do something for me that I need to be completed with the uppermost secrecy. A delicate matter I can entrust to you alone."

Aniskovach took a sip of brandy and waited for Prudnikov to continue.

"Something has come to my attention, something that you are particularly suited to dealing with." Prudnikov paused theatrically. "You remember the circumstances of General Banarov's demise?"

Aniskovach felt his pulse quicken. "Yes."

"And they were?"

"He supposedly shot himself in the head after drinking heavily."

"And you did not believe this."

"I believed he was murdered."

"Believed?"

"Believe," Aniskovach corrected.

"But you never apprehended the killer."

Aniskovach took a breath. "No."

"Why not?"

"At first it appeared to be a suicide, and no one questioned that explanation. It was only later I discovered a professional assassin was spotted in the area the week Banarov died. There was no direct evidence of his involvement, but Banarov had a habit of making enemies and was not known to be suicidal. I made some inquiries, but as it was a domestic matter, I had no authority to pursue the matter in depth. The FSB were not interested in my theory."

"You pursued it anyway, did you not?"

"As much as I was able. I believe in being thorough."

"And ruffled many feathers while doing so."

"It just meant I was getting close to a truth someone did not care to have revealed. I'd always suspected that parties within our own intelligence services had sent the killer, either us, the FSB, or the GRU. The unknown resistance I met during my investigation confirmed this."

"Indeed," Prudnikov said thoughtfully. "The assassination of one of our former generals by one of our own has potentially huge repercussions. None of us want a return to the bad old days where we feared our own colleagues might be plotting our demise over something we have done or might one day do."

"Quite."

"You spoke to a former acquaintance of this assassin as part of your own investigation."

"The only known acquaintance. Aleksandr Norimov, a former KGB, then FSB, agent. He's now a criminal operating out of St. Petersburg. He claimed to believe the assassin was dead until I proved to him otherwise. I would have liked to take him away for more intensive questioning, but I had no power to do so."

Prudnikov nodded. "Norimov's name has surfaced again."

Aniskovach was surprised and intrigued, but he did his best to maintain a detached composure. "In what context?"

"On the desk is a transcript of a telephone conversation. Read it."

Aniskovach walked to the large mahogany desk and picked up the piece of paper. He read it carefully, despite his growing excitement. When he was finished he looked at Prudnikov. His mouth felt dry. "What do you want me to do?"

"I want you to finish what you started. I want this Banarov matter closed neatly and with the utmost discretion."

"Why do you want me to do it?"

"Banarov may have had his fair share of enemies, but he was not entirely without friends. Some of those friends have become powerful in the time since his death and have influence in our government. His younger brother has risen highly within the GRU as well."

"I heard."

Prudnikov continued. "Recently, and with increasing frequency, I find that this Banarov matter is brought up in my company. I consider answering the questions of imbeciles who only through accident of fortune have become my superiors tiresome to say the least. Since it was your original probing that gave them reason to ask such questions, these parties will take much interest in whatever you say on the subject. You were the one who first believed Banarov was murdered; you pushed the case when no one wanted to know. Your integrity in this matter is without question." Prudnikov took a sip from his drink. "If you say this incident has been resolved, it will, finally, be left alone."

Aniskovach considered for a moment. The head of the SVR was asking him for a favor. If he completed this task with merit, he would find Prudnikov a most beneficial mentor for as long as his patronage had value. And when that value was spent, maybe these friends of Banarov or his brother would make better allies.

"I'll need resources," Aniskovach stated, careful to sound enthusiastic but not to sound too enthusiastic. "A team, agents with military backgrounds."

"You can have your pick of men and equipment."

Aniskovach's back straightened. "And authority."

"You shall receive any and all powers you might need. But there is a condition."

"Yes?"

"You must be satisfied with apprehending Banarov's killer. Question him, yes; kill him, of course. But your investigation ends there."

"But we can learn who sent him, who had Banarov murdered. Surely, that's the point."

Prudnikov shook his head. "I want this wound closed, not opened further. This is my condition. Accept, and you shall find your stock within the organization rapidly gains value. Decline, and wait for another opportunity of this magnitude to present itself."

Aniskovach had only pursued the Banarov matter as a means to create a name for himself. So the condition was an easy one to accept. Nevertheless, he stood silently for a minute in a pretense of deliberation.

"Then I accept the condition," Aniskovach said.

Prudnikov nodded. "Good."

"Tell me, though, why do you want this done so quietly?"

"Because," the head of the SVR said a moment after it became obvious, "it was me who had Banarov killed."

FORTY-ONE

Meridien Forest, Russia
Sunday
07:43 MSK

The earth squelched underneath Victor's feet. The forest floor was soaked from the winter downpours. He was fifteen miles west of Moscow, just north of Krasnogorsk, in the sprawling Meridien forest. The temperature was in the midthirties, average for the time of year.

Victor was dressed for the outdoors in thick cotton pants, boots, and a heavy coat over several layers. He had a black wool hat over his head and ears, insulated leather gloves over his hands. In his left fist he carried a shovel, in the right a pickax.

A mile to the east was one of Russia's most-famed country clubs, a carbon copy of those found in the West. It was complete with saunas, restaurants, golf courses, swimming pool, and tennis courts and offered cross-country skiing and Russian banya.

Victor had driven into the complex and set off on one of the many forest trails, usually busy in the summer, but in the winter gloom thankfully empty. At this time of year the club received few visitors, and he had seen no one else around.

He enjoyed being in the forest, alone, away from other people. The air was damp, clean, and the smell of trees, of nature, sweet. He savored his time away from the stress of civilization. He was cold, but he didn't care.

A quarter of a century before, he had been crouched down among trees not unlike those that surrounded him now, rifle butt pressing into his shoulder, its weight making his arms tremble. Numb hands clutched the weapon. His index finger just touched the trigger.

"Don't be scared," his uncle had said.

But he was scared, had never been more afraid. He didn't want to shoot the fox.

"Steady now."

The fox appeared out of the bushes, nose sniffing the ground. His uncle was still talking to him, but he couldn't hear what he was saying, the thundering of his heartbeat drowned out all other sounds. The animal moved slowly, nose testing the air. Victor wasn't sure if it could smell them or not. He thought what his uncle might do to him if he let the fox escape.

He fired.

There was a brief flash of red, and the fox disappeared from sight.

The whole world seemed to stop. Victor stared into the trees where the fox had been. He didn't know how long he had been staring before his uncle let out a roar that made him drop the rifle.

"WHAT A SHOT."

His uncle's voice seemed louder than the gunshot had been. "I can't believe you hit it. Why didn't you wait until the fox was closer?" His uncle was on his feet, trying to see the kill. He was laughing. "Did I teach you to shoot like that? I did, didn't I?" His voice was full of pride.

Victor didn't answer, couldn't. His heart was beating so fast he thought it was going to explode. He felt the flat of a hand slap him between the shoulder blades. It was the first time his uncle had ever touched him like that.

He squinted his eyes and forced the memory out of his mind. Already he couldn't remember the make of the rifle or what color his gloves had been. Over the years details had diminished, one after the other. One day he hoped he would forget that horrible flash of red as well.

After twenty minutes walking he crossed a narrow footbridge, and from the most northerly post he walked exactly fifty paces due north into the trees. He found the fallen trunk without any difficulty and headed east ten paces from its stump. Victor was up to his waist in bracken. It was dark under the canopy, the meager morning sun barely finding its way between the birches and pines. He started digging.

It was difficult work, but he was thankful of the rain that turned the earth, usually frozen hard at this time of year, into a workable mud. He used the pickax to loosen the hardened soil under the mud before digging with the shovel. About two feet down he dug carefully until he hit metal. He scraped the soil away until he could see blue canvas.

He found the edges and scraped the soil away until he cleared a rectangular area, two feet by three. The canvas sheet was tied together in the center with nylon rope. Victor undid the knot and opened up the sheet. The brushed aluminum briefcase was still shiny, if a little marked from the digging.

No matter. Victor cared nothing for the case itself, only what it protected. He pulled it out of the hole and placed it to one side. He took a pocketknife and lighter from his coat and used the disposable lighter to heat up the knife. He then cut through the watertight wax seal that filled the small gap where the two halves of the case met.

Victor opened the case, relieved to find that no moisture had gotten inside. The weapon was cold to the touch but could be assembled and fired at that very moment, and work.

Encased in sculpted foam rubber was a Snayperskaya Vintovka Dragunova. Known in the West as the Dragunov SVD. A sniper rifle. The first Dragunov was formally adopted into the Red Army in 1963, and rumor had it that the Soviet special forces, the Spetsnaz, had tested the weapon on American servicemen during the Vietnam War. Just an old soldier's tale, Victor had been sure. That was until he had met one of the snipers.

The rifle was disassembled into its component parts, with its stock, barrel, grip, and scope separate to allow it to fit inside a standard-sized briefcase. There was also the gun itself as well as a long suppressor. Victor's was the latest variant of the SVD, with stock and hand guards made from high-density polymer to lighten the weight, instead of the original wood furniture.

Though not as sophisticated or accurate at long range as some Western sniper rifles, Victor had a fondness for the Dragunov because of its reliability in all conditions and its no-nonsense mechanics.

As a semiautomatic rifle, the Dragunov had a much better rate of fire than a typical bolt-action sniper rifle, though the greater number of moving parts that made the rifle semiautomatic also made it less accurate than a bolt-action. But as a semiauto the SVD could also be used as an assault rifle and was fitted with conventional iron sights and bayonet mount for just such a use.

The Soviet philosophy on arms manufacture had been ease of use and reliability over accuracy, and Victor had found there to be a lot of merit in the ideal. Weapons that were world beaters on the range weren't much use if they didn't work under battlefield conditions. The Germans, Americans, and most recently British had all learned that lesson the hard way.

There were two magazines for the Dragunov. Each held ten 7.62 X 54mmR rounds that tended to make a nice mess of anyone unlucky enough to be on its receiving end. Victor had two types of ammunition for the rifle: the first was the standard lead encased in a copper jacket, the second were API rounds.

The armor-piercing incendiary rounds were made of solid steel with a hollow core. Inside the core was a small phosphorous incendiary charge, which would ignite when the bullet hit its target—typically a vehicle's fuel tank.

Victor closed the case and reached back into the

hole for the large leather sports bag that had been underneath the rifle case. Gritting his teeth, Victor hauled it up and out of the hole.

Inside, tied up in a waterproof sack, were a range of supplies and equipment, most of which Victor ignored. He took out a Glock handgun, a suppressor, a three-inch-thick wad of American dollars, extra ammunition for both the rifle and the handgun, and a Russian passport. All went into the pockets of his jacket.

The waterproof sack was then retied, the sports bag closed and lowered back into the ground. He refilled the hole and patted it flat before scattering dead bracken over where he'd dug. Back in the country club's parking lot he placed the metal briefcase in the trunk and slammed it shut.

He hoped he had wasted his time.

FORTY-TWO

Milan, Italy
Sunday
21:33 CET

Sebastian Hoyt spent money so fast it was lucky his company generated a small fortune each year. As the sole owner of a modestly sized but highly lucrative consultancy firm, Hoyt conducted his business interests across a wide range of fields. In these he almost always acted as an advisor, broker, or middleman. He traded mostly in information, information he harvested from one area and sold to another. Information, he had long ago discovered, was one of the world's most precious commodities, and it also happened to be one of the easiest to trade.

He advised the mafia on private investments to make the most of their money. He helped corrupt judges in Eastern Europe set up bank accounts for payoffs. He put arms dealers in touch with African militias. He supplied traveling Middle Eastern businessmen with access to call girls, alcohol, and narcotics. He brokered the dealings between contract killers and their clients. As long as Hoyt had access to people who needed information and those who could supply it, his bank balance would stay healthy.

The proposal he was checking through was boring him senseless, so he took a break and turned his attention to the Italian newspaper on his desk. It was a couple of days old and carried a small story about a shooting in Paris that was of interest to him. The article discussed what little the police had since discovered and named some of the dead. One of the fatalities was an American, James Stevenson, a hitman based in Brussels, whom Hoyt had conducted business with on several occasions.

One of Hoyt's most recent endeavors was acting as a broker between a nameless client and the American mercenary. Hoyt had given the American work before, and no client had ever complained about Stevenson's services. So when he was asked to hire an assassin who could assemble a team, Hoyt had gone where he had gone plenty of times before. He didn't expect the hitman to be killed in a mass murder in central Paris that received news headlines all the way to Italy.

It was a shame that Stevenson was dead, but only because Hoyt had lost an easy revenue stream. Just to be on the safe side, he'd put some of his underlings on the scent to see if they could find out anything about what happened. It wouldn't do his reputation any good if Stevenson had performed poorly. So far, the overpaid and undertalented simpletons working for Hoyt had given him nothing more than what he had read in the papers. In this instance it seemed no news was good news.

Even still, Hoyt had been expecting a communiqué from a pissed-off client for a few days now, but none had yet arrived. He was not overly concerned by this. The nature of such business meant that things could go bad and go bad publicly. The client obviously understood this, or maybe the hitman had been killed after the job's completion so that the client didn't care. Either outcome suited Hoyt. He didn't know what the job had been and was glad of that fact. It was easier to sleep at night when he didn't have to think about the messy consequences of his illicit dealings. Shame to have lost a revenue stream, but better to have maintained his reputation.

That last particular business arrangement had been obscenely profitable. The client had offered a $200,000 purse, of which Hoyt had passed on a mere $128,000 to the American mercenary. For a few e-mails and a delightful afternoon in Brussels, Hoyt had personally pocketed $72,000. If he rounded up his billable hours to a working day of seven, which he knew was being very generous, that became $10,285 an hour. Even for Hoyt that was an exceptionally good rate. If only all business deals could be so satisfying.

He opened his bottom drawer, took out a small black wooden box, and placed it on his desk. From the box he took out a hand-folded paper envelope. He tapped out some cocaine onto the desk and made a line of it with a razor blade. It was premium Nicaraguan, and the best money could buy—so finely cut it didn't need any more chopping. Using a silver tube designed for just such a moment, Hoyt sniffed up the drug.

He slumped back in his chair, eyes closed, pinching his nostrils. Christ, that felt good. He resisted doing another line and packed the cocaine box away. Hoyt prided himself on his self-restraint. It was time to head home. There was no one else at the office, so he made his way to the elevator in semidarkness. His corporation, though highly profitable, was a small affair and consisted merely of himself, his personal assistant, five analysts, and a receptionist. They all worked from Hoyt's plush offices in central Milan.

Hoyt had lived in Italy for so long that he could easily pass as a native. The decades under the Mediterranean sun had stained his skin a dark tan, and his Italian was fluent. His naturally dark hair and eyes aided the illusion. If asked where he was from he would say Milan. Hoyt loved Italy—the land, the culture, the language, the people. It just suited his tastes perfectly. It was perhaps not the best place to conduct business, but over the years he had found its location provided many advantages. With clients in both Western and Eastern Europe, Africa and the Middle East, Italy served as a fine centralized base of operations.

It was a short drive back to his townhouse. Hoyt lived alone, had never married. He liked women, but the idea of one day losing half of everything he owned did not appeal to his work ethic. Inside, Hoyt fixed himself a big martini and ran a bath. He was tempted to call up a particular prostitute who did a special thing with her tongue that he was particularly fond of, but he was probably too tired for anything like that. A few drinks, bath, and bed were all he needed. It was going to be another busy day tomorrow.

He was yawning heavily by the time he was on his second martini and getting into the bath. There was an unpleasant taste in his mouth that he dismissed on account of the large amount of cocaine he'd consumed throughout the evening. He lay with his head resting on a folded towel and his eyes closed, wondering why the hell he was so tired. He had been up late every night for a week, granted, but he had still gotten plenty of sleep. I'm getting older, he reminded himself.

The sedatives he had unknowingly consumed in the martinis ensured that he was sound asleep fifteen minutes later, that he did not hear the bathroom door open or the ever-so-quiet footsteps approach him.

A shadow fell across his unconscious face.

Reed squatted down next to the bath and took a large leather wallet from inside his suit jacket and rested it on his thigh. He unzipped the wallet and withdrew a small glass medical vial and hypodermic syringe. He unscrewed the cap and rested the vial on the floor before taking the plastic safety sheath from the syringe. He estimated Hoyt's weight to be no more than 180 pounds, so, after picking the vial back up, he inserted the needle through the membrane and pulled eight centiliters of potassium-chloride solution into the plunger.

Gently, Reed took hold of Hoyt's jaw with his free hand and opened his mouth. Reed placed the needle under Hoyt's tongue and pushed the tip into the lingual artery. With a slow, smooth motion, he injected the solution into Hoyt's bloodstream.

With calm efficiency Reed packed his things away in the order he had taken them out and stood. He washed out Hoyt's cocktail shaker to get rid of any trace of the sedatives before placing the half-empty prescription bottle next to Hoyt's glass. Reed then exited through the house the same way he had entered, disturbing nothing and seen by no one.

He checked his watch. It was 11:05 PM. The potassium chloride would induce cardiac arrest in approximately three minutes and would kill Hoyt within another two. The chemical would then break down into separate molecules of potassium and chlorine, both of which are found naturally inside the body after death, ensuring a pathologist would find no trace of the poison in Hoyt's system. There was a chance the needle mark might be detected if a complete autopsy was performed, but with no indication of foul play the chances of this taking place were extremely slim.

Should Hoyt survive the heart attack, which was

possible, albeit unlikely, he would still die. The attack would leave him in a massively weakened state and he would be unable to prevent himself from drowning in the bath. This would take no more than another two minutes, judging by Hoyt's poor physical condition. Either result would be perfectly acceptable to Reed.

Several streets away from the apartment Reed climbed into his rental car. He took his smartphone from the glove box and composed a message to confirm the success of the operation. He looked at his watch and waited until the hands read 11:12 PM before hitting send.

Reed liked to be exact.

FORTY-THREE

St. Petersburg, Russia
Monday
13:57 MSK

Victor, briefcase in hand, strolled through the crowds of Russians in the shopping mall, all dressed in heavy layers to protect against the cold that even the shopping center's heaters couldn't combat entirely. Victor took the escalator to the upper level, one gloved hand resting on the rubber handrail as he ascended. He moved the lollipop with his tongue from one side of his mouth to the other.

At a pay phone he called Norimov's bar and gave the

bartender who answered the location and time. He then made his way toward the main stairwell and climbed the stairs to the top parking-lot level. The parking lot was mostly empty, only a dozen or so vehicles parked beneath the sky above. He breathed in the crisp air, watched his breath form thick clouds of moisture. He was too focused to feel the cold. His pulse was perfectly steady.

The maintenance door was locked with a stainless-steel padlock that barely slowed him. On the other side Victor took the metal steps to the actual roof, one story above the top parking-lot level. The sky was near cloudless, the bright November sun making him squint. He drew a pair of sunglasses from his breast pocket and slipped them on. He moved to the edge of the roof, squeezing around the large ventilation pipes protruding from inside the building. The thrum of fans dueled with the rush of the wind.

Victor peered over the edge, saw the exterior parking lot six stories below him; at this time of day it was half full of cars. He turned, squatted down, and placed the briefcase on the roof. He unlocked it and opened the lid. It took less than a minute to assemble the Dragunov and calibrate the sight for the distance to the ground. He then selected the magazine containing the standard rounds and loaded it. Victor sucked on the lollipop while he waited, resisting the urge to crunch.

He saw the same black BMW he'd ridden inside two days before enter the parking-lot entrance. It meandered slowly and found a parking space close to the center, ten yards from a ticket machine as instructed. A moment later the rear off-side door opened and Norimov climbed out. Through the scope, Victor watched him as he walked up to the ticket machine.

There was at least one of Norimov's men in the car, the driver, but there could have been more. From Victor's position he couldn't see through the windows, but he doubted Norimov would have come with less than a car full. There could even be another car in the area, backup in case anything went wrong. Whatever their history, Norimov wouldn't fully trust him.

Victor scanned the area. New people were coming and going all the time, moving around the space, some walking to cars, some just taking shortcuts. He only paid attention to the men, those between twenty-five and forty. If Norimov's contacts had betrayed him or if Norimov had been compromised some other way, the FSB, SVR, or both would be in the parking lot. Russian intelligence had never made much use of women in the field, and Victor doubted they would have changed decades of tradition just for him. He used the scope to examine necks, searching for the spiraling wire that would give agents away. None of the likely suspects had them that he could see. Earpieces could be wireless, but Victor doubted the SVR or FSB could afford the latest tech.

If someone planned to make a play for him it would be from within the parking lot itself after he'd revealed himself. They would need to be within running or shooting distance of the ticket machine. The parking lot was flanked by roads on three sides, with numerous parked vehicles, most of which had been there for long periods. Surveillance could be anywhere. Victor had noticed three vans enter the area and park in the previous thirty minutes alone. There hadn't been enough time to get snipers in position, but he still checked every few seconds. Dozens more vans and SUVs had come and gone or had been parked since before he'd arrived. Any one of them could have a kill or snatch team in the back.

Or none at all. Maybe he was being arrogant, assuming he was still a wanted man after so many years. Arrogant or not, he spotted a potential twenty yards from Norimov. A dark-haired man in a long coat was chatting on a cell phone, loitering near his car. Similarly, there was a tall blond man making his way across the parking lot. He wasn't close to Norimov, but he was close enough. Victor couldn't wait it out though. If Norimov was being watched and he made no contact, any surveillance would be kept in place until the next time. But Victor was confident in his plan. Should anything go wrong, it wouldn't be because he hadn't been careful.

He hit a speed dial number on his phone, and through the scope he saw Norimov's head move, a confused expression on his features. It took the Russian a few seconds to work out where the sound was coming from, and he turned around and checked the ticket machine. He went around the back of it before finally reaching underneath.

Norimov found the phone and pried it from where it had been glued. He flipped it open.

"Very good, Vasily," he said instantly.

"How are you, Alek?"

Victor saw Norimov looking around, obviously trying to see where he was located, without luck. He even looked up to the building, but Victor had positioned himself such that anyone looking up from the parking lot would only see the glare of the sun in the sky above him. It was the reason he had chosen that particular time and position, where the sun was in the perfect place in the sky to disguise him.

"So what happens now?" Norimov asked.

"Could your contacts decrypt the information?"

"Yes, Vasily, they could. Everything went well."

"Thank you for this," Victor said.

"What are friends for?"

Victor couldn't answer. "Do you have it with you?"

"In my pocket." He tapped his chest.

"Under the ticket machine where you found the phone there is a padded envelope. Put it in there."

"Cute." Norimov fumbled under the ticket machine for a moment. "Hold on, I can't reach. I'm going to put the phone down for a second."

"You're getting old."

"I am old. You too will be one day."

"Not if I can help it."

Norimov found the envelope and placed the drive inside. At least Victor hoped he had. Through the scope Victor saw that the blond man had stopped walking. He now stood maybe ten yards behind Norimov, acting as though he was waiting for someone. But not very convincingly. Clear wire spiraled from his ear to his collar. Victor frowned.

"Don't make any movement. There's a man behind

you with an earpiece. Smile, laugh as if I had told you a joke."

Norimov did and asked, "What do we do?" The smile still on his face.

"They were waiting for me to show, but the phone's confused them."

"How did they know?"

"Whoever decrypted the drive either told them or was discovered decrypting it. They've probably got your bar bugged, your office. When you leave, they'll follow you."

"I'll lead them round half the country. See how they like that."

"Any victory, however small . . ."

"Exactly."

"Head back to your car and drive away normally," Victor said. "When they realize I'm not going to show, they could bring you in."

"I'll tell them you didn't show. Which is true."

"They'll make your life difficult if they can."

"Fuck them. I can take care of myself. I was thinking of moving anyway. The Caribbean maybe. I like the women."

He spoke lightly, too lightly.

Victor's jaw muscles flexed. "I'm sorry for getting you into this, Alek."

Norimov was still pretending to smile. "There's nothing to be sorry for."

It was crowded and hot inside the back of the removal van, but no one complained. There were four men in total, aged between twenty-five and forty. All professionals, all experienced operatives for the SVR. They all watched the images of Norimov and the parking lot displayed on the seventeen-inch monitor. Colonel Aniskovach watched too. A directional parabolic microphone was covering Norimov, but it was too far away, and the ambient sound too loud to decipher Norimov's words.

"He's definitely talking to him," an operative said. "Where the hell is he?"

"He must be nearby," Aniskovach replied. "He'll want to see Norimov with his own eyes to make sure he's alone. He's out there somewhere. When he is convinced everything is safe he'll show to collect the package." Aniskovach grabbed a radio to speak to the men outside. "Do not move until the target is identified and I give the command."

With less than an hour's warning of where the exchange was taking place, Aniskovach hadn't had the time to get snipers in position or a better plan put into action. Which was why, of course, the assassin had arranged things as he had. Aniskovach had to appreciate his cunning, but he had enough men in the area to trap him the second he showed.

On the monitor Norimov hung up the cell and placed it in his pocket.

Aniskovach spoke into the radio. "That's it; they're done talking. He won't show until Norimov has left. Kill him only if you are forced to, wound him by all means, but I'd like him alive." Aniskovach turned to his men. "Be ready."

Clouds obscured the sun. Victor closed the phone but kept watch over Norimov to make sure he was safe. It was the least Victor could do. Norimov strolled back to his car as if he had no care in the world. He moved to the passenger door and opened it. As he did so, Victor looked back to the blond man and saw he was talking, seemingly to himself. For a second the man glanced upstairs, straight at Victor.

The blond man must have eyes like a hawk. Victor took a breath, knowing he didn't have long before they locked down the location and trapped him. But for the moment he was up here and they were down there. With both hands back on the rifle, Victor swung it toward the plainclothes operative. He was already moving, knowing he had likewise been spotted, his right hand reaching to his belt.

Victor fired.

The bullet flew over Norimov's shoulder and hit the blond man in the face. When his body struck the ground most of the head was no longer attached to his neck.

The Dragunov's suppressor massively reduced the sound caused by the escaping gases, but the high-velocity round it fired created a sonic boom as it broke the sound barrier—unmistakably a gunshot. Victor watched the ensuing effect carefully. People in and around the parking lot ducked or flinched—shocked, scared, confused. All but two.

Victor killed the first with a bullet through the chest. The second, realizing what was happening, tried to run. He didn't get far.

Norimov's men pulled him into the car and the

BMW's tires screeched as it reversed out of the parking space and headed toward the exit. Victor risked standing up to get a better view. They knew where he was now, anyway. He looked around. Below him there were screams, hysteria, people running back and forth. Where were the others?

To his right, he spotted a white removal van. The man behind the wheel had a frantic look on his face and a spiral of clear wire descending from his left ear. Immediately Victor crouched back down, grabbed the Dragunov, and swung it to the right. The reticule rushed over the parking lot.

The driver's mouth was moving. Shouting something.

A small hole exploded through the side window, and the glass turned red.

Hearing the sound of breaking glass and a wet *thunk*, Colonel Aniskovach stopped barking orders and looked through the partition separating the driver's cab from the van's rear compartment. His mouth fell open at what he saw.

Bright gore plastered the front windshield. The operative behind the wheel was slumped to one side in his seat, his head split in two.

Aniskovach was already moving when he screamed, *"EVERYBODY OUT."*

Victor let the magazine fall out of the rifle and slammed in the second mag. He worked the action, ejecting the previous round and loading an API. Through the sniper scope Victor watched the van's rear doors swing open. He hovered the crosshairs over the fuel inlet.

A man leaped out of the back and ran. More boots dropped out of the back onto the road behind the first. Victor fired. The bullet punched a hole through the body work. Inside the van the incendiary charge ignited the traces of fuel in the inlet. Flames rushed through the fuel pipe, reaching the tank.

The van exploded.

It lifted off the ground, the force ripping outward, decimating it in a single instant. The fireball was huge, mushrooming upward, engulfing the operatives not fast enough to follow Aniskovach's lead. The shock wave blew out the glass of the neighboring vehicles.

Black smoke rose toward the sky.

FORTY-FOUR

Paris, France
Monday
10:07 CET

Rebecca returned to her apartment with a bag of groceries. She locked the door before walking to the kitchen, where she placed the bag down on a work surface, poured herself the last of the coffee from the pot, and drank it bitter and lukewarm. In the lounge she stood in the gloom for a moment before opening the drapes to let some light in. Outside Paris was gray and depressing. Her hair was wet and lank from the rain. She knew she looked awful without confirming it in the mirror.

Paranoia made her check that all the windows were closed and locked. The apartment was old, the walls, floor, and ceiling thick. Little noise found its way into the space and the quiet unnerved her. She took a breath in an attempt to control her anxiety. No one knew about the apartment. It wasn't hers. It had belonged to her uncle and was now the property of one of her cousins. She'd stayed for a few weeks a couple of years ago when she was given a set of keys and told to stay whenever she liked. Her cousin lived outside the city and didn't rent it out but was too sentimental to sell it.

She tapped the space bar on her notebook to get rid of the screen saver. She'd left it powered on before leaving for Switzerland. With only a laptop's processing power, the code-breaking software she was using could take several days, maybe even weeks, to breach the cipher on Ozols's memory stick. Unsurprisingly it hadn't found the code yet. The software displayed an ever-increasing count of the combinations tried. Billions down, billions more to go. Maybe tens of billions. Maybe more. If so, they would never crack it. Rebecca would die of old age long before the password had been discovered.

She considered e-mailing her friend at Langley who worked for the cryptography department. He had access to supercomputers that could smash open almost any cipher in hours, if not minutes. But her nameless companion was right, doing so would put them too close to their enemies.

Rebecca had entered into the software every word she knew that might have significance to Ozols. As part of the operation she'd been privy to much information on the Latvian, which in turn she'd passed on to his killer. None of those words had helped. The code was probably something with no significance, a blend of numbers and letters for added security.

After making herself fresh coffee, black with sugar, she sat down on a small, creaking armchair in front of a second, recently purchased computer. A similarly new printer rested on the floor.

On the screen was the home page for a financial consultant in London: Hartman and Royce Equity Investments. The home page was minimalist, elegant, with an artist's impression of the London skyline, at the center of which was Canary Wharf, where the offices for Hartman and Royce were located.

Rebecca navigated through the site until she found a page listing the company's executives with some biographical highlights and accompanying photos. She scrolled down and stopped at the name Elliot Seif in the middle of the screen. A click opened up Seif's details, complete with a larger picture of the man.

She right clicked and saved the picture.

At a nearby phone booth she entered the dialing code for the UK, followed by Seif's office number.

A woman answered in a polite but serious British accent. "Hartman and Royce, Melanie speaking, how can I help you?"

"I'd like an appointment to see one of your financial advisors please."

Five minutes later Rebecca left the booth with a next-day appointment booked to see a man called Brice to discuss private investments and her stock portfolio. The appointment would give her the perfect opportunity to get a close look at Seif and survey his offices.

She went back to her research. Already she had street maps of the Canary Wharf district in several scales, as well as photographs of the building and surrounding ones. She had a variety of CIA-supplied software on her computer that allowed her access, some legally but mostly illegally, to a number of useful sources.

Sharing a common language with the UK made things much easier than compiling dossiers on citizens of other European countries. She logged onto the UK electoral-register database to find Seif's home address. He had homes in both Surrey and London, and a second voter was registered at the Surrey address by the name of Samantha Seif, who Rebecca assumed was Seif's wife.

After a few minutes of clicking and typing, she had phone numbers and a credit history. Seif's résumé was next. A while later, she had surrounding area maps of the two addresses and a growing list of biographical information.

By the time her companion returned, Rebecca wanted to know everything about Elliot Seif there was to know. She glanced toward the other computer.

The software had stopped counting.

FORTY-FIVE

St. Petersburg, Russia
Monday
17:25 MSK

The amber-colored liquid sloshed into the glass, and Aleksandr Norimov threw the Scotch down his throat. He clenched his teeth and poured himself another drink. The heat from the whisky felt good spreading through his insides. He was surprised and glad to be alive. When the shooting started, he felt sure that he wasn't going to make it out of there. He put a hand to his chest. His heart was still thundering. He was too old, too out of practice for such excitement.

Norimov sat behind his desk, wondering what the hell was going to happen next, when he heard the cars pull up outside and poured himself a third drink. He'd finished his fourth by the time the office door was thrown open and the man walked in. There was an arrogance and casual menace in the way he carried himself, even with the fresh wound dressing that covered his left cheek from nose to ear and eye socket to jawbone.

"He killed five of our people this afternoon," Aniskovach spat. "Tell me where he is."

Norimov gestured to the dressing. "Bet that's going to leave a nice scar."

Aniskovach was still for a second before swiping his

arm across the desk's surface, knocking the bottle of whisky, glasses, and a stack of papers to the floor.

"WHERE IS HE?"

Norimov pushed his chair back and bent over to pick the bottle and two cracked tumblers off the floor. He set them back on the table and sucked the Scotch from his fingers.

"How the fuck would I know?" Norimov reached for the bottle. "You're the SVR, not me."

"If I thought for one moment you told him we were there . . ."

"Don't be so stupid." Norimov shook his head. "And don't assume that I am either. It was you who screwed it up by having men in the parking lot. I told you he'd spot them."

Aniskovach looked around, as if trying to formulate an appropriate rebuttal. After a moment he took the seat opposite Norimov, and placed his gloved hands on the table. He spread his fingers. "Yes, yes you did." He gave a crooked smile then grimaced and put a hand to his face.

Norimov hid his amusement perfectly. "Smiling stings, eh?"

Aniskovach frowned. "I guess I should have listened to your advice. You're not as over the hill as you look."

Norimov ignored the comment. He took hold of the whisky bottle. "Drink?"

Aniskovach regarded him for a minute. "Thanks," he said eventually.

Norimov took a new glass and poured Aniskovach a

Scotch. He took a sip. "He didn't try leaving via the airport," Aniskovach said.

"Did you expect him to?"

Aniskovach didn't say anything.

Norimov smirked. "Getting the first plane out of the country is exactly what you'd expect. So that would be exactly the last thing he'd actually do. He's good, or did you not pay attention to that lesson earlier?"

Aniskovach frowned. "So where is he?"

Norimov shook his head. "You're persistent if nothing else. Why would you think he would ever tell me where he was staying or where he was going? He never did in the past either."

"Would you tell me if you knew?"

"If there was enough money involved." Norimov sat back. "Speaking of which."

Aniskovach gestured to an SVR guy standing in the doorway. He walked over to the table and placed a briefcase in front of Norimov and opened it. Inside it was full of American dollars.

"I wasn't sure you'd actually pay," Norimov said as he examined the money. "When you came in here I thought you might kill me."

Aniskovach smiled as much as his injuries would allow. Norimov, who was studying his face intently, didn't join in.

"If I ever learn you have double-crossed me in any way, I won't hesitate to order your execution," Aniskovach stated evenly. "But I'm a man of my word. We had an arrangement and I will honor it."

Norimov brought the glass to his lips. "I didn't know you people had honor."

"Let's call it professional courtesy then. The end result is still the same." He paused for a moment, his finger gently touching his wound. "Did he have any idea you were working for us?"

"None."

"Then maybe in the future he will again need to contact you."

"I doubt it," Norimov said. "But I thought that the previous time. So what do I know?"

Aniskovach tilted his head to one side. "And you would have no problem letting us know again if he does? Even though he used to be your friend?"

Norimov thought for a moment. "He is my friend still. But business is business." Norimov paused. "He would understand that."

"I would never betray a friend."

"Then you won't get far in your chosen profession."

Aniskovach pulled the copied flash drive from his pocket and studied it in his hand. "Did he give you any indication what information is contained on this?"

Norimov shook his head. "He didn't know. That's why he needed my help. You haven't decoded it yet then."

Aniskovach stood. "It's a sensitive issue, so it's taking a little longer than usual." He headed for the door, but stopped. "And, just so there is no confusion, you're quite sure you have no idea where he might be?"

Norimov, who was counting his money, didn't look up. "He'll be out of the country by now, of that you can be certain."

FORTY-SIX

East of Kohtla-Järve, Estonia
Monday
16:45 CET

The service station was little more than a large café/bar with a surrounding area of uneven asphalt that served as a car and truck stop. On one side of the parking lot was a row of fuel pumps under a crumbling shelter. It was snowing, and the windshield wipers swept back and forth in front of Yukov sitting high in his truck's cab. The suspension was shot, and he bounced around in his seat as he maneuvered the big vehicle across the parking lot. The tires churned up brown slush.

Yukov stifled a yawn and pulled the truck to a stop. It had been a long drive from Russia, and he was desperate for a piss and a thick sandwich. He might allow himself a drink or two. Maybe even a nap if he thought he would have time.

There had been a delay at the border that had put him almost an hour behind schedule. He had no idea what was going on, but guards had been checking the identification of every vehicle heading out of Russia. They hadn't even had the courtesy to let him know why.

Perhaps the nap wasn't a good idea. He had to be in Tallinn before midnight, and if he overslept, he would be in for it. He pulled his coat from across the seat and put it on. It was blissfully warm inside his cab, but it would be far below zero outside. He grabbed his wool hat as well and pulled it down over his ears before slipping on his gloves. Kohtla-Järve was right on the northern coast of Estonia, and the wind blowing in from the Baltic could be murderous at the best of times. It was worse than normal tonight though—far worse.

When the door was open he shuddered instantly. The windchill turned his face bright red. He locked his truck as fast as he could and hurried across the parking lot toward the service station.

He had no reason to check his trailer before he left, and even if he had it was unlikely he would have noticed the split in the tarpaulin on the left side. It was a vertical cut about three feet in height held together on the inside by heavy-duty tape.

Slowly, one by one, the pieces of tape were removed, and the tarpaulin was pulled open by hands trembling in the cold. A shaking figure emerged through the gap and dropped to the ground, where he collapsed onto the asphalt, his half-frozen legs failing to keep him upright.

With enormous difficulty Victor pushed himself to his knees and, using the truck for support, pulled himself onto his feet. He was wet from the ground and knew if he didn't get inside soon the water would freeze on him.

His whole body shook uncontrollably. He couldn't feel his hands or feet anymore. The sound of teeth chattering stung his ears. The service station was maybe fifty yards away. He pushed himself from the truck and stumbled forward, walking fast to keep his balance. The wind, coming at his right, forced him to the left, and he leaned against it, jaw against his shoulder, hands pushed down the front of his pants because that was the warmest part of his body. He bounced back and forth off parked vehicles as he moved around them, unable to walk steadily.

He had spent several hours in the back of the truck with only his clothes to keep him warm. Victor wore a thick overcoat, hat, and gloves, but they hadn't been enough to keep the cold at bay. They should have been, but the weather conditions had been extreme, an unpredicted Baltic storm. Taking a flight or a train out of the country would have avoided the weather but also would have delivered him straight into the hands of his enemies. He couldn't risk driving himself, in case he was stopped by the authorities. Hiding in the back of the truck had seemed a good idea before the weather had turned. The trailer was transporting vegetables, and he had squatted down between crates to try and escape the wind that found its way under the tarpaulin. The cut he had made to gain access only exacerbated the windy conditions.

By the time the truck had reached the border, he had been in no state to defend himself had the guards been diligent enough to check the trailer. Knowing how cold the weather had been, he'd considered paying the driver to take him across so that he could sit in the cab, climbing into the trailer only as they neared the border. It would have kept him warm, but there was the risk that the driver would either give him up to the authorities or would give himself away by acting suspiciously.

Victor reached the entrance and pushed open the door. He received several glances from the Estonian and Russian patrons. His appearance and demeanor couldn't help attract everyone's attention, but there was nothing he could do about that. His priority was to get warm. There was no point dying of exposure just to stay unnoticed.

He made his way to the counter and said, "Coffee, please."

He didn't speak Estonian so he spoke in Russian instead. About a quarter of the population were ethnic Russians, and the city was so close to the border it was likely Russian would be understood. With his teeth chattering and his voice hoarse he had to repeat himself twice more before the woman behind the counter could understand him.

Victor downed the coffee in one gulp, not caring that he burnt his mouth in the process. He needed to raise his body temperature—and fast. He asked for another coffee and drank it as quickly before ordering sweet bread soup and some *pelmeenid*, steamed dumplings stuffed with beef and served with sour cream.

He ate the food quickly and didn't care about the mess he made. It took a while, but finally he started to regain feeling in his fingers. As the temperature of his torso increased, blood returned to the extremities. He had never forgotten the words of his drill sergeant.

Warm your insides, and your insides will take care of your outsides.

Fifteen minutes later he could flex his hands; after thirty minutes he could feel each of his toes again. Forty-five minutes after entering, he was ready to leave. He would have liked to have stayed longer, to have taken a room and rested, but he was still too close to Russia to relax. But he couldn't go anywhere dressed as he was.

He purchased a bottle of vodka and sat with it while he waited for the right moment. He didn't have to wait long until a man of similar height got up from his seat and headed toward the toilet. The man had no companions at the table he had vacated. Perfect. Victor waited a few seconds and stood up. He entered the toilet thirty seconds after the man.

It was a stinking, filthy room, but Victor was unconcerned about the lack of hygiene. The man moved up to the urinals and began to relieve himself. There was another man alongside him and Victor waited by the sink, pretending to wash his hands, until the second man had left.

Victor didn't have much time. Someone could come in at any moment. He moved up behind the man at the urinal. He was fast, the man noticing him too late. Victor grabbed his hair with his right hand and slammed his head off the tiles above the urinals. The man grunted, dazed.

Victor hoisted him backward, swung him around, and threw the man into a cubicle. Victor rushed in afterward, flung the door closed, and locked it.

The man was on his knees, groaning, trying to push

himself to his feet. Victor positioned himself behind him, feet on either side of the man's own. He wedged his left arm under the man's jaw, and pushed into his throat with the edge of his forearm. With his right hand, Victor grabbed the back of the man's head and kept him steady.

The man struggled desperately, but he was on his knees, Victor over him, and the concussion made him weak. He lost consciousness and Victor released him. Another minute and he would be dead, but since Victor was going to take his clothes, it was the least he could do to pay him back with his life.

When he was changed Victor dressed the unconscious man in his old clothes as best as he could before emptying the bottle of vodka over him. When he came round and started babbling about being attacked he would be ignored as a drunk. At least long enough for Victor to get a head start.

He exited the restroom. He kept his head down, but not too low, as he left the service station. The man's clothes gave him good protection from the weather, but the wind was still painful on his exposed face. He hurried across the parking lot toward the highway, where a group of people waited in a bus shelter.

"Excuse me, when is the next bus to town?"

The old woman he asked thought for a moment. "Five minutes."

"Thank you," he said.

He was exhausted, in desperate need of rest, but he couldn't stop yet. From Kohtla-Järve he could get transportation to Estonia's capital, Tallinn. Then the first flight out of the country. For the moment any destination would do before going back to France.

To the broker.

Victor hoped she had been more successful.

FORTY-SEVEN

Paris, France
Monday
19:54 CET

Rain splashed against the phone booth and ran down the glass in front of Victor. Headlights glimmered in the raindrops. He lifted the receiver and punched in the number with the knuckle of his index finger. He was glad when the line connected after three rings, glad when he heard her voice.

"It's me," he said.

The broker replied, "I know it is."

He was glad again at hearing those four words, the code for everything being fine. Just a single word difference and he'd have known she'd been compromised. There was no stress in her voice to indicate she was speaking under coercion.

"Where are you?" she asked.

"Back in Paris. I'll see you in one hour."

He replaced the pay phone receiver and exited the booth. Twenty minutes later he rang the broker's buzzer.

"You're early," she said when she answered.

He didn't respond. Of course he would arrive before he'd said. He climbed the stairs to her apartment and knocked on the door. He saw the spy-hole glass darken a second before the door unlocked and she took the chain off. Neither of which would stop a kill team, but maybe it helped her sleep better.

When the door was open she stepped aside to let Victor in, and he walked through the doorway, body half-turned so he didn't give her his back. She closed the door behind him, locked it and put the chain back in place.

"Do you want a drink?" she asked.

She was dressed in black jeans and a burgundy sweater that clung to the contours of her stomach and breasts. Her dark hair was loose and long, framing her face, making her seem softer, more vulnerable than when they had first met, even if her eyes were harder. Victor pulled his gaze from her and checked the apartment.

Aside from the new computer and printer and a few extra items in the cupboards and fridge it was no different than how he'd left it two days ago. He touched the screw heads on the electrical sockets and air vents. None were rough. In the lounge the lamp shade was still angled as he'd left it, and he was pleased she hadn't corrected it.

He found her in the kitchen fixing herself a cup of

coffee. There was a second tall cup on the work surface that she filled.

"You didn't answer," she said. "But I made you one anyway."

Victor said nothing.

"You look tired," she said.

"I am."

"You should rest."

"Later."

He picked up the cup and walked back into the lounge. He placed it down near her computers with no intention of even tasting it. He didn't seriously believe she would poison him, but some habits just couldn't be broken so easily. She followed him, sipping at her cup.

"How was your trip?" she asked.

"Unsuccessful."

She nodded. "I've had some luck."

"With the bank or the encrypted file?"

"Both."

Victor moved over to the window, stood with his shoulder to the wall, adjusted the drapes an inch to the side, and peered out. The street outside was empty. On the other side of the window he did the same to check farther down the street, where he hadn't been able to see. He looked back to see the broker standing expectantly.

"Aren't you going to congratulate me?"

"Maybe you should tell me what you've found out before patting yourself on the back."

She gave him a quick smile. "You'll be the one

patting me on the back." She moved to her computers and put her coffee down. "It's really good," she said. "Columbian. Drink it while it's hot."

Victor nodded.

The broker sat down in front of her computer and tapped the touch pad to bring it out of sleep mode.

Victor stood back and watched her work. Her fingers moved fluidly over the keyboard. Programs loaded. Commands were typed. She double-clicked the file and the password screen appeared. She typed something in. Ten asterisks appeared. She hit enter.

"That's it," she said. "I'm in."

On the monitor the file was extracting itself into a series of other files.

"You told me it could take days," Victor said.

"It did," the broker replied. "Two days to be exact. We're actually unlucky it took that long. Ozols only used standard 40-bit encryption. We should have realized, at least I should have. It's obvious with hindsight. The guy was a retired naval officer, right? He wasn't even retired intelligence. He had no access to advanced encryption software—hell, he probably doesn't even know the difference between low- and high-end encryption. I bet he used whatever his operating system came with. It wasn't like he was trying to make the drive spy proof. Remember, he had it with him to deliver. He probably only wanted a password in case he left the damn thing on a bus."

Victor remained silent. The broker had succeeded and he hadn't. He thought about Norimov and what the

Russian security services could be doing to him in a room without windows to make him talk. Maybe he was dead already, shot in the back of the head, revenge for the agents Victor had killed.

Victor made a promise to himself. To repay Norimov if he was still alive or avenge him if he was dead. He pictured a man's face. Around forty, pale skin, dark eyes, square jaw, authoritative. The man who had escaped the van before it exploded. Even if it took years Victor would find him.

He noticed the broker was staring at him.

He ignored her gaze and stepped closer. She opened one of the files and moved aside to let Victor see the monitor more clearly.

The broker said, "It took me forever until I figured out what I was looking at."

There was a picture filling the screen, some kind of computer-generated image, mostly blue with a grid, lots of numbers. A pixelated form lay in the center. The broker clicked a button and another appeared. Victor stepped toward it tentatively, the light from the computer reflecting in his eyes.

"What are they?"

FORTY-EIGHT

Moscow, Russia
Monday
23:05 MSK

"They're sonar pictures," Colonel Aniskovach answered.

He stood before Prudnikov's ridiculously large and phallic-enhancing desk. It was big enough for several computer terminals, but aside from the photographs, a modest flat-panel monitor, keyboard, and mouse, the desk was empty. Prudnikov sat behind the desk in an ergonomic leather chair.

They were in Prudnikov's office at the headquarters of the SVR. The building was the high-tech replacement to the KGB's former Lubyanka headquarters in Dzerzhinsky Square in central Moscow, now home to the FSB. The SVR headquarters was located in Yasenevo, on the outskirts of the city, and its passing resemblance to the CIA's Langley headquarters was no mere coincidence.

Aniskovach disliked the tasteless CIA-cloned headquarters at Yasenevo and would have preferred to spend his time at Dzerzhinsky Square. The old building was a masterpiece of beautiful Russian architecture that before the revolution housed an insurance company of all things.

The head of the SVR studied the photographs for a moment. "And what are they showing me?" he asked.

The tone of his voice lacked in patience. It was late to be working, even for spies.

Aniskovach wore his best suit, his tie razor straight, shoes polished to a mirrored shine. Every hair on his head was faultlessly combed. The horrid wound on his face couldn't be bettered, but at least the dressing covered it, and it showed his life had been endangered—even if now it meant he hated to look in the mirror when once he had reveled in it. He had made an appointment to see a cosmetic surgeon in Germany next week.

"The pictures show a sunken ship," Aniskovach answered. "From what my people tell me it has the dimensions of a frigate, a missile destroyer to be more precise."

Prudnikov shifted through the images and didn't look up. "Why am I looking at it?"

"Because the frigate is one of ours."

That made Prudnikov look up.

Aniskovach was a strong believer in the importance of the dramatic arts when delivering reports and especially when making requests. Simply telling and asking were usually enough to achieve the necessary goal of the discussion, but the outcome of almost any conversation could be improved with the proper implementation of timing and delivery. Aniskovach was very much aware he needed both working for him faultlessly if he was going to salvage his career.

The fiasco in St. Petersburg had made the headlines in the evening papers and was the biggest news story on Russian television, despite the SVR's best attempts to limit the damage. Dead bodies and exploding vehicles in broad daylight tended to get noticed. In one day

Aniskovach had been responsible for the loss of five lives and the hospitalization of another three. He felt it grossly unfair that he should receive any blame considering the circumstances. The operation wasn't officially sanctioned, and it had been a personal favor for Prudnikov. Which was the only fact saving Aniskovach.

The head of the SVR had even more to lose if the true motive behind the operation became known, and as such Aniskovach knew Prudnikov would do everything in his power to keep Aniskovach's head off the block.

How long that would last, Aniskovach didn't like to think about, but he knew it wouldn't be indefinite. Then the wolves baying for Aniskovach's blood would circle around him with teeth bared. He had fantasized about heading the organization on a number of occasions. Once it had seemed that one day his dream could realistically become a reality, but that was before he had gotten men killed, so many so publically. If he didn't fight for it, his reputation would be forever stained. He needed a victory and he needed one fast.

The only way he could hope to counteract the damage already done was with Prudnikov still on his side, but any alliance was tenuous at best and would quickly unravel the closer Prudnikov came to retiring. Unless he admitted his own role in the failed mission and exonerated Aniskovach in the process, Aniskovach knew his career was on borrowed time.

Once Prudnikov stopped protecting him and Aniskovach had to fend for himself, the best scenario he could hope for was to spend the rest of his SVR career sitting behind a desk doing mind-numbing analysis and pencil-pushing duties. He didn't want to think about the worst scenario.

"The frigate," Aniskovach began after an appropriate pause, "named *Lev*, was a missile destroyer built in 1984 that sank in the summer of 2008, not long after a joint naval demonstration with the Chinese. Her crew all lost their lives when she sunk."

"And?"

"The *Lev* was carrying eight Oniks antiship missiles."

There was a long wait before Prudnikov spoke again. "What happened to the ship?"

"A distress call was transmitted before she sank, wherein the captain stated there had been a catastrophic engine malfunction."

"This was confirmed by a recovery team?"

"There never was a recovery team."

"Why not?"

"A rescue team was sent, but it was reported that the destroyer had sunk in deep water, and recovery of the vessel and its armaments would not have been possible."

Prudnikov took off his reading glasses and placed them carefully on the desk. "The tone of your voice suggests you are unconvinced by that analysis."

"The captain of the rescue vessel that responded to the *Lev's* distress call was an officer by the name of Andris Ozols."

"That name means nothing to me."

"Ozols, who was retired, was murdered in Paris a week ago. He was carrying a portable hard drive that contained the pictures you're now looking at."

Prudnikov was looking at him attentively now, nearly hanging off his every word. "Go on," he said.

Timing and delivery, Aniskovach told himself. "The killer who met with Norimov and whom we attempted to apprehend, was in possession of the drive. He has the original. Those pictures were taken from a copy that our people decrypted earlier."

"What exactly are you telling me?"

"I would say that Ozols was planning to sell the information when he was killed."

"But what value does this information have if the ship is unrecoverable?"

"None."

"So why are we having this discussion?"

"Because Ozols lied in the original report. The destroyer sank on a continental shelf according to the coordinates shown in those sonar pictures. Off the coast of Tanzania in the Indian Ocean. It appears that Ozols fabricated the initial report so a recovery team would never be sent, allowing the missiles to remain on the seabed until he was ready to sell the ship's location to the highest bidder. Most nations would pay a fortune for those missiles and the technology they contain."

Prudnikov's eyes were as big as Aniskovach had ever seen them.

Aniskovach continued. "On the day Ozols was killed a mass killing also took place. Some eight people killed in addition to Ozols. According to Norimov the assassin was himself attacked by a team of other killers."

"What is the relevance of that?"

"I believe the killer was hired to retrieve the information but was targeted after completing the job by the same people who hired him. The motive for such an attack would likely be to keep the identities of those who employed him anonymous. This would be of particular benefit if those employers were, say, members of the CIA." He paused for effect. "The Americans would then be able to recover the Oniks and add the technology to their own inferior missiles. At the same time they would be able to deny any part in Ozols's death once we became aware of his identity and what he was up to. My sources in Paris inform me there has been much activity at the U.S. embassy this last week. Without the flash drive they won't know where to look for the missiles, but if they find the assassin first . . ."

"I need to pass on this information to the GRU straightaway." Prudnikov sat back in his chair. "I will make sure your name is mentioned when I do. You may leave now."

Prudnikov reached for his phone. Aniskovach remained standing.

"Did you not hear me, Gennady?"

Aniskovach, ever the showman, stayed silent for a few moments. "There is another possible course of action."

"Such as?"

"We recover the missiles ourselves."

Prudnikov's brow furrowed and he picked up the phone. "I have no need of the credit."

"I do."

The head of the SVR shook his head. "I gave you your moment to be a hero and you let the chance slip through your fingers. And got many good men killed in the process. What makes you think I would give you a second opportunity?"

"Those men were killed on a mission you personally requested."

"Be careful of your tongue, Gennady." Prudnikov's eyes were dangerous. "Do I need to remind you of the stain to my reputation I'm taking in defending you?"

"I only remind you because I know you are risking a lot to help me survive the backlash." Aniskovach missed out the important fact that Prudnikov had done so only to help himself in the process.

Prudnikov nodded. "I'm only doing what is right."

Aniskovach wanted to smile. Appealing to Prudnikov's deluded sense of duty and honor was a good tactic. "And I thank you for all you have done, sir."

Prudnikov accepted the thanks without his expression changing. "What are you asking?"

"Let me recover the missiles myself."

"For what purpose?"

Translated to, "what's in it for me?" Aniskovach thought. "Exposing Ozols's plans, recovering the missiles, and stopping the Americans from getting hold of them will help repair my reputation within our fine organization."

Prudnikov, unconvinced, started punching numbers on the phone. "If I were you I should not be so concerned with what's left of my reputation. I would be glad to have escaped incarceration and still have a career after such a disastrous mess."

Aniskovach continued as if Prudnikov had never spoken. "And by recovering the missiles and keeping them from the hands of our enemies I will have done enough so that I no longer require your protection. You would be able to distance yourself from my failing without fearing I will betray your hand in what happened."

Prudnikov stopped dialing. Aniskovach watched him reconsidering carefully. After a minute he put the phone down.

"Fine," he said. "I will let you do this one thing, but this is where we part ways. Regardless of the outcome, I stop protecting you, and you keep your mouth permanently closed."

Aniskovach had expected that at best he would receive such an offer. He just wished he could tell Prudnikov how he had managed to twist his own appeal completely around so that it was Prudnikov making the request to him. He stood in silence, pretending to weigh up the offer, and in doing so created a delicious measure of dramatic tension. Aniskovach nodded.

"We have a deal," he said.

It was all timing and delivery.

FORTY-NINE

Paris, France
Monday
21:01 CET

Victor looked away from the photographs. The broker was standing again, and he'd adjusted the computer and positioned himself so he could see her, the screen, and the front door at the same time while they talked. She was still frightened of him and was still trying to hide it. He could tell she didn't know what he was going to do at any moment. He liked it that way.

"So whoever hired us wants to get their hands on that ship," Victor said.

The broker nodded. "Or what's on it."

"Weapons?"

"Who knows?" she shrugged. "But whatever's on that ship is worth killing for."

Victor remained silent.

"Are you thinking about checking it out? Because if you are, according to the coordinates, the ship is off the east coast of Africa. Tanzania, I think."

"No. What's on the boat isn't my concern. We stick to the plan. We eliminate our enemies. Self-preservation. Nothing else matters."

"Okay," the broker said. "But we're getting somewhere. You could at least try looking happy about that."

"This is me looking happy."

"Then I really don't want to see you when you're mad."

"No," Victor said. "You really don't."

She smiled. She looked good smiling.

The lamp flickered and then went out, plunging the room into semidarkness. Light from the city found its way through the drapes.

"Damn wiring," the broker muttered. "Nothing works properly in this place."

"Shut up."

It wasn't just the lamp. The laptop screen had dimmed, switching to battery power. Victor saw nothing at the bottom of the front door. The lights were off in the hallway too. He grabbed the phone from the sideboard. No dialing tone.

In a second her hair was clutched in his left hand, the Benchmade knife in his right, the point of the black steel blade pricking the skin of her neck, carotid artery flexing beneath the pressure.

"You brought them here."

The whites of her eyes were large. "No, I swear."

The fear was real. So was the surprise.

Victor believed her. "Then they've been watching."

"That's impossible. I was careful."

"Then you weren't careful enough."

Victor released her and hurried over to the door. He pressed his ear against it, hearing nothing. He faced the broker.

"Where's your gun?"

She had a palm against her neck. Tears were in her

eyes. She hesitated. "I told you last time I haven't got one."

"You hid one in case you decided to kill me. Where is it?"

Silence, then, "Under the sofa cushions."

"Get it."

She did.

"Give it to me."

She tentatively held it out and Victor snatched it from her hand. A compact HK P2000. He released the mag, checked it was loaded, slammed it back in, and pulled the slide to chamber a round. He flicked off the safety.

He looked around quickly. The front door was the only viable entry point for an assault. Even now they could be in the corridor outside preparing to do so.

Victor pointed. "Grab as many things as you can and barricade that door."

He dragged the sofa across the room with one hand. The broker picked up the armchair and placed it on top. He took the table where the lamp had stood and threw that on as well. The barricade wouldn't stop anyone, but it would slow them down.

"Follow me."

The broker hesitated. "My computer . . ."

"If it's not going to save your life, leave it."

"I've got hard copies, but we need those files."

She grabbed a shoulder bag and slung it, before opening a drawer and fumbling inside it. She removed her hand after a few seconds with a memory stick between her fingers. She plugged it into the laptop and copied a folder across.

"I'm setting the computer to wipe the hard drive."

"Hurry."

The instant she'd finished, Victor led her into the kitchen, took her by the shoulders and guided her to where he wanted her to stand.

"What are you doing?"

He then wrenched the string to pull up the blinds and shoved the broker out of the way of the window.

She grunted, fell, but the window was still intact, the wall opposite unmarked. No sniper.

The broker scowled. *"What the hell was that for?"*

He didn't answer her, opened the balcony door, stepped out, looked around. There was a drainpipe. If it was strong enough, it would take him straight down to the ground in less than a minute. He grabbed it, pulled sharply. It moved, but not much. It would do for the short time it would take.

Victor turned and saw the broker pulling herself upright and knew there was no way she would be able to climb it. He hated having to compromise his course of action to take into account the abilities, or lack thereof, of another. He had to find a different way.

There it was. At the end of the building a black metal bar protruding from around the corner. A fire escape. There were two more balconies between them and it. Victor turned to the broker.

"Take off your shoes."

"Why?"

"If you want to live just do as I say."

She kicked them off and he pulled her out onto the balcony. He pointed.

"I'm going to jump across." He tucked the HK into the front of his waistband and climbed onto the rail, holding onto the drainpipe for support. "When I'm over there I'll reach back for you."

She shook her head violently. "What? No way, I can't do it."

"Then you stay here and die. Either way I'm gone."

He was glad she had a cheap apartment; there was only a gap of a few feet between each balcony. If he had no other choice, he could do a standing leap from the railing to the next balcony. But the railing was wet. If he pushed off too hard, there was a chance his shoes might slip and he could fall. He looked down. It was a long way.

Instead of jumping, he stood on the railing, body twisted, facing the wall. He gripped the drainpipe hard with his left hand and reached out with his right leg until his foot touched the railing of the next balcony.

Victor extended his right arm as far as it could until he had a grip on the brickwork above the other balcony. He then pulled with his right arm and pushed off with his left leg. His left foot touched the railing just in front of his right.

He looked back to the broker. "Come on."

The broker climbed up onto the railing the way he had done, only painfully slowly. Her breathing was heavy. He could see her fighting not to look down.

He reached out to her. "Give me your hand."

"*Oh God.*"

"He can't hear you. Now give me your hand."

She reached out a shaking hand across the gap. He grabbed her wrist hard.

"You're hurting me."

"Then you won't fall. Leave your left foot on the railing and reach out with your right. I'll keep you steady."

She stretched, but couldn't reach her foot all the way across. "*It's too far.*"

"It's not. When I say, push off hard and I'll pull you the rest of the way. Okay?"

"Yes."

"Are you ready?"

She nodded.

Victor tightened his grip. "*Now.*"

He pulled hard, and she pushed, but she lost her balance, and her left foot slipped. She cried out. Victor grunted under the strain but managed to swing her into the railings. She banged into them—crying out—but he heaved her up, and she scrambled over them, finally collapsing onto the balcony.

She lay gasping on the wet stone, eyes squeezed tight. He dropped down beside her and pulled her up by the armpits. He climbed up onto the railing on the far side.

"Same again," Victor said. "And then it's not so easy."

A figure turned into the hallway, his eyes staring down the iron sights of his MP5SD submachine gun. He was dressed in black combat fatigues, heavy Kevlar body armor, tactical harness loaded with grenades and spare magazines. A handgun was strapped to his right thigh. Over his eyes protruded night-vision goggles.

Four identically equipped men followed fluidly down the corridor, each covering a different field of fire, no one crossing the path of another's weapon.

They reached the target's apartment, taking up their positions, one on either side of the door, the others spaced out along the hallway, waiting for the ram to be brought over. The bearer was 240 pounds of muscle and temper and he hurried down the corridor, ram held in both hands. Sixty pounds of black steel with a crude white skull painted on the business end.

He stopped in front of the door, saw his commander give the hand signal, and swung the heavy ram back.

Victor heard the crash as he crossed to the second balcony. The broker, still on the previous balcony, startled at the sound, immediately pressed herself harder to the wall, clearly terrified.

Victor pointed. "Get onto the railing."

"I can't."

"Do it."

The broker shook her head. "*I can't.*"

She'd barely made the first one without the pressure of enemies bearing down upon them. It would be even harder now. There wasn't enough time as it was. He looked to the jutting bar of the fire escape. He could get to it or take a drainpipe and be on the ground in thirty seconds. But it would take minutes to get away with the broker slowing him down. Minutes they didn't have.

It would be so easy to abandon her. His instincts told

him to leave her and just go. What else could she really know that would be of any use to him? A lot was the answer. But together they wouldn't make it. She'd heard his voice, seen his face, knew more about him than probably anyone alive, and that was before they'd actually met. Victor couldn't allow her to be taken.

He looked at her. Her eyes were still closed. Victor drew the HK and leveled it at her head, took a breath. Held it. But didn't fire.

He kicked open the balcony's French window and charged through even as shards of glass were still falling away. He hurried through the apartment's kitchen, into the lounge. The layout was identical to the broker's rental two doors down.

Victor peered through the spy hole into the corridor outside. There was just enough light from a window farther along the hallway for him to make out the black-clad figure standing directly in front of the door. He could discern the shape of the MP5, the bulk of the bullet-proof vest, the edges of the night-vision goggles.

Victor took a deep breath. Assassins with pistols were one thing, a fully armed and armored tactical team was another. He could hear the grunts and crashes as more were trying to fight their way through the barricaded door farther along the corridor. They were assaulting the wrong room, had no idea he wasn't there.

If he was going to do something it had to be now.

Victor flicked the latch, flung open the door, grabbed the stunned gunman by the arms, and pulled him into the room. He was taken completely by surprise, didn't even cry out. Victor swept his feet out from under him and smashed the butt of the broker's handgun into the floored man's jaw.

Victor slammed the door shut again, locked it.

The other gunmen in the corridor heard the noise, spun around, saw that one of their own was no longer there.

"*What the fuck was that?*"

"Shit, shit, he's got Xavier."

"He's in a different fucking apartment."

"Withdraw, withdraw, he's in 305."

In the broker's apartment the gunmen withdrew before they'd completed the search. They hurried back out into the hallway, taking up new positions to assault the target's apartment.

"Right," the commander whispered. "Let's nail this fucker."

Victor wedged a chair under the door handle and grabbed stun grenades from the gunman's tactical harness, stuffing them into the pockets of his jacket. He took a handful of spare magazines for the suppressed MP5.

The guy on the floor was out cold, face bloodied. Victor pulled the night-vision goggles from him and put them on. His vision became a pixelated green blur. He took the sidearm and gave the unconscious man two swift kicks to the head to make sure he wasn't going to wake up anytime soon. If he fired a shot the team would assault immediately. As it was, he had a few seconds while they readied themselves and composed an ad hoc plan to rescue one of their own.

He recognized the insignia the man wore on his uniform and drew a breath of relief. The gunmen weren't CIA but French police, members of Recherché Assistance Intervention Dissuasion, or RAID, the French police's counterterrorist unit. Maybe they'd had the broker under surveillance or he'd been spotted at the airport and followed. Or maybe a civilian had recognized him and called it in. Either way he was paying the price for coming back to Paris.

With the MP5SD in hand, Victor ran back through and out onto the balcony. He grimaced for a second, looking straight at a street lamp across the road, the goggles magnifying the light to uncomfortable levels. He saw the broker was as he had left her, pressed up against the wall on the other balcony, trying not to hyperventilate.

Victor stood up on the railing and leaped back to the next balcony, then did the same again to take him back to the first. His foot slipped on the railing, but he grabbed the drainpipe to stop himself from falling, dropping the MP5 to do so. He breathed a sigh of relief when the gun landed on the balcony.

He scooped it up and hurried through the kitchen and into the lounge. He had the weapon up in both hands, the stock pressed firmly into his shoulder, his eyes looking straight down the sights, his head and gun moving in unison.

The sofa, desk, and chair were broken, pushed to one side of the door. There were no RAID guys in the lounge. They were outside in the corridor.

Preparing to breach the wrong room.

Again.

FIFTY

Two stood to one side of the door ready to go in, a third and fourth waited on the other side, the commander had a pump-action shotgun in hand, ready to blow the hinges off the door with Hatton rounds. The ram had been abandoned.

The shotgun-armed commander held up five fingers, then four, three, two . . .

Something rolled into the corridor from the apartment they'd just left. Something metal.

Through the grainy-green night vision it took the commander a second to realize what it was. When he did he inhaled to scream a warning. It was too late.

The stun grenade exploded with an excruciatingly loud bang and an incredible flash of light.

The gunmen started yelling, blinded, disorientated, senses overloaded. One dropped his gun, another stumbled backward down the corridor, bumping into walls, trying to get away. The commander screamed for his men to hold their positions, but his ears were ringing so much he couldn't even hear his own voice.

Amid the chaos Victor stormed out of the broker's apartment and into the corridor, emerging through the stun grenade's smoke, MP5 raised, set to three-round burst. He squeezed the trigger ten quick times, the MP5 making a series of rapid clicks, his aim shifting as targets fell. He aimed for faces and guts, where the heavy body armor offered the least protection. The gunmen appeared out of the darkness with each shot, illuminated for an instant by the strobelike flickers from the MP5's muzzle flash. Bodies flailed and contorted. Blood misted in the air.

Within three seconds the breach on Victor's MP5 had blown back for the last time, and all four gunmen lay slumped in the corridor. The smell of cordite and blood filled his nostrils. Smoking shell casings crunched underfoot.

No one was moving, so he reloaded and slung the MP5 over his shoulder. He grabbed the commander's shotgun and used it to blow the lock off the door to the apartment next to the broker's rental.

Victor threw the shotgun away and kicked open the door. He ignored a terrified Algerian woman huddled with two children in a corner and moved through into the kitchen. He opened the balcony door and grabbed the broker by the arm. She screamed for a moment until she realized it was him.

"Come on," he said. "We're leaving."

Victor dragged her back into the kitchen and out into the corridor. She took a sharp intake of breath, stumbling over the bodies of the four gunmen.

"*Oh Christ.*"

"Hold it together; there'll be more of them. Stay directly behind me."

Victor had the MP5 back in hand and the broker's gun in the front of his waistband. He led her through the corpses and down the corridor toward the elevator.

He hit the button and the door opened. Stepping inside, he pressed for the ground floor and stepped back out. The broker was left standing in the elevator.

"Out," Victor ordered.

"What?"

He grabbed her wrist and pulled her back into the corridor. The doors closed behind her. Victor headed back toward the stairwell, moving quickly, staying to the right, his shoulder brushing the wall.

"The elevator . . ." the broker said.

Victor ignored her, led her quickly to the stairs. He pushed her against the wall next to the stairwell door.

"Stay here."

He squatted down in front of the door, gun ready in his right hand. He reached up and opened the door with his left, peering in. The stairwell was empty.

"Come on."

He rushed down the stairs, gun up, pausing at each floor to stop, listen. The broker followed him closely. Victor stopped on the first floor, opened the door into the corridor, and guided her through.

The broker looked back. "This isn't the bottom."

"I know." Victor didn't slow down. "Stop talking."

He could hear heavy footsteps rushing up the stairwell below. Victor pulled the pin from another stun grenade but kept the striker lever pressed down. He wedged the grenade behind the door handle so that the lever was held in place. At least until the door was opened.

Victor hurried along the corridor to a window at the opposite end of the building. He smashed it with the butt of the submachine gun and knocked out the shards of glass left. He climbed through, dropped.

He landed in an alley ten feet below, in a crouch, immediately going into a roll, absorbing the impact through his whole body. The soles of his feet stung, but there was no injury. He came to his feet, turned, looked up. The broker was leaning out the window.

He gestured. "Let's go."

"I—I can't; it's too far."

"Don't jump out, just drop. When you hit the ground, roll. Do it."

"I can't."

Victor turned around, opened a Dumpster, grabbed half a dozen refuse sacks, and threw them underneath the window.

"Come on."

She took a breath. "I'll break my legs."

"In five seconds I'm gone. Now do it."

She did, landing awkwardly, feet first, falling backward. The trash bags burst but slowed her fall. She groaned, tried to stand, failing and fell backward. Victor extended a hand over her and she took it. He heaved her onto her feet.

"I think I've sprained my ankles."

"You can stand so you haven't. Move."

A small explosion made the broker startle.

She looked up toward the window. Victor didn't react, moved to the mouth of the alley, and pressed his back to the wall, listening. The noises of any street: cars and pedestrians. He pulled out his wallet, taking out a matte-black metal tube with a small spherical mirror attached to the end. He extended it out, held it up and looked in the reflection.

There were several vehicles outside the front of the building, two assault-team vans, four marked police cars, three unmarked. There were around a dozen figures, some suits, some uniformed officers.

He grabbed her by the wrist and hurried to the opposite end of the alleyway. He used the mirror again to look round the corner. One marked car. Two officers. Much better.

"Listen." He pulled the broker closer. "They're outside. As soon as we leave this alley they're going to see us."

"What are we going to do?"

"You have a car?"

"I rented one, but it's a block away at least."

"That doesn't matter. I'll go out first and get their attention. They'll come after me. Thirty seconds later you get to the car and get out of here."

"What about you?"

"I'll think of something. Here." He took out a newly purchased phone and gave it to her. "Get out of central Paris. Keep the phone on. I'll call you."

"We shouldn't split up."

"This is the only way."

"There must be something else we can do."

"If you have a better plan, now's the time to tell me."

She shook her head meekly.

He grabbed her by the shoulder. "You understand what you're doing?"

She nodded.

"Then say so."

"I understand."

He dropped the MP5SD. It was a shame to be parted from it, but his objective was to get away, not have a running gun battle. And walking around with an 800 rounds-per-minute submachine gun wasn't the best way to go unnoticed.

Victor gave the broker her gun back. "Just in case." He still had the knife, a 9mm SIG P-228 with a full mag and a single stun grenade. Not much if he ran into more guys in body armor with submachine guns, but it would have to do.

"Thirty seconds after I've gone, you go. Count the seconds."

He stepped out of the alley and ran.

He heard the first shout as he reached the middle of the road, heard the shot when he was on the opposite side of the street. A chunk of brickwork blew out of a nearby wall.

Across the road, Victor ran straight for a side street too narrow for the cars to drive down. They would have to chase him on foot. He ran down the alleyway, dodging around trash cans, boxes. He hurried around a corner, took another immediately, finding himself in a wide back alley that ran between a line of stores. He headed straight down its center, veered off as soon as another way appeared.

On a main street he slowed to a jog to avoid attracting too much attention. One of the best ways to find someone trying to run away was to follow the trail of confused pedestrians looking over their shoulders. He made his way around the block, doubling back to the broker's street. If anything they would expect him to run farther away. The last thing they would expect him to do was head back.

On the same side of the road as the broker's apartment he headed down a side street, cut across a main road, dodging around the slow-moving traffic. On the other side he took another alley, emerging from it into a casual walk across the next road.

Four blocks later he found a late-night café full of noisy patrons and sat down at a table with a good view of the window. As he waited he kept his eye on the alley he'd come out of, but no one came that way. No one he recognized passed on the street outside. He'd lost them. By the time a waitress arrived at his side his pulse and breathing had returned to normal.

"Ice tea," he said, when he was asked for his order. "With lime if you have it."

FIFTY-ONE

23:03 CET

He called the broker. She gave him the name of a bar and its location on the outskirts of the city. He hailed a cab, told the driver the destination, but had him stop a couple of blocks away. It could have been any low-income Parisian neighborhood. Winding streets seemed to blend into one another. Quiet.

He circled the block where the bar was located a couple of times, checking for anyone waiting who looked out of place. If the broker had been successfully shadowed before, she could be so again. It was not the kind of area where people would choose to just sit parked along the curb. He saw no one.

The bar was a run-of-the-mill drinking house. Linoleum-covered floors, faded wallpaper, and a long polished bar, marked and scuffed from thousands of glasses and bottles. The broker was sitting in the corner, facing the door. He expected she did so in order to see him enter instead of to look out for any threats like she should be doing.

Victor sat down on a stool next to her, adjusting it so he could watch the entrance and see the broker without moving his head. She had smartened herself up, cleaned her face, and reapplied her makeup. She was dressed differently too. There was a shopping bag next to her feet.

"I got us both a vodka tonic," she explained, before adding with her eyes lowered, "I drank both though. Sorry."

"That's okay."

Two glasses stood in front of her on the table, half-melted ice cubes lay in the ashtray. She saw him looking.

"Unless I have a straw, I can't drink out of a glass with ice in it. They don't have any straws here."

Victor nodded as though it mattered. The broker was badly shaken up, that much was obvious. The adrenaline

was all gone, and she was getting her head around what
had just happened.

"First time you've been in a situation like that?" he
asked

"Yeah." She took a deep breath. "Do you ever get
used to it, people trying to kill you?"

"They weren't trying to kill us."

"It was still terrifying. And you know what I meant.
So," she said, "do you? Get used to it?"

"Yes," he answered, even though he'd wanted to lie
and say no. "You deal with it better each time."

"So I won't feel this bad if it happens again?"

"Some people deal with it more easily than others."

"Will I?"

Victor saw the fear in her eyes at what his answer
might be. He wasn't sure why, but he decided to spare
her. "I'm sure it will get easier for you."

The broker told him how she'd driven away without
a problem and wasn't followed. "I found a store that
was still open and bought some new clothes. I—"

"Let's just continue where we left off."

"We need to go somewhere else to talk."

Victor stood. "Okay, but we go where I choose."

The neon sign above the door announced the hourly cost
of the rooms. Inside, the lobby was dark and small, deliberately poorly lit. The short man behind what served
as a reception desk stared leeringly at the broker while
Victor counted out the money. A condom machine was
attached to the wall in the corridor outside.

The room was small and featureless except for the

double bed that took up nearly all the available space. There was a metal box next to the headboard that took coins to make the bed vibrate. Victor couldn't believe people really used those things anymore. Had they ever? The last time he'd witnessed one in action it had made him feel sick.

The broker was standing in front of the window, looking out of the half-opened drapes. Victor was about to tell her she shouldn't be doing that, but if there was a sniper out there, she would have been shot already.

She was nervously toying with the fabric. It didn't look thick enough to actually prevent anyone from peering through. Victor supposed that was the point, an extra thrill for those who used the room. He guessed the fact that the only eyes likely to be looking in belonged to pigeons would hardly matter.

"It makes my spine crawl just being here," the broker said, not turning around.

Victor closed the door behind him, locked it. That made her face him. "I don't care if you don't like being here," he stated without emotion. "No one will find us. These kind of places don't like to advertise who stays."

She didn't argue. He was right, and he knew she understood that. She folded her arms in front of her chest. He left the main light off and turned on a lamp by the bed. It had a thin red shade and cast a dim crimson glow over the room.

Neither talked for a moment.

The broker spoke first. "Back at my apartment, if they weren't trying to kill us, why did you kill them?"

He'd been expecting such a question. "Flashbangs work for a few seconds only."

She responded quickly, already knowing that fact. "But they had night vision. Surely they would have been blinded longer."

When he finally answered he didn't try to hide his displeasure at being questioned. "NVGs have a cutoff mechanism for bright light."

"Okay," she said eventually.

"If I hadn't killed them, we couldn't have escaped."

"But they were just cops, right? Good guys."

"It was either them or us," Victor said. "And they knew the risks when they signed up." He gave her a minute before speaking again. "What do we do now?"

She snapped out of whatever temporary anxiety or guilt had gripped her and straightened up. "Elliot Seif," the broker stated with surprising venom. "He's the first port of call."

The broker withdrew a computer printout from her shoulder bag. It was low res, black and white, a head-and-shoulders shot of a thin, suited man in his fifties or older. His forehead was a mass of deep lines, lips thin, eyes dark under bushy eyebrows. He looked like an accountant.

"Who is he?" Victor asked.

"An accountant."

Victor raised an eyebrow.

The broker looked at him closely. "Did I miss something?"

He shook his head. "Continue."

"Seif is a senior partner at a large financial firm in London, Hartman and Royce Equity Investments. He handled the account that paid me the money, which I in turn used to pay you."

"You're certain?"

"You're good at what you do. So am I."

She was good—Victor knew enough about her to know that. He trusted she knew exactly what she was talking about. Victor reached into his coat for his cigarettes and matches.

"Could you not do that?" the broker asked.

He looked up. "Sorry?"

"Can you not smoke, please?"

He hesitated for a moment, then put the packet back. "I'm trying to quit, anyway."

"You'll feel better for it."

"I don't so far."

She smiled briefly before getting back to business. "But Seif is just a stepping stone," she said. "He's a middleman, nothing more. A conduit for the money to provide an extra layer of protection for whoever's behind this. We have to know who owns the account that paid me, or we've failed before we've really begun." She paused to get her breath back, continuing after a moment. "And to do that I need access to his files."

"Can you outside line it?"

"An agency cryptography team and a supercomputer would help."

"Point taken."

"The transfer was done electronically. I'm guessing

from a front company or dummy corporation somewhere. Seif will have it on record. On a hard drive there'll be a name. That's all I need."

"Why not just speak to Seif?"

"I would be amazed if he knew where the money really came from and even more amazed if he knew where it went after it left his hands. And if he did, he wouldn't tell us."

"I can be very persuasive."

She stared into his dark eyes. "We don't need to go there."

"You mean you don't want to go there."

"That's right, I don't. It would be too difficult anyway. We'd have to snatch him, which can't be easy. And he could lie, send us in the wrong direction. We don't have time for that. Getting his files would be easier surely."

Victor nodded after a few seconds thought. "Then we'll break into his firm."

"If it's viable, but we're against the clock, so hopefully we won't need to. He's bound to have a laptop or PDA with client information. I don't need much to get us a lead."

"How long have we got to get this done?"

"They could be targeting Seif as part of the cleanup, so we have to get to him before they do. My control was dead within days of this op going wrong. I don't know how many other people are involved, but we've got to assume not many. So if we can't get Seif's files by to-morrow, then it has to be the next day at the latest."

"That isn't long."

"I can't do anything about that."

Victor's jaw flexed. It had been a statement, not a critique. It wasn't in his nature to complain. "With this short a time frame, there is no way I can take the computer from him without his knowledge."

The broker nodded, grudgingly accepting the implication.

"We'll need an appointment at Seif's firm for tomorrow," Victor said. "Plus his home address and every piece of pertinent information we can find on him."

"I'm seeing one of his associates at two thirty tomorrow afternoon."

"That was fast."

He caught the trace of a proud smile before she said, "Can't say I'm looking forward to it, though. I've got a thing about bad teeth."

"That's just a stereotype Americans like to perpetuate. Teeth are no worse in Britain than anywhere else. "

She shook her head. "Dammit."

"Excuse me?"

"I thought you might have said 'we' at some point in there."

"Why would I say that?"

"You wouldn't necessarily, but if you had it would have told me where you're from."

"You think I'm British?"

She shook her head. "Or you could have said it instead of 'Americans.' "

"So I'm American?"

"You speak like you're from the United States

sometimes, like a Brit at other times, transatlantic sometimes, too. Your accent switches all the time, though, so
I really don't have a clue."

"I move around a lot."

"I figured. But when we spoke on the phone, I'm
sure I detected an Eastern European accent in your English. But when we met, I thought I could hear a trace
of French. I'm guessing your accent reflects whichever
country you're in at the time."

"Very observant."

She smiled, shyly but proudly at the same time. "So
I thought I'd test you, see if you'd slip and give it away."

He liked her guile. "Better luck next time."

"Thanks, I'll make sure I'm more subtle."

"You'll have to be."

She was still smiling, as though they were just normal people talking, a man and a woman getting to know
each other, chatting easily. He reminded himself that
was a dangerous course of action. There were good reasons he had no one in his life. Now was not the time to
start letting his guard down.

He noticed her expression was different. She stared
at him.

"What?" he asked eventually.

"I didn't thank you for earlier. At my apartment."

"You don't have to thank me."

"You saved me. If not my life, my—"

His voice was hard. "We don't need to discuss it."

The broker's face changed. It looked like he'd hurt
her feelings. Victor told himself he didn't care why.

No one spoke for a minute. The broker reached into

the shoulder bag again and took out a file. She handed it to Victor without looking at him.

"Seif's dossier," she explained. "I'm sorry; it's all I could get in the time frame."

The file was a quarter inch thick. She had done a lot in just two days. He flicked through, surprised. Impressed.

"It'll do."

FIFTY-TWO

Falls Church, Virginia, U.S.A.
Monday
16:54 EST

Sykes climbed out of his Lincoln and gave the door a good, satisfying slam. He squinted against the low afternoon sun, pointed the key fob at the car, and watched as the indicator lights flashed twice. It was hardly necessary. Crime in this government and CIA-heavy part of the state was virtually nonexistent, even though over the river it was rampant, but Sykes was a cautious man. He just wished he had been more cautious when Ferguson had said those immortal words to him *How would you like to be rich?*

Yes had been the answer, hell yes. Sykes was on the last few zeros of his trust fund and didn't much like the idea of having to downgrade his lifestyle. But that had been then; now Sykes would be happy if he managed to stay out of jail. It was supposed to be simple. A retired Russian navy officer was selling the whereabouts of some extremely valuable missiles to the CIA. Kill him and steal the information. Have the killer killed to prevent the rest of the CIA from finding out who hired him. Recover missiles and sell them on the black market. On paper it had sounded easy, but everything that could have gone wrong had gone wrong.

Hunting an assassin around Europe while trying not to get busted by his own organization wasn't what Sykes had signed up for, and it certainly wasn't what he'd sold his honor for. Ferguson, old fearless bastard that he was, was hardly breaking a sweat. For him it was just one more messy operation in a lifetime of messy operations. Ferguson may have done this kind of illegal shit plenty of times before, but Sykes was as green to it as could be.

The air was still but cold. He could feel his insides jumping around all over the place. It was saying something that his stomach hadn't exploded yet. For the last week he hadn't dared leave home without a pocket full of antacids.

At the end of the drive was Ferguson's beautiful three-thousand-square-foot colonial. The house was nestled within four wooded acres and was in immaculate condition. Sykes took a heavy breath as he approached. If things had been bad yesterday, today they were desperate.

Ferguson opened the door. He was dressed casually in a polo shirt and slacks and did not look pleased at the interruption to his sandwich. Sykes couldn't remember the last proper meal he'd been able to finish that hadn't played murder with his guts. With a monogrammed handkerchief Ferguson wiped the corners of his mouth while he finished chewing.

"I figured you'd want to know straightaway," Sykes said.

"That sounds decidedly ominous, Mr. Sykes."

Sykes shifted his weight. He spoke in facts. "Tesseract returned to Paris a few hours ago. He met up with the girl, Sumner. There was a firefight. They're both gone."

There was an agonizingly long pause before Ferguson spoke. His voice was too calm and sent a chill along Sykes's spine. "You had better come in."

Sykes followed Ferguson into the hallway. It was the first time he had been in the veteran CIA officer's house. For some reason Sykes would have expected it to be cold inside, but instead it was almost uncomfortably warm. Sykes unbuttoned the jacket of his dove-gray suit and let it fall open.

Ferguson's house was sparsely decorated. A pure guy's place. He'd been divorced for at least ten years, and as far as Sykes knew there wasn't some crusty love interest. He noticed golf clubs near the door.

"What the hell has been going on?" Ferguson asked when the door was closed.

No foreplay then, straight to the ass raping.

"Exactly as I said. Tesseract was spotted in Paris. I'm not sure exactly how at this moment." Sykes cleared his throat. "He went to Sumner's apartment. Obviously we had no one on her after you had me redirect Reed after Hoyt."

Sykes was pleased to be able to pass the blame so early in the conversation.

Ferguson was silent for a moment. "Then what?"

"The French police tried to take him down. Needless to say, it didn't work."

Ferguson weighed the response for a moment. "I've just spent the afternoon teaching the director of national intelligence a lesson in the art of putting and this has somewhat soured my good mood." Ferguson pushed a hand through his hair. It was so thick Sykes used to think it was a wig. From the amount of hairs Sykes discovered each morning in the shower, he expected to be bald as a plucked chicken by the time he was Ferguson's age.

"This is the kind of complication we could have done without."

"We're still safe," Sykes offered, more to satisfy his own anxiety than Ferguson's.

The old guy huffed. "Thank you for that small assurance. I'm assuming we have more dead bodies."

Sykes nodded. "He killed three, two more are in the hospital. I don't know if they'll make it."

"What do the Frogs know?"

"As far as I know they don't know anything. They don't know why Tesseract was in Paris or who the girl was. The apartment isn't hers and the one in Marseilles was rented under an assumed identity, so they won't be able to connect her to the agency. Her cover is good. It should hold."

"Let's hope so," Ferguson said.

They stood without speaking for what seemed like a

long time. Sykes could almost see the wheels turning inside Ferguson's mind. When he couldn't stand the silence any longer, Sykes said, "I don't understand how Tesseract tracked her down."

"Have you heard anything about the police finding her body?"

"No."

"Then think again."

Sykes couldn't keep still. His fists were clenched down by his sides, knuckles white. "I don't understand."

"He didn't find her," Ferguson said.

Sykes was as confused as he looked. "What?"

Ferguson explained it for him. "Either he contacted her first or perhaps she contacted him, but that hardly matters. What matters is she realized she'd become a target so agreed to meet him."

"But why? And how did she know before Reed got to her?"

"Because she's smart. Tell me if I'm wrong, but that's why we used her."

"Yeah, but . . ."

"Maybe she's smarter than we thought. Maybe Kennard made a mistake and revealed his identity, so when he died she put two and two together. Or either of them could have become suspicious and deliberately broken protocol. Who knows?"

"I guess that makes sense."

"So," Ferguson continued, "she runs to her cousin's apartment in Paris, unaware that we know about it. She's frightened; she doesn't know what to do; she's got nowhere else to turn, and so she goes to Tesseract for help. Maybe offering to tell him what she knows if he gives her the drive. Either he's desperate and agrees or goes there to kill her and changes his mind and they decide to work together. She knows more, he's more capable, so each can help the other. I would say that's a pretty shrewd course of action."

Sykes frowned hard. He'd been frowning a lot recently. "So what are we going to do?"

"We sit back and wait," Ferguson said with annoying calm. "Either Tesseract will kill her as a precaution or maybe just for revenge once she's no longer useful. That'll solve one little problem if nothing else. Then Tesseract will disappear with the flash drive, and we'll never hear from him again. We won't get the missiles and we won't get rich, but we'll get to keep our freedom. Considering everything that's happened so far I would consider that a victory."

"Or?"

Ferguson walked out of the hall and into the spacious kitchen. Sykes followed.

"Drink?" Ferguson asked.

"I'll take a beer," Sykes answered after a second's deliberation.

Ferguson's thick eyebrows moved closer together. "I was thinking more like juice or water."

"I'll skip then."

"Suit yourself," Ferguson said. He opened the fridge and took out a carton of grapefruit juice. He poured himself a tall glass. "Or," he continued eventually, "they'll contact us and try and do a deal. I think this is more likely. They'll offer us the information if we leave them alone."

Sykes exhaled heavily. "Okay. And if they do, will we?"

Ferguson looked shocked. "Of course not, you idiot. Where's your head? No, we won't leave them alone. If we do this right we can manipulate their coming together to give us an opportunity to take them both out and retrieve the drive in one go. We get our hands on those missiles and come out cleanly."

"You really think we can still pull this off with everything that's happened?"

Ferguson stared at him with something approaching disgust. "I've got myself out of deeper holes than this, Mr. Sykes, and still managed to smell of roses."

"What about Alvarez?"

The old CIA man sighed as though the whole conversation was beginning to bore him. "Alvarez is nothing more than a Boy Scout. I've never thought particularly highly of him. All he does is follow the path of least resistance. Look, what's just happened is actually a good thing for us in a way. It'll give the idiots in the department some more wild geese to chase. And all the while they're being led farther and farther away from us. If Procter, Chambers, and Alvarez had a brain between them they would be looking for how someone could have found out about Ozols in the first place. Instead they're trying to do things the other way around. They'll never get anywhere that way. So keep your cool and this will all be over soon enough. And, with a bit of luck, when it is, there will be tens of millions of dollars waiting in numbered accounts for us both. I take it you still want to be rich? I know I do."

Sykes nodded his agreement. "I was thinking," he said, "it's almost a shame we've got to kill Tesseract. I mean, the fact that he's come this far shows how good he is. We could really use him on our team, couldn't we? He'd make a great asset. Maybe we could bring him on our side."

"I'll forget you said that."

Sykes swallowed the dry nothing from his throat. "Sorry."

Ferguson glared at him. "Have I not taught you anything, Mr. Sykes? Never apologize. Ever. At worst it's an admission of culpability, at best it just makes you look like a fucking chump."

FIFTY-THREE

London, United Kingdom
Tuesday
13:56 CET

Rebecca sat on a comfortable leather sofa in the reception area of Hartman and Royce Equity Investments, feeling a little nervous but confident those nerves weren't showing. Seif's company was located on the nineteenth floor of the striking Canary Wharf tower—fifty stories of glass and steel that loomed over the rest of London's skyline. The view was stunning. Rebecca concentrated on the glittering flow from the reception area's tranquil water feature and let the hypnotic reflection of light relax her.

The click of heels caused Rebecca to turn her head. Approaching her was the receptionist, Melanie, a stunning brunette with a delightfully friendly manner and a porn star's physique squeezed into a flattering pinstripe. Melanie had greeted Rebecca courteously, all big white smiles and practiced small talk, insisting on fixing her a coffee while she waited. Rebecca found it very hard to say no to her.

Melanie offered the espresso in a small china cup with a saucer. Rebecca took it and wasn't surprised to find Melanie made a killer espresso. Strong with just a hint of bitterness. Rebecca couldn't remember having a better one.

"That's fantastic, thank you."

"My pleasure." Melanie's glossy lips formed a smile. "Anything else you fancy, just let me know."

While Melanie walked back to her desk, stiletto's clicking and a certain strut to her walk, Rebecca wondered whether there was more to the offer than the obvious. No, couldn't be.

"She seems friendly," the voice in her ear said.

Rebecca brought the espresso cup to her mouth. "Very."

"I think she likes you."

"You jealous?"

She took a sip while she waited for his reply.

"Of what?" he asked after a moment.

"Nothing, it was a joke."

"I don't get it."

She sighed. "Never mind."

"Don't get on too well with her. We want her to forget you the second you walk out the door."

"Got it."

Rebecca sipped her espresso while watching partners and employees exiting the elevator after long lunches. Nobody gave Rebecca a second look as they passed through the reception, sometimes pausing for a word with Melanie on their way through. Rebecca was just another client or visitor. One of dozens of new faces that must appear every day. There was little need to disguise herself.

His voice came through Rebecca's earpiece again. "Still no sign of him yet."

"Okay," Rebecca said without moving her lips.

He was outside watching for Seif's return. He'd been in the area since the morning performing surveillance, observing Seif arriving, leaving for lunch. They'd left Paris in the early hours of the morning. Tesseract had stolen a car and driven them to Calais, where a ferry had taken them across the Channel. A train had brought them to London.

They traveled as a couple, even though her companion wasn't doing that great a job of pulling it off. Rebecca could tell he was used to operating alone and had limited personal experience to draw on. She was better, helping to pick up his slack, but she could tell he didn't like the physical contact it entailed. She expected he wasn't used to people touching him except those he had to pay to. He had tried hard not to let his unease show, and Rebecca did her best not to let on that she noticed.

He didn't trust her either, that was obvious, even if she had shown herself an ally, and it was hard to be a convincing couple when one partner was constantly looking out for signs of betrayal. Well, maybe looking out for signs of betrayal was part of being in a relationship, but Rebecca imagined most men worried more about their partners cheating than organizing their deaths. Thankfully the situation was only temporary. Rebecca wasn't exactly keen on his company either.

It was clear he disliked everything about what he was doing too, even if he didn't explicitly say. All his actions were controlled, and she knew that rushing his work was something he usually did everything to avoid. He preferred to plan his actions meticulously, the kind of operator who'd learned a long time ago that the more time spent on the drawing board, the fewer surprises in the field. Now he had to operate with half the facts in a quarter of the time.

His voice came through the earpiece again. "Okay, he's walking through the lobby now."

"Gotcha."

Two twenty PM and the elevator doors opened. A large man stepped out, his considerable bulk encased in a tight-fitting navy blue suit. He had a square face and a flattened, off-center nose, the legacy of a life of brawls. He wore a serious expression that matched his very serious build. Rebecca noticed he was wearing a gun under the left arm of his suit. In Britain he wouldn't be able to carry it legally, bodyguard or not. Tut, tut.

Following him came a man she recognized instantly as Elliot Seif. He was short and thin and looked just like he did in the Web site picture. His skin was heavily wrinkled and looked as if it didn't get to see much of the sun. What was left of his hair was combed over to the side. He carried a black leather laptop case.

After Seif came a second bodyguard, similarly sized and dressed as the first. Seif acted as though they weren't there, simply chatting away on his cell. The bodyguards walked at his pace, stopping when he stopped to exchange a few words with the receptionist, keeping his phone muffled against his chest as he gazed adoringly at her. Melanie flirted with him shamelessly.

Rebecca could feel the eyes of the bodyguards skim over her quickly, but she continued to read through the latest copy of *National Geographic* as if she didn't even know they were there. The article on elephant-seal migration patterns was fascinating, if a little on the condescending side.

Leaving Melanie faking a laugh, Seif continued on his way between his bodyguards. It was quite a statement to have not one but two personal bodyguards. Seif evidently felt a considerable need to protect himself, or perhaps the bodyguards were there more for show. Rebecca thought they probably made a good impression on certain less-desirable clients who no doubt had bodyguards themselves.

As soon as they had left she stood and turned toward the receptionist.

"Restroom?"

Melanie pointed in the direction Seif had gone. It was the only corridor. "That way, third door on the left—it's marked."

Rebecca smiled. "Thank you."

She walked with brisk, long strides, heading down the corridor, reaching the corner in time to see Seif and his bodyguards enter the last office at the end of the hall. The second bodyguard took up position outside the door, adopting a comfortable pose, legs slightly apart, hands clasped before him.

She imagined that while Seif was in his office there would always be a bodyguard outside the door. The bodyguard looked Rebecca's way but she was already heading into the restroom.

Back in the foyer Melanie caught her attention.

"Ms. Oswald," she began, showing an earnest look, "I've just had Mr. Brice on the phone. I'm afraid he's been unavoidably detained and won't be back today. He apologizes profusely for the inconvenience."

Rebecca looked disappointed. "That's a shame."

"Mr. Brice wonders if you'll be able to reschedule for later in the week."

"I'm flying back to New York tomorrow so that won't be possible." She paused for a second, pretending to think. "But when I'm here next month I'll make sure to book another appointment."

Melanie nodded. "Okay, I'll let Mr. Brice know."

"Good-bye."

"Good-bye, Ms. Oswald."

Rebecca noticed her expression change as Melanie slipped out of receptionist mode and into her real self. "And maybe when you're here next I can show you around the city. There are some fantastic sights to see."

Rebecca nodded, slowly, uncomfortably. "I can imagine."

She headed to the rendezvous point, a bar/café alongside the plaza outside of Seif's building. There were maybe a dozen tables outside and probably a dozen more between the plate-glass windows that served as the shop front. All the tables seemed to be occupied, men in suits, women in suits, the odd casually dressed person looking severely out of place and feeling it.

She'd tried to spot him as she approached, and even standing right outside didn't help. He'd specifically said he would be on a table out front. For a long horrible moment she thought they'd got to him, and she looked around frantically, sure she would be next. But instead she saw him nursing an espresso with a copy of some London newspaper open next to his cup. He hadn't seen her; his focus was purely on the newspaper, and she was glad he hadn't seen her panicking. She didn't call or gesture to get his attention, but stood observing him for a moment, enjoying the rare feeling of watching him in secret.

He turned over a page, took a sip of his coffee. In the sunlight he was almost handsome. She was surprised to find he looked so normal sitting alone with his newspaper, no different from the city workers surrounding him.

Rebecca reminded herself he was quite literally the exact opposite of normal and made her way between the tightly packed tables and people. She sat down across from him. A steaming espresso was waiting for her.

"Why were you watching me like that?" he asked without looking up.

"Oh, uh, sorry. I didn't mean to. It's just I didn't see you straightaway."

"If you had I'd need to consider changing my profession."

She wasn't sure if it was a joke or if he were serious. He tilted his head up to look at her. His expression showed nothing. It never did. He was as close to inanimate as she imagined a person could be.

"Seif takes his computer out to lunch with him," she said.

"Then he'll take it everywhere."

Rebecca said, "I think you can rule out the office as a strike point."

"Elaborate."

"There are a lot of employees and one of his bodyguards stands outside his office door, and he's not going to let you past in a hurry. I'm sure you could force your way past, but if anyone else enters the corridor, which is highly likely, they're going to see the two-hundred-plus pounds of meathead lying slumped on the floor."

"I wouldn't do it that way, but my way wouldn't be easy. The same bodyguard won't be posted there all day. The tedium would make him lose focus. They'll rotate, probably once every couple of hours. If they're smart, these times will seemingly be irregular and changed on a daily basis. There's no way of anticipating a change-over. How did Seif's bodyguards behave inside the office?"

"Alert, watchful, even with a hot receptionist to stare at."

He nodded. "They evidently paid attention during their protection class about the danger of complacency in familiar environments. If they didn't let their guard down in the office they won't anywhere."

"Then they're good."

He shrugged. "They're good and bad. Big and scary is great for pushing through crowds but makes them bulky and slow, but while they look like dumb apes they're armed and very observant. Seif didn't hire them just for show."

"You saw that they were carrying?

He nodded, showing no surprise, no alarm, nothing.

"Handguns?" she asked.

"Yes," he answered. "What were they wearing under their raincoats?"

"Suits."

She smiled. "You looking for fashion tips?"

"What kind of fit?"

"You *are* looking for fashion tips."

"Loose, tight, what?"

"Tight enough to need repairing if they bend over too fast."

He nodded.

"Is that good?" Rebecca asked.

"It might help."

"Listen, I really think this is a bad idea. If it was just

Seif it would be different, but these two guys change everything. They're like hawks, big mean hawks with guns. You won't get near him without them making you."

"If Seif is a target of the cleanup, I'll have to take any opportunity that comes my way. Seif owns a London apartment as well as the mansion in Surrey, right?"

"Right. We're going to have to split up," she said. "I'll reconnoiter his apartment, you his house. If he turns up at the apartment, I can call you. Either way, you can avoid the bodyguards. Stealth it."

"And how are your breaking and entering skills?"

She sighed. "Okay, good point. But what are we going to do now? We didn't anticipate he would have two armed guards."

She took a sip of her espresso. It wasn't a match for Melanie's.

The man she knew only as Tesseract said, "When you've finished that, I want you to wait a little while and get yourself a large cappuccino or something that you can drink slowly while you watch Seif's building. Let me know the second you see him leave. If he does, phone his office and ask to speak to him. They should tell you if he's coming back or not. If he's not, try and follow him, but better you lose him than one of his bodyguards sees you."

"Okay, but where are you going?"

"I'm going to get a gun."

"You have access to one in London?"

He looked at her. "Is that a question?"

"I knew where you lived, nothing more," she said. "If that's what you mean."

"It is."

"Whether anyone else does is another matter."

"Seif's bodyguards are armed, so it's a chance I'll have to take."

"It's still two against one."

His expression didn't change. "Poor odds for them."

"What exactly are you planning?"

"We don't know whether he's going to be at the house or apartment later, and, like you said, his office is out. That leaves one option."

"Which is?"

"I'll have to get to him somewhere between all three."

FIFTY-FOUR

Central Intelligence Agency, Virginia, U.S.A.
Tuesday
08:17 EST

Procter walked at a pace slightly faster than normal, which for a guy of his size and age wasn't an easy feat. He was late for the morning briefing and getting his fat ass into one of the skinny agency chairs three minutes late instead of four was his priority. He entered the elevator and rode it up to the top floor. He nodded and grumbled greetings to colleagues as he strode down the corridors. When he pushed open the heavy soundproof door to the briefing room, three sets of eyes looked his way.

"Sorry I'm late. Patricia's been up half the night with her head hanging over the toilet and looking like an extra from a zombie movie. I got stuck with the school run."

Chambers smiled and gave him a look that said no problem. For once she was looking a little rough around the edges. Ferguson and Sykes were sitting together on the opposite side of the conference table and looking like they were their own private boys' club. Procter pulled out a chair between the two camps.

There was some perfunctory small talk before Alvarez began his report.

"Last night, Paris time, agents from the French police's counterterrorism unit attempted and failed to apprehend a male suspect who they believe murdered Andris Ozols and seven other foreigners a week ago. During the attempt a shootout ensued that claimed the lives of several police officers and left others in the hospital."

"How sure are we that this suspect is Ozols's killer?" Chambers asked.

"The French certainly think so. As I understand it, an agent with the DGSE at Charles de Gaulle on other business identified the individual as he left passport control. He was put under immediate surveillance until he left the airport when he entered a taxi, after which he was followed around the city by a police helicopter. I doubt they knew for certain when he was first spotted at De Gaulle, but they wouldn't have tried to take him down if they weren't sure. And the fact that he shot his way out of a RAID assault definitely fits our guy's MO. I think there can be little doubt."

Procter asked, "What was he doing back in Paris?"

"That's yet to be established," Alvarez replied. "But he was observed entering an apartment occupied by a woman. That's where the RAID team attempted to take both persons into custody. It's unclear at the moment exactly how they managed to escape."

"I don't suppose that makes much difference," Ferguson muttered.

"At the moment those details aren't the most important point," Chambers said. "What I want to know is, Who's the woman?"

"The French claim she's an unidentified Parisian and not much else," Alvarez answered. "But they know a lot more than they're telling us. They're aware we weren't exactly forthcoming about Ozols, so until we enter a little quid pro quo I think we've reached the limit of what they'll tell us just yet.

"The authorities have managed to keep the press at bay so far, so we've got no intel that way, but a second major shooting in a little over a week is a pretty fucking big deal in that part of the world. More details might come out in the news. However, we've been lucky, and the NSA has grabbed us a few useful intercepts. According to the French Secret Service she's an American."

Procter, who had been looking out of the window, straightened in his seat. "An American?"

"Her name is Rachel Swanson, but the DGSE believe this is an alias."

"What else do we know about her?" Chambers asked.

"That's it so far."

Sykes asked, "Do we have anything to indicate why he met with her?"

"That's the question," Alvarez said. "Maybe she's his lover or just a friend, but I'm thinking business associate is more likely."

"Employer?" Procter asked.

"It's a possibility."

Chambers gestured to Procter: "I want to know everything there is to know about Miss Swanson, alias or not."

Procter nodded.

"In light of this Swanson development," Alvarez said. "I think we should check past and present CIA employees."

Chambers's eyebrows rose.

"Excuse me?"

"Something's been bugging me for a while now," Alvarez began. "We assumed that another prospective buyer for the missiles or the Russians had Ozols killed. But we can't dismiss that it's someone within our own walls."

"I've already had words with the director to make sure it wasn't us who put the contract out on Ozols," Chambers said.

"I'd dig anyway. Someone might be operating off the books. Before, there was no reason to suggest this was the case."

"And what is there now to suggest otherwise?" Procter asked.

"A hunch."

"A hunch?"

"My hunch, to be more specific. Sebastian Hoyt is dead."

Chambers leaned forward. "Say again."

"Hoyt, in case anyone has forgotten, paid the American hitman, Stevenson, that briefcase full of cash to kill Ozols's killer. He died of a heart attack on Sunday night while he lay in the bath. According to the autopsy, there are no signs that his death was anything other than natural, but it's a hell of a convenient coincidence for whomever Hoyt was working for."

Procter couldn't disagree. "I'll say."

"Chances are Hoyt was murdered simply as a precaution, but the timing of it, just after we found out his role in all this, makes me suspicious."

Ferguson shook his head. "Hardly enough reason to think we have a mole."

"I'm not saying we have a mole—maybe a leak, maybe a rogue operation running under our noses."

"Okay," Chambers said. "There's no harm in trying to find out if this Swanson is or was affiliated with us. I'll authorize full access to our personnel records, asset lists, and so on."

"And may I suggest that any information found goes no further than the people in this room."

"Of course."

Sykes tried not to shift in his seat.

FIFTY-FIVE

It was getting dark outside when Elliot Seif and his bodyguards reached the parking garage beneath the building. His spot was in an area reserved for the building's elite, and there were only a scattering of cars under the hard white glare of the fluorescent lights.

Seif would be arriving home late tonight. Work rarely kept him beyond his scheduled hours, but his latest mistress—the very young and very nubile Isabella—often ensured he missed dinner with his wife. After years of serial adultery, he was as discreet as ever and believed his wife still had no idea of his escapades. Although Seif could lie and mislead with the best of them in the boardroom, he was utterly unconvincing when lying to his wife. He knew it; she knew it; but they both pretended otherwise.

The smell of exhaust fumes hung in the air. There had been some ventilation problems earlier in the week, and it still wasn't quite fixed. Seif had complained on several occasions. It screwed with his asthma, and he needed every ounce of stamina his aging body could muster to keep up with Isabella's youthful insatiability.

He knew she was only his for the endless stream of expensive gifts he lavished on her, but Seif didn't care. He was well aware he had no charm to go with his frail body and wrinkled face, but a certain breed of woman found his wallet irresistibly erotic. Money, he had long ago discovered, was the world's number one aphrodisiac. He considered it perfectly fair that Isabella desired him only for his money as he wanted her purely for her tight young body. Above all else, Seif was a deal maker, and he considered theirs to be a very good arrangement.

The echoes of heavy footsteps interrupted the silence as the bodyguards stepped out of the elevator. They took the most direct route across the expanse of concrete, one bodyguard walking in front of Seif and to the right, the other behind and to the left. Under normal circumstances they could get Seif from the elevator to the car in under forty-five seconds. Seif never walked fast.

His bodyguards were alert. The underground garage was a dangerous space, but they knew it well. Their gaze constantly shifted between potential places of concealment where someone might be hiding. Just because they'd done the same thing a thousand times and more without incident didn't mean they ever got complacent.

Any face or vehicle they didn't recognize in the area was watched closely. More than once Seif had found himself apologizing on his bodyguards' behalf after they'd been rough with someone who'd made a seemingly threatening action. It may have been a ballpoint that time, one of the bodyguards had told Seif, but next time it might be a gun. Did he really want to wait to be sure? Better to apologize for a mistake than to die for one. Seif had readily agreed.

They were there for show more than anything else. Seif dealt with plenty of less-than-reputable individuals, some of whom were uncouth enough to try to intimidate their way into a better deal, or at least they would do so if Seif didn't have two mean motherfuckers in his corner. And if one day any of the Euromafia scumbags realized he was stealing their money, to get to Seif they'd have to get through five hundred pounds of pure badass first.

Neither of his bodyguards liked the location. It was designed to be as pleasant a space as possible with no mind to security. As such, it was full of blind spots that had to be watched with care. Still, it was far safer than an exterior parking area. In here they could protect their client.

At least that's what they believed.

The silver Merc SUV was parked at the far end of the garage in the most secure location. It had been reverse parked so that Seif, who rode in the back, had the bodyguards in front of him and the wall behind him when they were most vulnerable, as well as for a quick exit. In addition, the car was armored and all windows fitted with bulletproof glass by a specialist firm in Germany.

Seif gripped his mobile phone to his ear and gulped as he listened to Isabella describe in lurid detail exactly what she was going to do to him when he finally arrived at her apartment. The volume on the phone was turned high to compensate for Seif's poor hearing, and his bodyguards listened to every explicit word and groan Isabella uttered. They never let on that they could, except to each other.

The first bodyguard unlocked the car with an electronic key fob while Seif waited with the second bodyguard a few yards away. Alongside the driver's door, the first bodyguard peered through the windows before lowering himself into a press-up position to check underneath the SUV for explosive devices. The bodyguard had done it hundreds of times. It was boring, a pain in the ass. And a waste of time.

Suppressed gunshots echoed in the close confines of the parking garage.

The bodyguard collapsed onto his stomach, screaming.

There was a second of stillness before the other bodyguard went for his gun, struggling to pull it out from under his jacket. It was tight against his chest to better show off his muscles.

He yelled at Seif, "*GET DOWN, GET DOWN.*"

The bodyguard dropped to one knee, unsure where the shot had come from. His first instinct was to look behind them for the shooter.

Seif just stood there, open mouthed, unable to react, staring at his injured bodyguard. He was lying on the concrete, face down, right arm and leg thrashing around but his left limbs, those alongside the Merc, were bizarrely still. Seif realized the man had been shot in both his left arm and leg. He was too big, too heavy, and in too much pain to right himself. He tried to get his one good hand beneath his jacket, to his gun, but his arm was too bulky to squeeze beneath his chest. He was trying to speak, but he couldn't get his words out among his cries. Glistening blood crept along the ground.

The second bodyguard kept a tight hold on his own gun. He looked around frantically, eyes searching their surroundings, checking the likely points from which someone could have taken a shot. Aside from cars the place was empty. He could see no sign of any attackers. Where the hell were they?

He gestured to Seif. "Get back to the elevator. I'll—"

He cried out, bullets catching him in the knee, thigh, and ankle, rounds shattering bone and sending explosions of blood across the concrete. He fell backward, all thoughts of the .45 forgotten as he clutched at the bloody mess of his legs.

Seif hadn't moved. He looked on with horror at the two guys writhing around on the ground. He heard a noise, saw a man in a suit slide out from underneath the Merc and come to his feet. He was wearing a black ski mask. He had a gun. With a silencer.

Seif still had the mobile phone clutched to his ear, the incessant sexual drone of his mistress not missing a beat. His gaze was locked on the masked gunman. He couldn't move, couldn't talk, couldn't even think. He'd hired bodyguards so they could protect him from a day like this, but he'd never seriously entertained the notion that anything this bad might actually happen.

The gunman walked past the face-down bodyguard, who had given up trying to get his weapon, and now lay still and quiet, tilting up his head as much as he could to watch what was happening. The other bodyguard stayed where he was, on his back, face screwed up with pain. Blood soaked his trousers. He was trying to hold his splintered knee together with his left hand while his right stretched across the ground for his pistol.

Victor walked slowly toward Seif, angling his gun for a second at the guy reaching for his .45.

"Don't be stupid," Victor said.

The bodyguard pulled his hand back, and Victor kicked the gun away as he passed. He stopped directly in front of Seif, holding the handgun at arm's length, the end of the suppressor no more than an inch from the terrified accountant's face.

Victor's request was straightforward. "Computer."

His eyes unblinking, Seif didn't hesitate and raised his left arm up toward Victor. His right still held the cell phone to his ear. Victor took the computer from him.

"Password?"

"Isabella."

Seif was sweating. Somehow he managed to speak. "Is that all you want?"

On the other end of the phone his mistress thought he was speaking to her. She groaned louder. His eyes never leaving Seif's for an instant, Victor took the laptop from him with his free hand. He saw no harm in replying.

"What do you think?"

Seif gasped, trembled, misunderstanding. The phone fell from his fingers. "Don't hurt my family."

Victor didn't hesitate. "I wouldn't."

He gave Seif a moment to process the remark, stepped

back, lowered the gun, and turned around, watching Seif's and the bodyguard's reflections at all times on the Merc's bodywork. No one tried anything. Groans emanated from Seif's cell. Victor took another step, stopped, turned back, and shot the phone. It exploded into a thousand pieces.

He considered shutting up Seif's mistress for the price of a bullet to be money well spent.

FIFTY-SIX

Amsterdam, The Netherlands
Wednesday
21:37 CET

The hotel was popular with British tourists and run by a mostly British staff. There was a stag party occupying several rooms on the same floor, whose guests weren't inclined to respect the peace and quiet of other guests. This suited Victor perfectly. The more attention focused elsewhere, the less directed at the broker and him.

The city had been Victor's first choice when leaving the UK. Numerous flights and ferries transported countless Brits across the North Sea every day of the year. It was easy to slip out of the country among the crowd. Before going to the airport they had emptied Seif's laptop case. It contained his computer and its peripherals, several newspapers, and a film entitled *Naughty School-girls Must Be Punished*.

"I've seen that one," the broker said. "It's crap."

Victor did his best to keep his lips straight.

"I knew it," the broker said.

"Knew what?"

"That you could smile."

"Don't get used to it."

"I won't."

Her eyes were mischievous. He liked that.

They'd both slept during the day, and now he stood guard while the broker worked on Seif's computer. There were thousands of files on the hard drive, the complete financial records of dozens of companies, a huge amount of information. It was an electronic maze.

"We're looking for money," the broker had explained. "The transfer of money. The money to pay us came to Seif from one of these companies." She pointed at the huge list on screen. "One of those will have records that coincide with your previous contracts. You were always paid the same way, half before, half afterward."

"Correct."

"So we're looking for pairs of payments."

"It'll take hours going through all those files."

"Yes, it will," she agreed. "Do you want to do it for me?"

Victor shook his head. "I'll leave it in your capable hands."

"Thanks."

He stood to one side of the window, peering into the night through the slim gap between curtain and wall.

He could see the small parking lot, its entrance, and he watched those cars that arrived and the people who climbed out. They were couples mostly, no one he deemed a danger. He didn't have a weapon, and it played on his mind. If anyone came for them he had only his hands to defend himself.

Outside, Amsterdam was alive. The narrow streets were full of people, drinking and smoking and having a good time. There were cafés licensed to sell marijuana nearby, and with the window open Victor could smell the drug in the air. It made him remember long nights out on maneuvers.

"Why don't you try and relax," the broker said from behind him. "You freak me out just standing there."

"I can't relax."

"Why not?" she asked. "You can't really believe anyone's going to come for us here."

He didn't turn around. "I spend every day expecting to be killed," he stated. "Because the day I don't, will be the day I am."

She exhaled loudly. "Then you might want to re-think what you do for a living."

"What I do for a living is keeping you alive."

She went back to her work.

This part of the city, away from the infamous red-light district, was beautiful, even in the winter. The canals and quaint architecture made the city seem cozy and welcoming. Victor had visited a few times before, always passing through, never staying. He decided when this was all over he would make a point of coming back.

The clicking of the laptop keys had been a constant

background noise for the last two hours. The stag party had finally moved out into the city, and Victor found the quiet rhythmic clicking of keys soothing somehow, the sound relaxing, making his eyelids heavy.

Occasionally, in his peripheral vision, he saw the broker look up from her work toward him, but not with the watchfulness she had once shown. The broker talked a lot more, even though he responded infrequently. Now, when she looked his way the fear was gone, even if the wariness wasn't fully. She was less concerned with what he might do, more comfortable in his presence now. Victor wished he could say the same thing about her.

If it came to it, Victor told himself, he would kill her as painlessly as possible. She'd done enough to warrant that at the least.

He noticed the people in the crowd on the street below seemed to blend into one another, colors evening out. The sound of the broker typing became quieter. He realized his head had drooped forward, and he snapped it back in line with his spine.

"I need some air."

Victor headed for the door.

"Okay," the broker said, looking up.

He made a point of not looking back.

Outside the hotel he welcomed the night air. The street was noisy, full of people, and he let the flow of the crowd steer him until he found a bar he liked the look of. He went inside for a bottle of beer and drank it slowly while he walked back to the hotel. He wanted to stay out longer, to be on his own, but he couldn't leave the broker by herself for too long for both their safety.

Having a partner, if she could be called that, was not something he would get accustomed to any time soon. He'd worked alone for so long he felt strangled operating so closely with someone else. She wasn't used to this either; her field skills were basic at best. He had to use one eye to watch her back, leaving only one to watch his own. The fact that she was a woman, an attractive woman, didn't help either. She was the kind of distraction he wasn't used to having.

He took a swallow of beer and sidestepped to avoid a trio of cocktail-fueled young women stumbling along the sidewalk. They jeered at him as he passed, one offering herself in a less-than-sophisticated manner. He found it amusing and simply raised an eyebrow at her. They stumbled on laughing.

When Victor entered the hotel lobby he noticed the clock and realized he'd been gone far longer than he'd planned. He took the stairs to the second floor and approached their room. They each had an electronic key and had agreed that they would knock once and pause before entering. He did so and opened the door. She looked up from her work at him and they made eye contact. She half smiled at him. It made Victor feel uncomfortable.

"How long is this going to take?"

She didn't like his blunt tone. "I don't ask you to explain your methods," she said. "Please extend me the same courtesy."

Victor headed toward the bathroom. "I see you're developing a backbone."

She was just as sharp. "And I see you're developing a sense of humor."

Victor had briefly smiled then, despite himself, knowing she couldn't see it with his back to her, but he was quick to remind himself that she was just a tool. Nothing more. Just an aid to his own survival. No different from a gun. Useful, but to be discarded as soon as its usefulness was spent. Nothing good would come of his thinking about her in any other way.

He walked into the bathroom to splash some water on his face. He heard the broker's voice from the other room.

"You were gone a long time," she said.

He stared at his reflection. "I had a beer."

"You're joking," was her response.

Victor dried his face with a towel. "I don't joke."

"I didn't think you guys drank alcohol."

"You watch too many movies."

She said something else, but he was already closing the bathroom door and running a bath. He bathed quickly, reentering the bedroom dried and dressed.

He found the broker was leaning back in the chair, arms folded behind her head. She was smiling casually. It suited her.

"I've found it," she announced without fanfare. "The money was paid to Seif by an outfit called Olympus Trading."

"How do you know for certain?"

"Olympus has made some noteworthy transfers to

Seif recently. The latest one was a week before you killed Ozols."

"And the others?" Victor asked, seeing where she was going with this.

"A month before Ozols, what job did you do?"

"An arms dealer, in Sweden."

"Two payments were made to Seif at that time, one about a week before he was killed, and a second identical amount a week afterward. Do I need to go on?"

Victor shook his head.

The broker continued, "Whatever Olympus Trading is, it also doubles as the front company for whatever part of the CIA we're dealing with."

"A slush fund."

"Exactly. To pay for black ops."

"Maybe it only exists on paper."

"Looks genuine to me. And a real, functioning company is far better for washing money than a paper one."

Victor felt his body relax, happy, relieved, knowing they were one step closer to ending this thing. He showed no outward signs of this.

"We'll leave tomorrow," he said. "What's the destination?"

"Put it like this," the broker said with a grin. "You'll look good with a tan."

FIFTY-SEVEN

Washington, DC, U.S.A.
Wednesday
19:40 EST

Most people Ferguson knew of his own age were starting to really feel it, but Ferguson felt as fit and healthy now in his sixties as he did in his forties. He may have lost some weight with the passing years, but his body showed no signs of packing in on him anytime soon. He planned to enjoy a long and relaxing retirement, and, with a bit of luck, a very wealthy one. He pictured himself lazing on a beach in the Seychelles with nothing more troublesome to worry about than his tan lines.

Of course all that hinged on the thorny problem of cleaning up a rogue operation gone wrong. Ferguson had yet to be panicked by the events of the last week and a bit. He had faced both metaphorical and real bullets in his lifetime, and he saw this as just another awkward knot to slip out of. He was still two steps ahead of being found out. And he planned to remain so.

It was a short walk from his car to the memorial. He'd seen it up close a hundred times or more, but still it never failed to impress him. The huge Greek-style building that housed Lincoln's statue was brightly illuminated, and though it was almost eight at night, there were still dozens of people on the steps leading up to it.

Ferguson began ascending the steps, looking for

Sykes. He couldn't see him, but he supposed that was testament to the precautions they were both taking. Finally, more out of breath than he would have expected, Ferguson reached the top of the steps. Still no Sykes. Ferguson checked his watch. He would give him five minutes maximum, then call his cell phone.

He saw him after no more than three minutes. The man looked downright scared. It was clear to Ferguson that he had judged Sykes's mettle incorrectly. He had a sharp mind and a deft shrewdness for intelligence work, but he wasn't cut out to be involved in an operation where tangible risk was involved.

"Pleasant night," Ferguson said when Sykes reached him.

The younger man was taller, bigger built, and had on a thicker coat, but he looked far less comfortable in the cold evening. "Is it?"

Ferguson began walking, Sykes automatically following at his side. "We have a situation you need to be aware of, Mr. Sykes."

Sykes rubbed his hands together. "What situation?"

"Elliot Seif was killed earlier today."

"So? That's a good thing, right? Oh shit, did Reed screw up?"

"No, of course he didn't. The police believe Seif shot his wife and then turned the gun on himself. A domestic dispute gone wrong."

It took a few moments before Sykes spoke again. "Then what?"

"The day before Seif was killed, he was robbed."

"Robbed?"

Ferguson nodded. "Someone shot and wounded his bodyguards and took Seif's notebook computer."

Sykes processed the information for several seconds. "Tesseract?"

"I would think that a fair assumption."

"What the fuck happened?"

Ferguson walked at a slow pace. His small eyes moved from side to side, checking for anyone who looked out of place before he spoke.

"From what is in the police report it appears that someone got to Seif in the parking garage underneath his building. The robber wore a mask. No other witnesses, security cameras had been disabled, both bodyguards didn't so much as get a shot off. And Seif reported his computer had been taken. Nothing else, no wallet or watch, just his computer." Sykes didn't say anything. Ferguson stopped and faced him. "What information would Seif have on him?"

Sykes looked confused; he struggled to speak for a second or two. "I'm not sure what you mean."

"Tesseract didn't rob him to pass the time, and he didn't take his laptop as a souvenir. He took it for a reason. What can they do with it?"

Sykes shook his head. "I don't understand, why did he go after Seif at all? You said they would contact us to try and return the drive. You said they'd try and deal."

"Well," Ferguson began, "that's evidently not what they're doing."

"Then what the hell are they doing? I don't get it. None of this makes any sense."

Ferguson sighed. "Use your head, Mr. Sykes. Isn't it obvious?"

"What? What's obvious?"

"They're coming after us."

Sykes's mouth dropped open. "*What?*"

"If they'd wanted to try and exchange the drive for their lives, they would have done so by now. They haven't."

"But that doesn't mean—"

"Tesseract couldn't have found out about Seif without Sumner's help," Ferguson interrupted. "And the only logical reason for them collectively going after Seif would be if they thought they could get information, something they could use to get to us, something from his computer. So, I'm asking you again, what could that something be?"

Sykes wasn't thinking, he was reacting, panicking. "Oh fuck."

"Kindly calm yourself."

"Just how am I supposed to remain calm when I've just found out I'm at the top of an assassin's hit list? I don't want that fucking sociopath after me. Have you forgotten he's killed a dozen people in the last week alone, and that's only the ones we know about. I don't want to be lucky number fucking thirteen."

Sykes continuously looked around as if he expected Tesseract to be hiding in the shadows. It was embarrassing to Ferguson that he'd ever thought Sykes could handle this kind of operation. Quite simply, Ferguson had known eunuchs with more balls.

He went to speak, but a couple, arm in arm, walked

close by. He led Sykes farther away until they were out of earshot.

"They must have worked out some way to track us down; that's why they took Seif's computer. Think, why would they do that?"

"Seif's just an accountant. He handled the transactions to the accounts Tesseract used. He doesn't know anything."

"There must be something," Ferguson prompted.

It took him a few seconds before Sykes muttered, "Ah."

"What?"

"They're trying to follow the money."

"Explain," Ferguson demanded.

"That's the only trail there is," Sykes explained. He was talking quickly. "From one account to the next. Seif'll have records of the transactions made. They could find out where the money came from."

"And where did the money come from?"

"Olympus."

The already-deep lines in Ferguson's forehead deepened. "I'm assuming you don't mean the home of the Greek gods."

"Olympus Trading," Sykes corrected. "It's one of the front companies we use."

"And what is it?"

"It's an import-export outfit in Cyprus. It's just a skeleton, a couple of employees, a building, some warehouse space. The money was washed through its books on the way to Seif."

Ferguson absorbed the information for a few seconds. "What can they find out from it? Worst-case scenario."

"Worst-case scenario is they find nothing, I think."

"You think?"

"I know." Sykes almost sounded sure. "There's nothing there that can lead back to us. Just account after account. Olympus must have a hundred clients and customers. It would be impossible to get anything from its books."

"Are you positive of this?"

He nodded. "I set up Olympus myself. The paper trail will take them to the moon and back before it leads to us."

"Good. Then we have nothing to worry about."

Sykes looked far from convinced. "Unless they've worked out some way to do it that we haven't thought of."

Ferguson offered no further reassurance. He began to walk away when Sykes called after him. Ferguson turned around. "What is it?"

Sykes caught up with him. "Olympus is a dead end, but they don't know it is, do they?"

"I'm not sure I follow you."

"Isn't it obvious?"

Ferguson had said the same thing to Sykes earlier, and Ferguson noted Sykes's smug tone. He liked having the knowledge, the power.

"No," Ferguson said. "It's not."

"My point," Sykes explained with more than a little

cockiness, "is that if they went to Seif, they'll go there, to Olympus."

Ferguson nodded, understanding, impressed. "Very good, Mr. Sykes. Very good indeed."

FIFTY-EIGHT

London, United Kingdom
Thursday
04:02 CET

Reed stood next to his hotel-room window, peering into the city through the crack between wall and curtain. In the sliver of glass he could see the reflection of bare skin, limbs splayed on the sheets. The girl had her face toward the door, away from him, the golden waves of her hair spread across the pillow. The diffused light smoothed away what little imperfections she carried. Except to roll over, she hadn't moved since he had climbed out of bed. He could see in the window the rise and fall of her chest, intermittent, not regular. Awake.

He took a sip from his drink as he watched her. In silence they had played this game for some time, of her pretending to sleep and his pretending not to watch. Reed slowly flexed the muscles of his arms from shoulder to wrist.

When she finally broke the silence, her voice was quiet. "Why are you watching me?"

Reed took another sip from his drink. "Why do you allow me to watch?"

She turned her head to look at him from over one slender shoulder. "Do you want to do me again?"

And she had displayed such elegance on arrival. Reed shook his head. He pivoted and leaned against the wall next to the window. It was cool against his naked back.

"I shall respectfully decline."

She laughed. "I just love the way you guy's talk."

Reed found it quite derisory that his acute Englishness impressed her. She claimed to be twenty-one, but she was certainly younger. An Australian. He kept his contempt to himself and acknowledged her remark with a small nod. After finishing his London assignment Reed had remained in the city while he waited for the next update. The girl helped pass the time.

She reached for the remote and turned on the television.

"You don't mind, do you?"

Reed shook his head once. "Be my guest."

She flicked through the channels with barely a half second's pause on each. Her eyes were transfixed by the flashing images and constantly changing sound. He watched in quiet bewilderment of her simple pleasure.

There was a flash of blue in the dim light that immediately grabbed his attention. Reed walked to the source and took the smartphone from where he had left it on the sideboard. He opened the e-mail. He read the message carefully, then a second time before opening the attached files. He would go through them as soon as he had left. He started picking up his clothes from the floor.

"I have to leave," he said.

She pushed her small breasts together with her arms and pouted. "You *sure*?"

"Alas, yes."

To his surprise the girl looked genuinely disappointed. She sat up to better watch him dress. "Why?"

"Work."

"But it's late. Do you have to?"

"I'm afraid so."

She sighed. "You never told me what you do."

Reed's answer was honest.

"I solve problems."

FIFTY-NINE

Rotov, Russia
Thursday
17:50 MSK

In the good old days all it took to get an operation moving was the will of a high-ranking officer. While the Soviet empire stood strong, the KGB moved fast and decisively, answering only to the very top. Things moved much slower these days, Aniskovach thought bitterly, and the power of the SVR was but a shadow of that which the KGB enjoyed. In twenty-first-century Russia, as in the SVR's Western counterparts, layer on layer of bureaucracy strangled every command.

The tall SVR colonel rubbed his gloved hands together while he waited for the plane to be loaded. Grim-faced soldiers took aboard rucksacks full of supplies: diving gear, weapons, salvage equipment, and explosives. The plane was an Ilyushin Il-76, a venerable workhorse of the Soviet and now Russian air force. This particular plane was owned by the SVR and used exclusively by the organization. The original military insignias were still visible through the thin layer of paint that covered them. The hammer and sickle still endured, albeit faintly.

In his youth, Aniskovach had witnessed firsthand the last breath of Communism pushed from the lungs of his beloved nation. That system may not have worked as intended, but at least it had given his country its own ideology and a fiercely strong national identity. These days Russia was but capitalism's poor adopted child struggling to take its first unassisted step. If Russia was a tree, it had already bathed in summer's warmth and now was embraced by winter's chill. Spring's regrowth was a far off dream. Aniskovach hoped he lived long enough to see the restoration of Russia's rightful place at the head of the world.

He stood silently observing. There was nothing to say. The soldiers did not need his instructions. They were members of the Spetsnaz, the Russian army's special forces, but they were all, like Aniskovach, dressed in civilian clothes. Each member of the six-man team had been selected because of his exemplary record in both diving and demolitions. Each one was a highly trained and superbly disciplined warrior, adept at planning and logistics as well as fighting. After Aniskovach had briefed the team on the mission's objectives, they had selected their own equipment and supplies.

The SVR had no control of the Spetsnaz, which were a regiment of the Russian army, but at times the elite soldiers were loaned out to the SVR on a per-mission basis. Any such operations were usually kept off the soldiers' records. The GRU, the army's own intelligence service and a fierce rival of the SVR, would often be aware of these activities, but the GRU had no knowledge of this particular mission, thanks to Prudnikov's influence.

Bypassing the usual channels was slowing the whole operation down considerably. Aniskovach, if it had been purely up to him, would have left for Tanzania at least twenty-four hours ago, but Prudnikov was playing it safe. He had been burned once recently and was not willing to feel the fire a second time so soon, even if Aniskovach was confident the mission would be a complete success. Securing both the services of the Spetsnaz without the knowledge of the GRU and a plane to fly the equipment had taken three whole days. It would be another day before the plane was able to fly.

The wind blowing from the east stung Aniskovach's face, especially his wounded right cheek. The base had little protection from elements. The single strip of runway and three hangars that constituted the airport were the skeletal remains of a Soviet air force base, long aban-

doned by the military and now used privately. Tonight
the only customers were the SVR.

It didn't take long before the plane was loaded. The
equipment, though too much for individuals to carry,
did not require a plane with a cargo capacity of forty
tons to transport. Without using such a plane, however,
it wouldn't be possible to get the equipment over several international borders and to its destination.

The plane was supposedly set to embark on a humanitarian mission, flying to Tanzania to deliver medical supplies for charities working in Rwanda to the east.
The fact that, aside from the equipment required by
Aniskovach's team, the plane's cargo consisted of empty
crates would not matter. The appropriate officials in
the Tanzanian government would be offered cash in-
centives for going along with the charade.

Aniskovach and his team would travel commer-
cially to Tanzania in two separate groups before joining
up at their destination. Seven Russians traveling together
would attract undue attention, especially when only three
spoke languages other than their own. The first team
would pick up the equipment from the plane and drive
north from Tanzania's capital, Dar es Salaam. Once they
had rejoined as a team they would collect the equipment
that would be waiting for them and hire a suitable boat.
They would then take the boat and locate the *Lev*.

The SVR colonel had no plans to recover all the
missiles, impressive as that would be; just the guidance
systems would do to provide proof of Ozols's traitorous
deception. The rest would be destroyed along with the

frigate to ensure no other parties gained Russian technology. Aniskovach could then reveal the entire plot to Moscow and his role in preventing it. The stain caused by the St. Petersburg blunder would be washed clean away.

With a gloved finger Aniskovach absently stroked his damaged face. The pain was still intense at times, but he made sure no one witnessed him taking his pills or those moments where the pain got the better of his will. It was bad enough to be disfigured without appearing weak as well.

A stocky Spetsnaz corporal approached him.

"The equipment has been loaded and secured, sir."

"Very good."

The corporal stepped back and rejoined his colleagues.

Though it was unnecessary for the operation's success that he accompany the team, Aniskovach would nevertheless take direct command. He had absolute faith in the abilities of the Spetsnaz, but it would look better to the powers that be if he was there personally.

The plane would arrive in Tanzania in the early hours of Saturday and the supplies should reach Tanga by midday. It wouldn't take long to locate the sunken frigate or to complete the recovery and blow up the *Lev*.

Facial movements hurt him severely, so Aniskovach didn't look anywhere near as pleased as he felt. Within a few short days he knew his honor would be restored.

SIXTY

Nicosia, Cyprus
Thursday
15:49 CET

After the chill of London and Amsterdam, the warmth of Cyprus was a welcome change. Even in November the temperature hovered in the seventies. The flight from Amsterdam to Larnaca International Airport had been pleasant enough and had taken just over four hours. Rebecca had arrived only a little fatigued.

She was amazed she didn't feel worse. The last ten days had been the most stressful of her life, and the days weren't getting easier. She had teamed up with a ruthless contract killer in an attempt to eliminate the people trying to kill her, people who just so happened to be not only her employers but also a rogue element inside the CIA. Six months ago it would have been unreal, ridiculous even, but it was all too real. She had never felt so anxious, so scared.

Tesseract, or whatever the hell his name really was, was almost unreadable. If he had any concerns about what they were doing he didn't let it show. He was completely self-confident, and his utter calm helped control her nerves. If she could keep doing her part, she was sure he could do his. But even if they did pull this off, what was she going to do then? Rebecca had spent the last seven years working as an intelligence analyst for the CIA before she had been pulled out of service for this gang fuck of an operation. In the remote chance that she didn't get prosecuted for her role in a highly illegal op, she would never be given her old job back. No one would trust her again. She wouldn't blame them either.

She tried not to think about it too much. There were more immediate concerns to overcome before she considered her career. Like staying alive.

They had traveled separately. He'd told her before they'd left Amsterdam there was a chance their enemies would be looking for both of them, assuming they were together, so it was safer to fly on their own. She wasn't sure she believed him; after all, they'd traveled to London together and then to Amsterdam together and had stayed in the same hotels both times. She assumed he wanted to be on his own but didn't say anything. The one thing Rebecca could read in him was that she made him uncomfortable. Wasn't it supposed to be the other way around?

The hotel where they were staying was located in the southern Greek half of the city. So was their destination. The sun-faded sign that announced *Olympus Trading* in both Greek and English was mounted on an innocuous warehouse, whitewashed, though looking anything but. Grime caked the windows, the paint on the shutters flaked.

He adjusted his sunglasses. "Very classy."

They stood in a side street in a poor neighborhood in the southeast of the city. The district was out of the way of the main tourist areas, full of warehouses and small shops; market stalls seemed to be everywhere.

Only a few white clouds floated through the deep

blue sky above. She could tell her companion didn't like the heat. She imagined that he did most of his sleeping in the day; seeing the world under the cover of darkness had given him pale skin that was already starting to burn, and from the way he breathed she could tell he had a low tolerance for high temperatures. He'd covered his face, neck, and exposed arms in sunscreen but, even still, he wasn't comfortable out of the shade.

Conversely, Rebecca relished it. Her skin was brown already, and she had put the sunscreen straight down when he had handed her the bottle. She had some flesh on display, bare legs protruding from her skirt, naked arms and stomach, but on his request she'd wrapped a shawl around her to cover the cleavage on display from the bikini top. It would draw too much attention, he'd told her. She'd given him a look in return that he quickly shied away from. She grinned briefly.

In this part of the city there were mostly locals, market stalls selling fruit or fish. Farther down the street a drunk sat propped against a wall sipping from a bottle of rum while a tourist examined peaches at a trader's stall. A skinny kid pushed a wheelbarrow full of old newspaper past an old man with a thick beard who grilled prawns on a rusty barbeque.

A wide-brimmed hat and sunglasses provided her with a basic disguise, one that would work against a cursory glance but nothing more. She'd cut her hair shorter and bleached it too, on his instructions. Being a bottle blonde definitely didn't suit her complexion, but even Rebecca didn't recognize herself in the mirror anymore.

"You think it's deserted?" he asked and took a bite from his vanilla ice cream. He'd asked for a double-sized one from the vendor.

Rebecca stood next to him. She had a guidebook in her hand and tilted her head forward as if reading it.

"Olympus is more than just a paper trail, it's a working front, so there are people in there. Probably only a handful of employees by the looks of it. I doubt any will know who they really work for."

Rebecca moved her free index finger down the page as if she were searching for information.

"That's a nice touch, by the way," he said.

She kept her eyes on the page. "I'm a fast learner."

He had to be quick to prevent half his ice cream from collapsing. "Do you really think we'll find anything there?"

"Don't talk with food in your mouth." She turned over a page in the book. "We don't know until we look."

He walked down the street a few steps, held his hand out as if pointing. "Okay," he said. "I'll come back tonight after I've picked up some things."

Their hotel was only a half-hour walk away. They left the way they had come, negotiating the maze of side streets at a leisurely pace. Rebecca took his hand in hers as they walked and felt the tension in his touch, but she didn't let go, and together they looked like any other couple enjoying some winter sun.

The tourist, eating his perfectly ripened peach, was never far behind.

SIXTY-ONE

The bar was noisy with conversation, laughter, and traditional Greek music. Rebecca sat alone at a small table along one wall. She had a feta cheese salad in front of her, untouched except for the odd black olive. It was hard to eat when she was so tense. She looked at her watch every few minutes. He'd been gone for hours. He needed to get "equipment." It would have been nice to have some idea of how long he was going to be.

She didn't like being on her own, knowing she was vulnerable, knowing that without his help, if anyone made a play for her, she was dead. Initially she had been terrified to be in his, a hired killer's, presence, but the rational part of her brain told her that she was safer with him than alone. He had survived two CIA-sponsored attempts on his life, and she had witnessed firsthand how he'd dealt with the French RAID team. At the moment he was the best and only friend she had. Rebecca was desperate to be near him again, to feel safe again.

She felt a little better being around lots of people. The bar was full of dining couples and partying tourists, only a few locals. There was an especially loud group of guys at a table close to Rebecca's playing drinking games. The bar was across the street from her hotel, and from where she sat she could just about see the hotel entrance. He'd told her to wait in such a place.

Maybe he was testing her. Rebecca could tell he didn't trust her. She wouldn't have been surprised if he was watching her right now and had been minutes after he'd supposedly gone off to get whatever the fuck he needed. *Bastard is waiting for me to set him up,* she thought. If he didn't trust her by now, then, not to put it too bluntly, he could go to hell.

A couple of times a guy from the group nearby would shout something to her. They looked like navy types. Brits by their accents. They seemed pretty harmless, just guys out getting drunk. She didn't respond, just smiled the polite but uninterested, universally recognized, leave-me-alone smile and averted her gaze. Some men just couldn't take a hint.

Rebecca stabbed her fork into a piece of feta and again into a slice of tomato. She forced a small amount of food into her mouth. Her clothes were starting to feel a little loose. It took a long time before she finally swallowed and then felt immediately full. She hailed a waiter for another glass of wine.

When the guy got up from his seat with the encouragement of his buddies, she kept her gaze directly at her food, silently hoping he would lose his nerve at the last second and walk away. He didn't.

"Hey, I'm Paul," he announced as he took the seat opposite her.

"Hi," she said, giving him just a second of eye contact. He wasn't bad looking but wouldn't have been her type even if she had been in the mood.

"You got a name, love?"

She hesitated, partly because she didn't want anyone

to know her real name, but mostly because she just didn't want to talk to him.

"Rachel," she answered eventually

He smiled. "Cute name."

He did the talking, asked the questions, made the jokes. Rebecca responded each time in as few words as possible. She tried her best to discourage him, but Paul had too much Dutch courage inside him to give up without a hell of a fight. Occasionally he would receive leery encouragement from his friends.

"Listen," he said, eventually coming to the point. "My distinguished colleagues and I are moving on to another bar. I would be honored if you'd join me."

"I don't think so," she said.

He hadn't expected that. "Why not?"

"I'm just not interested."

"Sure you are." He was persistent, if nothing else. "I'm a good-looking guy, you're a good-looking girl; think of all the interesting things we could do."

When charm failed, the desperate ones always tried a deluded appeal. "Just leave me alone, Paul."

He scowled for a moment. "All you Yank bitches are the same; you think you're so superior."

"That's probably because we are," Rebecca said, finally losing patience. "Now do us both a favor, and, if you can find it, go fuck yourself."

He stood up fast, glaring, and for a second she thought she'd pushed him too far. A voice interrupted the standoff.

"I got us both a drink."

Rebecca glanced up. It was him. Tesseract. The killer.

With complete nonchalance he placed a couple of glasses on the table. "Vodka tonics," he said. "No ice in yours."

Paul looked him up and down. "What are you, her boyfriend?"

"We're business associates."

"Then you won't mind me and Rachel here getting to know each other."

"You're in my seat."

Paul sneered. "Just fuck off, mate. Let a fella work."

"I'll say this as simply as possible so you don't get confused." His voice was icy cool. "Leave."

Paul stood, turned, reached a hand out as if to push him. Big mistake. In less than a second he was on his knees, his arm twisted and locked, ready to be snapped with an ounce more pressure. Paul yelled in pain.

His drinking buddies were out of their chairs. Tesseract applied a fraction more pressure to Paul's arm and they froze at his scream.

"*Whoa, whoa.*" Rebecca was on her feet, palms up. "Easy, we don't have to do it that way." She looked at Paul. "Do we?"

"*FUCK NO.*"

She looked at her companion. "Let him go."

His eyes were focused on the four other guys, but he spoke to Paul. "Do you promise to behave yourself?"

"*Hell yes.*"

He released him. "Find another place to drink."

Paul pulled himself to his feet, cradling his sore arm. He went back to his friends, and, while they threw threats and insults, they backed off out of the bar. Everyone else was quiet. People were looking at them. Her heart was thumping. Equal parts relief and anger surged through her.

He took her by the shoulders and pulled her against him and into an awkward hug. Rebecca resisted for a moment before wrapping her own arms around him, her chin resting on his shoulder, any anger vanishing as she felt their bodies together, the protection of his embrace. He stank of smoke, but she didn't care. It felt good.

She noticed she was holding him tighter than he was her and realized it was for show, for the people watching, to maintain the couple act.

Rebecca pulled away. She could see the surprise and awkwardness on his face. She sat down, embarrassed. He sat down opposite her, picked up her fork, and started eating her salad. Slowly, the bar's noise levels began to rise back to normal.

"What the hell was that?" she asked quietly.

His tone was frustratingly casual, "What was what?"

Rebecca frowned. "Are you making a joke?"

"I told you I don't make jokes."

She shook her head. "Look, you didn't need to do anything. I was taking care of it."

He looked up and paused chewing. He said nothing.

"I was taking care of it," she said again.

He raised an eyebrow. "I would say that's a flatteringly positive assessment."

She glared at him. "When I want your help, I'll ask for it."

"When I deem it necessary to help," he began, "I'll do so whether you ask for it or not."

She noticed something in the way he said it, an unexpected protectiveness. He saw that she'd noticed it too and looked away. He continued attacking her salad so he didn't have to look her in the eye. She took a drink of the vodka tonic.

"Thanks for getting it without ice."

He nodded without looking at her.

Rebecca watched him for a minute. "Did you get everything you needed?"

He nodded, said nothing.

"So, what next?" she asked.

He continued eating for a few moments before speaking. "I'll break into Olympus and get the files."

"Just like that?"

"Just like that."

She nodded. "Then we're one step closer to the bad guy."

He gave her an expression she didn't get. Rebecca looked at him quizzically. "What?"

He raised an eyebrow at her.

"I am the bad guy."

SIXTY-TWO

Just to make Alvarez's day more frustrating it was raining. Hard. He didn't carry an umbrella, never had, never would, and he walked quickly with his wide shoulders hunched up around his neck. Rain pelted the top of his head and ran down his face and neck and soaked his coat and shirt. He'd only been out of the cab for three minutes, but already he was wetter than a coed on spring break. The rain suited his mood though. The investigation was quickly running out of momentum. With Hoyt dead and the only solid lead gone with him, Alvarez was virtually stalled. Ozols's killer and the location of the missiles were getting further and further away.

It took him another minute of getting drenched before he spotted the right café on a street that seemed to have dozens and hurried inside. The interior was small with a low ceiling and every table was taken. Alvarez swiped some of the rain from his hair and face and looked around the room. He saw Lefèvre sitting on his own and reading a newspaper. The short, meticulously groomed French lieutenant looked exactly the same as when Alvarez had first encountered him a week and a half ago outside the killer's hotel. His manner seemed different now though; then he had been all arrogance and superiority. Now he just looked like a regular guy. He hadn't seen Alvarez enter and only looked up as Alvarez was pulling out a chair opposite him.

"I'm glad you didn't stand me up," Alvarez said as he took his seat. "Because after getting this wet I would have had to hunt you down."

Lefèvre closed his newspaper. "Drink?"

"Yeah. Coffee, please."

The Frenchman called over a waitress and ordered two coffees and a *pain au chocolat* for himself. Alvarez smiled. Cops were the same the world over. They all ate their national donuts. Alvarez took off his saturated coat and hung it over the back of his chair.

"You wanted to see me?"

Lefèvre nodded. "That's right. Thank you for coming."

"No problem."

"I believe we can help each other."

"I tried to tell you that over a week ago."

Lefèvre shrugged. "And I should have listened. But I had a hotel full of dead bodies to deal with. Please accept my apology for any rudeness on my part."

"Accepted."

"I'll keep this short."

Alvarez wiped some rain from his head. "Suits me."

"Andris Ozols," Lefèvre began, "was a retired officer of the Russian and Soviet navies. Correct?"

Alvarez didn't respond.

"I'll take your silence as a yes," the French lieutenant said with a half smile. "I know this is true, and I'm quite sure you do too. Anyway, we both know that he was murdered last week by a professional killer. A killer who was himself targeted only two hours later at his hotel, where he shot a large number of people. This as-yet unnamed killer then returned to Paris a few days ago. He was recognized and followed but escaped arrest, and in the process killed several police officers. Before his escape he met with an American woman."

"Why are you telling me all this?" Alvarez asked.

Lefèvre leaned back. "Because you can do more with it than I can."

"Why do you say that?"

"John Kennard," Lefèvre said.

Hearing the name made Alvarez picture the guy in his head. Dead. Stabbed to death and lying on a shitty bathroom floor. "What about him?"

"He worked with you, yes?"

"Listen, I'm not here to answer your questions, okay?"

Lefèvre nodded. "That's up to you. I'm telling you what I know, and I'm asking for nothing in return. But I hope when I have finished you will be more forthcoming with me."

The waitress returned with their order. Alvarez took a sip of coffee. "Go on."

"A day after Kennard was murdered, a homeless man, well known to my people, tried to use his credit card to buy alcohol. He was picked up by an officer and questioned. On his person, among other things, was a cellular phone that had belonged to your colleague. After extensive interrogation the man claimed to have retrieved the items from a trash can after seeing another man discard them. I believe him. He has no history of violence, and there was no knife on him nor any blood on his clothes, clothes he neither washes nor takes off."

Lefèvre continued, "The man who threw the phone and credit card away is described as wearing a suit and speaking with an English accent. As you might expect this did not sound like a typical Parisian mugger to me. There was clearly more to the murder than anyone first thought. As part of the investigation Kennard's most recent calls were all checked. They were to friends, family members, colleagues, and so on—nothing suspicious except a single French number that called Kennard's phone twice after he had been killed."

Alvarez did his best not to react to what he was hearing.

"That number corresponds to an apartment in Marseilles where we found sophisticated communications equipment. My equivalent in Marseilles found this residence abandoned. Fingerprints were taken there that match those found in an apartment here in Paris. The same apartment where Ozols's killer escaped with that American woman."

Alvarez was stunned. He put his coffee down.

Lefèvre continued, "As you can see, there is some connection between your colleague, this American woman, and the man who murdered Andris Ozols. I don't know what this connection is, and I'm taking a big risk in telling you all this information. For all I know you're involved, too."

"I can assure you that is definitely not the case."

Lefèvre nodded as if he didn't need to be convinced.

"I'm a police officer. It's my job to bring criminals to justice. But I know how the intelligence business works. I know there are things I will never be told, things that I need to be told, and without all the evidence, how can I solve anything? "

Lefèvre took a brown leather briefcase from the floor and removed a file.

"What's that?" Alvarez asked, looking at the file.

"For you," Lefèvre explained, "everything we have so far. All the evidence."

Alvarez picked up the file. He asked a simple question. "Why?"

"Because you can do more with it than I can. I would prefer one of us to succeed than us both to fail. Justice matters more to me than credit. People are dead. They deserve to be avenged. For this, I am deferring to you. All I ask in return," Lefèvre said, "is that you tell me, off the record, when you are successful."

It was a small price to pay. "I will," Alvarez said and meant it.

Lefèvre gestured to the file. "Inside you'll find the fingerprints of the American woman. I suggest you start by finding out who she really is."

"I don't know how to thank you."

Lefèvre smiled. "You don't have to."

SIXTY-THREE

Rebecca sat on the end of the bed, flicking through the hotel's satellite-television channels. It was a bizarre mix of both English and Greek language channels with local Cypriot TV. Tesseract was packing his backpack. Her curiosity had made her ask what the equipment was for and, to her surprise, he'd told her. First there was a portable high-capacity hard disk to clone the contents of computer hard drives. Next a transmitter, radio receiver, and tape recorder to bug a phone should he not find what they needed. Items she didn't need explained were screwdrivers, pliers, a wrench, hexagon keys, pencils, and paper. Lock-picking tools, a glass cutter, and a suction cup were placed together in a separate small bag, which was then added to the backpack.

"Do you think you'll need all that?" Rebecca asked.

He shook his head. "But better I take what I might not need than find myself without what I do need."

When everything was securely packed away, he took a set of clothes with him into the bathroom and closed the door. It wasn't closed all the way, and through the crack she could see his reflection as he changed. She glimpsed his bare arm, lean but with ridges of hard muscle. She continued watching to sneak a peek at the rest of his body but instead flinched at what she saw.

She caught a glance of his torso and the scars that marked his flesh. A huge circular bruise the size of a fist dominated the center of his chest. She saw two scars that could have been bullet wounds and more that she guessed were caused by blades. There were others, but she didn't look long enough to identify them. Rebecca turned her head away, shocked and horrified.

"That pretty?"

She looked up and saw he was looking at her through the mirror. Her face flushed with embarrassment, and she averted her eyes. Before she had worked up the courage to respond, he closed the door fully. She heard the bolt slide across.

He came out a few minutes later, and she watched him take the folding knife from the bedside table and slip it into his pocket. He'd bought it from town. Trying to find a gun would have attracted too much attention, he'd told her.

"I expect you hate instant coffee as much as I do," Rebecca said. "So I made us both a tea."

He took the mug from her and sipped. It must have been okay because he took a longer sip a second later.

"I still think I should go with you," she said.

He didn't look at her. "I work alone."

"That hardly matters. I—"

"Besides," he said, interrupting her. "It's safer for you if you stay here."

She sighed. It was useless trying to argue with him. He was like a child. Stubborn and narrow minded, too used to doing things his own way to accept that someone else might be able to help.

"Remember," he said, "don't leave the room until morning. If I'm not back by sunrise, something has happened to me, and I'll never be coming back. Get off the island straightaway and disappear. Take a boat not a plane—"

"I know, I know. We've been through this once already."

"And we'll keep going through it until I'm convinced you understand everything."

"It would be nice if you could give me some credit."

He looked at her for a moment. "This is what I do."

Rebecca could see she was breaking through the wall he surrounded himself with, even if the only way to penetrate it was to make him lose patience. She wanted to chip away more at that wall, but instead she found herself saying something else.

"And why do you do it?"

He looked at her blankly. "What?"

"I said, why do you do what you do?"

Rebecca examined his face while he struggled with her question. She'd expected some kind of quick retort or dismissal or downright refusal to answer. Not this. He looked confused, pained even, and she instantly regretted asking him.

"It's okay," she said, trying to lighten the mood. "You don't have to say."

"It's the only thing I've ever been any good at."

She could see that it hadn't been a justification or even an admission. It had been a confession. He turned his head away and grabbed the backpack from the bed.

She watched him, finding herself starting to see the man instead of the killer.

"How do you manage to sleep at night?"

"First I close my eyes," he explained, deadpan. "The rest comes naturally."

Her nostrils flared. "I thought you didn't make jokes."

"I'm learning."

She saw the trace of smugness in his face. He was pleased with himself, but she saw his responses for the avoidance they were. "Tell me your name."

"What?"

"I've known you for almost a week," she said. "And I still don't have an actual name to call you."

Rebecca had wanted to ask him before but had never been brave enough to do so. Now, she found she didn't need courage. She saw the vulnerability in him, the fear she had put into him by making him talk about himself.

She watched him fidgeting with the backpack, acting as if he was checking something. "You don't need to call me anything."

"Just tell me."

He stopped what he was pretending to do and looked up at her. "If you want to call me something, call me Jack."

"That's not your real name."

"I go by whatever name is on the passport I'm using."

She frowned. "So I should start calling you Jack?"

He slung the backpack over his shoulder. "At least until I change passports."

Rebecca stood up and faced him from across the bed. "If you go by so many other names, what difference does it make if you tell me your real name?"

"I am whoever my passport says I am," he explained. "I'm more convincing if I think of myself as that person."

"You say that like you're trying to convince yourself more than you are me."

"A name in itself means nothing." He was speaking louder now, angry but trying to hide it. "No one alive knows my real name. That's the way it's going to stay."

"What does family call you?"

He didn't respond. She could've guessed he wouldn't.

"What about your friends, then, do they know your real name, or do they all call you the same false name, or do different ones know you by different names?"

She used the remote to mute the TV while she waited for the answer. He adjusted a strap on the backpack and reslung it over his shoulder. He didn't answer her question.

"God," she said, understanding. "How can you live like that?"

"It's better than dying," he answered simply. "Or having someone innocent die because of me." He headed for the door. "It's getting late," he said. "I have to go."

Even with less than state-of-the-art lock picks, getting through Olympus's back door took seconds. Victor had seen no evidence of alarms, so there was no need to disable the building's power. There were no street lamps in this part of town, and the streets were deserted. Victor slipped inside and closed the door behind him. He stood in the darkness by the door, listening. He remained motionless until he was sure there was no sound except his for own breathing.

He flicked on a slim flashlight and used its beam to examine the interior. He was in a warehouse space that was empty but for a few crates stacked together in one corner. He could see an armchair, TV, and table behind them—someone's own little hideaway—but there was no one there. Making no noise, Victor moved to the far end, keeping close to a wall at all times. A narrow set of steps led up to offices above the warehouse. He took them slowly, one careful step at a time.

The office wasn't locked. In the beam of the flashlight he could see a few desks and a couple of computers—workspace for two or three staff members. There was a tall filing cabinet against one wall and a small safe buried into the brickwork. A newspaper sat folded next to one of the monitors.

He went to the filing cabinet first, working his way through the drawers from bottom to top. There were invoices, purchase orders, delivery notes, licenses, correspondence, memorandums. He looked for specific dates—his past contracts—any sizeable sum of money that was handled just before or just after those dates. He took anything that looked remotely useful.

He copied the contents of the two desktop computers to the portable hard drive before turning his attention to the safe. If there was anything else to find, it would be in there. In his backpack he had a slim but powerful laptop, installed onto which was a special piece of software designed specifically for cracking electronic key codes. The software conducted a brute-force attack through a wireless connection, interfering with the lock at its programming port before running a continuous string of numbers until the combination was found. Victor had downloaded the software from the company's Web site at considerable expense, but without an effective countermeasure it was worth its price. Though against the traditional dial-face combination lock that Victor faced it was completely useless.

The safe looked thirty years old. Thankfully it looked like a group 2—the most common of the two safe types, and the least secure. There would no countermeasures he would have to worry about, no antitamper acid release to destroy the contents. Still, without the proper tools, it could take him hours to crack. Trust a CIA front company to have a safe almost as old as he was. The powerful laptop in his backpack was no more use to him than a paperweight.

Which left Victor with three ways of breaking into the safe: explosives, drilling, or lock manipulation. He had neither explosives nor a drill, so he was going to have to do it the old-fashioned way. Victor laid out the high-tech tools for the job: a pad of graph paper, a pencil, and a stethoscope.

Traditional combination locks all worked in the same tried and tested manner. When the dial was turned, an attached spindle turned the drive cam, which then turned the combination wheels. Into each wheel a notch was cut, which when the correct combination was dialed, would all align perfectly. Resting just above the wheels was a small metal bar, called the fence. When all the notches aligned, the fence fell into the created gap, allowing the bolt securing the safe door to slide across and the safe to be opened.

Victor took off his jacket and folded it to use as a makeshift cushion. He was going to be kneeling down for a long time.

The first step in cracking the safe was to determine how many wheels the safe contained. Each wheel behind the dial corresponded to a single number in the combination. Just like the wheels, the drive cam had a notch cut into it, for the fence to fall into when the correct combination was dialed. Between the fence and the door bolt was a lever, which, as the drive cam was turned, would make a small clicking sound when the nose of the lever made contact with the drive cam's notch.

Victor used the stethoscope and listened carefully for the clicks—one when the nose of the lever fells into the notch, called the right click, and a second when the nose exited the notch, called the left click. The numbers on the dial corresponded to these clicks, and the space between them was called the contact area.

Once he had determined where the contact area was, Victor set the dial to the exact opposite position, known as parking the wheels. Then, slowly, he turned the dial clockwise. Each time the dial passed the parking position there was a small click. Victor counted how many clicks there were before they ceased. Victor counted three clicks, one for each wheel, so he knew he was dealing with a safe that had a three-number combination.

Victor reset the safe by turning the dial clockwise several times. He then parked the wheels at zero and slowly turned it counterclockwise. Each time there was a click, one for both the left and right side of the notch, he plotted the numbers on a graph until he had completed a single circumference.

He started the process again, resetting the wheels, slowly turning the dial counterclockwise, but starting at three numbers counterclockwise from zero. This way meant that the contact area where the lever and notch met would be different. He again plotted the position of the clicks on the graph.

Victor repeated the process at intervals of three until all the points on the dial had been plotted. Finally, the laborious and painstaking process was finished and he had two graphs, one showing the positions of the left clicks, the other showing the positions of the right clicks. He joined up the points until he had two zigzags.

The numbers plotted on the two graphs converged exactly at three points, one for each wheel and therefore combination number. Victor made a note of these three numbers and wrote them down in all six different combination possibilities. He tried them out one at a time. On the fourth combination the safe opened. He looked at his watch. It had taken him seventy minutes. Not bad.

Inside the safe were five taped stacks of cash, a

folder, and a bottle of gin. Each stack of cash equaled five thousand euros. Victor placed them in the backpack and opened the folder. It was full of files. They followed the cash. He exited the office and began descending the stairs.

Paperwork had never been Victor's strong point, but the broker would be able to dissect the files in no time and find out what they needed. He was glad he'd teamed up with her. Alone he would have never gotten this far. He would still be running blind, going nowhere, waiting for the CIA to find him. Several times she had proved herself to be an extremely valuable associate— partner even, though it felt strange to accept that she was.

He didn't want to admit it, but she was more than just that. Not a friend yet, but a companion, someone he actually wanted to talk to, though he still found it difficult to communicate with her. This was partly because of the effect she had on him and partly because of Victor's nature. When he played a role, he could be articulate and charming with the opposite sex if it was necessary, but when playing himself he was clumsy and awkward. He was badly out of practice, though he had never really been in practice.

He'd been denying the attraction, but he knew it was there. His gaze lingered on her whenever she wasn't looking. The glimpses of her body made his pulse quicken more than any hooker ever had. But it wasn't just the desire she stirred in him. She was the only woman in his life, ever in his life, who knew what he really was, and even knowing that she didn't look at him with disgust. Before he'd left he even saw empathy in her face as she looked at him, even if compassion didn't normally sit well with his loner survivalist mentality.

Victor had told himself over and over that he didn't need anyone in his life, for anything. Maybe that had been the case once, but maybe it was wrong now. Or perhaps it had always just been easier to convince himself that he didn't need anyone than to admit the truth.

He exited the warehouse, realizing he was looking forward to seeing her when he got back to the hotel. He frowned. It was a bad idea, Victor told himself, don't go there.

Only he wasn't listening to that particular voice anymore.

SIXTY-FOUR

01:10 CET

Rebecca yawned. Her eyes were sore. He'd been gone about an hour, and she had no idea when he was coming back. He had been evasive when she had pressed him for a time. As long as it takes, was the best answer he gave her. She wanted to be awake when he came back, so she picked up the phone and called room service for a triple espresso. If that didn't keep her awake, nothing would.

She had settled on watching a news channel. It

helped her eyelids stay up, even if the stories held no interest for her. Hurry up and get back, she thought. She didn't like being on her own, even in the relative safety of the hotel room. Don't open the door to anyone, he'd told her. She was starting to find his paranoia unbearable.

But then she had seen his scars. It had been a revelation. Rebecca couldn't imagine the kind of existence that would cause someone to carry so many injuries. And if he carried that may physical wounds, how many psychological scars were there inside his head? She realized, almost to her amazement, that she actually felt sorry for him.

She thought back to what happened in the bar, the way he'd intervened on her behalf. Was that because he actually wanted to help, or was it just to maintain their low profile? At the time she'd been insulted that he hadn't let her fight her own battle, thinking maybe even hitmen could have chivalry, misplaced as it was, but then she had realized he was more than likely just protecting himself by keeping her out of trouble. Now, she was sure he had simply been looking out for her and that thought touched her.

Twice now he had, in a way, rescued her. She smiled. Like a guardian angel. Though a guardian angel of death would be a better description.

Would he kill her when this was all over? It was a question she'd asked herself a dozen times or more over the last few days. Initially, even after he'd said she would never see him again, Rebecca had expected he would put a bullet in her skull the second he didn't need her anymore. The idea of seducing him in an effort to keep her off his list of targets had once been in the cards—she'd seen the way he looked at her—but she hadn't had the courage.

Now, after the way he'd avoided telling her his name, she was certain he didn't intend to kill her. If he'd told her, she would become even more of a risk to him, and his professional mentality would force him to eliminate that risk. He didn't want to do that. Maybe he had once planned to kill her but not anymore. She smiled at that, knowing he liked her, even if he would never admit it.

She was under no illusion about who he was or what he did for a living, but maybe there was something approaching a human being behind all that, after all. Maybe, when this was all over, she might find out what that human being looked like.

When her coffee arrived she was already half asleep. Rebecca opened the door and took the cup and saucer from the guy, her eyes squinting from the hallway lights behind him. She went back into the room to get some money for a tip.

Turning around she saw that he was now inside the door. Though her vision was blurry she realized he looked too old to be a hotel waiter. His hair was black but his skin tone was light, not Greek. Suddenly afraid, she stepped back away from him, further into the room.

His expression showed nothing as he closed the door behind him. He moved forward smoothly, unrushed. She saw his eyes: icy blue. They were the eyes of a man without a soul.

Rebecca prayed that the man whose name she didn't know would come back at that moment, but there was no sign of him.

This time he wasn't going to save her.

SIXTY-FIVE

01:49 CET

The main light was off when Victor returned to the room. Good. He'd told her not to put it on. Secondary lights only. They were off too. He heard the shower running. He hadn't told her never to use a shower. If someone came for her he doubted it would make a difference either way.

"It's me," he said.

No answer. She couldn't hear him over the noise of the shower. There was a crack in the curtains. A trace of moonlight shined through into the room. Light from the bathroom slipped under the door. There was just enough illumination for him to see that nothing was out of place. He was cautious, though—he always was. In the darkness he walked over to his bed, the one farthest from the door. He flicked on the lamp. The room stayed dark.

Sighing, he walked around the bed to the second lamp next to the broker's bed. They always used double rooms with two beds. It was hard enough to sleep knowing she was in the same room without her being in the same bed too. After all the years of sleeping alone Victor didn't know if he could with someone next to him. He didn't want to try and fail, to know just how far removed from normality he really was.

He flicked the switch but it stayed off too. Victor turned around. The light in the bathroom was on, so the electricity was working, but both lamps were out. It seemed like too much of a coincidence.

The knife appeared in his hand.

He moved over to the main light switch. It was against protocol to turn it on if a smaller light source was available, but there wasn't one. His hand reached out, his finger touching the switch. But he didn't flick it down. Something was very wrong.

It felt as if he had been guided toward it. He could be mistaken, but he wasn't about to take the chance. He moved his hand away from the switch and took the slim flashlight from his pocket. He shined the light at the switch. It was just an ordinary light switch, no different from how it had been when they had first entered, except the screw heads looked scratched. He shone the light at the floor underneath the switch. It took him a few seconds before he noticed the miniscule white speck on the carpet. He squatted down and touched it with his finger. Plaster.

The room had been immaculate when they had arrived.

His pulse started to rise. There were no sizeable wardrobes, no room underneath the beds. That left the bathroom.

Victor turned on the TV, cranked up the volume. He moved back to the bed. He had the flashlight in his left hand, the knife in his right. He moved silently over to the bathroom door, standing facing it. He had a horrible feeling about what he was going to see inside. His stomach was tighter than it had ever been.

He kicked the door open.

The bathroom was small. There was no one hiding in there, no one waiting.

No one alive anyway.

She still looked good, even with wet hair draped across her face. Her head was resting on the lip of the bath as if she were resting, but at an impossible angle from the rest of her body. The water from the shower splashed on her face and the wide, open eyes. Victor approached slowly and turned off the shower.

No amount of controlled breathing could slow down his heart rate. Victor squatted down next to the bath, the knife slipping from his fingers. He knew it was pointless, but he checked her pulse anyway. Her skin was still warm. He reached out a hand and brushed the blonde hair from her face. She'd complained when he'd ordered her to bleach it. He gently closed her eyelids. She looked asleep, peaceful. He stayed looking at her far longer than he knew was prudent.

He retrieved the knife from the floor and stood back up, his knuckles white. He felt sick. Victor left the bathroom, cold anger in his eyes.

There were no defensive wounds, no evidence of a fight of any kind, no traces of blood, no skin under her nails, nothing to suggest she had even fought back. Victor knew her well enough to know she wouldn't have died without a fight. But against whoever killed her that fight had been over the second it had begun. The killer was good. And he was still near. The broker wasn't the only target. He had come for them both. Victor turned around, looking back at the light switch.

There would be a trip switch behind it, rigged up to a detonator that would explode when electricity was passed through it. In turn the explosion would detonate the plastic explosive packed behind the wall, enough to ensure no one inside the room survived the blast. It would have killed them both, had she gone to Olympus with him. But she hadn't. He'd told her to stay. It was safer.

The killer was outside. He wouldn't have just set the bomb and left, hoping it would be successful. He would need to make sure. He was nearby, watching, waiting. He would only leave when the fireball burst through the window.

Victor wasn't going to keep him waiting.

He used the knife to unscrew the light switch, and carefully he removed the front plate. Inside it was exactly how he imagined it would be. A detonator was attached to the main wiring and implanted into a large quantity of what looked like American C-4. It wasn't in a block; it had been carefully kneaded and pushed into the cavity behind the wall. There looked to be several pounds' worth. With it were plastic soda bottles filled with diesel to ensure the explosion caused a relentless fire, presumably to incinerate their corpses and leave no trail back to whomever started this. He expected other bottles were hidden around the room and in the bathroom too.

The killer, watching from nearby, would have seen Victor enter the hotel. If he did not see the explosion soon he might work out what had happened. Victor couldn't allow that. He unplugged the TV, cut the lead from the back of the set, and stripped off the plug, leaving him with three feet of cable. He unplugged the room's phone and moved it closer to the door. He then tore off the phone's plastic exterior and attached the wires at the end of the TV cable leading to those inside the phone. The other end he attached to the detonator after carefully removing the original wires. When everything was secure, he plugged the phone into the socket next to the TV.

When the phone rang, the electricity passing through its wires would blow the detonating charge. The plastic explosive would follow. Victor quickly gathered his things and left. He didn't have time to waste.

He had a call to make.

Even in the middle of the night the various bars and cafés that lined the street were still open and busy, Cypriots and tourists having a good time. Reed sat at a table outside one of the least-raucous establishments, quietly sipping from a tall glass of freshly squeezed orange juice. He had a book on the table before him that he hadn't read but that helped explain his unsociable presence. He knew the waitress still wondered why he had been sitting there most of the evening, but this time tomorrow Reed would be back in England enjoying a large glass of Hennessy Ellipse Cognac.

From where he sat he could see the dark rectangle that was the window to Tesseract's room. Reed's pulse was three beats per minute higher than normal as he waited for the big bang. He was expecting it soon since only minutes earlier he had watched Tesseract arrive back at the hotel. That he had no other name to call his prey caused a small measure of annoyance to Reed. Rebecca Sumner had been unable to tell him despite his considerable efforts to convince her to. In the end he believed her that Tesseract had refused to tell her his real name. Which was fitting he supposed. Men like Tesseract, like himself, did not have real names.

He had asked her other things as well. How old was he? What was his history, his training, his background? Reed liked to have such information about his targets, and even more so when a target was a fellow professional killer of obvious, if in no way comparable, skill. The dossier his employers had provided on Tesseract was woefully inadequate, and Reed took no pleasure in killing people he felt he did not properly know. Alas, she had not been able to tell him anything aside from the barest of details, nothing of significance he had not already known. She had not lied. People never lied to Reed. He was most persuasive.

The shockwave ruffled his shirt and made his ears pop. Glass rained down on the street. Bricks punched through windshields of parked cars. Flames spewed from the blasted-out windows. Thick smoke billowed into the night sky.

Reed closed his eyes and pictured the delicious moment when the light switch would have been flicked and the flesh stripped from Tesseract's obliterated bones. It would have been quite a sight, Reed was sure, even if he had never been comfortable using bombs. They went against his doctrine as an assassin. They were too obvious, too indiscriminant, with too much chance of collateral damage. They were the weapon of a terrorist, not a contract killer of unparalleled ability.

The initial stunned silence that followed the blast was quickly replaced by hysteria. Another one of the deplorable side effects of explosive devices. They had a nasty habit of upsetting bystanders. Around him everyone was on their feet, staring, pointing, some screaming. He was pleased to see that the falling debris had injured no one on the street, though if anyone was unfortunate enough to be walking past the room's door when the bomb went off, they would have been disintegrated. At least they would have died instantaneously. No suffering. That mattered to Reed. The adjacent room would also be demolished, but there had been no guests next door. Reed had checked first. He never killed innocents unless it was unavoidable. He was a professional, not a psychopath.

It had been just enough C-4 to guarantee ripping Tesseract into countless unrecognizable chunks and sufficient accelerant to make certain both sets of remains were incinerated. That had been the unmovable stipulation from the client. He wanted absolutely no traces. With limited time and resources, and with an accomplished adversary to consider, Reed had no choice but to use explosives and fire to make the bodies unidentifiable.

Reed took a moment to finish his drink before standing. There was no way Tesseract could have survived a blast of such magnitude, so Reed's work was complete and another worthy scalp added to his already-impressive résumé. It was lamentable that it was such a good trap that his prey would never have known he had walked straight into it. The Englishman collected the book and the newspaper and left an especially generous tip.

He made his way through the shocked crowds outside the hotel, walking slowly, enjoying the warm night air in a charming city, unaware he was not the only person on the street unconcerned by the blast.

SIXTY-SIX

Arlington, Virginia, U.S.A.
Friday
12:30 EST

Ferguson sat chewing quietly at a corner table in the lounge of his gentleman's club. He was enjoying his favorite meal, a steak tartare accompanied by a large glass of Burgundy. He had his phone switched to silent so that he could eat his food without interruption. Growing older Ferguson had discovered he preferred to do more and more things alone. Too much of his life had been spent in the company of idiots for him to waste his remaining years. He particularly liked to eat by himself without having to chat business or banalities between swallows.

His phone flashed, but Ferguson ignored it. The club was mostly empty, just a handful of retirement-age men like himself spread throughout the grand mahogany-paneled room. There was a huge real fire roaring in the marble fireplace set into one wall. The club was his personal retreat, and he had been frequenting it for nearly two decades watching the other faces grow older, the waistlines wider, and the conversation quieter.

Ferguson felt tired. He hadn't been sleeping that well. He maintained a persona of utter calm, and for the vast majority of the time that calm was genuine, but there were occasions when his interior was not quite as steady as his exterior led people to believe. With so much at stake and playing so close to the line it was hardly surprising.

It almost defied belief that Tesseract had managed to stay alive so long. But, Ferguson reasoned, in his own past he had received his fair share of good fortune with operations, so he supposed it was only natural to have such bad luck with this one.

Ferguson placed another piece of uncooked meat into his mouth and chewed. He hoped that it was only a matter of time before Tesseract and Sumner were dead, and, once he no longer had to worry about some assassin who refused to die, he could look forward to a very rosy retirement. Just so long as he got his hands on that flash drive.

Sitting on the bottom of the seabed was at least a hundred million dollars worth of technology. Ferguson was so close to being rich beyond his wildest dreams he could taste it. So far he had simply been unlucky, that was all. Ferguson was sure of it. The tartare steak was difficult to swallow.

His phone flashed again, and Ferguson saw Sykes's name on the screen. The gutless fool had been trying to get through to him all morning. It was obviously something important, or in Sykes's mind important, but Ferguson wasn't in the mood to hear about another screwup just yet.

If anything else went wrong, Ferguson would be having some more difficult nights. Should everything be wrapped up cleanly, there would still be all that came before it to tidy up too. Even if Alvarez ended up nowhere, Chambers and Procter wouldn't simply let things lie. As much as Ferguson disliked them, Procter in particular, he was painfully aware that the fat fuck and anorexic bitch were shrewd and determined individuals.

With Procter's great big nose sniffing around, Ferguson knew he was going to have to draw this thing to a resolution with absolutely no loose threads. Otherwise Procter would keep tugging away until the whole thing was pulled apart. The only way to put the issue to bed was if someone took the heat for hiring Tesseract. There had to be a bad guy.

A conversation a few decibels on the wrong side of rude interrupted his thoughts. He looked up to see Sykes arguing with the maître d'. Ferguson sighed and gestured for Sykes to be allowed to pass.

Ferguson made a point of eating and not looking at him as Sykes took a seat opposite. A file dropped onto the table.

"Merry fucking Christmas."

"I beg your pardon."

Ferguson glanced upward to see Sykes's smiling features. His face looked like it belonged in an ad for a range of male grooming products for the not-so young and not-so good-looking.

"Christmas has come early," he announced. "It's over."

"What?"

"It's over." Sykes declared again

The sixty-seven-year-old heart inside Ferguson's chest started to beat faster. "He's dead?"

Sykes's face stretched even further. "Blown to fucking smithereens."

"Sumner?"

"Dead too. Reed got them both. There's not enough left of either to identify. Nothing will come back to us. Ever."

Goose bumps rose down Ferguson's back. "*Thank God*," he said, joining Sykes with a smile of his own. "That boy is worth every penny. I do hope Her Majesty appreciates his skills." He paused for a moment to enjoy the sweet taste of victory. "I was almost concerned there for a moment."

Sykes laughed. "You're telling me. My heart's been in my mouth for over a week."

"Relief feels good, doesn't it, Mr. Sykes?"

"Fuck, yeah. But it gets better."

"He has the drive?" Ferguson asked, excitement in his voice.

Sykes nodded. He pointed at the file.

Ferguson raised his eyebrow and his forehead wrinkled. He reached for the file. "Already?"

Sykes nodded. "I've been trying to get hold of you for hours. I had plenty of time to sort it."

Ferguson discreetly opened the file and glimpsed the sonar pictures inside. "Where is it?"

"About eighty miles off the coast of Tanga, Tanzania," Sykes explained in a low voice.

The veteran CIA officer thought for a few moments. "You'll need to be on the soonest possible flight out. I'll think of some reason for you to visit the embassy on my behalf."

The reluctance in Sykes's face was obvious. "You want me to go personally?"

Ferguson nodded. "There have been far too many mistakes made on account of using third parties already. I need you there." The subtle but flattering appeal worked instantly. Ferguson could see Sykes warming to the idea. He continued. "Take a couple of divers—some former SEALs based on the Continent shouldn't be too hard to find."

"I gathered a list of suitable personnel some time

ago," Sykes said with seeming nonchalance but lashings of thinly disguised smugness.

"Very good," Ferguson said. "Plan for them to meet you there and brief them only when you're on the boat. Enough money should allay any reservations they might have about agreeing to a mission before they have all the facts."

"Okay."

"And let's make sure we know enough about them so that, should it be necessary, we can arrange for some unfortunate accidents to befall them, of the Reed variety." Sykes nodded, but a little uncomfortably. "And once you have everything organized it's time we started contacting potential buyers so we can make the sales as soon as possible. The longer we have those missiles in our possession, the more at risk we'll be."

"I'll sort it."

"Good man."

Sykes started to rise.

"Ah," Ferguson began, "given this last week's unfortunate events I think it would be wise if we cross off any Western buyers from the list."

Sykes sat back down. "Excuse me?"

"To be on the safe side," Ferguson assured. "It's best if we sell the missiles outside of Europe or the continental U.S."

"But the whole point was to sell them to the Pentagon. Our country will pay more than anyone by far."

Ferguson took a sip of wine. "Things have changed," he said. "It's too risky now. It was always going to be extremely difficult to deal with our own country and remain undetected, and that was before that massacre in the middle of Paris went down. We have Alvarez sniffing around like a bloodhound and spreading suspicion that this whole thing might be an illegal op as it is. What do you think will happen when we send an invoice to the military? And if we sell them in Europe our people over here will hear about it pretty fucking quickly too. Best we stick to other parts of the world only, I think."

"What other parts of the world? No North America, no Europe—Russia and China's already got them—the only countries left who would want them are in the Middle East or North Korea."

Ferguson took a sip of wine and nodded.

"Whoa, hold on a minute," Sykes said, leaning forward. "Now you're talking about selling arms to rogue states or fucking terrorists. That's as good as painting a bull's-eye on our nation's back. Fuck that. I'm not having the sinking of one of our carrier fleets on my conscience. I'm no traitor; I love my country."

Ferguson frowned. "Mr. Sykes, may I remind you those missiles can be used in anger against us already, whether we sell them or not. And, let me tell you, this planet would be far more stable if America loses some muscle mass."

"That's a rather unpatriotic view to take."

"Try not to mistake your own lack of balls for patriotism, Mr. Sykes. I've spent my life fighting this country's battles and had my blood spilled in the process, so don't presume to lecture me on patriotism now."

Sykes scoffed. "Spare me the hero speech."

If they'd have been in private, Ferguson's knuckles would have connected with Sykes's excuse for a jaw.

"Hero speech?" Ferguson spat. "How dare you? I gave twenty-five years and my marriage to fighting the cold war so you could sit there sporting your polished veneers and designer face cream. This country is still alive because of men like me, men who went the extra mile just to shovel the shit no one else would go near."

Sykes went to speak, but Ferguson cut him off. "But I've never considered myself a hero, not once, do you understand me? And I'll tell you now, I went into that fight knowing I would have to wear my medals on the inside, that it would be whisky in place of parades and instead of a twenty-one-gun salute it would be being left to rot in some shitty corner of hell the average Joe didn't even know existed. Keeping America safe has been my life, and it's sucked me dry, consumed every waking moment of my life—of my existence.

"Then the cold war ends, and guess what happens? Hey, you've done it, you've won the battle. It's over. Your hand gets shook and your back gets patted and the thanks last as long as they take to give. And before long you're forgotten, obsolete, a relic. You keep your job, but no one really wants you to do it anymore. Your expertise is worthless now because you actually won your fight. And what are you left with? No money. You got paid peanuts and didn't care. You took the job because you loved your country. But what happens when you find your country doesn't love you back? What do you have left?" He took a deep breath.

"I'll tell you," Ferguson said. "Nothing. That's what. You're surplus, a has-been. Old. You don't speak Arabic; you speak Russian. What good are you now?"

Sykes's shocked expression told Ferguson what he already knew, that he should have kept quiet. Ferguson grabbed his glass of Burgundy and took a big swallow.

"This isn't about the money," Sykes said eventually. "You were never going to sell those missiles to our military, were you? You want to get revenge. You want to get back at Uncle Sam for forgetting about you."

Ferguson put his glass down. "That's where you're wrong. I don't care enough about my country anymore to want revenge. This *is* about the money. I want to be reimbursed for all my years of loyal service when I did care."

"Well, I'm not helping you do it if it means selling those missiles to fucking North Korea or worse."

"That's where you're wrong again, Mr. Sykes. You're going to do exactly as you're ordered to the absolute best of your abilities. Do you know why? Because you've been party to multiple murders. American citizens are dead thanks to you, or had you forgotten? The only way out of this is through lethal injection."

Sykes glared hard at Ferguson.

Ferguson drained the last of the wine. "Don't look at me like that, Mr. Sykes. Once you've sold your soul to the devil you can't then ask for it back."

SIXTY-SEVEN

Exercise always cleared his head and focused his mind. The simple pleasure of physical exertion was one that most people did everything in their power to avoid. Reed could not understand that, but he could not understand most people anyway. He grunted. He had his toes resting on his room's high bed to increase the resistance of his one-arm pushups. He breathed hard. Sweat dripped from his nose.

His smartphone flashed, breaking his concentration and interrupting his rhythm. He squeezed his eyes shut to regain his focus, determined only to stop for death itself. Training was about beating his body with his mind, and with a body so perfectly honed it was never easy.

He fought on—breathe out, push, breathe in, lower, repeat, repeat, repeat. Finally he collapsed, no longer able to continue. He lay with his face on the carpet for a minute while he regained his breath.

All the lights were off in his hotel room, and he operated only from his natural night vision. The phone felt heavy when he lifted it, but he knew the fatigue would pass shortly. Reed was at the peak of physical fitness. The new message was from his most recent client. He sat down on the end of the bed to read it.

Another contract. Reed absorbed the details and considered for a minute. The stipulations of the job required him to go to Africa immediately, but the target could only be dispatched once Reed had been given the green light from the client, who noted the target to be an easy feat for Reed's skills. The Englishman shook his head. The appeal to his vanity was particularly transparent, even from a client he guessed to be American.

The idea of taking another contract so soon after killing five others was not something Reed would normally do. He needed to return to the Firm's employment as soon as possible. He could only take so long an absence at one time without it creating problems. Plus, he did not particularly like the sound of flying to Tanzania and then waiting until the client gave him the go-ahead. The prospect of another sizeable donation to his bank account was, however, particularly appealing.

Reed composed a reply and sent it to the client. He checked his watch. It was too late to travel, so he decided to sleep for a few hours first. He took a pillow from the bed and placed it on the floor. He lay on his back, palms flat by his hips, knife within easy reach.

He woke precisely three hours later and phoned the front desk, asking for travel arrangements to be made on his behalf. He then showered, dressed, and packed his things. He checked out and collected the flight details from the concierge.

He climbed into a taxi in front of the hotel and told the driver to take him to the airport. Reed had never been to Tanzania before. If nothing else, the trip would broaden his horizons.

* * *

As Reed's taxi pulled away from the curb, a man on the opposite side of the street lowered his newspaper. He was dressed like a tourist: long shorts, T-shirt, sunglasses, and ball cap. He waited until the taxi crossed an intersection and headed into the distance before dropping the newspaper into a trash can and crossing the road. It was a warm afternoon.

The man took the cap from his head as he entered the hotel. He walked through the spacious lobby and took the elevator as though he were a guest returning to his room. He used the key card he had stolen from a maid the day before to open a hotel-room door. Inside, he closed the door behind him and reached underneath the bed frame. After a moment his hand gripped the device and pulled it free from the tape that held it in place.

The device consisted of two components: a small radio receiver and an attached digital audio recorder. Sitting down on the bed, Victor scrolled through the noise-activated recordings, ignoring the sounds of a maid's vacuuming, a door being slammed, and several TV news broadcasts. It was the last recording that he listened to twice, making notes on a small pad of paper.

He unscrewed the caps at either end of the room's telephone receiver and opened up the case. Inside, the ends of two new wires were tightly wrapped around exposed sections of copper wire running the length of the receiver. Those wires formed a circuit that transmitted the sound waves of a voice as fluctuating electrical currents between the phone's speaker and microphone.

The new wires were in turn attached to a small transmitter the size of a bottle top fixed to the telephone casing with superglue. The transmitter worked by emitting the electrical signal running through the wires as radio waves. Because the transmitter was so small, the signal sent was weak and could only be picked up from short distances. To be sure of an excellent recording, Victor had placed the receiver only a few feet away beneath the bed.

He removed the transmitter and wires from the phone before fixing the receiver back together. Victor left the hotel room and made his way back to the lobby. Outside, the keycard, radio receiver, and transmitter joined the newspaper.

The night of the explosion Victor had recognized the assassin straightaway. There could have been no mistaking him. No one who witnessed a bomb blast behaved like that. Not unless they also happened to be the bomber. He had walked away casually, seemingly without a care in the world. He was dressed in khaki pants and a white long-sleeved shirt. He looked like a tourist, not a killer. That was the point.

Victor saw the telltale signs of countersurveillance in the assassin's manner, even though he believed his job to be complete. He never walked at the same pace for long, sometimes crossing the road for no apparent reason, sometimes crossing back suddenly. He frequently paused to look in shop windows, to check in the reflection for anyone who might be following him. He was good, very good.

Victor had kept pace with him, mirroring his movements, staying out of sight. He stayed close but not too close, his face lost in the crowds that lay between them. Despite his precautions, the killer wasn't as thorough as he could have been. But letting your guard down when the job was done and the danger past was a mistake everyone made at some point.

Victor corrected himself. Nearly everyone.

Once he had discovered where the assassin was staying, Victor had bribed an unhappy-looking concierge to find out which room was his. After stealing the key card, Victor had bugged the room when its occupant was eating dinner in the hotel restaurant. Now he knew that his mark was leaving Cyprus and where he was heading, even which flight he would be taking.

That he was leaving proved Victor's enemies believed he'd died in the bomb blast. He was no longer a target. With such extensive fire damage, the authorities might never be able to conclude that only one out of the two guests were present in the room at the time of the blaze. All Victor had to do was get off the island and disappear. Even if his enemies eventually realized he was still alive, he would be ten thousand miles away with a new face and a new life. They would never find him.

The plan had been to kill whoever wanted him dead, to erase the threat, to stay alive. Now he didn't need to do that. He could live his life without expecting an assassin's bullet.

He'd won.

Victor hailed a taxi and told the driver to take him to the airport. He sat in the back, silently staring out the window. He thought about where he might go, thinking of those countries where he had never set foot, where he had always wanted to go. For prudence it would be best to go to somewhere in South America first. His Spanish was good, and he would quickly become fluent. He could pay for a new identity there, a genuine identity, become a citizen of Argentina maybe. Then from there, Who knew where he would go?

But he wasn't going to South America, sensible as that idea would be. Because there was something he needed first. Something he couldn't live the rest of his life without. Something he'd never wanted before.

Revenge.

SIXTY-EIGHT

Harrisonburg, Virginia, U.S.A.
Saturday
08:12 EST

"I always wanted to ride when I was younger," Procter said. His arms were folded and resting on top of a sturdy wooden fence. In the field on the other side grazed two bay quarter horses. "Never got the chance though. Now I'm too old and too fat to start." He didn't look unhappy about this declaration. "They're amazing creatures, full of character and grace."

Alvarez stood to the side of Procter. "All I see is two big dumb animals eating grass."

Procter laughed and looked at him. "Never wanted to be a cowboy, then?"

"I hear horse meat tastes pretty good."

They were in the heart of rural Virginia, farm country. Their cars were parked on a narrow road flanked by fields. No other vehicles had driven by so far. The sun was shining, but the air was crisp. Procter was dressed in jeans and a casual shirt underneath his coat. Alvarez wore a suit and overcoat. He'd barely worn anything else for weeks.

Procter turned around. "How was the flight?"

"Long."

"I can tell. You look worn out."

"I'm tired as dead dog."

Procter rubbed his hands together. "You should try going to bed. I hear it's the recommended cure for tiredness."

"I'll sleep later."

"I've got a thermos in the car. You want a cup of coffee?"

Alvarez shook his head. "I'm trying to reduce my caffeine intake."

"Really?"

"It's not good for the body."

"And how's that working out for you?"

"Not so good."

Procter turned around again and leaned his considerable weight against the fence. The wood made a loud, threatening creak.

"You didn't hear that," he said.

"Hear what?"

The associate deputy director had always been a chunky 3XL kind of guy, but without a suit to thin him out a bit he looked like he was carrying more weight than was good for two people, let alone one. Alvarez, who measured his own body fat in the single percentiles, saw a heart attack waiting to happen.

"It's Saturday," Procter stated, "the weekend."

"I know."

"You know what a weekend is?"

"I used to."

"What's on your mind that couldn't wait until Monday?"

"A woman."

Procter smiled. "My dad used to say behind the scowl of every man lurks a member of the fairer sex."

"That's probably true," Alvarez said. "But this isn't just any woman." He drew a notebook from inside his coat and opened it. "Her name's Rebecca Sumner, aka Rachel Swanson, American citizen, used to be one of ours, formerly of the Directorate of Intelligence working the Europe office until around four months ago."

Procter's face became serious. "The woman who met with Ozols's killer?"

Alvarez nodded. "She was a good analyst, a hard worker, on the rise, ambitious, all that shit. She resigned her post to work in the private sector. On the surface nothing more than a government employee off to land a bigger paycheck. Only she didn't take a job with any of the usual suspects. In fact, she left the country under a false passport three weeks after leaving her desk with the company. She went to France and rented a small apartment in Marseilles, paid for six months' rent in advance. In cash."

Procter looked skeptical. "On an analyst's take home?"

"If it was," Alvarez said, "then I'm in the wrong job and you can take my verbal resignation right now. But no, there were no withdrawals from her bank account to match the deposit. Someone else gave her the money. She had no means of employment in France, but monthly donations were made into her U.S. bank account to the amount of her former salary."

"No kidding?"

Alvarez flipped over a couple of pages. "On Wednesday, French police entered her apartment and discovered a few things of note, such as a sink full of burned documents and communications equipment. Half her clothes were gone. Drawers were left opened. The front door hadn't been locked."

"What spooked her?"

"A neighbor confirmed she left her apartment in the early hours of Friday morning. Before she left, Sumner made several calls to John Kennard's cell phone. He was already dead by then, of course, and Sumner didn't leave a message. It was the first time she'd ever phoned him. They had never worked together at the agency or trained together at the Farm. They lived twenty miles apart, had different social circles, no family in common, no reason to explain why she had his phone number. Seems when he didn't answer her call, she packed her bags and disappeared."

"To Paris."

Alvarez nodded. "Her cousin owns an apartment

there that she was using. Anyway, she's there less than a day when French authorities try to apprehend a suspect they believed to be the man responsible for the hotel massacre. He was seen entering the building with Sumner. Obviously we know what happened next.

"The killer knows Sumner, who knows Kennard. For argument's sake, let's say they've been working together. Kennard was in Paris with me working on getting the location of those missiles from Ozols. He had access to all my notes. More important, he was there when Ozols gave me the time and location of the meet. Maybe he passed that on to Sumner, who did the same to the killer. A nice arrangement. Efficient. Fewer risks.

"But something goes wrong because Kennard is killed, which spooks Sumner into leaving Marseilles. She thinks she's next, so she's meets with Ozols's killer, who survived an assassination attempt. Hoyt drowns in the bath."

"A cleanup."

"Exactly."

"So who's behind it?"

"I don't know for certain," Alvarez answered honestly. "I can't see Sumner and Kennard, two young CIA employees, turning mercenary. Kennard maybe, but the fact that Sumner continued to receive a pay packet equaling her old salary tells me she could have been tricked into thinking she was part of a legit, albeit off the books, op."

"Only someone within the agency could pull that off," Procter stated. "You've got a suspect, haven't you?"

"I've no proof."

"Go on."

"Remember: Russian missiles, only six people knew about Hoyt. I'm one of them, a techie in Paris is another, and the rest are the four people in the briefing room when I gave my report."

"And I'm one of those," Procter said.

Alvarez nodded.

Procter blew out some air. He shook his head. "Old bastard's retiring next year."

"Maybe he wants to add to his retirement fund."

Procter looked thoughtful. He didn't speak for a long time.

"You've done a good job, Antonio," he said eventually. "But given the sensitivity of what you've just told me, I don't want you to speak of this to anyone again. That includes me."

"What are you saying?"

"I'm going to tell you this because I like you, not because you need to know," Procter explained. "I've known for some time that we had a problem in NCS, someone playing by their own rules. This isn't the first time something like this has happened. I've had people looking into this whole thing for a while, from other angles." They watched a car drive past until it became small in the distance. "I've never been able to get close before. And I never would have guessed Ferguson would be who I'm after, but now we might just have made that all-important break. You've helped immeasurably already, but you're too close to this. You—"

Alvarez scowled. He adjusted his footing. "Sir, don't take me off this now when I'm this close to nailing this fucker. If Ferguson really is behind this and we get him, we'll be able to catch Ozols's killer next, then whoever murdered John. Everyone."

Procter put a hand on Alvarez's shoulder. "I respect your dedication but you've done as much as you can. If it is Ferguson, then he knows you are on his trail. He's probably got people watching everything you do."

"You seriously believe that?"

"Why not? Ferguson has been so careful about covering his tracks that he's killed or tried to kill everyone who even knows a piece of the puzzle. If that's the case, he's sure as shit going to keep an eye on the person trying to put those pieces together."

Alvarez looked around. He thought back, trying to remember if he'd seen anything that could be surveillance. There wasn't, but he just might not have detected it. Alvarez was a good operative, but he wasn't deluded about his skills. He couldn't guarantee no one had tailed him.

"So what do we do now?"

"If you continue openly investigating, we may force him to abandon his plans and might never get this close to him again. We can't have that. We're going to pretend the matter is closed and make Ferguson feel secure while we look for evidence. You can't be involved in that. Look what happened when you found out about Hoyt. He was dead twenty-four hours later."

Alvarez couldn't hide his disappointment. "I've worked my ass off for the last two weeks on this, losing a good five pounds in the process of trying to track down Ozols's killer and that goddamn flash drive—not to mention the five months it took me to get Ozols to play ball so we could get those missiles and stop any evil fuckers from getting their fingers on the technology. A colleague of mine is dead, killed by the same people who murdered Ozols. That person is someone inside Langley, if it's Ferguson then he's a fucking traitor whose hand I have shaken, and you want me to let it go?"

It had taken all his will to keep from raising his voice.

Procter looked at him sympathetically. "Not let it go, hand it over. You've done everything you can."

"Sir, I still think I can be involved without anyone knowing. We can—"

Procter moved away from the fence and pointed his key fob at his car. "My mind's made up, Antonio." He took a few steps before turning around. "Get me hard copies of everything you have and drop them off at my office Monday morning. Destroy your own copies. That's an order."

Alvarez took an almighty calming breath.

In the field the quarter horses were running. Procter watched them for a moment before looking back at Alvarez.

"Go home," the big guy said. "Go home and get some sleep."

Alvarez's knuckles were white on the steering wheel of his Dodge sedan. His eyes stared ahead, seeing the road, the traffic, but focused on a point far away. His nostrils flared with each big, regular exhale. The anger inside him made his heart thump hard. He wasn't sure how long he'd been driving, an hour at least, maybe two. He didn't know where he was heading but he was going nowhere. He passed the same landmarks, took the same intersections, circling the countryside so he could talk—try to talk—himself out of doing something stupid.

But it wasn't working. The more he thought, the angrier he got, until he made a right where he'd taken a left three times before, and twenty minutes later he was slowing down to drive past the big colonial house where a certain traitorous a-hole made his home. It was a nice place, that much was obvious, and Alvarez wondered how much had been paid for by dollars other than Uncle Sam's. Ferguson was home, judging by the two cars on the drive.

Alvarez pulled up on the opposite side of the road a couple of houses along. He turned off the engine and adjusted his mirrors so he could see Ferguson's driveway. He checked his watch, figuring he wouldn't have to wait long.

If he'd been anywhere else he'd be asleep by now, but anger, adrenaline, and determination kept the tiredness from taking hold. It happened ten minutes later, one guy in a tan-colored Ford. He pulled up on the same side of the road as Alvarez, two properties along, the other way back from Ferguson's. Through his mirrors Alvarez watched the guy adjusting his own mirrors.

Good. Alvarez had been worried Procter wouldn't act soon enough, but he'd made a call and got someone watching Ferguson pretty damn quick. Very good. Now it would be impossible for Alvarez to kick Ferguson's door down and threaten to plug the old fuck if he didn't come clean.

Alvarez gave it a minute or two before starting up the engine. He saw the guy in the tan Ford register him and expected a note would be made. Procter would probably give him crap about it when he found out, but Alvarez had been forced to eat enough crap today that some more would just seem like dessert.

He headed for DC, a little above the speed limit, and reached his destination in good time. Again he pulled up on the opposite side of the road and used his mirrors to watch the building. Sykes was on the third floor of the plush brownstone that was a good way above what he should be able to afford. Alvarez knew that Sykes's parents were wealthy, so he wasn't about to jump the gun and assume the guy was rotten just because of where he lived.

Cars came and went, but Alvarez didn't see any surveillance. That figured. It cost a lot to watch people, especially agency people, and Ferguson was the suspect, not Sykes. But Alvarez was convinced that if this whole thing was a rogue op run by Ferguson, he sure as hell wasn't running it alone.

Ferguson was too thorough and too careful to have gotten his hands dirty personally. There had to be a conduit between him and the assets on the ground. If it wasn't Sykes, then Alvarez was going to have to look elsewhere, but if it was Sykes, then Alvarez was working a lead just sitting in his car. Procter had told him to keep off Ferguson. He hadn't said anything about Sykes.

After an hour Alvarez was starting to need to piss something bad, but ten minutes later he'd forgotten about his bladder entirely. Sykes was coming out of the building's front door. He was carrying a suitcase and looked in a hurry. Alvarez sat up in his seat, watching Sykes intently as he hailed a taxi, starting the engine as one pulled up, putting the Dodge in gear as Sykes climbed in.

The taxi was easy to follow. Alvarez hung back two cars, quickly realizing that it was heading for Dulles. Maybe Sykes was going overseas, somewhere sunny on the coast of the Indian Ocean.

Alvarez took out his cell phone and cycled through his numbers until he found the name he was looking for. He hit dial, switched the phone to speaker, and put it in his lap so he could get both hands back on the wheel.

After seven rings a man answered. "Yeah?"

"Joe, it's Antonio. I need a favor, fast."

"Man, I'm only a Fed on weekdays. I'm at the park with my kid. Can't it wait?"

"Would I be calling if it could?"

A pause. "Okay, what can I do?"

"I need you to check credit-card transactions in the name of Kevin Sykes." He gave Sykes's address and social security.

"What am I looking for?"

"He's bought an airline ticket, and I need to know where he's going."

"How long have I got?"

"He's on the way to the airport now, so not long."

"My wife is giving me dirty looks. I'm not going to get any tonight."

"Spare me the details. Just hurry, please. It's important."

"I'll phone the office now."

Alvarez thanked him and hung up. His phone rang after eleven minutes.

"Okay, your friend Mr. Sykes used his AmEx to buy a roundtrip from Dulles to Kilimanjaro, Tanzania, by way of Paris and Amsterdam. Air France leaving at four fifteen. That's a twenty-four-hour flight. And I figured if you wanted to know where he's flying to, you'll want to know where he's going when he gets there."

"Yeah. Where?"

"Some city in Tanzania, Tanga. It's on the coast. He's booked himself a room at a hotel there."

"How the hell do you know that?"

"Same way I know about his flight. His credit card."

"Shit, I didn't even think."

"Well, you sound tired."

"I am."

"There you go then. Plus, you never were very smart to begin with."

A few seconds later Alvarez was calling the airport. He couldn't risk taking the same flight as Sykes, even if the two had only met a couple of times in person. Alvarez learned that the next Air France flight left six hours later, which would give Sykes too much of a head start. He also learned that a Northwest flight leaving an hour after Sykes could get him direct to Amsterdam in time to join the same flight down to Tanzania. It was also cheaper.

Surprised but pleased, Alvarez gave his credit-card details to the operator without hesitation. If Sykes was going to Tanzania, it could be for only one reason.

He knew where the missiles were.

SIXTY-NINE

Eighty Miles East of Tanga, Tanzania
Sunday
17:27 UST

Sykes squinted against the glare of the afternoon sun. He stood on the deck of the commercial salvage vessel hired by Dalweg and Wiechman. The pair were former Navy SEALs who ran their own diving-and-salvage company based a few hundred miles up the coast in Kenya. They didn't have the greatest of service records before leaving their respective teams, Dalweg in particular. He'd left the navy with a dishonorable discharge for beating a prostitute so bad she almost died. But the retired special-forces guys had been used by the company before on deniable operations and knew how to keep their mouths shut.

The pair had arrived in Tanga a day before Sykes and had hired the boat and purchased equipment they weren't able to bring across the border. Before Sykes had even arrived, a sizeable chunk of cash had been wired into Dalweg and Wiechman's company bank account. They would get the same amount again when the mission had been completed.

As Ferguson had made clear, Sykes had first informed them of the rough details of their task and had only given them a full briefing when they were on the boat.

"That'll increase the fee by twenty-five percent," Dalweg had said.

Sykes had assured him that he would see to it when the job was done. Figuring that would happen, Sykes had only offered them half of what Ferguson was willing to pay. Even with their increased fee, Sykes would still walk away with a fat few K's of the total in his own pocket. He was pretty pleased with his brokering skills, and it felt good to be ripping off that fucker Ferguson too.

Sykes found Dalweg and Wiechman to be typical ex-military types, particularly ex–spec ops guys. They were built big and tanned, with lined and weathered faces and stares that could curdle cream. Both were around forty and had the scars and stories that only men who had fired rifles in anger carried. Despite their penchant for expletives and bad taste in jokes, Sykes found them to be all business.

The temperature had slowly been on the increase since the boat had left port, and Sykes was sweating more than he had in years. He wore long shorts and a T-shirt that was showing dark stains under the armpits and at the center of his chest. He would've taken his shirt off, but, despite his weekly gym visits, he felt very body conscious alongside the two former SEALs, who both had arms as thick as his thighs. He knew, even without their taking a look at his love handles, that they already looked down on him as a soft CIA pen pusher who had no place in the field.

They had dropped into the sea twenty minutes ago and had assured Sykes their recon dive would take no more than half an hour. With the aid of standard dive tanks, they had descended to the seabed to examine the frigate and the missiles. They would then surface and plan how best to extract them from the sunken ship. With luck they would be back at port before dark, and anything they couldn't get today would be extracted tomorrow.

There was a big hydraulic winch fitted onto the deck, next to which was a large amount of equipment that Sykes didn't recognize, and he didn't want to show his ignorance by asking for it to be explained. He knew it was salvage-and-demolitions equipment, but that was the extent of his knowledge. He unscrewed the top from a bottle of water and took a long drink.

The ocean was far calmer than he expected, but Sykes was a certified land lover who much preferred a swimming pool and a deck chair to a beach and surf. He'd popped a couple of sea-sickness pills just in case, and it was almost time for some more.

Normally waiting around with nothing to do would have frustrated Sykes, but he was deep in thought. It wasn't long ago that he was fantasizing about briefcases full of dollar bills and bank balances with lots of zeros. Not anymore. The close calls and narrow escapes of the past couple of weeks, combined with the new insight into Ferguson's plans, had left him feeling scared and regretful. If he wasn't in so deep, Sykes would have gone straight to Procter to fess up. Ferguson's comment about the lethal injection was never far from Sykes's mind.

Whatever else happened, Sykes was sure of one thing: It wasn't going to end well. Ferguson had shown himself to be a thoroughly unscrupulous and spiteful bastard who Sykes could barely trust. After the way Ferguson had made sure everyone who knew anything about his plans had met with the grim reaper, how did Sykes know he himself wouldn't end up being a similar liability that needed silencing?

That thought had meant he'd barely slept since Ferguson had ordered him to fly to Tanzania. He put a hand to the back of his shorts and checked that the SIG was still there. He'd kept it on his person every second since landing. Dalweg and Wiechman didn't strike him as the kind of guys who would turn hitman for a few extra bucks, but he wasn't about to take the chance.

He knew he was probably just being paranoid. Ferguson needed him. But Sykes, who was aware of his own considerable usefulness and the irrationality of having him killed, was also perfectly aware that Ferguson had shown himself to not always be the most rational of individuals.

Until things had calmed down, Sykes would stay on guard. If anyone so much as looked at him funny, he would turn himself in. Maybe he'd be able to cut a deal, testify against Ferguson to avoid the needle. Better to spend his life behind bars than end up a victim of Ferguson's madness.

He stared off into the distance. All around was water. Endless blue sea that met the sky at the horizon. He felt utterly alone. There was a splinter of worry at the back of his mind. What if Dalweg and Wiechman got chowed on by sharks or their tanks ruptured? Sykes didn't know how to drive the boat, and he certainly didn't know how to navigate.

He took another gulp of water and turned around as he heard a noise. A head emerged from the sea a few feet from the boat. Wiechman. He pulled his goggles up from his eyes and removed his mouthpiece. He pushed sandy blond hair away from his face.

"What's it like?" Sykes called.

Wiechman shook his head. "It's a wreck."

"I know that."

The former SEAL swam the short distance to the boat. When he reached the back he pulled himself on board. "It looks good," he said. "Hull's split open real nice, so we've got an open channel straight to the missiles."

"Yeah?"

"There's eight on board, four are crushed, smashed, or otherwise totally fucked up. The casings on two more have ruptured, and the seawater has corroded them to hell. We can get two for sure. It's going to take all day, though, because of the amount of other crap down there burying them."

"Two's good." Sykes's eyes squinted behind his sunglasses. "We never figured on getting them all."

"Looks like they're just practice warheads."

"Doesn't matter."

Dalweg surfaced and swam to the boat. Wiechman wiped the water from around his eyes. "Fuckers are big, though, bigger than I thought; we're never going to get them up here in one piece. We'll have to dismantle them as best we can first. Then bring them up with balloons before we winch them on board."

"Whatever it takes."

"Okay."

Dalweg joined them on the deck. "Reckon with a little luck we'll get you the two good ones up before we have to head back later. Can always come back tomorrow to see if anything else is recoverable."

"That's fine," Sykes said. "Just make sure you don't blow yourselves up."

Dalweg laughed, but Sykes hadn't been joking.

He took a seat while the two divers sorted through their gear. He didn't understand how the hell he'd gotten himself in such a mess. He'd thrown away his honor for nothing more than money. It wasn't as if he was even poor to begin with. He'd just wanted more than he had. Sykes put a hand to his chest, feeling the sudden burn of rising acid. If his insides didn't melt away before the end of this thing, he was going to be very surprised.

Luckily it was almost over now. They would have two extremely valuable missiles within twenty-four hours, and they'd sell them to jihadists or North Korea or whichever psychos paid the most. Then they could develop their own arsenals of antiship cruise missiles, and Sykes would spend the rest of his life praying one was never used to sink an American vessel.

Sykes knew he was greedy and stupid and a coward.

But at least he was going to be rich.

SEVENTY

Tanga, Tanzania
Sunday
19:03 UST

The target was quite clearly troubled. His manner bespoke of a man anxious and distressed. His movements were rushed and awkward, his face a picture of concern. What perturbed him Reed could only guess, but even if he could guess correctly, he wouldn't care. Reed stood with his arms folded in front of his chest, leaning against a low wall. At least two dozen people were between Reed and his prey. Reed's eyes were hidden behind a pair of mirrored sunglasses.

Two large men, one blond, the other dark, disembarked from the cab of a three-ton truck caked with dirt. They were the target's traveling companions. Both had deep tans and bulky limbs. Along with the target, the two men walked around to the back of the truck and peered inside. Seemingly satisfied, they crossed the road and approached their hotel. None of the three saw the Caucasian man who stood within a crowd of locals, watching them with an amoral gaze.

The hotel was a decent one, or at least it was for this part of the world. Tanga was large and sprawling, but seemed quiet and sleepy, almost deserted in its center, where once-impressive German colonial buildings had succumbed to age and disrepair. Around the bustling market Tanga was more vibrant and crowded, with colorful, busy streets lined with more modern but less-grand structures.

Here the roads were laid with asphalt, gravel or hard-packed dirt formed the surfaces. Reed had yet to see a pavement. The air was hot and humid, somewhere in the low eighties. He could smell grilled chicken, frying fish, and marinated mishikaki kebabs from the nearby market. Vendors used seed rattlers to advertise their wares and customers haggled for better prices.

A thin film of sweat covered Reed's skin. The time in Cyprus had taken it a few shades up from the pasty complexion he normally sported as a typical Englishman. He was dressed like a tourist in loose-fitting cargo trousers and a light linen shirt. Long sleeved. Sandals would have been appropriate but didn't afford the kind of grip needed when moving with haste, so he opted for some conservative-colored athletic shoes.

The target rushed up the hotel steps with his two companions following behind. Each had a backpack over their shoulder and one carried a large sports bag in each hand. The dossier had stated that they would be armed. Both were former commandos, and that alone gave Reed cause to respect them, but they were on a diving-and-demolitions expedition and were not bodyguards. Reed had no plans to kill either unless they were unfortunate enough to get in his way.

The client had arranged weapons for him to collect on arrival: a rifle and a handgun. The rifle, an Armalite AR-15 assault rifle equipped with an optical sight for sniping, was hidden under some discarded tires half a mile away. The handgun, a Glock 17 with attached suppressor, was in Reed's shoulder bag. Both had already been checked, stripped, and thoroughly cleaned by Reed. Given such firepower, his employer's note, that the target's death should not appear natural or accidental, was somewhat redundant.

Reed did not plan on using either weapon. The locale was not a good one for sniping—narrow, busy streets that offered little chance of a clean line of sight. The handgun was more appropriate to the environs, but given the choice Reed preferred the more intimate effect afforded by a blade.

He was still waiting for the order from the client and had already decided the hotel would be the best strike point. Executing the target on the street was an option, but Reed didn't want to create a scene unless he had to. A quiet execution in a hotel room was considerably more appealing. He was eager to complete this job without creating a commotion. That he had used a bomb in Cyprus continued to gnaw at his professional sensibilities.

The target disappeared through the hotel's front entrance, and Reed checked his watch. A Tanzanian man in an oil-stained T-shirt tried to sell him coconuts. The man spoke in his native Swahili. Reed spoke several languages fluently, had a reasonable grasp of several more, but Swahili was, and never would be, one of them. When Reed shook his head, the man tried broken English, the language of Tanzania's post-German masters. Reed removed his sunglasses, and the man, unnerved by the look in Reed's eyes, turned and left him alone.

Reed replaced his sunglasses and approached the hotel. The bright sun prevented him from seeing through the glass of the windows or doors. He gave the target a generous four minutes to leave the lobby and then crossed the street. He pushed through the revolving entrance. The lobby was several degrees cooler than outside, the large ceiling fans working hard to keep the room a pleasant temperature. Immediately Reed became more aware of the sweat on his skin.

As he expected, the target and his companions were absent. Reed approached the front desk and paid for a single room with cash and took the stairs to the fifth floor. The hotel used regular metal keys, and Reed found a quaintness that at least one corner of the world had yet to be modernized. It would also make it easier to get through locked doors if he had to be quiet. Reed's room was functional and clean, but the décor was bland. No matter. Reed was not there to enjoy himself.

He unslung his shoulder bag and removed the handgun. He placed the weapon under one of the bed's pillows. Carrying the bag around was to be avoided. It would draw attention. He spent ten minutes examining the room before he opened the window to let in some air. He had no plans to stay in the hotel, but the room gave legitimacy to his presence. His white face made him too recognizable to linger in the vicinity otherwise.

The dossier already told him that the target was staying in room 314. The two divers were down the hall in 320. There was an elevator and two sets of stairs. Reed always preferred to use stairs if it was practical to do so. In an elevator he was virtually trapped and completely exposed when the doors opened to whomever was waiting. He exited the room and returned to the lobby.

There was a modest hotel bar that seemed pleasant enough. He bought a bottle of mineral water and took a seat where he could see enough of the lobby to know if the target left. Reed had been informed that his prey would be in Tanga for at least a couple of days, but the Englishman was nonetheless prudent. The mineral water was refreshingly cold. He was a little bored.

Though Reed had killed five people inside a week and was due to kill another shortly, only killing the target he knew as Tesseract had given him anything close to satisfaction. Even that was limited, since dispatching him had placed no real demands on Reed's considerable skills. He had originally given Tesseract credit for his performance in Paris, but now concluded that surviving that attack had more to do with the incompetence of the assailants than with Tesseract's own ability. A truly capable professional would not have been killed so easily in Cyprus. It was a shame that a potentially worthy adversary had been found so wanting—lamentable, but Reed had yet to encounter anyone who lived up to such a mantle. In short, Tesseract was an amateur compared with Reed.

The bar was almost empty except for some foreigners who were grouped in a corner and laughing over a few drinks. Reed took a small sip from his water. Maybe it was time to only take challenging contracts. It was more befitting to his abilities that way. Perhaps until the new year he should perform only for the Firm and decline any private offers that came his way. Well, unless they appealed to his sense of adventure. Reed was getting ahead of himself, he knew. He still had this job to complete, and untaxing as it was, he still needed to keep his focus. When one's concentration waned, mistakes followed. Reed's smartphone was in the pocket of his trousers. He took it out and placed it on the table before him.

He waited.

SEVENTY-ONE

Falls Church, Virginia, U.S.A.
Sunday
12:05 EST

It took a few seconds for the ringing phone to pull Ferguson from his sleep and another few before he understood what had woken him. Decades had passed since Ferguson had needed to be on guard while resting, and his once-acute senses had dulled with age and inactivity. He reached out a thin hand to grab the phone.

His voice was croaky. "Yes?"

"It's done."

"Who is this?"

It was Sykes. He spoke hurriedly, frantically. "We've got the missiles, well two of them, what we could get from them. We'll go back tomorrow, see what else we can salvage. They doubt we'll get anything though."

"Slow down," Ferguson said. "And tell me again."

Sykes spoke more slowly, describing exactly what had been extracted and the situation regarding the remaining missiles. Ferguson took a few moments to digest what he was being told. He sat up.

"You have two of the missiles? In your possession?"

"Not one hundred percent of them, but propulsion, electronics, etcetera. In a truck outside."

Ferguson stared into the shadows of his bedroom. The drapes were closed to stop the sun from interrupting his nap. He felt as though someone had injected him with pure joy.

"That's tremendous news. Well done, Mr. Sykes."

"Thanks."

Sykes's toned echoed none of Ferguson's own happiness. Not that it mattered.

"Stay in your hotel and keep a low profile tonight, and tomorrow you can see what else can be recovered."

"Okay."

Ferguson hung up. He climbed off the bed and made his way downstairs and into his study. He felt tired, both in mind and body, but at least it was almost over. Just another messy assignment in a lifetime of necessary but untidy service to his nation. A nation that had registered him obsolete. After all those years of faithful service it was surely only right that he receive a generous retirement package.

It would be nice to have more missiles, but the greater the number, the harder it would be to transport and store secretly. Two missiles were plenty. Hell, he only needed to sell one to bank more money than he could ever spend.

Once the dust had settled, Ferguson would be whiter than white. There wouldn't even be the barest hint he had anything to do with Tesseract or Ozols or the missiles. He thought about all the events that had conspired to create this result while the computer powered up. What could he have done to have made things work out more smoothly? Even with the benefit of hindsight there wasn't much that should have been done differently. No one could have foreseen Tesseract's surviving that ambush in Paris. Things had only become messy after that. The one mistake Ferguson knew he'd made was in using Sykes, but fortunately he was in a position to correct that.

His loyal deputy would take the blame for everything. Sykes had the power to have seen this thing through thus far—the ambition—and the idiocy to get himself killed in the process.

Dalweg and Wiechman had been contacted the day before and briefed on what was about to happen and what they were to do afterward, so Ferguson had only one message to send. The e-mail took him seconds to write and gave him considerable satisfaction to send. The e-mail contained just one word.

Proceed.

SEVENTY-TWO

Tanga, Tanzania
Sunday
19:17 UST

The kitchen was even hotter than outside and carried the loud noise of busy work. There were maybe a dozen members of the kitchen staff working frantically, preparing and cooking food, washing up, cleaning. A huge chef was shouting orders with the vigor of a drill sergeant. Victor, with a small crate of fruit on his shoulder, drew neither looks nor words as he dodged around the working bodies. He appeared to have a purpose and a reason for being there, and busy people rarely interrupted their work to challenge someone else who also seemed to be working.

Victor kept his head tilted slightly forward so it was hard for anyone to see his eyes. Eye contact helped people remember. His gaze passed over the work surfaces as he moved, trying to find a knife to palm. He saw none and didn't want to risk loitering and attracting attention just to get one. A weapon was always useful, but for what he was planning he could go without. He left the crate on the floor by the interior door before he slipped through.

The assassin had still been waiting outside when Victor left him. He'd taken the same flight to Tanzania, flying coach while the assassin flew first, and had followed the man since. Under normal circumstances he wouldn't have fancied his chances at shadowing so skilled a target, but Victor had one considerable advantage. He was supposed to be dead.

Victor had imagined sliding a knife into the assassin's flesh alongside the spine and piercing the heart or maybe hamstringing the man first to watch him writhe on the ground before finishing him off. But that wasn't what Victor did, even if he had been able to. He didn't stab people in the street in front of dozens of witnesses, no matter how much he wanted to. That's what amateurs did, and amateurs got themselves killed.

Even if the opportunity presented itself, Victor

couldn't kill him, at least not yet. The assassin was nothing more than a hired gun, a paid killer no different than himself. Victor hated the comparison. The man he'd followed wasn't his true enemy; he was just a limb. Victor wanted to cut off the head.

The back corridors of the hotel were narrow but reasonably cool. In places the plaster on the walls was cracked and the doors thin and poorly painted. There were no cameras in this part of the hotel. No security guards either.

Victor stopped when he came to a door and passed his ear close to it for a few seconds. He heard people talking. He moved on, pausing to listen at another door. This time there was no noise. He moved on. He tried three more before he heard the quiet hum of electronic machinery. He slowly tried the handle. It was unlocked.

Inside the room was tiny, barely more than a closet. There was just enough room for the chair, table, two television monitors, and accompanying recorders. On the TV screens were the simultaneous live feeds from the hotel CCTV cameras. Each screen carried four feeds; one at the front entrance, lobby, elevator, and one for each of the floors.

Victor sat down and pressed rewind, watching the time until he reached midday. He then hit play and watched. A couple of minutes later he saw the assassin's target and two companions enter through the front. They disappeared from one feed and appeared on the other as they crossed the lobby. The elevator took them to the third floor, and the camera there recorded them as they entered their respective rooms.

The picture quality wasn't good enough to see the room numbers, but Victor counted how many doors were between the camera and the rooms, specifically the room where the lone man entered.

He was the key. It was obvious the other two were just the hired help. Victor's first instinct was that they were bodyguards, but he had seen how the three operated together and dismissed that idea. Earlier in the day Victor had followed the assassin while he in turn followed the man to the harbor, where the target had joined the other two men. The equipment Victor saw on the boat indicated that the men were divers.

That the nameless target was being shadowed by the assassin meant he was important. By the way he carried himself, he wasn't a case officer. He was someone's subordinate sent out to personally oversee the last part of the operation. To salvage whatever was on that sunken ship that was so valuable and that was no doubt now in the truck outside.

He left the room and closed the door behind him. He made his way to the stairs and began ascending to the third floor. The assassin's target knew something, something that made him a target, something that was a liability to whomever was in charge. And that something Victor needed to hear.

He just had to get to him before the assassin did.

Reed closed the e-mail and stood. He placed the smartphone back in his trouser pocket. He left the water on the table. The lobby was peaceful. Noise of merriment drifted out from the bar as he reached the stairs and took them to the fifth floor. He walked down the corridor and entered his room.

The gun was under the pillow as he had left it, and he pulled back the slide, loading a bullet into the chamber. He tucked it into the front of his trousers so the suppressor extended down along his left thigh. His shirt, hanging loose, disguised the gun's handle.

The trousers were likewise loose enough so that, if he was careful how he walked, no one would notice he was armed; though descending stairs was not possible with a big piece of metal down the front of his trousers. No matter, he could take the elevator down the two floors instead.

Reed took the spare magazines from the satchel and placed them in the pockets of the trousers: two in the left, one in the right. He did not expect to even use a single magazine of bullets, and only then if circumstances were truly against him. But Reed had risen to the very top of the killer's ladder by being meticulous and prepared for the worst at all times. He was not about to change his habits now.

He left the room and headed for the elevator. He pushed the call button and waited patiently. Reed knew himself to be very good at waiting. He also knew, however, that he was considerably better at killing.

Victor reached the third floor and stepped out into the corridor that formed a rough square around the hotel. He walked around the circumference, getting his bearings while he located the camera. There were around fifteen rooms per floor. The corridor was wide but un-carpeted. The floorboards were polished and clean.

He found the camera near the elevator, positioned so it could see the elevator doors and the adjoining corridor. Victor counted the doors and saw the room he wanted halfway between the elevator and the far inter-section. Victor knew the man was alone, but there was always the chance that one or both of his companions had joined him in the room since Victor had watched the CCTV footage.

If they had guns, which Victor had to assume, things could quickly turn bad. But if he was fast he could get the information he needed, probably just a name or an address or maybe a phone number, and, he hoped, get out before anyone else realized he was there.

It took mere seconds to reach the door, but, before he had a chance to make a move, another door opened far-ther along the corridor. Victor kept walking as one of the two big guys exited his room. He was marginally shorter than Victor with blond hair and a scrappy beard. He wore long shorts and a loose T-shirt. His strength was obvious. The man's gaze stayed on Victor as they passed each other.

Victor kept his pace and turned the corner at the end of the corridor, resisting the natural urge to look back. The man would be watching him until he left his vision. Victor stopped when he was out of sight and listened. He heard a knock, then a few seconds later a door opened. Hushed voices before the door closed again.

Two in the same room complicated things, but at

least it meant each would be a distraction to the other. It would give him a better chance of gaining the element of surprise. Victor carried on down the corridor instead of doubling back. He didn't want the camera to get a shot of his face, poor quality or not.

He walked as fast as he dared without appearing to hurry. The hotel seemed relatively empty. He didn't imagine it did much business even at the best of times. His pulse was slow and steady.

Victor approached the turning where the elevator was located. He heard the chime as it reached the floor. That was all he needed, another guest or hotel employee nearby to give him more problems. He slowed, wanting the person to leave the elevator in front of him instead of behind. He heard the doors open.

The man who stepped out was in his early forties, tall, fair skinned, with Slavic features, carrying a suitcase. He could have been considered handsome but for the recent wound stitched shut on the right side of his face.

That face Victor had seen before a week ago in St. Petersburg through the scope of a sniper rifle.

Victor didn't slow his pace or react in any way. He hoped he was somehow mistaken, even though he knew he wasn't. The SVR were here. The first thought that entered his mind was that they'd tracked him down, but that made no sense. The organization had a fraction of the resources and technology of the CIA, and outside the old Soviet bloc its influence was limited. Unless they had been shadowing him since Russia, it was beyond their capabilities. And if they had followed him here he wouldn't have just encountered one of their number by chance.

The Russian turned his head and looked Victor's way. Just a casual glance, and for a few seconds it seemed as if he'd failed to recognize him. He turned his head away and took another step from the elevator. Then his head involuntarily snapped back to look in Victor's direction, whole body stiffening, expression changing as he identified the man walking toward him.

They were no more than three yards apart when Colonel Gennady Aniskovach thrust a hand inside his jacket. Victor sprinted forward, closing the distance fast. Aniskovach drew his handgun, but Victor was within his reach before he could fully extend his arm.

Victor grabbed the Russian's wrist and twisted sharply. At the same time he threw his free fist at Aniskovach's face. The punch connected on the nose, breaking it instantly and sending a spray of blood from the nostrils. Aniskovach grunted with pain, and the gun dropped from his hand. His eyes filled with water. Victor kicked the gun into the elevator and flung the dazed Russian in too.

Inside, Victor grabbed Aniskovach by his shirt and slammed him against the mirrored wall. Blood flowed from his nose, dripped rapidly from his chin. Water spilled from his eyes. Victor frisked him, finding a spare mag and pocketing it.

"How did you find me?" he demanded in Russian.

It took a second for Aniskovach to speak. "I . . . didn't."

Victor took a hand from the Russian's clothes and

grabbed his throat, Victor's fingers on one side of his esophagus, thumb the other. He started to squeeze, hard, cutting off the air intake. Aniskovach choked.

Victor gave him ten seconds without oxygen before releasing the pressure enough for him to talk. He coughed for a moment. "I've only just got here . . ."

He started coughing again. Victor understood—they weren't here for him. The flash drive. The SVR had found out what it contained and had come to collect whatever was on that sunken ship. That meant they had taken it from Norimov. The elevator doors closed and it started to ascend.

Victor tightened his grip on Aniskovach's neck. "Did you kill him?"

The Russian looked confused. "Who?"

With his free hand Victor pressed his fingers into Aniskovach's wounded cheek. He screamed and Victor squeezed harder on his throat. The Russian gasped and spluttered, his face reddening until Victor eased his grip enough for him to talk.

"You know who."

Aniskovach spat phlegm and blood from his mouth. "Norimov?"

"Yes."

"We didn't kill him." The Russian took a series of deep breaths and raised his head. "He was working for us."

"What did you say?"

"Norimov . . . sold you to us." Aniskovach took great delight in the effect his words had. His face twisted into a smile, thin lips shining with blood. He spoke between coughs. "And he did so . . . for much less than . . . I would have paid."

Victor's grip unintentionally weakened. For a moment he couldn't speak, couldn't do anything. Norimov, the only person he would even come close to considering a friend, had betrayed him. For nothing more than money. He felt hollow.

The elevator doors opened on the fifth floor and the noise brought Victor crashing back to the world. He glanced over his shoulder, ready to incapacitate whoever was waiting. A man stood outside the elevator. He had a lean, muscular physique, dark hair, and blue eyes, dressed casually.

Reed.

SEVENTY-THREE

19:22 UST

The two killers stared at each other for a single long moment. Reed held the advantage, his enemy was half-turned away, hands gripping another man, pinning him against the back of the elevator. But Reed didn't move.

Reed was rarely surprised, but he was as good as paralyzed. Tesseract was dead. He had died in a hotel room in Nicosia, blown into atoms by an expertly placed bomb. Tesseract was dead, yet he was standing no more than four feet away. Reed stared forward blankly, his expression one of disbelief as his brain tried to rational-ize what was obvious. He had failed.

Reed reacted second, only beginning to draw the Glock as Tesseract was already wrenching the other man away from the wall.

Victor swung Aniskovach one hundred and eighty degrees and threw him out of the elevator just as Reed extended his arm and fired; the man took the bullet meant for Tesseract in the chest, momentarily contort-ing before crashing into Reed. Both men were sent flailing.

Reed hit the floor first, on his back, Aniskovach's body landing on top of him an instant later. He didn't have time to brace himself, and the impact momentarily stunned his body but reignited his mind.

He couldn't see Tesseract, and there wasn't time to get out from under the dead weight, so Reed angled the Glock and fired blind.

Victor hit the button for the lobby and threw himself to the side of the elevator, back pressed flat against the paneled wood a split second before bullets struck the back wall. The mirror smashed, and Victor shielded his face with his arm against the explosions of glass. Jagged pieces rained down onto the floor. The doors closed.

A triangle of indentations appeared in the metal on Victor's side. The elevator descended and the firing ceased. Avoiding the broken glass, Victor grabbed the Russian's gun from the far corner. A 9 mm Browning.

He ejected and checked the magazine, slammed it back in, worked the slide, and thumbed off the safety. Ready.

In seconds the elevator reached the ground floor and the doors opened. Before Victor stepped out into the lobby he used his knuckle to hit the buttons for the second, third, and fourth floors, and quickly stepped out before the doors closed behind him. There was no one nearby.

He had the Browning tucked into the front of his waistband with his shirt hanging loose to cover it. His right hand hovered by the grip as he walked cautiously forward. His gaze was fixed to the stairwell entrance, figuring the assassin would race down after him. It would take him considerably longer than Victor to reach the lobby, but still not long.

The assassin would know that too, and he would also calculate that Victor knew it. Taking the stairs would be the fastest way down, but in doing so the assassin would have to take the risk that Victor was waiting for him. There were other safer ways to the ground floor that would take longer. If their roles were reversed, Victor wasn't sure what he would do.

He had no time to think about it further since he saw seven men exit the hotel bar. They were all white, skins sunburned or shiny and starting to tan. The men were dressed as civilians but had the unmistakable bearing of military types. Victor knew they were Russians even before he heard them speak.

A couple of them glanced his way, but the others didn't pay Victor any attention. Some carried backpacks and looked weary from travel, while the rest seemed fresher. They'd obviously traveled separately in two groups to avoid suspicion. It made sense. It was the largest hotel in town and close to the port. Tourists were commonplace here, making it the ideal location to remain anonymous.

Any desire Victor had to wait and ambush the assassin disappeared now that there were seven, most likely armed, Russian soldiers in the lobby. The new arrivals started walking toward the elevator. Victor headed straight toward the exit at a measured pace, just a guest hurrying on his way into town. A few of the Russians looked his way but nothing more. The ones without rucksacks congregated in the center of the lobby.

As Victor passed the first group he hoped none of the seven had been involved in the St. Petersburg's incident. They would have seen that photo Norimov mentioned. If they had and Victor was recognized, he wouldn't have much chance of escaping. He approached the middle of the lobby, veering to the right to avoid the Russians, estimating there had been enough time for the assassin to reach the bottom of the stairs. But the door remained closed.

The assassin clearly had something else in mind.

Reed made his way down the stairwell, taking deep, quick breaths as anger threatened to explode through his calm exterior. Tesseract was alive. Reed had failed to kill him. He had survived the bomb. No, Tesseract had found the trap and set it off to fool Reed into thinking he had been successful. The Englishman's teeth ground together. He remembered thinking of Tesseract as an amateur, but if Tesseract was an amateur, What did that make Reed?

Reed could not remember the last time he had lost his temper, but now he felt the purest rage. Tesseract had beaten him, made a fool of him. Reed needed vindication.

He knew he would never beat the elevator to the lobby, and, if he took the stairs to the ground floor, Tesseract would be waiting to ambush him. Reed had no intentions of rushing into a trap.

He reached the third floor and entered the corridor. He quickly moved toward a window at the opposite end that he knew would give him a perfect vantage point. It overlooked the street outside the front of the hotel, and from that position Reed could wait for Tesseract to emerge from the main entrance and place two hollow points into the back of his skull.

Reed ejected the half-empty magazine from the Glock, the muscles in his jaw flexing periodically beneath the skin. He had never experienced emotion toward a target before, but now it overwhelmed him. Reed turned his head, hearing a door opening behind him, and saw the target he was in Tanzania to kill enter the corridor from his room. He was heading for the elevator when he looked Reed's way and spotted the gun in Reed's hand.

Sykes backed off, wide eyed, openmouthed, retreating inside his room.

Reed placed the ejected mag in a pocket, reloaded a full one. He opened the window and stood with the

Glock out before him, aiming at where he expected Tesseract to appear.

In his peripheral vision he saw one of the target's hulking hirelings emerge from same room where the target had just fled to. He moved well, fast, a pistol clutched in both hands, held down, and to the side, the safety grip people are trained to use to stop them shooting someone by mistake. The downside was that it took an extra split second to acquire a target.

Without moving his head Reed shot the guy twice in the chest. The impact sent him tumbling backward, deflecting off the wall before hitting the floor as a dead man.

Reed reestablished his aim on the street outside and waited patiently. It would have taken seconds to kick the target's door open and fulfill the contract, but that would give Tesseract enough time to escape. Reed did not care about the job he was in Tanga to complete. He cared only about the man he had failed to kill. The man who had beaten him. He cared only about winning.

He cared only about killing Tesseract.

Two floors above, Aniskovach regained consciousness and pulled himself to his feet. Each breath was agony. He pressed his left hand against a wall for support while his right found the bullet embedded in his armored vest. He checked underneath for blood, but the bullet hadn't gone through the other side.

The SVR colonel had always been a cautious man, but after coming close to death in St. Petersburg Aniskovach had adopted a safety-first approach to operations. Despite the pain, it felt good to be alive. He wasn't sure how long he'd been out but hoped there was still time. He reached into his pocket and pulled out his phone.

The ringtone echoed throughout the lobby. It was some novelty tune that, if circumstances were not so perilous, would have made Victor frown. He saw one of the Russians reach into a pocket of his jacket to answer. Victor walked past, feeling the urge to increase his pace. The exit was directly ahead. He was so close.

The Russian answered the phone and a second later looked Victor's way. Victor saw the reflection of the man's face in the glass windows before him.

It took the Russian another second before drawing the breath into his lungs to shout, but Victor was already running. Two seconds to cover the distance to the main entrance, another to get through the door. Three more to reach cover outside. Six seconds. Too long if any of the Russians had a gun within quick reach. He would be dead with bullets in his back long before he reached safety. The bar was less than half the distance. He sprinted toward it.

The other Russians were slow to react to the unexpected commotion, and he reached and was through the bar entrance before he heard movement behind him—more shouting, the sound of bags opening, the metallic reverberation of weapons being drawn.

Victor dodged round the tables and chairs, making

his way to the far end of the long room. He heard a Russian chasing after him, not as agile as he—knocking into tables, spilling drinks—but still fast.

Victor pushed open a service door at the far end of the bar and ran down the corridor on the other side. He headed for the kitchen, charging into the swing door, knocking it aside.

The kitchen was even busier than before, full of noise, steam, heat. The narrow walkways between work surfaces were blocked with people.

Victor backtracked, knowing he wouldn't be able to force his way through before the Russians caught up and filled the kitchen with lead. Either that or he would give them the time to head him off.

He emerged back into the corridor to see the pursuing Russian sprinting toward him. Victor's sudden appearance surprised him, and for a split second he hesitated. Victor didn't.

He dashed forward, timing his attack so that the heel of his shoe connected with the running man's stomach at the apex of the kick's force.

The Russian gasped, doubled over. Victor grabbed him by the shoulders and sent his head crashing into the closest wall. There was a dull crack of plaster, and the Russian's head bounced backward. He stumbled, arms flailing.

Victor leaped at him while he was dazed, driving his elbow into the Russian's face, and the man collapsed silently.

He heard a noise, wasn't sure where it originated,

but drew the Browning and fired two shots at the door leading to the bar. Victor didn't wait to see if he'd been right and started for an adjoining corridor.

Automatic fire tore through the bar door. Victor was already jumping out of the trajectory as bullets struck the walls and floor, blowing wood, plaster, and dust into the air.

He scrambled back to his feet, and a second later he was racing up the same stairwell he'd ascended earlier. Going up when he needed to get out was a bad idea, but his first two avenues of escape had been cut off and he needed another.

He moved fast but cautiously, gun held out straight before him, always in sync with where he looked. The Russians were below him, and the assassin above.

Trapped.

Sykes stood in the center of his hotel room completely still, gaze locked on the door, the SIG clutched tightly in one sweaty hand. The sound of gunshots echoed around the room. He'd never been more afraid in his life.

One minute he'd been on his way to the bar to get a drink and the next he was staring at a seriously mean-looking guy with a gun. Wiechman, like an idiot, had charged out, gun in hand, to see what was happening. Then there had been the sound of silenced shots and the definite thump of a heavy man-sized object hitting the deck.

After that, there had been no more noise for what

seemed liked minutes. Sykes wasn't sure how long. He stood staring at the door, waiting for the guy with the gun to come and kill him.

Something crazy was going on, and Sykes was caught right in the middle.

A horrible realization started to take shape in Sykes's mind. The man with the gun had recognized him.

No, it couldn't be.

Dalweg burst into the room, and in his panic Sykes almost shot him. Dalweg's face was twisted with anger.

"Jack's dead," he spat. "What the fuck is going down in this place?"

Sykes was about to say he didn't know, but then more shooting started.

Reed heard the commotion in the lobby seconds after the moment when he judged Tesseract should have reached the street outside. Reed lowered his arm, turned, and headed away from the window and down the corridor. The sound of unsuppressed automatic fire echoed from below. A submachine gun by the high cyclic rate. Bizon probably.

The Englishman did a quick evaluation of the circumstances. The man Tesseract had been assaulting in the elevator clearly had friends, and those friends were armed and now after Tesseract. Reed remembered the foreigners in the bar. Russians. Why they were here in Tanzania Reed did not know, and neither did he have any interest in knowing. What did interest him was that they were trying to kill Tesseract and were interfering in his own attempt to do so. If they continued to, which was likely, they would find themselves between Reed's gun sights. Reed would allow nothing to get between him and his prey, and he would allow no one but himself to make the kill. Reed was the best. He had to prove that. If someone else killed Tesseract before Reed, his own life would continue on as a mere shadow of its former existence.

The Russians had prevented Tesseract from leaving through the main entrance. The only logical avenue of escape from the lobby would therefore be the hotel bar. That would lead him to the kitchen and the service stairwell.

Reed hurried. His prey was close.

SEVENTY-FOUR

19:24 UST

Victor reached the second floor and rushed down the corridor, Browning gripped in both hands, arms extended and bent slightly at the elbow, gaze looking directly along the 9 mm's iron sights. The fire alarm started blaring. He could hear people screaming. He couldn't be sure what they were screaming at, but the voices sounded more scared or horrified than pained.

He turned a corner, found a door in the right location, kicked it open, entered fast, completed a quick sweep of the room. A single, neatly made bed, no personal effects.

Unoccupied. Empty. Victor headed straight for the window, grabbed a chair, hurled it.

The glass shattered. He stepped forward, leaned briefly through the open space. Below him was a row of neatly parked cars glittering with shards of glass, behind them the chair, smashed. The parking lot extended for maybe twenty yards. A low wall marked the edge of the hotel compound. No Russians. No assassin.

The drop was too far to risk, even with the cars to break the fall, but next to the window was a drainpipe. Victor slipped the Browning into his waistband, climbed up onto the windowsill, balancing on the balls of his feet, using his hands on the frame for support. He swiveled round so he was facing into the room, reached for the drainpipe.

A shadow appeared on the wall through the open doorway. The shadow of a man with a gun.

Victor immediately let go, lurched backward, seeing the assassin appear and the brief muzzle flash off the handgun as it fired.

The bullet snapped through the air above him and for a serene split second Victor fell, the broken window rushing away from him. He landed on a parked sedan, crumpling the roof with the force of his impact. Side windows exploded, the windshield cracked, air was forced from his lungs.

He sucked in a breath, ignoring the pain, and pulled the Browning from his waistband, limbs aching but still working, so no bones broken.

He squeezed the trigger the instant Reed showed himself, but he was still shaken, his posture awkward.

He missed. Victor shot again twice more, missing but forcing his enemy back into the room before he could return fire.

Victor rolled off the car roof, landing on his feet. He spun around, gun trained on the window, crouching to steady his aim. Adrenaline surged through him. He breathed steadily in a futile attempt to control its effects. If he was injured he felt no pain. Five seconds past. Ten.

No. The assassin had withdrawn, moving to another position. Victor scanned the other windows on the same floor overlooking the parking lot. The next attack could come from any of them. There was no way he could watch them all. Wherever he looked created a blind spot from which the assassin would receive a perfect shot.

His gaze searched for a way to escape. The parking lot was too empty, running through it would leave him too exposed. There was a door, but too far to risk making a break for. A fire exit was closer, but closed.

The fire door swung open, banging against the wall as two Russians emerged, both armed with PP-19 Bizon submachine guns.

Victor dropped down behind the wrecked car, his body positioned behind the back wheel on the driver's side. He felt vibrations through his back as bullets struck the bodywork. He didn't wait for the firing to stop, dropped onto his stomach, and extended his arms under the car.

He fired twice, one bullet catching the closest Russian in the shin. Both retreated back through the open fire exit, and Victor sprang to his feet, put another round their way, and ran across the lot, weaving between parked cars, heading toward the road, hoping the assassin was similarly distracted.

Asphalt exploded around his feet.

He took cover behind another car, pivoted. Victor returned fire, but the uninjured Russian had ducked back into the cover of the doorway.

Movement on the floor above caught Victor's eye, and he reacted in time to avoid the bullets that came his way. One smacked into the uneven ground where he'd been kneeling, another blew out a window of the car next to him.

Victor threw himself out of the line of fire, going onto his front. He took a breath, considered his choices quickly. He had two separate attackers at two different firing points, one with the higher ground, and there were more enemies nearby who would join the fight in mere moments. It was a battle he wasn't going to win. He needed to move. And fast.

Victor slid beneath an SUV, grazing his elbows on the hard ground. He did the same under another. No more bullets were fired. No one knew where he was.

He sprang up, shot at the window where the assassin had been and into the fire exit without waiting to acquire targets. A bullet struck the uninjured Russian as he moved out of cover.

Victor ran, heading straight across the parking lot, away from the hotel, trusting to speed to keep him from being hit. He covered the remaining ground fast, leaped onto the small wall that divided the parking lot from the street beyond. He heard the spit of the suppressed shot and a piece of brickwork disintegrated under his shoe.

He lost his footing, fell forward, off balance, landing awkwardly, stumbling into the road to keep his momentum from knocking him over.

A horn blared. Tires screeched. The bumper hit him mid-left thigh, catapulting him up onto the car's hood. He slammed into the windshield, cracking it, tumbling up and over the roof, bouncing off the trunk before hitting road, instinctively rolling to ease the impact.

The car skidded and lost control, mounted the sidewalk, and continued over the low wall, crashing into a stationary SUV on the other side.

Everything seemed slow and quiet. Victor pulled himself from the hot ground and to his feet, grimacing as he put weight on his left leg. He hurt all over. He tasted blood in his mouth. His vision was blurry. He squinted through the haze, his eyesight returning, shapes coming back into focus. There were maybe four or five people standing openmouthed nearby. He saw the crashed car, steam rising from the hood, the shocked female driver stumbling out. Behind her a man was climbing down a drainpipe on the side of the hotel.

Victor realized the Browning wasn't in his hands. He frantically looked around.

He saw it lying near the crashed car. He limped hurriedly over to the gun, vaulting awkwardly over the wall, aware that his whole body was moving more slowly than he was telling it to. He scooped the 9mm up into both hands and spun round to where he had seen the assassin.

Victor fired, his aim terrible, the bullets striking the wall well to the side of his target, who dropped the last couple of yards, disappearing out of sight behind the row of parked cars. He reappeared an instant later, firing and moving, using the vehicles as cover. Victor shot back, taking cover himself behind the crashed car. Bullets thumped into bodywork.

Click.

The Browning was empty.

Victor immediately dived back over the wall behind him, going into a roll to break the fall, coming out of it fluidly into a sprint despite the pain. A four-wheel-drive Jeep with sun-faded paint and dried mud caking the wheels and sides was pulling away from the curb farther down the street. Perfect. Victor jumped up onto the hood, took two steps, dropped down on the other side, taking the drop with his right leg to spare the left. The Jeep stopped sharply. The driver was already fleeing before Victor had the chance to order him out.

A bullet flew past his head.

Victor climbed inside and slammed the door shut. The interior was filthier than the outside, seats split with padding spilling out in several places, instrument panels cracked, upholstery ripped, everything dusty. Victor glanced to his right, saw the assassin hurrying across the hotel parking lot, reloading his pistol on the move.

Victor ducked in the seat, put the Jeep's stick shift into first, transmission creaking, and accelerated. The passenger door's window blew out, scattering fragments of glass over his head and back. More bullets came his way, flying through the broken window, slamming into bodywork.

Victor reloaded with one hand as he drove. The last

magazine. The Browning held thirteen bullets. Good, Victor thought.

Unlucky for anyone who followed him.

Reed watched the Jeep race out of the Glock's effective range, lowered his weapon, and scanned the area for a suitable vehicle to chase Tesseract. There were several cars, mostly old sedans with neither the horsepower to catch up with the Jeep nor the four-wheel drive to handle Tanga's less-than-even roads at speed. Anger threatened to explode through his calm exterior. Tesseract had survived yet again, and once more Reed suffered the indignation that his skills had been found lacking. He needed affirmation that only blood could provide.

He heard Russian voices nearby and glanced in their direction to see several men entering the parking lot from an open fire exit. All were armed with Bizons and looked hungry for blood. One of their comrades lay dead on the ground in front of them.

The Englishman held the Glock out of sight down by his thigh and acted like a shocked bystander as the Russians hurried out into the street. They shouted at locals, but the Tanzanians did not understand them, and in turn the Russians did not understand what was said back.

There were four Russians so similar in appearance and movements they might as well have been military-bred clones of one another. Spetsnaz, Reed assumed. He had much respect for the highly trained and fiercely capable Russian special forces, considering them third only to their British and American counterparts. A fifth man appeared, clearly their CO, but not military, probably GRU or SVR. He was the man Tesseract had thrown at Reed and who Reed, in turn, had shot.

Reed turned his body and head away. He did not want to risk being recognized, unlikely as it was. The officer ordered his soldiers to get to their vehicles and continue the pursuit. He did not follow as his men split into two pairs and rushed off. He leaned against a wall, a hand on his chest. He must have been wearing a vest to have survived Reed's bullet to the sternum. Most fortunate.

Reed walked quickly until he was out of sight of the Russians before breaking into a run. He dodged around pedestrians, sprinting around the hotel's exterior until he emerged on its front side. Cars were parked along the half circle of driveway that linked the hotel to the main road. He knew that he did not have time either to hot-wire a car or to find keys for another. But he didn't need to. A man was closing the door of a well-kept-looking Land Rover.

Reed threw the driver from his seat and climbed in. He started the engine.

SEVENTY-FIVE

Sykes hurried down the stairs, trailing behind Dalweg. The big ex-SEAL had his Beretta held out before him and moved fast and assured while Sykes breathlessly stumbled after him, one hand loosely gripping his own gun and the other on the banister to help keep him on his feet. Fear and acid reflux made for a lethal cocktail.

Gunshots made Sykes hesitate. They were loud, seemingly originating from outside the back of the hotel. Dalweg was unfazed, reaching the bottom of the staircase and taking up position to peer into the adjoining corridor. He looked back at Sykes.

"Come on," he said. "You need to keep up, or I'm just gonna fucking leave you here. I don't care."

Dalweg headed down the corridor and Sykes followed, trying not to startle at every bang. It sounded like a full-scale war was being fought, but he was glad that those who were trying to kill one another were not doing so inside the building anymore. Sykes's palm was moist around the SIG's grip.

The lobby was deserted apart from a couple of members of the hotel staff cowering behind the check-in desk. Dalweg picked up speed, almost jogging across the open space of the lobby before reaching the main entrance. He put a shoulder to a wall and glanced through a window. He moved to another and looked out again.

"Looks clear. I think we're good."

Sykes swallowed and used the sleeve of his T-shirt to wipe his sweaty face. A sustained barrage of automatic fire made him freeze in place, and even Dalweg flinched. Shouting came next. It sounded like Russians in the adjoining bar and corridors.

A barrage of thoughts assailed Sykes's mind. If Russians were here, they must have found out about the missiles. But who were they fighting? Who was the man who shot Wiechman? What the hell was going on? The answer terrified him.

Sykes felt Dalweg's hand on his shoulder. He looked at him.

"Listen, you worthless little shit," Dalweg said. "If you want me to get you out of this I'm going to want more money. A hell of a lot more."

Sykes nodded several times. "Of course, whatever you want. Just get me the hell out of here. Please."

Dalweg looked at him contemptuously and pushed through the main hotel door. Sunlight flooded through the doorway and made Sykes squint. He'd left his sunglasses in his room along with the rest of his belongings without a second's thought.

Dalweg rushed out into the glare and took up a covering position behind a car parked in front of the hotel. Sykes ran after him and squatted down nearby, panting, terrified.

Dalweg looked left and right down the street. Locals were gathering in response to the gunfire. They appeared curious more than scared.

"I don't see anyone," Dalweg said.

Sykes kept low anyway. "What about the truck?"

"It's still there."

"No one's near it?"

Dalweg shook his head. "If they were I would have said, idiot. Whatever's going down here isn't about those missiles."

"It must be."

Dalweg looked at him, scowling. "Then why, genius, are those clowns shooting the shit out of one another around the back and not making off with the truck?"

Sykes shrugged.

"Exactly," Dalweg said.

"What are we going to do?"

"We're leaving."

Dalweg stood and hurried across the street and over toward the truck. He stopped and motioned for Sykes to follow. It took three deep breaths and a half-hearted prayer for Sykes to get his legs moving. He sprinted out from behind the car and across the street, heading toward where Dalweg was climbing into the truck's cab.

Sykes heard the sound of a vehicle approaching and flattened himself against the truck as a Jeep hurtled closer. He stared at the driver, in shock. The Jeep sped past and Sykes watched it, openmouthed, disbelieving. Tesseract.

Movement caught his eye. A man emerged from out of a side street. The man had a buzz cut and a neck like a tree trunk, skin too light to be a local. It took a few seconds for Sykes's brain to catch up with what he was seeing, and in that short time the man charged straight at him.

Sykes raised his gun hand, but he was nowhere near

fast enough, and 205 pounds of angry Latino struck him shoulder first in the gut, sending Sykes flying backward, hitting the dusty blacktop on his back, hard. The gun flew from his hand and clattered out of sight.

Sykes wheezed, red faced, trying desperately to pull air into his deflated lungs.

Alvarez was on his feet in only a few seconds. He was a big guy, but he still had more speed than most people expected. A small crowd of Tanzanians were watching him, but he ignored them and looked around for Sykes's gun. He couldn't see it anywhere, and there was no more time to search.

He took a step back, turned around. A tall square canvas cover shielded the back of the truck and had a secured door in the middle of the back panel. Alvarez ripped the door open and peered inside. Two pickup trucks sped past him. The sickly strong smell of saltwater made him wince. Thick canvas sheets covered the cargo. Alvarez pulled them aside, seeing an assortment of items: dive tanks, regulators, an underwater cutting torch, lanyards, fins, open-bottom lift bags, underwater lights, a box of flares.

Lying among the equipment were huge tubular sections of white-painted metal that ran the entire length of the cargo box and that were as wide as Alvarez's shoulders. They had obviously been dismantled to allow them to be brought to the surface, but the missiles were still much larger than Alvarez had imagined.

"Jackpot," he whispered.

Alvarez heard the driver's door open, pressed his back flat against the tailgate, and waited.

Sykes tried to call for help, but he didn't have enough breath to make words. He struggled on the hot ground, scared and in agony. He watched a Land Rover accelerate out of the hotel's driveway and heard Dalweg's voice.

"What the fuck?"

Sykes tried to look up to see Dalweg, but he didn't have the strength. Instead he rolled his head to the side, seeing the world at a skewed angle and watching Dalweg approaching him along the side of the truck, on his way to help. Sykes rolled his head to the other side and saw Alvarez waiting behind the back of the truck, out of Dalweg's sight.

"What happened to you?" Dalweg asked.

Sykes rolled his head back again and tried to warn Dalweg, but his shouts came out of his winded chest no louder than whimpers. He tried to point, but Dalweg didn't understand.

The second Dalweg reached Sykes, Alvarez was upon him. He threw himself at Dalweg from behind, tackling him down to the ground, hitting the road to the left of where Sykes lay. Orange dust wafted into the air.

Sykes tried to shuffle out of the way as the two men grappled and punched each other next to him. He was still wheezing, but the intense pain in his chest was slowly fading with each second. He managed to roll to the right, first onto his front, and then onto his back

again. He heard the grunts and sickening *thwack* as fists
hit flesh no more than a few feet away. Blood specks
landed on Sykes's face.

Sykes pulled himself slowly to his feet and staggered backward until he found a wall to lean on. Some
locals started cheering the fight.

Straight in front of him Alvarez and Dalweg
pounded the crap out of each other. Both guys were
strong, and both knew how to fight. Alvarez wrestled
his way on top of Dalweg, using his left hand to pin
Dalweg's right arm to the ground while he punched
and elbowed Dalweg with his own right. Blood erupted
from a gash on Dalweg's cheek. He was already bleeding from the mouth. Sykes could see it was all going to
be over in a few seconds.

He couldn't see his own gun, but Dalweg's Beretta
was lying close by in the road, just out of reach of either fighting man. Sykes pushed himself away from the
wall and rushed over to the gun as fast as he could. He
circled round where Alvarez and Dalweg fought, stag-
gering to keep his balance.

Alvarez saw what was happening, let go of Dalweg,
and scrambled after Sykes. He caught up with him before Sykes reached the weapon, wrapped his arms around
Sykes's thighs, hoisted him off his feet and brought him
back down to ground. Hard.

Sykes's arms cushioned the fall, but not enough to
stop his face from finding the asphalt. He went limp and
groaned quietly.

Alvarez got to his feet. He turned around to face

Dalweg, only to see him heading back to the cab. The door was already opened, and he reached inside. When Dalweg pulled his arms back out, he had an Uzi in his hands.

Alvarez scooped up the Beretta and sprinted out of the line of fire before Dalweg had the submachine gun raised. Alvarez looked around frantically for some cover, realized there wasn't any close enough for him to get to in time, turned back, and shot at Dalweg through the truck's canvas backing, hoping for a lucky hit.

The Uzi roared in response, and a cluster of smoking holes appeared through the canvas. Rounds blasted chunks out of the masonry around Alvarez. He dropped down to his hands and knees, bending low to see underneath the truck. Dalweg was behind one of the rear wheels, only his shadow visible. The Uzi rattled off another burst, and more bullets sailed over Alvarez's head.

Alvarez steadied his aim as much as he could and squeezed off a round.

The bullet blew out the truck's tire, passing through the rubber and striking Dalweg in the leg on the other side. He howled in pain and abandoned his position. Alvarez fired another shot after him, but Dalweg was out of his field of view.

Alvarez got himself vertical, moved closer to the back of the truck, and tucked himself behind one of the big wheels like Dalweg had done. A second later more rounds came his way.

He stuck his head out of cover long enough to see that Dalweg was positioned behind a small wall on the other side of the road, and then pulled his skull back down. He felt the reverberations as bullets struck the truck and silently prayed that an unlucky round wasn't going to set one of the warheads off. Alvarez didn't know if they were armed or duds, and it had to be a long shot anyway, he told himself, but he didn't want to wait around to test the theory.

He shuffled to the side and reached his arm backward and around the wheel to fire off a couple of shots in the general direction of Dalweg. His odds of hitting were probably longer than those of one of the warheads going bang, but he couldn't have done too badly since the Uzi stopped blasting for a few seconds.

Alvarez didn't waste the opportunity and changed positions, hurrying to the front of the truck and taking cover behind the wheel there. In a hunched-over crouch he moved around the front fender, leaned out of cover, and took a shot. He watched as the bullet plugged a hole in the wall shielding Dalweg.

The returning hail of 9 mms forced Alvarez back to behind the wheel. Rounds pinged off the truck's hood, cracked the cab windows, whacked into the ground. Alvarez heard what sounded like running water and looked to his left to see fuel spilling out from a ruptured fuel tank, bullet holes through both sides.

Alvarez would be first to admit that his understanding of chemistry was nothing special, but he knew that diesel had a higher flashpoint than gasoline and was much harder to ignite. Even a match wouldn't do it. But that fact was little comfort when a pool of the stuff was forming next to him.

He edged away from the diesel, wanting to make a

run for it but aware he was completely pinned down. Moving out of the cover of the truck meant braving a storm of lead. Alvarez was brave, but he wasn't stupid.

He popped out from behind the truck to fire another bullet at Dalweg, but, before he could fully squeeze the trigger, he felt a searing pain in his right shoulder and his legs gave way underneath him.

Alvarez landed on his back, grimaced against the unbelievable pain when he tried to move his right arm. He put his left fingers to the wound, feeling a small entry hole in the front of his outer deltoid. He stretched his fingers around to touch the much-larger exit wound at the back of his shoulder. A through and through. No bone damage, but when Alvarez withdrew his left hand, he saw that it was drenched with blood.

"Oh shit."

SEVENTY-SIX

19:26 UST

Victor followed the dusty road as it curved around and away from the hotel complex. Up ahead it joined onto the main road leading deeper into the city. The main road would be the quickest route out of the area, but it was also the most obvious choice. It would have to do. Victor didn't know the area well enough to take to the side streets unless he had to.

He slowed down to blend in, joining the traffic waiting at the intersection. He checked the rearview.

Two pickups, a Toyota and a Ford, raced toward him.

Victor accelerated, maneuvered out from the line of cars onto the wrong side of the road, changed up a gear, and sped out across the intersection. He swerved around the cross-traffic, switched back to the right side of the road, and changed up again.

The pickups followed his lead, speeding across the crossroads, leaving clipped and crashed cars in their wake.

Victor released the throttle; slammed the brakes, power sliding the Jeep into a right; then immediately accelerated, the rear end slipping, vehicle rattling under the strain. He raced down a side street. Seconds later he saw the pickups following, taking the corner more slowly, glancing off parked cars as they tried to keep up with him.

Victor took another corner, sped across an intersection. He kept his eyes on the road, following it as it rounded a block of densely packed buildings, whitewashed stone colonials interspersed with shanties. Bald truck tires lay discarded in loose heaps on the side of the road. He moved around slower vehicles, hearing horns and seeing drivers expressing their anger at him.

The road straightened out and split in two. For a second Victor hesitated, but then he veered left onto a wide street that sloped downward. He looked in the mirror. Behind him the pickups overtook other cars or barged them out of the way.

Looking forward again he saw a grime-smeared

taxi speed out from a side street, pulling onto the road directly ahead of him. There was no time to brake, no room to dodge. Victor floored it, smashing into the taxi's front end, the bigger, heavier Jeep knocking the taxi back, sending it spinning into an oncoming car, wrecking both. Victor was thrown forward in his seat, but the seat belt kept his head from colliding with the steering wheel.

He struggled to keep the Jeep under control, swerving wildly, finally straightening out in time to see the first pickup, the Toyota, fifty yards behind, swerve onto a sidewalk to avoid the mangled car and taxi. Sparks flew off the wall as the truck scraped along, side mirror obliterated. It skidded back onto the road, dust pouring from its wheels.

The second pickup slowed down earlier, easily avoiding the crashed vehicles, and was gaining. In the rearview Victor could see the face of the Russian behind the wheel, grim and determined.

Ahead of Victor the street banked to the left. He followed it onto a wide tree-lined avenue full of traffic. The road surface was smooth and even. Rundown two-story residences with pillared verandas flanked the street. Some were painted in flaking pastel shades—creams, yellows, and blues. Vervet monkeys played in the vegetation alongside the road.

Victor, hands locked on the wheel, flicked the Jeep through the slow-moving cars, denting a wheel arch as he squeezed through a gap just before it closed again. The pickups were right behind him now, smashing their way through the other smaller vehicles. Horns blared.

The Toyota was close enough for Victor to see inside the cab and the Russian in the passenger seat readying his submachine gun.

Reed followed the destruction. The Land Rover was only a couple of years old; perfectly maintained; and, combined with his deft driving skills, took him quickly along Tanga's roads. He had the Glock resting in his lap, loaded, cocked, ready.

He had not spotted the Jeep, but he knew he was on the right path. He raced past damaged vehicles and those that had pulled over to avoid crashing or those already crashed. The roads were clearer for him as a result.

He was gaining with every second, and it would not be long now until Tesseract was back in his crosshairs.

The Russian passenger in the first pickup leaned out of the window and attempted to get into a firing position with his Bizon. Victor didn't give him the chance. He pulled off the road, down a narrow street, the gap between the parked cars just wide enough for one vehicle at a time. Brightly patterned clothes and bedding hung from washing lines stretching between the buildings.

The pickup followed, swerving as it took the corner too fast, its back end losing traction. The gunman managed to pull himself back into the cab just before the Toyota scraped along a stationary car, metal screeching against metal.

Victor accelerated as he crossed an intersection, not daring to slow down and give his pursuers a chance to catch up. He lurched to the side, another car smashing into his back end from the right, spinning the Jeep around, force pinning Victor against the door until the vehicle stopped dead. The other car skidded and crashed through a storefront.

The lead pickup came out of the intersection fast but then braked hard, tires billowing smoke. The driver swerved to avoid the Jeep in the middle of the road. The second pickup was traveling even faster and followed the first, rushing past Victor. The driver stamped on the brakes, and the pickup slowed before it clipped the back of the Toyota and careered to the side, vaulting up the curb and through a row of market stalls protected from the sun by seaweed-thatched roofs. Exploded passion fruit and coconuts flew in all directions. Traders fled.

Victor put the Jeep in gear, reversed, crushing another market stall in the process, then changed to first, turned the wheel, accelerated. He saw the first pickup pull a three-point turn to chase after him. The passenger was already out of the window this time. Victor ducked in his seat as 9 mm rounds sprayed the Jeep.

He changed up again, trying to put some distance between him and the first pickup, but something was caught under the Jeep and slowing him down. He switched to reverse and accelerated, going backward down the street toward the pickups. A broken wooden crate appeared in front of him, deposited from under his vehicle.

Victor braked, changed back to first, and swerved around the remains of the crate; he then turned quickly back into the narrow street lined with cars, knowing the pickups would have a hard time maneuvering back into it.

The Jeep's back window blew out. Glass pebbles scattered around the interior. Bullet holes cracked the windshield.

Victor emerged from the intersection, glanced both ways down the street. In one direction, vehicles blocked the road, stopped in reaction to the chase. In the other, a Land Rover was speeding toward him.

He saw the dark silhouette of the driver and knew who was coming.

There was no other way to go. Victor turned toward the oncoming Land Rover. He kept one hand on the wheel, and the other grabbed the Browning from his lap. The Land Rover raced down the opposite side of the road. Victor raised the handgun, and, when they were five yards apart, fired through the windshield. At the exact same time rounds came back at him.

For an instant Victor glimpsed the driver's emotionless face as the vehicles passed each other. In his rearview Victor saw the Land Rover braking. He heard a horn, looked to his front to see a rust-spotted dala-dala bus turning a corner into the street. He was heading straight for it, no room to swerve around. He slammed on the brakes and pulled the hand brake. All four tires screeched and spewed out smoke. He came to a stop, close enough to see the terrified expressions of the bus passengers looking down at him.

The driver was giving him the finger as Victor put the Jeep into reverse and did a fast three-point turn. The pickups emerged from the intersection, turning his way, the Ford ramming into the side of the Land Rover as it performed a one-eighty.

Victor turned off the road at another intersection, not seeing the result of the collision. The Toyota pickup braked hard behind him, took the same corner, gaining quickly until it was almost at his bumper.

He took another turn, hard, fast, hoping to send the pickup the wrong way, but the Russian driver wasn't so easily fooled. He followed but lost some distance. Victor joined a dusty highway. There was little traffic, and he accelerated. The Jeep shook under the strain. It was pulling slightly to the right, and Victor compensated.

The pickup followed after a second, gaining with its newer, more powerful engine. In his mirror Victor saw the passenger lean out and steady his submachine gun.

Rounds punctured the safety glass of the Jeep's windshield, spreading cracks across Victor's view. There were holes close to his head. Far too close. Victor hit the brakes and the speedometer needle swung counterclockwise.

The Toyota was forced to brake as well to avoid crashing into the back of him, and the Spetsnaz gunman flailed around, unable to fire.

When the needle hit forty, Victor wrenched the steering wheel left. He released his foot from the brake pedal and, at the same time, pulled the hand brake. The Jeep slid sideways and Victor took off the hand brake, turned the wheel hard, accelerated, tires were screaming and smoking, losing traction as the Jeep fishtailed, one-eighty completed.

The first pickup braked again, its wheels locked, but

Victor was in the opposite lane, whooshing straight past it, his arm extended out the window, firing the Browning, two rounds at the driver. Ten left.

He kept accelerating, unsure whether he'd hit anyone, not willing to slow down to check. In the mirror he saw the pickup perform a clumsy U-turn. By the time it had completed the maneuver, Victor was half a mile away. Perfect. He performed his own U-turn, faster, going back into the other lane. He accelerated.

Two hundred yards ahead of Victor, the Toyota cut across into the same lane. Victor continued accelerating, saw the passenger lean out of the side window, Bizon raised. Muzzle flashes exploded from the barrel of the submachine gun. Both vehicles were moving too quickly for the gunman to get an accurate shot, but the distance was closing fast. The Russian ceased firing, readied his aim.

One hundred yards. Fifty.

At twenty, the shooting began again, and Victor flicked the steering wheel, swerving left into the other lane, passing the pickup on the opposite side to the gunman. This time Victor didn't miss.

Blood splashed on the inside of the Toyota's windshield.

The pickup lurched to the side, out of control, smashing side to side into a semitruck, crushing the Russian passenger before he could pull himself back inside.

The Toyota rebounded off the semi, swerving erratically, going onto two wheels, flipped once, twice, sliding down the highway on its roof, the flattened body of the Russian gunman hanging limply through the window.

Victor dodged around the oncoming traffic and left the pickup spinning slowly in his rearview.

He breathed deeply and concentrated on the road ahead and where it would take him. For now it was over. The road was wide, empty, heading north to Kenya, just twenty miles to the border. There was no way he could risk going back for the assassin's target. By the time he got back to the hotel it would be swarming with the authorities as well as Russians. Plus, the guy would be long gone by now anyway. Victor would have to use what he'd found from Olympus to continue his hunt, go through the paperwork. Do it the broker's way. He kept the needle at sixty.

A vehicle appeared in his rearview, fighting to get through the traffic bottlenecked by the crashed pickup.

The Land Rover.

Victor pushed down on the accelerator pedal, and in seconds the Land Rover had disappeared into the blur behind him. All Victor had to do was keep the accelerator down, and, by the time the assassin had negotiated his way out of the tailback, Victor would be too far gone to catch.

He pictured droplets of water bouncing off dead eyes.

The muscles in Victor's jaw flexed, his gaze hardened, and he eased his foot on the accelerator. The needle swung counterclockwise to thirty. Ten seconds went by, then twenty, and Victor saw a dark speck in his mirror appear, growing larger, clearer, closer. Good.

He took the next exit off the highway, again easing the pressure on the accelerator, drawing the assassin nearer. The street he turned into was wide, lined with one-story houses made from cinderblocks and roofed with corrugated tin or seaweed thatch. Power cables hung low across the road. Graffiti was scrawled along the walls.

The Land Rover followed seconds later. Through the rearview Victor's eyes locked with Reed's. Victor saw hatred in his gaze and knew the assassin saw hatred returned.

Victor accelerated and skidded round the next corner, back end sliding out. He fought the wheel as the Jeep pulled right, driver's side grinding against a line of parked cars, denting a fender, crushing lights.

He veered back into the center of the road. He was on a narrow, dusty street, flanked by shanties. There were no turnings visible. In the distance the shanties thinned out into rocky scrubland. Old row boats sat upturned along one side of the road, bottoms cracked and warped from the sun. Behind him, the Land Rover was close enough for him to see the assassin's weapon raised.

Victor heard the abrasive pop of unsuppressed gunfire. New holes appeared in the windshield. A bullet tore a chunk from the dash, and Victor drove evasively, swerving left and right. The firing stopped, and in the rearview Victor saw his attacker had both hands back on the wheel.

The Land Rover rammed into him from behind, jolting Victor in his seat. A few seconds later another impact forced the Jeep to the right, and before Victor recovered the Land Rover sped forward, coming up alongside him so that both vehicles occupied all available road, thick dust clouding behind them.

Reed had one hand on the wheel, the other firing the Glock, eyes flicking between Victor and the road. Victor returned fire when he could—eight rounds left, six, four—but the angle was bad, he couldn't get a good shot.

He didn't have the ammunition to waste, so he dropped the Browning into his lap and swung the wheel to the right, slamming sideways into the Land Rover. Metal shrieked. Bullets raked the Jeep.

Victor pulled to the left and then back right, hitting the Land Rover hard, then again, and again. The firing ceased. Victor stared into the assassin's unblinking eyes.

Both vehicles sped down the road, door to door. Victor's arms were locked on the steering wheel, muscles taut, teeth clenched, gaze alternating back and forth between the road ahead and his enemy.

Victor waited until the assassin had his gun back up to fire and then released the accelerator, dropping back sharply, Jeep scraping alongside the Land Rover. Rounds punctured the hood. Steam hissed through the holes.

Victor swerved right, moving directly behind the Land Rover. He controlled the wheel with his left hand, took the Browning in his right, and fired his last four rounds, straight through his own windshield. Two holes appeared in the Land Rover's rear bumper, dust blew out from the road, but the fourth bullet hit its mark.

The driver's side rear tire exploded.

The Land Rover swayed erratically, spun around, kicking up dust, going onto two wheels for a second before tipping and rolling off the road and into the brush.

Victor discarded the empty Browning and took the pressure off of the accelerator. The Jeep didn't slow down. It started to shake, steam pouring from the engine. Victor tried the brake, but the acceleration was locked. The brakes squealed, brake dust clouding from the wheels, but the Jeep was still doing fifty. Smoke spewed out from under the hood. Followed by flames. He hurtled toward a T-intersection, going too fast to take the corner. The hood blew open, covering the windshield.

He tried to guess the corner and swerved to the right, the Jeep shooting off the road and into the vegetation. He wrestled with the wheel, unable to see with the hood up, traveling fast, tall grasses and trees rushing past the door windows.

Victor jerked in his seat as the Jeep's suspension fought the uneven ground. Without warning the earth seemed to smooth out perfectly for an instant until the Jeep tipped forward and Victor realized he was falling just before everything went black.

SEVENTY-SEVEN

Alvarez used the truck for support to help himself stand back up. His right arm swung uselessly at his side. Blood stained his shirt and made it cling to his skin. With the pain and the nausea Alvarez didn't have the energy to collect the Beretta from where it had skidded under the truck, but, one hand held against his head, a cut above his left eyebrow, he saw Sykes approaching it.

Sykes knelt down and picked up the gun.

"What are you doing here?" Sykes asked him.

"I was going to ask you the same thing."

Sykes didn't answer. He wiped the dust from the Beretta with his T-shirt. Alvarez watched.

Dalweg rounded the back of the truck, limping, his left calf red with blood from where the bullet had grazed his flesh. He held the Uzi casually in one hand.

"Unlucky shithead," he said to Alvarez. "Got you with my last round."

Dalweg's face was a bloody and swollen mess. He walked up to Alvarez and hit him in the stomach with the butt of the Uzi. Alvarez sank to his knees and Dalweg smirked.

"Now we're even," he said. He looked to Sykes. "Who the hell is this guy?"

"He's agency," Sykes explained. "It's a long story."

It took a few seconds before Alvarez had stopped

coughing enough to see the barrel of the Beretta aimed straight at his face.

Alvarez's eyes locked on Sykes's. "You don't want to do this, man."

"Well, I am doing it," Sykes said. "And don't blame me. You didn't have to come here; you didn't have to get involved."

"Yes I did."

"Then you don't leave me much choice."

"You know what's in that truck?" Alvarez asked, looking first at Sykes and then at Dalweg.

Dalweg spat blood out from his mouth.

"Of course I know," Sykes said.

Alvarez pulled himself back onto his feet and wrapped his good arm around the truck's side mirror for support. He looked to Dalweg. "You're really going to help him do this?"

"That's what he's paying me for."

"I see that navy tat on your arm. You going to say that after we lose ten thousand sailors when one of our carrier fleets gets blown up?"

Dalweg scowled. "Fuck the navy. I got kicked from my team just because some hooker ended up with a few shitty bruises." Dalweg smiled. "I'm owed some payback."

"Those things—"

Dalweg stepped toward Alvarez. "Shut up."

Alvarez looked back to Sykes. "I always thought you were a patriot, Kevin. You really going to sell out your country just to fatten your bank account?"

Dalweg slammed the Uzi into Alvarez's gut, and

Alvarez dropped back to his knees, gasping. "Did I stutter? I said shut the fuck up."

Sykes frowned and sighed. "I'm too deep in this to get out now."

Alvarez stopped coughing enough to say, "There's always a way out."

Dalweg spat more blood out of his mouth and stepped away. He gestured to Sykes. "Just shoot the prick so we can get the fuck out of here."

Sweat glistened on Sykes's face. He leveled the gun down to where Alvarez was kneeling.

"Hurry up and do it," Dalweg said, stepping closer.

Sykes lined up the iron sights over Alvarez's left eye and took a deep breath.

Dalweg stood next to Sykes. "Shoot him."

Sykes held his breath.

"Do it," Dalweg said.

When Sykes released the breath from his lungs it came out as the word, "No."

"*Fucking do it.*"

"No." Sykes lowered the gun. "I'm not crossing that line."

"Are you out of your mind? You can't just let this guy live. This time tomorrow you'll have the whole CIA gunning for you."

"I don't care," Sykes said to Dalweg without looking at him. "Get in the truck. We're going."

When Dalweg didn't move or answer, Sykes turned his head. He was just in time to hear Dalweg say, "Well, I care," an instant before a big fist hit him square on the cheekbone and he crumpled to the ground.

"Pussy-ass faggot. I knew you didn't have no balls the moment I met you. I'm not having this boy and his crew coming after me." Dalweg stepped over Sykes's writhing body to retrieve the Beretta. "Want a job done, you gotta do it yourself."

He faced Alvarez, raised the gun.

"Any last requests, hombre?"

Alvarez stared up at Dalweg, eyes narrowed, jaw clenched, no fear, only hatred. "Go to hell."

Dalweg sneered, showing cracked and bloody teeth. "Ladies first."

Dalweg cried out as Sykes kicked his heel into the back of Dalweg's injured calf with as much strength as he had left. Dalweg didn't go over but stumbled forward toward Alvarez, who sprang up from his knees, launching his forehead into Dalweg's unprotected face. Bone, cartilage, and teeth gave way, and Dalweg lurched backward, hitting the side of the truck, falling to the ground and into the pool of diesel, conscious but dazed, Beretta still in hand.

"You're fucking dead," Dalweg screamed.

His arm extended in Alvarez's direction, and the gun went off. The bullet buried itself into the wall to Alvarez's right, a wide miss, but Alvarez didn't hang around until Dalweg recovered his senses enough to shoot straight. Alvarez hurried away while Dalweg writhed on the fuel-slick road and Dalweg took another three shots in rapid succession. Alvarez flinched but wasn't hit. He headed down an alleyway, left palm pressed over the exit wound on the back of his shoulder. There were no more gunshots or sounds of pursuit, so he paused to lean against a wall and catch his breath. He tugged an incisor from the skin between his eyebrows.

He heard the truck's engine start up a moment later and shuffled back to the corner where the alley met the street, glancing out. Sykes was still lying prostrate on the road surface, his left cheek bruised and probably fractured. He wasn't going anywhere anytime soon.

Fume clouds rose from the exhaust and the truck tried to pull away from the curb. There were vehicles parked in front and behind it, making the maneuver tricky. The blown-out rear tire slowed it down further. Diesel continued to spray from the ruptured fuel tank.

Alvarez knew that if he didn't do something soon, the truck would be gone and the missiles with it. He pictured them being sold on the black markets of the Middle East within days. He took a breath. Last-chance time.

Alvarez wiped the blood from his left hand onto his pants and ran out into the road, staying on the driver's blind side. He moved round to the back of the slowly turning truck and, with his good hand, grabbed the tailgate. With a grunt he jumped up and tumbled over into the cargo deck.

He already knew what he was looking for and where to find them. He quickly opened the box and took a flare. He lost his balance when the truck stopped sharply, knocking his injured shoulder against one of the dive tanks. He cried out and lay for a few seconds, trying to force the pain from his mind while the truck started to reverse slowly. *Move.*

Alvarez sucked air into his lungs and put the flare

between his teeth so he could unlatch the tailgate and drop out onto the road.

His knees took the impact, and his face contorted against more pain. He twisted onto his back as the truck reversed over him, stopping with the rear tires at either side of his shoulders. The air stank of diesel fumes.

Alvarez grabbed the flare in his mouth, used his teeth to hold on to the cap while he pulled the flare from the grip tube. The truck changed gear into first above him. He unscrewed the cap with his teeth and spat it away, reserved the flare so that he was holding the bottom with his teeth, hooked the ignition cord with his index finger, and pulled.

The flare ignited and thirty thousand candela's worth of light and heat poured out from the end that was pointing away from Alvarez's face.

The truck started to move forward again, and Alvarez rolled onto his right side, accepting the agony in his shoulder so he could thrust the burning end of the flare into the pool of diesel collecting on the road.

The fuel set alight instantly, and Alvarez's face was flooded with heat. He lurched backward away from the fire. It quickly spread up to the fuel tank and both ways along the road. The diesel-soaked tires started burning, leaving a strip of molten rubber on the ground.

A second later the truck had passed over Alvarez, leaving him lying on his back on the road, choking on thick tire smoke.

Alvarez knew that although diesel wasn't explosive like gasoline, it burned much more fiercely. In seconds, flames engulfed the truck's entire right side and the vehicle stopped abruptly.

Still on his back, Alvarez used his feet to push himself away from the ever-growing fire. His face felt as if it was sunburned, and he smelled burned hair. He saw locals edging closer to check out the burning truck. He shouted at them to get back, but they didn't understand him. A compressed-air tank exploded, and the resulting bang and fanning of flames convinced the crowd to back off. Sykes had managed to get back to his feet and was stumbling down the road.

The driver's door opened and Dalweg leaped out, landing on his hands and knees before frantically scrambling away from the burning truck. When he was at a safe distance, he looked back at the flames licking high up the sides of the canvas backing and screamed in anger.

Alvarez didn't have the strength to move but raised his head for a second to see Dalweg turn toward him.

"You fucking happy now, ese?"

Alvarez wanted to say yes, but instead he coughed. Dalweg strode closer, menace etched into his smashed-up face. His fists were tight at his sides.

"I may not get my money now," he spat. "But I'll settle for cutting your fucking heart out."

He pulled a dive knife from a belt sheath. It glimmered in the light of the burning truck.

Alvarez looked up again to judge the angle, raised his left hand, and tossed the flare.

It hit Dalweg in the center of his diesel-soaked chest.

SEVENTY-EIGHT

Victor's eyes opened, and for a few seconds he couldn't understand what was happening. Everything was wrong. Colors and sounds didn't make sense. The world was brown, blurry, strange. His head hurt. He took a breath but breathed in only water through his nose.

He leaned up, coughing, raising his eyes and nose out of the river. He hung upside down for a moment, gasping. He didn't know for how long he had been unconscious, but he guessed it could only have been a few minutes. He did a quick assessment of his body, flexing his hands, arms, legs, toes and moving his head, feeling stabs of pain as he did, but his limbs performed as he had commanded. No major injuries.

He unbuckled his seat belt, dropped onto the ceiling—now the floor—going underwater and then scrambling out of the smashed driver's window. Glass sliced his arms and legs. The river was slow moving, shallow, two feet deep. He struggled to his feet, staggered a step away from the upturned Jeep, soaking-wet clothes clinging to him. He held his arm up to shield his eyes from the sun.

Victor felt a sharp pain on the top of his head as he squinted. He reached up and pulled a long sliver of metal from his scalp. Blood mixed with water and ran down the side of his face. He leaned against the Jeep while he tried to get back his bearings. He felt shaky, senses all over the place. He breathed heavily. His left leg especially was in pain where the car had hit him, and in response he kept his weight on his right foot. The many minor knocks and scrapes didn't seem to hurt that badly; the adrenaline surging through him was a perfect inhibitor. If he survived until the morning, he knew he was going to feel terrible. He looked forward to that feeling.

Looking around, he saw the far bank of the river was maybe twenty yards away, the near side less than half that. Victor could see crushed shrubs and small bent-over trees, the path where the Jeep had smashed through the foliage before shooting off a high section of bank. The metallic taste of blood filled his mouth.

He couldn't see where the assassin had crashed, and maybe he was dead, but if Victor had survived, then so could his enemy. He had to be sure. He needed to see the body. After a few moments of rest, he pushed himself off the Jeep and headed for the near riverbank, wading through the knee-deep water. It was thick and dark with soil, growing shallower the closer he made it to the shore. He felt naked without a gun.

He'd taken two steps up the muddy bank when he saw a Russian emerge from the tree line, half-crouched, movements confident, Bizon in hand.

No 9 mm bullets ripped through Victor, so he stopped and waited. The Russian smiled at Victor and gestured for him to come forward. They were five yards apart.

The Russian said, "You're lucky he wants you alive. For now."

Victor said nothing.

There had been two Russians in each pickup. Where was the second? Victor approached slowly, shuffling, acting more injured than he was. He glanced around. He couldn't see the road through the trees and vegetation, but he knew it was there, maybe a hundred yards farther back at the top of the slope. Despite the sun it was dark beneath the canopy. Three yards.

The Russian motioned for Victor to come closer still, and he continued to walk forward, grimacing with every step as though he could barely stand. He needed to be close to try anything, but as soon as he was within range he knew the butt of the submachine gun would slam against his skull. He didn't control his breathing, letting the adrenaline surge heightening his senses, supercharging his muscles. Two yards.

Another step and Victor would charge, trusting the Russian had bought the pretense of weakness—a slim chance, but his only one.

From behind the Russian a chill voice said, "No one kills him but me."

Suppressed gunshots. Two. A double tap.

The Russian splayed forward, his features contorted into shock, fear, and pain for a single second before his body went limp and he collapsed face-first into the mud, directly in front of Victor. Two holes side by side in his spine so close together they touched.

No more than ten yards away Reed stood motionless in the undergrowth behind the body. He was holding the Glock in a two-handed combat grip, aiming straight at Victor's chest. Reed didn't speak. He didn't blink.

Victor took a breath, realizing he was a dead man. Killing the Russian might just have been possible, but this enemy didn't want to take him alive. At such close range Victor wouldn't miss, even injured, and he knew the assassin wasn't going to either. The only cover to run to meant heading closer still in order to get into the tree line. Even without a leg he could just about walk on, he wouldn't get close. Moving back into the river to try and reach the Jeep would be even more hopeless. Even if he could somehow make it to the vehicle without getting shot, what would he do next?

Nothing was the answer. There was nothing Victor could do to stay alive.

He supposed there was something fitting to be killed by one of his own kind. Norimov had told him for someone so careful to stay alive he lived as though he had a death wish. If he did have such a wish, it was about to come true.

Victor stepped forward and stood up straight, showing his enemy he wasn't going to cower or beg. It wasn't much, but it was all Victor had left as he waited for the bullet to the heart or brain. He didn't have to wait long.

Reed fired.

SEVENTY-NINE

But he didn't fire at Victor.

There was a sound, the crackling of vegetation. Reed spun instantly to its source, ninety degrees to his left. He shot once into the darkness beneath the canopy, dropped to one knee, reducing the size of his body while at the same time providing a more stable firing position. Shot again. Suppressed automatic fire came back at him, mud flying up as bullets raked the ground around his position.

Victor didn't hesitate, moved while Reed was distracted by what had to be the second Russian from the pickup. He sprinted toward Reed, toward the dead Russian, toward the Bizon still clutched in the Russian's hand.

Reed fired again at the unseen gunman, and a cry emanated from the trees. Victor covered the ground quickly, but Reed was already spinning back toward him. Victor tensed, anticipating the bullet's impact, but then he saw the slide was back on the Glock in Reed's hand.

Empty.

Victor reached the Bizon and scooped it up into his hands. He leveled it to fire, but Reed was already on him, pushing the gun's barrel to one side before he had it in line. A hand grabbed Victor's shirt a split second before a foot looped around his leg.

He crashed to the ground, on his back, right arm extended, hand still gripping the submachine gun. Reed landed on top of Victor, his weight knocking the air from Victor's lungs.

Flames spat from the muzzle of the Bizon. Ejected brass cases struck the mud. The recoil made Victor's arm shake and flail about wildly. Reed forced Victor's index finger down on the trigger. The magazine was empty in just over three seconds, the last bullet escaping the gun into nearby vegetation.

Victor reached for Reed's hair, found it too short to grab hold of, went for his eyes instead, but Reed was already rolling. He came to his feet a few yards away and Victor likewise rose.

For a moment the two stared into each other's eyes. Victor assessed his opponent while he knew he was likewise being assessed. The assassin before him had a compact frame, but Victor could tell that every pound was honed for strength and speed. He wore his hair short and with no care for fashion or style, no more than a centimeter or two in length all over. Too short for an enemy to grip in his fingers, as Victor had found out.

Blood ran from the assassin's right ear. Superficial wounds on his torso and arms, Victor assumed from the crash, were visible where his shirt was red. His face was damp with sweat, chillingly empty of expression, conveying no anger or excitement or even determination. It was as if no thought or feeling existed behind his eyes.

With a slow, casual motion, Reed reached his right thumb and forefinger up his left shirt sleeve. He drew out a knife from a wrist sheath and smoothly opened the folded blade.

It had a four-inch, partially serrated kriss blade with a gladiator point. It was matte black, precision crafted ceramic, strong as folded steel but much lighter and sharper, invisible to metal detectors. Victor had never seen the model before. Custom made, then, for an expert.

Victor took a step backward.

They were five yards apart, far enough away for Victor to tear off his shirt and wrap it tightly around his left arm. He gripped the end of the shirt tightly in his fist to keep it secure. Reed nodded to him—the killer's bow—a mark of respect between enemies.

Victor didn't nod back.

There was a pain growing in his lower back, bruised vertebrae from the crash or the earlier fall. It was getting worse, but he showed no sign of it on his face. Reed likewise stood as if he was not injured and bleeding in several places. Neither man displayed any weakness lest their opponent take the advantage.

Reed held his knife loosely in his right hand, the point up, thumb resting along center of the blade. He kept it at chest level, arm bent at the elbow, standing with his feet shoulder-width apart, knees bent slightly, balance ready to shift in an instant. Victor stood with the same stance. He was taller than his enemy. It didn't matter.

He took another step backward, instinctively retreating away from the blade but also moving toward the river where the water would help support his leg.

Reed rushed forward, covering the distance fast, jabbing upward at Victor's neck. His speed was incredible. Victor dodged backward, hearing the *whoosh* as the blade sliced through the air. He used his shielded forearm to ward off a follow-up thrust to his stomach, hitting the blade from above with the back of his wrist. Victor punched with his right arm, hoping to hit his opponent's exposed jaw.

Reed pulled back, used his left arm to block the blow, and whipped the knife up. Victor saw it coming, moved, but felt the blade cut his right arm. The knife was so sharp it barely hurt.

They stepped away in unison, both equally vulnerable to the other, neither willing to take uncalculated risks. Each face was a blank mask, impassive.

Victor was considering his tactics as he knew his opponent was also. The assassin may have had a knife, but he was no fool. He wouldn't commit himself blindly until the moment was exact, and neither would Victor. But in their first engagement Victor was cut and the assassin uninjured. All his enemy had to do was repeat the process, each time wearing Victor down. But he'll try something else, Victor thought; he won't repeat the same attack.

Reed leaped forward, the knife held high and wide, bringing it across for a wild slash at Victor's eyes. Victor didn't take the bait. He jumped back out of his opponent's reach as the assassin's arm pivoted, driving the knife downward. Instead of plunging into the side of Victor's neck, the blade hit only air.

Victor knocked the knife hand to one side, kicked at Reed's stomach. Reed threw his left arm in the way, accepting the blow where it had little effect.

Victor edged backward, his feet now under water. The next attack came with frightening speed, more following as Victor dodged. Reed didn't slow his momentum, coming forward with every thrust, keeping Victor on the defensive. All Victor's effort was focused on stopping the knife point from entering his flesh. He blocked and dodged, always retreating. The water reached the midpoint of his shins. He took a slash to his abdomen when Reed changed his attack and Victor wasn't fast enough to avoid it.

The wound made Victor wince, and he cursed himself for showing pain. Moving through the water slowed him down but was easier on his injured leg. His enemy's speed was likewise affected, but his reflexes were still blindingly fast. The warm blood on Victor's stomach and arm proof those reflexes were faster than his own. The slash to his stomach wasn't deep, but he could feel it tearing more every time he moved. He wouldn't allow it to slow him down. If he tore himself apart, so be it.

Victor concentrated on parrying, hoping to wear his opponent down while he waited for the opportunity to counterattack. The shirt wrapped around his arm was cut in a dozen places, but so far it had protected his arm from the knife's edge. It was razor sharp, as he expected it would be, but still couldn't penetrate all the way through the thick layers of cloth in a single slash. But each attack took its toll, and, as Victor parried, his shield was slowly being destroyed. With luck it might last another few minutes before it would be useless. When it did, Victor would use his bare arm as the shield.

Reed stopped suddenly, allowing Victor to back off a few steps. The water was almost knee deep. His enemy was playing it safe, not willing to continue the relentless attack and drain his own energy. He knew what Victor knew, that defending was less strenuous. He was pacing himself, knowing the duel would not end quickly. As fatigue increased reactions slowed.

Victor risked taking his eyes off his enemy, quickly glanced around, looking for anything that might help him. On the bank, unseen in the trees, was the second Russian shot by the assassin. There would be a submachine gun next to him, but there was no way Victor could get to it. He couldn't go backward either. The far bank was too far away. He'd never make it. If it was dark he would have a chance of escaping if he could put some distance between them, but at this rate he would be dead long before then. Blood was slick on his arm and stomach. The pain in his back and leg was relentless. Think. *Think.*

Reed came forward again, thrusting and slashing at Victor's waist, trying to get the knife under Victor's arm after he'd failed to get above it. Victor blocked awkwardly, forced to twist his forearm so his palm was upward. He couldn't risk using the underside, where arteries flowed just below the skin.

Victor pushed an attack aside, felt the hot sting as the knife bit deep into his forearm. The blade caught for a second among the folded layers of the shirt, and

Victor used that advantage to throw himself forward, slamming his elbow at his opponent's chest, hoping to crack ribs.

Reed sacrificed his balance, shifting all his weight to one leg to pull himself away in time. The elbow only glanced his rib cage. Victor blocked another blow with his protected forearm. Red stained the shirt.

The knife came again, in a blur, but Victor knocked the assassin's hand up with his left forearm, accepting another cut as he tried to grab hold of the wrist with his right hand. Reed was faster and intercepted Victor's arm, catching the wrist in his left hand. Victor propelled himself forward, going inside the assassin's reach. Before Reed could counter, Victor drove his forehead into his enemy's face.

Reed grunted, stumbled backward, releasing Victor's wrist. Reed's eyes filled with water, blood flowed from the split on the bridge of his nose. He swung frantically with the knife, slashing the air in front of him, keeping Victor at bay.

Victor kept his distance from the lethal blade, welcoming the chance to get his breath back. Blood dripped from Reed's chin. Victor took two heavy breaths, but he only needed one.

The assassin attacked, aiming high. Victor sidestepped, threw an elbow at the side of Reed's head. Reed parried with his left arm. The knife came at the side of Victor's face, in a slash, but Victor ducked down low to avoid it, springing back up, kicking with his right leg. Reed lurched backward, dodging the attack, but was unable to keep his balance.

Victor knocked the knife to one side with his left hand and punched straight out with his right fist. His knuckles connected with the assassin's jaw, but it was a glancing blow, sliding away, force redirected—his enemy too fast.

Reed recovered his footing and leaped at Victor from a low crouch. Victor caught the incoming arm in both hands, turned it away, but had to let go and pivot out of the way to avoid Reed's counterpunch. Both men stepped back. The riverbed was hard and rocky underfoot.

Even Victor's opponent was looking tired now, his mouth open, taking in large gulps of air with each inhale. It had become a battle of attrition, each man's abilities evenly matched, neither capable of ending the fight quickly. With each attack and parry the stamina of both was wearing away, working to the point where fatigue would create the inevitable mistake. But Victor, bleeding from both arms, stomach, and ribs, knew that as things stood he would reach that stage sooner.

The pain was extreme. He could no longer keep it from his face even for a second. His arms felt heavy. The shirt was shredded, soaked with river water and blood—more of a hindrance than anything else. Victor released it and shook it off his arm. He thought about throwing it at his opponent, but it would be a pathetic gesture. He wasn't about to humiliate himself.

His chest heaved; his mouth hung open. He blinked the sweat from his eyes. Reed lunged forward. Victor used his left bare forearm to block the blade, feeling it enter his skin. Reed felt it too, and his eyes glimmered.

Victor threw him backward, went to attack but stumbled, his face contorting in sudden agony. Both actions faked.

Reed lunged again, sensing the kill, lured into overeagerness. He neglected protocol, overextending his thrust. Victor sidestepped easily, pushed the blade away with his right forearm, and brought his left fist across and into Reed's face.

There was a satisfying *smack*, the blow knocking Reed sideways. Reed's arms sagged, stunned. Victor twisted, throwing a heavy punch, trying to capitalize on the change in initiative while he had the chance, but Reed was already dropping into a low crouch, and Victor realized he'd been fooled, his own tactic used against him.

Reed sprang up inside of Victor's reach, the knife racing straight toward his neck.

Victor did the only thing he could and threw his left arm into its path.

He felt the knife point pierce the underside of his forearm, slicing through skin, muscle, and blood vessels, scraping between his ulna and radius bones.

The gladiator point came right out of the other side of his arm, the matte-black blade utterly red. Drops of his own blood splashed Victor's face. He gasped, fought not to scream. His legs buckled.

He grabbed hold of his enemy's wrist, tried to pull the knife free but his strength was gone. Reed pushed the knife from side to side, increasing the size of the wound, magnifying the agony. Blood poured from Victor's arm. It took all his will to keep standing. He had nothing left. A cruel grin formed on Reed's face.

That smile stung Victor more than the blade in his arm. It stabbed something deep inside him, reminding Victor he wasn't dead yet. He had one last chance to save his life.

He tipped himself backward, deliberately falling.

Reed grabbed hold of Victor with his free hand to stop him, to keep him upright and impaled, but he didn't have the leverage. Letting Victor fall meant letting go of the knife, but falling too meant he would land on top of Victor, cushioning his own fall and trapping his prey underwater. It would make finishing him off all the more easy.

Reed fell too.

Before they hit the water, Victor brought his right leg up and managed to wedge his knee at the base of Reed's breastbone.

Victor disappeared beneath the river, taking the pain of their combined weight, the water cushioning the fall but the rocky riverbed intensifying it. That force was directed straight through Victor's knee and right into his Reed's solar plexus.

Reed let out a cry as his diaphragm collapsed and the breath expelled from his lungs. In that instant his strength left him completely.

Immediately Victor pushed upward with his left arm. It emerged from underneath the water, and he drove the point of the knife protruding from his forearm into the Reed's exposed neck. The inch of blade disappeared entirely into the Englishman's flesh.

Reed's eyes went wide.

Victor, head still underwater, wrenched the blade

from side to side, crying out against the agony in his own arm as he tore through his assailant's neck. Reed gagged. For a moment there was resistance against the blade. The thick walls of the carotid artery.

Reed threw himself away, pressing his hands to his neck, but it was too late.

A torrent of blood erupted from the wound.

Victor's watery sky turned red. Reed fell backward into the river, water splashing up around him.

Victor heaved himself up and sucked in precious air. He struggled to his feet, cradling his impaled arm. Reed was floating in the river before him, a crimson cloud rapidly expanding around him, both palms pressed over his throat, trying desperately to stem the spray of blood and do the impossible—stay alive.

Victor ignored him. The knife was buried to the hilt in his arm, blood leaking out from the top and bottom, all around. Using only his right hand, Victor slid off his belt and wrapped it around his upper-left bicep as tightly as it could go. He forced the metal catch through the leather to create a new hole to fasten it.

It would be suicide to remove the knife, so he left it in place. The belt would help, but it was only a temporary respite. At the rate it was coming out, most, if not all, the major blood vessels in his arm had been severed. At his weight, and with just the belt to help him, Victor estimated he had less than half an hour before he bled to death. He would probably be unable to walk after fifteen minutes, twenty if he was lucky.

Reed was making a croaking sound, blood bubbling

from his mouth. His face was white, blood vivid, almost black against his skin. He looked up at Victor without blinking. There was no fear in his eyes, no hatred, just a cool acceptance of his fate. Victor wondered what his own eyes would betray when his turn eventually came. He turned away from Reed for the last time and thought of Rebecca.

He waded through the water and up the bank, unsteady on his feet. He made his way through the trees, following the path the Jeep had carved until he saw the Russian's pickup parked along the road. He stumbled toward it. The keys were still in the ignition.

Victor's eyes flicked between the analog clock on the dash and the road ahead as he drove back to the city. Ideally he needed to get as far away as possible before going to a hospital, out of the country preferably. But there wasn't time. He would bleed to death behind the wheel if he tried.

He drove with heavy eyelids, feeling colder and colder. He was yawning as he pulled up outside a Tanga hospital. He felt himself going as he stumbled into the emergency department. He was greeted by a brief scream.

A nurse's hand gripped his right arm and pulled him down a corridor. He sagged to his knees as he struggled to keep up with her. She was shouting and asking him questions. He couldn't understand what she was saying. Then he heard English and somehow Victor managed to make his mouth work and he shouted out his blood type as loud as he could. He would have fallen, but unseen hands pulled him on his feet. His vision was failing as he lay down on a bed. There were other people around him, more nurses, maybe doctors.

He heard wheels squeak.

EIGHTY

Dar es Salam, Tanzania
Tuesday
12:03 UTC

Sykes did everything in his power to maintain a calm persona, but he knew that he was failing. He had barely slept for two days but was too on edge to feel any tiredness. Despite the fact that the building was perfectly air conditioned, Sykes was trying to ignore the dampness gathering under his armpits.

After the disaster at the hotel, Sykes had gotten out of the country, crossing the northern border into Kenya. He'd rolled options around in his head while throwing antacids down his throat and vomiting periodically when they ran out. In the end he realized he didn't have the balls for life as a fugitive or the know-how to last as one.

If he really tried, there was a slim chance he might be able to sort things out enough to survive the inevitable fallout. But Reed had been at Sykes's hotel. He was sure of it. The man who had shot Wiechman. And the only explanation for Reed being there was that Ferguson had sent the assassin to kill Sykes. It was enough to change Sykes's priorities. Getting rich and his career came a clear second to staying alive.

He gave himself up at the embassy on Sunday afternoon. He'd been in CIA custody since then. Ten minutes ago he'd been led from his room to an agency office in the basement of the embassy compound.

Sykes stood silently before Procter, who sat behind a desk in a chair obviously too small for him. Ten seconds past. Twenty. Procter saw he was struggling to start.

"Would you like to sit down?" he asked.

"I would like to stand if it's all the same to you, sir."

"They're your legs."

Sykes kept his hands clasped behind his back. He would do this with some dignity. In fact, he reminded himself, it was about the only thing he had left. Sykes spoke without pause for almost thirty minutes. He started with just the highlights: Ferguson's coming to him with the plan; his agreeing; recruiting Kennard and Sumner; using Sumner to hire Tesseract and to identify him through dummy jobs; getting Hoyt to hire Stevenson; hiding the money trail through Seif and Olympus; using information supplied by Kennard to help Tesseract kill Ozols; having Stevenson's team attempt to kill Tesseract; sending McClury after Tesseract when Stevenson failed; dispatching Reed to kill Kennard, Hoyt, Seif, Sumner, and Tesseract; thinking Reed had been successful in Cyprus; decrypting the flash drive and locating and recovering the missiles; and how it all went wrong.

When he had finished, Procter seemed far too calm considering what Sykes had just told him.

"And," Procter began, "the purpose of his highly illegal course of action, one that resulted in a large number of deaths, was to sell the Oniks missiles to the highest bidder?"

"Yes," Sykes admitted. "We did it for the money."

"Okay, good." Procter seemed pleased at his cooperation. "And you were involved in this operation from the start, were you not, Mr. Sykes?"

Sykes knew he was going down hard. And he deserved it.

"I was instrumental from the very beginning."

"I appreciate your honesty. I can certainly understand how difficult this is for you."

What was going on? Did he just hear some sympathy? Procter was obviously softening him up for the killer blow.

"Now," Procter continued, "it may surprise you to learn that I already knew much of what you've just told me."

Something exploded inside Sykes's stomach. "How?"

"How doesn't matter. What does matter is that you've come in voluntarily. If I'd been forced to bring you in unwillingly, this conversation would have been decidedly more unpleasant. Tell me more about what happened yesterday."

Sykes's throat was dry. He explained about Dalweg and Wiechman and the recovery of the missiles from the sunken *Lev* and their return to the hotel, the conversation with Ferguson. "That's when everything went bad." He explained things as he remembered them.

Procter took everything in silently and made the occasional nod. When Sykes was finished, Procter asked, "Why was Tesseract in the country, at the hotel?"

Sykes shook his head. "The only thing I can think of is that he was coming after me."

"But how did he even know about you?"

"Somehow Sumner got wind that she was a target and avoided Reed. She then teamed up with Tesseract to come after me and Ferguson. I guess she worked out who we were. I don't know how."

Procter was silent for a moment then started asking questions. Lots of questions. Sykes answered. All the gory details. He left out the fact that he'd seen Reed in Tanga, since it wouldn't do any good if Procter knew that the reason why Sykes was confessing was that Ferguson wanted him dead. If that information came out later, so be it, but for now, Sykes wanted to feel like he wasn't quite as low as Ferguson on the traitorous-scum ladder.

"You have filled in a great many blanks to this sordid and despicable affair," Procter said, "and for that I am greatly appreciative. However, you have knowingly engaged in criminal activities that constitute the highest penalties allowed by law."

"I understand that, sir. And I accept the consequences."

It felt good to be honorable, if only for a few minutes.

"But," Procter continued, "it could be seen that you

are guilty of nothing more than obeying orders. Ferguson was the instigator in this ridiculous mess, and you the victim of his lunacy." Sykes wasn't sure how to respond, so he didn't. "I can see that you had no wish to conduct this operation, but you were put in an impossible situation. Ferguson was your superior, a hero of this organization. You had no choice but to do as you were told, and I can appreciate that.

"From day one we teach you to obey your superiors, to follows orders that you may not understand because you are not always in possession of the full facts. And you have to obey them, to the letter, even if you don't agree with them. Because if you do not, you could destroy something of vast importance."

If Sykes wasn't mistaken a flicker of light appeared at the end of the very dark tunnel.

Procter continued: "The loyalty you have demonstrated to your superior is to be commended. But now you must chose where your true loyalty lies. To the agency or to your mentor?"

There wasn't even a second's deliberation, but Sykes mentally counted to ten to make it seem as if the choice had not been an easy one. He felt the pause perfectly demonstrated the internal conflict that was supposedly within him.

"My loyalty is to this agency, sir."

Procter nodded solemnly. "I'm very glad you said that. Very glad indeed. Because I need your help."

"I'm not sure I follow."

"Most of what you have told me cannot be substantiated, can it?"

Sykes thought carefully for a moment. "No, sir."

"And therein lies the rub."

"I'm still not sure I understand."

"It's your word against Ferguson's."

Sykes nodded. "Yes, sir."

"And his word is worth more than your own."

The thought of Ferguson's getting away clean made his blood boil, but his words came out pathetic instead of angry. *"That's not fair—"*

"Fair or not, that is the situation. So we must be smart, mustn't we?"

Sykes was confused. "Yes, sir."

"Ferguson won't be aware of what's happening, and neither will he find out what you've told me. So what I want you to do is this. I want you to carry on as normal, and do what Ferguson tells you to do. Just record it." Procter stood and placed the flats of his palms on the desk. "I need proof, enough proof to string Ferguson up by the throat so tightly even he cannot wriggle free. We need the case against Ferguson to be so overwhelming and the charges so severe that it's impossible to keep it quiet. People need to know what's happened."

Sykes was starting to understand. Procter was desperate to make sure this wasn't swept under the carpet.

"And bringing Ferguson to justice will mean I can forget about any indiscretions you have performed up until this point," Procter continued. "I won't forget those people who helped in its course. But I don't want to put you under any pressure to do anything that you don't want to do."

Sykes straightened his back, knowing that he could

gather more than enough proof already to hammer the nails in Ferguson's coffin. It would be a pleasure to do so. Sykes smiled inwardly. He knew what Procter was up to, the sly fucker. Procter would be the crusader who cleaned—no purged—the CIA of corruption, who showed that one of the organization's greatest heroes was rotten to the core. That kind of achievement would accelerate him straight into the director's chair in just a few years. After that, Who knew? Procter was going places, that much was certain. And if Sykes continued to be as smart as he knew himself to be, he would be going there too. Sykes had a plan.

"I want to make things right," he said, and he meant it.

Procter smiled. "Good for you."

EIGHTY-ONE

13:13 UTC

"How are you feeling, Antonio?"

Alvarez blew out some air and, in answer, raised his slinged right arm as much as the pain would allow. He had some pills in his system, and they took much of the edge off.

"I'm told it should heal good," Procter said.

"Won't be pitching anytime soon though."

Procter stepped into the hotel room, and Alvarez

closed the door behind him. The room wasn't particularly big to begin with, but with Procter now taking up a good amount of the available space it was positively cramped.

"You know how much blood you lost?"

Alvarez shook his head. "No, but I'm betting I'm half African now."

With one arm Alvarez moved his bag to one side and sat down on the room's single bed. The bag was small and only contained some dirty laundry and Alvarez's few personal effects. The clothes he was wearing had been bought for him while he spent most of the night on a hospital bed. He'd been flown to Tanzania's capital by an embassy chopper and given a hotel room to rest in.

"But you're lucky you didn't come away with worse," Procter said, tone noticeably more serious. "Going off on your own like that. What were you thinking?"

"I didn't have a whole lot of time to think."

Procter frowned. "As an officer of the CIA you should probably have answered differently there."

"I'm high on painkillers."

Procter showed some teeth. "Then I'll let it pass."

Alvarez didn't say anything. He reached across to the bedside table and grabbed a bottle of mineral water. He switched it to his right hand to twist the top off with his left, but the bottled water was damp with condensation and too slippery in his weakened grip.

"Let me get that for you," Procter offered, stepping closer.

Alvarez kept the bottle away from Procter. "I got it."

He pushed the bottle against his chest and, with the extra support, managed to get the top off. He took a small sip and placed it back down.

"Not as thirsty as you thought?" Procter asked.

"Guess not."

"You know," Procter said, "a part of me wants to shout my big mouth off at you for disobeying my commands."

"So why don't you?"

"Because I'm not sure if it would be just ego talking. After all, you did a good, if unconventional, job."

"We didn't get the missiles."

Procter shrugged. "The second Ozols got killed and the drive went missing we were never going to get those missiles. It was a lost cause from the get-go, no matter what spiel came out of Chambers's mouth."

Alvarez rubbed his shoulder.

Procter continued, "You stopped anyone else from getting them. That's the most important thing."

"Status quo maintained?"

"That's the business we're in."

"What happens to Ferguson and Sykes?"

"Sykes turned himself in. He'll cut a deal, help the case against Ferguson."

"When's Ferguson going to get the good news?"

Procter chewed on his answer for a moment. "That's going to take some more legwork. But don't worry, he'll get what's coming to him." He reached a hand for the water. "Mind?" Alvarez shook his head, and Procter took a long drink. "And don't think about going solo again," he said after screwing the top back on. "I won't be such a nice guy next time you pull this kind of shit."

Alvarez half raised his arm again. "Couldn't if I wanted to."

Procter looked at him closely. "But do you want to?"

Alvarez thought for a moment, then shook his head. "Once was enough."

"Good. Because you're going to be behind a desk for a while. Partly because you need time to heal and partly because I've got to be seen giving you a telling off. The agency doesn't have time for mavericks."

Alvarez nodded.

"What time's your flight out?" Procter asked.

Alvarez turned his wrist over to look at his watch. "Soon."

"Make sure you're on it."

"I will."

"What are you going to do when you get back?"

"Normal stuff. Have a barbeque, go to a ball game. See my kid."

"Sounds nice," Procter said.

EIGHTY-TWO

Moscow, Russia
Tuesday
14:11 MSK

Colonel Gennady Aniskovach passed through the corridors of the SVR headquarters and, with a controlled amount of anger, accepted that his face now drew more glances damaged than it had when beautiful. Prudnikov's secretary, who had previously always gazed at him with brazen longing and desire, averted her eyes when he arrived at her desk. Aniskovach waited while she announced his presence by an intercom and, despite the pain it caused, gave her his best smile when she finally glanced his way before he entered Prudnikov's office.

The director was reading a report of some variety and did not look up. There was no small talk. Aniskovach knew he had exhausted that particular pleasure. Eventually Prudnikov placed the report to one side. He adjusted it so it was square to his desk.

He poured himself a glass of water and took a drink. "My throat is hoarse from the amount of explaining I have been forced to do on your behalf. As you may expect, the GRU in particular are not exactly happy that four decorated members of our special forces have lost their lives and that another two were injured during an operation we told them nothing about—an operation that should have been theirs to conduct in the first place."

He rubbed his brow before looking up, gray eyes narrow. "I do not appreciate that you have put me in this position yet again. I did as you requested, and I gave you the task of recovering those missiles, at the same time allowing you the chance to repair your tarnished reputation. And what do you do? You are responsible for yet more deaths; you create yet more problems for me. And you didn't even come back with so much as a handful of bolts."

"I'd like to remind you of the unforeseen circumstances that interfered with the mission," Aniskovach responded calmly. "Yet I still managed to successfully destroy the missiles and therefore deny America acquiring our technology." Aniskovach stood straight backed. "And I offer my sincerest regret for the loss of life, sir."

The head of the SVR smirked. "Even you cannot make that sound sincere, Gennady. Though others may not see past your charm, I am not so easily misled. I've spoken to the soldiers at the hospital, and I know what really happened. You had nothing to do with the destruction of the missiles. That was but a fortunate coincidence, so don't try and claim credit. I always knew that you were ruthless, but now I know that you have no conscience, not even when good men die to serve your ambition. If it were purely up to me, I would have you thrown out of the organization or, at the least, I would confine you to a desk for the rest of your career where you could do no more damage."

"Sir, I—"

"Silence." Prudnikov waved his hand. "Do not spill your veneered words on me. There is no need for it. I say this honestly: Your ability to capitalize on your own mistakes is extremely impressive. Even at my best I don't believe I could have wriggled from the fisherman's net as well as you have."

"I don't understand."

"I'm sure you don't. But it seems the GRU were not the lone recipient of information relating to the Tanzania operation. That we very nearly lost our missile technology to the Americans has created ripples in the pools of power above my head. It was an especially clever move of yours to leak what happened to those who know no better so that the illusion of success can shield you from your failure. If nothing else, I must respect your guile."

Aniskovach had originally planned to appear shocked at news of the leak but now chose to stand emotionless. There seemed little point in acting ignorant.

"There are many who care only for headlines who are extremely pleased with your actions. Press releases are already being prepared to boast of our victory." Prudnikov sighed. "Quite the hero, aren't you?"

"I do my duty as well as I can."

Prudnikov laughed bitterly and leaned back in his chair. "It appears that your stock has risen sharply and that you have some new friends in the Kremlin, friends who inform me that you've done Russia proud, friends who inform me that it would weaken our very nation if I were to downgrade your responsibilities. Apparently the lives of four distinguished soldiers, four real heroes, is but a small price to pay for keeping our missile superiority. I have been instructed that I should congratulate you, reward you even."

The SVR colonel tried not to look too pleased with himself. This was going even better than he had expected.

"Thank you, sir."

"There is no need to thank me, Gennady, when this has been entirely of your own doing. Any thanks you receive should therefore be directed purely toward yourself."

"Then I thank myself."

Prudnikov's eyes narrowed to slits. "Your arrogance will be your downfall."

"Perhaps," Aniskovach began, "but so far any arrogance has been more than justified. There is no reason to suggest that justification shall not continue. In which case confidence would have been a more accurate choice of word. Sir."

Prudnikov, showing a look of pure disdain, considered Aniskovach for a long time. He didn't retort, and Aniskovach took his silence as a sign of concession in the verbal battle. Eventually the head of the SVR adjusted his glasses and cleared his throat. "Since I cannot demote you," he said, "I may as well make use of you. You are to continue your hunt for General Banarov's assassin. Hopefully on this matter you have already reached the limits of any damage you may have caused. Do we know anything more of him?"

Aniskovach had not told Prudnikov the full extent of what happened in Tanzania and had completely left out the involvement of Banarov's killer. Such information was too valuable to give up until the most opportune moment. For now, though, one minor detail to placate Prudnikov wouldn't hurt.

"Well," Aniskovach began with a carefully measured quantity of drama. "We've had a very interesting development in that regard."

EIGHTY-THREE

Tanga, Tanzania
Tuesday
16:50 UTC

When Victor awoke, he wanted to be sick, but he forced himself to take stock of his surroundings as soon as consciousness allowed. He was lying in a hospital bed, a mosquito net surrounding him. His vision was blurry, but it was bright, daytime. A ceiling fan thrummed overhead. The room was small. He was alone.

Every inch of him seemed to hurt. There were bruises everywhere. Wounds all over his body had been dressed. A ring of bandages was wrapped tight around his stomach, but his left forearm was the most heavily bound. Nothing was splinted or cast, so he knew there were no broken bones, but fearing tendon damage he tentatively flexed his left hand. He winced at the pain, but all his fingers seemed to move correctly. He hoped that there wouldn't be any long-term damage. If he made it back to Europe, he would get it looked at by a specialist just to be sure.

He felt weak; it was difficult to sit himself upright. He guessed he was suffering the side effects from any painkillers and sedatives as well as from his injuries. He brushed the mosquito net aside. Since there were no tubes inside him, he swiveled his legs out from under the blanket, and the soles of his feet touched the cool floor.

He didn't know why he was in a private room instead of a ward, maybe just on merit of his skin color. It was an effort to stand, and he moved slowly over to the window. Looking out he saw that he was on the first floor, no more than fifteen feet from the ground. Not far, but in his current physical state he doubted he'd be able to support his own weight, let alone climb. The window was a potential escape route, not his first choice of exit.

He would have to be careful how he elected to leave. If he slipped away unnoticed, it could create a fuss; people's memories would be keener if questions were asked about him at a later point. If he took his time, discharged himself without incident, then if anyone came asking questions, no one would really remember him except for his race and wounds. After he left, he would come back and pay an intern to steal his records.

He enjoyed the feeling of the sun on his skin. It was good to be alive, better than he could have believed. But he wasn't safe. He was surprised there were no guards outside his room. Maybe the Tanzanian authorities didn't know his part in the killings of the previous night. He realized his sense of time was off. He didn't know what time of day it was or how long it had been since that knife fight in the river. He remembered waking up before, maybe twice, but couldn't remember any details. He hoped it was only the next day.

The door opened, and he turned quickly to see a doctor enter. Victor could barely see the face, his eyes having trouble focusing. The doctor was tall and overweight. White. He looked to be in his fifties.

"How do you feel?"

His accent was strange. Victor couldn't place it.

"Groggy," was his reply.

The doctor seemed agitated. "You should be resting."

"How long have I been here?"

"Almost two days."

Victor knew he was fortunate that people who mattered didn't yet know he was here after so long a time. But any further time spent in the hospital gave any enemies more chance to zero in on his position. He needed to leave, now, regardless of causing a commotion. Victor opened the cupboard near the bed and found some of his clothes.

"I need to go," he said.

"I'd like to talk to you before you do."

"I haven't got time."

"Are you quite sure?"

There was something in the tone that made Victor look up. The face started to come into focus. There was a curious expression etched on the doctor's features. His white coat looked pristine. There were no pens in the pocket, no stethoscope around the neck, no identification.

Victor stopped getting dressed. "Who are you?"

"I'm not a doctor."

"I worked that part out for myself."

The man who wasn't a doctor smiled. "I would have been disappointed if you hadn't."

"If you're here to kill me you've waited too long."

"You think I'm a killer?" He laughed to himself. "Hardly."

"Then what are you?"

"Think of me as an administrator."

Victor continued putting on his clothes. "Is the accent necessary?"

"Is this better?" An American.

"Where's your backup?"

"I don't have any."

A lie.

"Then what's stopping me from killing you?"

"In your current physical state, I think even you would struggle with that. But, more notably, the same thing that would prevent me from doing likewise." The administrator pointed, gestured through the door's window to the corridor outside full of patients and hospital staff—a janitor, nurses. Witnesses. "I just want to talk."

"We're talking," Victor said. "You have the time it takes me to get dressed."

"Then I'll be curt."

Victor kept his gaze on the administrator the whole time. He couldn't see signs that he was armed. "Please do."

"I'm here because we can help each other."

"How?"

"We both want the same thing."

"Which is?"

"This thing to be over."

"And?"

"I can make that happen."

"Why?" asked Victor, genuinely intrigued.

"Don't be fooled by the cuddly exterior," the administrator said. "I'm really not a very nice man."

"I wasn't fooled," Victor said. "And you haven't answered my question."

"My reasons are my own. But this whole mess should never have been created. I want to clean it up."

Things were starting to make sense. "And whom exactly are you representing?"

"The government of the United States of America."

"I doubt that very much," Victor said.

"I represent the U.S.A. in my own way," the administrator corrected.

Nether spoke for a moment, and the administrator took an object from a trouser pocket and threw it to Victor. He caught it in his right hand. The assassin's knife. Victor unfolded it slowly. His left forearm throbbed.

"That's a pretty special weapon," the administrator said. "Custom made. No metal. Ceramic blade, carbon-fiber fittings, gladiator point, kriss edge."

"You know your knives," Victor said.

"I wasn't always a desk jockey," the administrator explained without emotion. "What happened to the man who stabbed you with it?"

Victor folded the blade away. "I stabbed him back."

A smile appeared on the administrator's fleshy mouth. Victor went to return the knife, but a palm was raised his way. "Keep it. It's more use to you than me."

Victor kept it in his hand. "Since you're being generous," he said, "do you have a cigarette?"

The administrator shook his head. "I can probably get one for you."

"Forget it," Victor said after a few seconds. "I think I've just quit."

"Good for you," the administrator said. "So is your answer a yes?"

"It's a maybe. But that isn't the only reason why you're here, is it?"

The administrator smiled. "Very perceptive. You're right; there is something else I want. I would like to retain your services. From time to time."

"I'm thinking of retiring."

"I would hope you might reconsider."

"Why do you need someone like me in your service?"

"My colleague made a mistake in using you as an expendable asset. I recognize your potential is far higher."

"My ego doesn't need massaging."

"Be that as it may, there are times when being able to subcontract delicate assignments out of house is necessary. Going through the conventional channels to get the job done is not always the most efficient use of time or resources. Especially when that job is, technically speaking, illegal."

"You must have the contact details of a thousand men like me. Why do you need another?"

"Because those people exist and you don't. Despite all that has happened these last two weeks, you still have your anonymity as well as your life. The agency still knows nothing about you; no one does. That's some accomplishment."

"You still found me."

"Not really such a tall order after yesterday. But, even so, I don't know who you are, and I doubt I'll ever find out. I consider this past fortnight to be your interview. You've proved yourself extremely qualified for the position I need to fill."

"I've been very lucky."

"I don't believe in luck. I don't believe you do either."

"And how would this arrangement work?"

"You'll perform no other work besides that which you do for me. Those contracts will come directly from me or an associate of mine. And that's it. Simple."

Victor showed nothing in his expression. "I know what you're getting out of this, but how do I benefit?"

"Money, of course."

"You don't know what my fee is yet. I think I'm about to increase my rates."

The administrator smirked. "I'm confident we'll be able to afford you."

"What else do I get besides money?"

"Immunity. We can help you avoid any unnecessary

complications with other nations. The French are still busy looking for you after Paris, and I'm sure the Swiss would like to ask a few questions as well. And let's not talk about the Russians."

"You make a compelling pitch."

The administrator continued. "Most important, if you do exactly as instructed and don't flaunt yourself, I can make sure that no one on my side of the Atlantic bothers you either."

"What if I say no?"

"I don't believe you will."

Victor held his gaze, knowing exactly what would happen if he said no. The broad-shouldered janitor who was trying to look busy in the corridor outside would be reaching into his too-clean toolbox for something other than a screwdriver.

"All right," he said. "I accept."

"I thought you would."

"On one condition," Victor added.

"Name it."

"I want the person who started this. And that isn't negotiable."

There was barely any change in the administrator's face. "I thought you might say something to that effect. You can have him." He took an envelope from his clipboard and laid it down on the end of the bed. I'll contact you in a couple of weeks once you've had time to rest so we can discuss how to proceed."

When the administrator was almost at the door, Victor spoke. "There is something else."

"I was wondering when you were going to ask." The

administrator stopped and faced him. "You want to know what was on that boat, don't you? You want to know what all this has been about."

Victor didn't look back. "I couldn't care less about that. I never have."

The administrator's broad forehead wrinkled, and he folded his arms across his chest. "Then what is it?"

"There was a woman." Victor was near the window. "Rebecca."

"Rebecca Sumner," the administrator said, the curiosity in his voice obvious. "She was killed in Cyprus."

"That's right," Victor said slowly.

"So what do you want to know about her?"

The bright sunlight warmed Victor's face.

"Everything."

EIGHTY-FOUR

17:02 UTC

The administrator closed the door behind him and walked down the busy hospital corridor. He made sure not to look at the janitor lingering close to Tesseract's room. A simple nod would have been the signal for his man to enter and execute the injured assassin, and Roland Procter did not want his new employee killed unnecessarily.

Locating Tesseract had been relatively simple. After

Sykes had finished briefing Procter, he had used local assets to do the searching. It hadn't taken that long. There were only so many recently hospitalized white guys in the city.

Procter thought about Ferguson. This whole thing had happened because the old bastard hadn't had enough slaps on the back for doing his job twenty years ago. It was no excuse to turn traitor for a few million. It was a sorry end to a once fine man's career. Procter wasn't driven by money; it was power he wanted. Power could buy everything that money could as well as everything that it could not.

He exited the hospital in an excellent mood. Within a few short days he would have compiled a case against Ferguson so compelling even the hacks on the Hill couldn't brush it under the carpet. With careful leaking of information to the press, Procter would ensure his face was seen at every breakfast table in the city. Savior of the CIA was quite a catchy title, he'd decided.

He expected to be promoted within six months. Chambers was only there until they found someone else, and Procter would soon make himself the perfect candidate. With Ferguson dead, it would give even more weight to Procter's ascension. Sullying the name of a dead hero would be worth even more than destroying a live one. Everyone who mattered, in the agency and on Capitol Hill, would want a scandal of that magnitude kept under wraps. If he elected to keep quiet, the amount of political currency Procter could gain from the top brass was immense.

Having Ferguson killed barely caused a tremor on

Procter's moral compass, broken as it already was. Ferguson was a traitor and a murderer and it was only just that he be executed for his crimes. Procter had ordered far-more-honorable individuals killed than Ferguson and still slept like a chubby baby. Plus, this killing came with an extra bonus: it brought Tesseract on side. Now Procter had his very own pet hitman.

He smiled. It would all work itself out beautifully, though Procter reminded himself not to be too cocky. He was good, that much was certain, but it was always the ones who didn't realize they weren't invincible that failed to achieve their fullest potential. He wasn't about to make the same mistakes Ferguson had made.

Procter knew he was far too good for that.

A gaunt man joined him on the street outside the hospital. He wore a white linen suit and seemed particularly uncomfortable under the Tanzanian sun. Sweat made his pale face shine.

Procter walked alongside him. "How did it go?"

"Nothing recoverable," the man said. "The frigate is a mess and the missiles onboard are in pieces, corroded, or both. As for the truck, well, the missiles were half-rusty anyway. The fire finished them off. If anything survived it's been looted."

"Would have been nice to have brought one back," Procter said. "But you can't win them all."

"No, you never can."

"What about Tesseract?"

"Our people got here too late to get fingerprints without his noticing, but we have a blood sample from when he came in and, more important, photos. And there are a few other things to follow up on when we get back." The gaunt man sidestepped a group of laughing children heading the opposite way. "It's all in here."

He handed over a slim file, and Procter opened it briefly. "Good job, Mr. Clarke."

Clarke showed little in his expression. "You don't really think he'll stick to the deal, do you?"

"He doesn't have a choice."

Clarke looked anything but convinced.

Procter spoke: "When you bring a dangerous dog into your home, waiting until after it takes a chunk from your ass is leaving it too late to establish who's boss." He glanced Clarke's way. "We'll make sure to let this animal know right from the start he's at the very bottom of the pack. If he doesn't stay house trained, there's a simple solution. We have him put down."

"If you remember," Clarke said. "The last time someone tried that things didn't work out too well."

"True," Procter said with a nod. "But we have one irrefutable advantage over our predecessors. With this," Proctor tapped Tesseract's new file, "we own him."

EIGHTY-FIVE

Falls Church, Virginia, U.S.A.
Saturday, three weeks later
22:49 EST

Curtains rippled. The breeze from the open window was light and cooling. William Ferguson lay in his bed, hair damp from the shower, a Scotch and water sitting on the bedside table, a copy of his favorite daily open across his lap. If he hadn't had the chance to read it fully during the day, he made a point of finishing it before going to sleep.

His house was quiet. It had been a long time since anyone else had lived with him, and he preferred his own company. On rare occasions, though, he missed hearing the noise of others. The small green light caught his attention. It meant everything was okay. Ferguson's house was fitted with a state-of-the-art security system supplied and installed by the agency. The light would flash red if anything, person or otherwise, broke the perimeter. He'd never yet had to hit the panic button.

It seemed a very long time since Sykes had come back from Tanzania with his hat in his hands. A simple operation had turned into a huge mess, even Ferguson had to admit that, but it was over now. So he wouldn't get rich, not yet anyway. There was still enough time for one last scheme before he retired. He had managed to prevent his country from getting their fat undeserving hands on Oniks missiles at the very least. It wasn't much, but it was some small revenge for the way he had been ignored and unappreciated. Ferguson would let things settle down before he considered his next move.

Sykes, lucky SOB that he was, had somehow managed to avoid being murdered by Reed but thankfully had no idea he had ever been a target. Reed had dropped off the grid, and the only explanation for his disappearance was that he had been killed, incredible as that may be. Ferguson had no way of finding out more about events in Tanzania without raising suspicions.

Ferguson knew that he was in the clear, though. Alvarez was no longer hunting for clues, and Procter and Chambers had more pressing issues to deal with. So long as Ferguson kept his head down, he was safe.

Sykes still needed to be removed. The metrosexual wimp just didn't have the wits or the stomach for this kind of work, and he was now nothing more than a walking liability. He was the final link between the failed operation and Ferguson and couldn't be allowed to stay alive. Ferguson would have to find someone else to do the job now that Reed was dead. He would even do it himself if he had to. He would probably enjoy it.

The veteran CIA officer turned the page of his paper and took a sip from the whisky, savoring the taste in his mouth before swallowing. He put the glass back down and frowned, noticing that he was chilly. Blasted open window.

He tried to ignore it, but by the time he'd turned the next page he acted. Ferguson threw back the duvet and marched across his spacious bedroom and into the adjoining annex. Huffing in annoyance, he slammed the window shut, trying to remember when he had opened it in the first place. He prayed to the god he had never believed in that his mind wasn't going.

Back in bed, he finished off the Scotch and dropped his newspaper on the floor. He settled himself into his usual sleeping position and flicked off the lamp. He searched with his cheek for a smooth area of the pillow. Ferguson sighed, contented.

Cool metal pushed against his temple an instant later. He gasped.

A man spoke to him from the darkness. It was the last voice he ever heard.

"It's a pleasure to finally make your acquaintance."

Read on for an excerpt from
Tom Wood's next book

WAR OF LIES

Coming soon in hardcover from
Thomas Dunne Books

ONE

Bucharest, Romania
Wednesday
07:11 CET

It was a good morning to kill. Impenetrable gray clouds obscured the sun, and the city beneath was dark and quiet. Cold. Just how he liked it. He walked at a relaxed pace, in no hurry, knowing he was making perfect time. A fine rain began to fall. Yes, a particularly good morning to kill.

Ahead of him, a garbage truck made its slow way along the road, hazard light flashing orange, windscreen wipers swinging back and forth to flick away the morning drizzle. Garbage men followed the vehicle, hands buried under armpits while they waited to reach the next pile of trash bags on the sidewalk. They chatted and joked among themselves.

He interrupted the group's banter as he passed through the spiraling cloud of exhaust gases condensing in the spring air. He felt their gaze upon him, taking in his appearance for the few short seconds before he'd gone.

There was little for them to note. He was smartly dressed—a

long woolen coat over the top of a dark gray suit, black leather gloves, thick-soled Oxford shoes. In his left hand he carried a metal briefcase. His dark hair was short, his beard neatly trimmed. Despite the cold, only the bottom two of his four overcoat buttons had been fastened. Just a businessman on his way to the office, they would assume. He was a businessman of sorts, but he doubted they would guess the nature of his uncommon profession.

Behind him, a trash can clattered into the road, and he looked briefly over his shoulder to see black bags split open and refuse spilling across the asphalt. The garbage men groaned and rushed to gather up the trash before the wind could spread it too far.

After a short walk, the businessman arrived at a large apartment complex. It stood several stories taller than the surrounding buildings. Balconies and satellite dishes jutted out from the dull brown walls. He made sure not to appear rushed as he took the half dozen steps up to the front door. He unlocked it with his day-old key and stepped inside.

It was dark in the hallway. Only half of the strip lights in the ceiling worked. There were two elevators, but he ignored such things whenever he could and headed for the stairs. He climbed twenty-two flights to the top floor. He reached his destination with little trace of fatigue.

Close to the stairwell door, he heard an elevator open on the other side and the clatter of stiletto heels. He waited until the noise stopped, replaced by the jangling of keys. Hinges creaked. A moment of silence before a door banged shut.

The man with the briefcase continued. The corridor beyond the stairwell door was long and featureless. Spaced at regular intervals were numbered, spy-holed doors. Dirty linoleum lined the floor. The paint on the walls was faded and chipped.

The cool air smelled of strong detergent. Somewhere a baby cried softly. At the end of the corridor, where it intersected with another, was a door marked MAINTENANCE. He placed his briefcase down, and from a pocket, removed a small packet of butter taken from a nearby diner. He unfolded the wrapper and carefully smeared the butter onto the hinges of the door. He placed the empty wrapper back into the same pocket.

From inside his coat, he removed two small metal tools: a

tension wrench and a slim, curved pick. The lock was significantly better than most, but the businessman unlocked it in less than sixty seconds.

A door opened behind him. He slipped the lock picks back into the pocket.

Someone said something in gruff-sounding Romanian. The man with the briefcase spoke several languages, but not this one. He stayed facing the door for a moment in case the speaker was talking to someone inside the apartment. A slim chance, but one he had to play all the same.

The voice called again. The same guttural words, but louder. Impatient. His back still to the speaker, the businessman reached inside his coat. He withdrew his right hand and kept it out of sight by his side. He turned side-on to look at the resident, keeping his head tilted forward, eyes in the shadow of his brow.

A heavyset man with several days' worth of stubble was leaning out of his front door, fat fingers white on the frame. A cigarette hung from thick lips. He looked over the man with the briefcase and removed the cigarette from his mouth with a shaking hand. Ash fell from the end and onto the marked linoleum.

He swayed as spoke again, words slow and slurred. A drunk then. No threat.

The businessman ignored him, picked up his briefcase and moved down the adjoining corridor, walking away from the drunk before he made any more noise. When a door clicked shut behind him, he stopped and walked silently back, peered around the corner, saw no one, and placed the suppressed 9mm Beretta 92F handgun back inside his overcoat. He reset the safety with his thumb.

Total darkness enshrouded the room on the other side of the maintenance door. Water dripped somewhere unseen. The businessman flicked on a slim torch. The narrow beam illuminated the room—bare brick walls, pipe work, boxes, a metal staircase along one side. He negotiated his way across the space and ascended the staircase. His shoes were quiet on the metal steps. At the top, a padlock secured the rust-streaked roof access door. The lock was marginally harder to pick than the previous one.

Eleven stories up the icy wind stung his face and every inch of exposed flesh. It subsided within a few seconds as the pressure equalized between the stairwell and roof. He crouched to reduce his profile against the sky and moved across the roof to the west edge. The wind was pushing the clouds northward, allowing the glow of the rising sun to spread across the city. Bucharest extended out before him, slowly awakening. Present location aside, a particularly beautiful city. This was his first visit, and he hoped his work would bring him back before too long.

He turned his attention to his briefcase, unlocked it, and opened it flat. Inside, a sheet of thick foam rubber surrounded the disassembled Heckler & Koch MSG-9. He removed the barrel first and attached it to the body of the rifle. Next, he fixed the Hendsoldt scope in place, followed by the stock and finally the twenty-round box magazine. He folded down the bipod and rested the weapon on the roof's low parapet.

Through the scope he saw a 10x magnification of the city—buildings, cars, people. For fun, he positioned the crosshairs over a young woman's head and tracked her as she sipped her morning coffee, anticipating her movements to keep the reticle in place. She passed beneath the branches of a tree, and he lost sight of her. Lucky girl, he thought with a rare smile. He took his eye from the sight, repositioned the rifle, and looked through the scope once more.

This time he saw the entrance to the Grand Plaza hotel on Dorobantilor Avenue. The eighteen-story building had a modern façade, all glass and stainless steel, appearing both strong and sleek at the same time. The businessman had stayed in several hotels of the Howard Johnson chain while plying his trade around the globe, but not this particular one. If the Grand Plaza met the reasonable-to-high standards of the rest of the franchise, he imagined the target would have enjoyed a pleasant stay. He thought it only fitting that the condemned man should get a good night's sleep before his morning execution.

The man with the rifle took a laser range finder from his briefcase and aimed the beam at the hotel entrance, finding it exactly six hundred and four yards away in central Bucharest. Well within acceptable range, and only six yards under his estimate. He rotated the elevation wheel to correct for the distance and elevation.

Outside the hotel entrance, a craggy-faced doorman revealed his bad teeth by yawning. Close to him, tied to a nearby streetlight, a purple ribbon fluttered in the breeze. The man with the rifle watched it for a moment, calculating the wind speed. Five, maybe five and a quarter miles per hour. He adjusted the Hensoldt's windage wheel, wondering how long it would be before someone realized the significance of the seemingly innocuous ribbon. Maybe no one ever would.

He adjusted the scope's power ring, decreasing the magnification to see a wider view of the hotel. There were few other people nearby. Some pedestrians, the occasional guest, but no mass of people. This was good. His marksmanship was excellent, but with just seconds to make the kill, he required a clear line of sight. He had no compunction against shooting whoever was unfortunate enough to stand between the bullet and its true mark, but such killings tended to give targets advance warning of their own impending demise, and as long as the target wasn't mentally deficient, they moved.

The man with the rifle checked his watch. Today's unfortunate subject was due to appear shortly, if the itinerary included with the dossier was accurate. The businessman had no reason to doubt his client-supplied information, even if this was his first assignment for his new employer.

Another adjustment of the scope and he saw the entire width of the hotel's front side and two-thirds of the way up its single tower. Light from the rising sun reflected off the windows of the top three floors within the scope's view.

The rain had ceased by the time a limousine pulled onto the hotel's drive from the adjoining road and stopped outside the main entrance. A large white guy dressed in a beige jacket and dark jeans climbed out and ascended the steps with the brisk efficiency of a bodyguard. His head swept back and forth, fast but efficient, gaze registering every nearby person, assessing for threats and finding none.

The man with the rifle felt his heart rate begin to speed up as the time grew rapidly closer. He breathed deeply to stop it climbing too high and negatively affecting his aim. He waited.

After a minute, the bodyguard reappeared and took up position midway down the steps. He looked around before gesturing back up at the entrance. In a few seconds the target would come into view. According to the dossier, the target—a Ukrainian—typically traveled with several bodyguards who would naturally have stayed at the same hotel. The bodyguards were all ex-military or ex-intelligence, who would no doubt surround the Ukrainian and make an otherwise completely clear shot difficult.

The man with the rifle had selected the MSG-9 as it was semi-automatic and would allow him to fire several times inside of just a few seconds. The 7.62×52mm full metal-jacketed rounds carried enough power to pass through a human body and still kill someone standing behind, and these particular bullets incorporated a tungsten penetrator to account for the body armor the target and his guards would likely wear. A wall of flesh two-armored-men thick could shield the Ukrainian and he would still die.

Before the businessman could zoom in closer to prepare for the shot, a tiny flicker of light from a window of the hotel's thirteenth floor caught his attention. He quickly raised the barrel of the MSG-9, angling up the scope to check out the light source. He feared a guest was better enjoying the view of the city through a telescope or pair of binoculars. From an elevated position they might inadvertently spot him, and if so, he would have to forget about the contract and make a quick escape. No point completing the kill if the police apprehended him afterwards.

Once the reticule centered over the window he increased the magnification of the scope, and saw the source of the flicker was not the reflection of sunlight on the lenses of binoculars or a telescope, but a rifle scope like his own.

A suppressed muzzle flash transformed the businessman's surprise to alarm for the two-thirds of a second it took for the bullet to reach his head.

Pink mist swirled in the air.

07:36 CET

Victor watched the body fall out of sight and took his eye away from the scope as the crack of the shot slowly faded into nothingness. The rifle's long sound suppressor had negated the muzzle report, but could do nothing to stop the sonic boom emitted when the bullet broke the sound barrier. A person with the right ear would know there had been a shot fired, but without the accompanying muzzle blast and flash, however, its point of origin would be all but impossible to decipher. Subsonic ammunition would have almost eliminated sound altogether, but it was windy in Bucharest, and at a distance of six hundred yards, Victor didn't trust the slower round's accuracy.

The hotel room window hadn't opened far enough for his purposes so Victor had unscrewed the pane. As a result it was cold inside the room, but the flow of air would help disperse the tang of cordite. Shooting with the rifle barrel outside of the window would have helped with the smell, but it would also have helped give him away. Only amateurs operated like that.

Quickly, but not hurrying, Victor unscrewed the suppressor from the rifle's barrel and disassembled the weapon. He placed the individual parts back inside the foam rubber insert of a leather briefcase. The process took less than twenty seconds. Using a handkerchief, he retrieved the hot brass shell case from the floor and placed it in a pocket. He then moved the armchair he'd been sitting on away from the window and back to its original corner. With his foot, he rubbed the depressions from the carpet where the chair legs had rested near the window.

He screwed the windowpane back in place and used a small piece of sandpaper to smooth the heads of the screws. He surveyed the room for signs of his presence. It was contemporary, neat and very clean. Neutral colors. Lots of stainless steel and lightwood. No personality in the décor but no offense either. He saw nothing to be concerned over. He hadn't used the bed or the bathroom, or so much as turned a faucet. Hard as it had been to resist the pull of three-hundred-thread-count sheets, the room was a strike point—nothing more—and tasting its comforts wasn't worth the implicit risk. Sleeping in the same place where he fulfilled a contract was simply not how Victor conducted business.

Happy he'd left no physical evidence to tie him to the room, Victor placed the briefcase inside a larger suitcase, closed it, and exited the hotel room. His pulse was two beats per minute above his resting heart rate. He didn't have to worry about fingerprints as a clear silicone solution covered his hands to prevent oil from his skin leaving prints on anything he touched.

He walked to the stairwell to avoid the security camera near the elevator and descended to the first floor. He passed through the lobby, ignoring the commotion, with his head angled slightly downward so the cameras there would only see his forehead and hair.

Near to the hotel entrance, a tall, wide-shouldered man in jeans and a beige suede jacket was speaking frantically to a similarly sized, but older man. Both looked Eastern European, Slavic—Russians or Ukrainians maybe. The older man looked to be in his late forties, clothed in a fine black pinstripe suit that was perfectly cut across his large, muscular frame. He had short-cropped black hair that was gray at the temples, and a clean-shaven face. He stood left side on to Victor and the jagged line of scar tissue forming the bottom of the ear was clearly visible. There was no earlobe.

Four other men surrounded the two Slavs. All were pale-skinned Eastern Europeans, all in dark suits, all muscular but not overly so, all with the bearing of ex-military high-end bodyguards. They formed a tactical screen around the man in the suede jacket and the older man in the pinstripe suit, each looking in a different direction—overlapping fields of views, alert, good, primary hands hovering near their waists, ready to earn their paychecks.

As Victor approached the desk, he heard the large man in the suede jacket explaining in Russian why the man in the pinstripe—the VIP—needed to wait inside. Victor pretended not to understand the topic of conversation as he reached the front desk and stood at an angle so the nearest camera only caught the back of his skull.

The receptionist behind the desk looked flustered, staring at the group of Slavs, and didn't notice Victor's presence until he held a hand across the guy's field of view.

"Sorry, sir," he said in Bulgarian-accented English, "how can I help you?"

"I'd like to check out early, please."

Victor gave his details, handed back his keycard, and waited while the receptionist completed whatever receptionists had to do, all the while listening to every word of the conversation between the head bodyguard and his VIP.

As he checked the bill and went to sign the paperwork, heavy footsteps approached from behind. Normally, Victor never allowed anyone to walk up behind him, but with the security camera limiting his movements, and in the process of signing out, he couldn't reposition himself without drawing attention to what he was doing. And the bodyguards looked observant enough not to let such telling movements go unnoticed.

So Victor stood still as he finished putting his alias's signature on the bottom of the form, and received a predicted shove to the shoulder from the bodyguard as he arrived at the desk to bark orders at the receptionist. Victor didn't dodge and he didn't resist the shove—again to preserve his cover as a forgettable guest—but the bodyguard had to weigh two hundred and thirty useful pounds and Victor stumbled. He recovered his footing easier than a surprised businessman might have, but only to stop himself crashing to the floor.

Before he could make an expected angry—but not too angry—comment, he heard the man in the pinstripe suit shout a very angry, *"Nikolai."*

The guy in the suede jacket turned from the front desk to look at his boss. Victor looked, too.

The forty-something VIP stormed towards his head bodyguard, the other four guards rushing to maintain a full screen around him, five paces out, no corner of the lobby not covered by at least one set of eyes.

"Nikolai, you disrespectful brute," the man in the pinstripe said as he neared, "apologize to this man immediately."

He gestured to Victor, and Victor recognized the Ukrainian accent.

The bodyguard called Nikolai looked at Victor and said, in inflectionless English, "Sorry."

"It's fine," Victor said back.

The Ukrainian in the pinstripe suit turned to him. "Forgive me, please. My friend here has yet to be civilized. Are you hurt?"

"I'm fine."

He took a step away, eager to end the interaction with the man whose life he had saved. Each second here increased his risk of exposure exponentially. The Ukrainian looked at Victor with an intensity Victor rarely experienced, a familiarity despite the fact Victor had never seen him before. He wasn't sure why, but it made him uncomfortable. He was forced to make a conscious effort not to let his unease show.

"Oh, no," the Ukrainian said as his gaze dropped, "your suit."

Victor looked, too, seeing the small tear in his right jacket sleeve. It must have caught on the corner of the front desk as he stumbled.

"It's all right," Victor said. "It can be fixed."

"No, it's ruined." The Ukrainian turned to Nikolai, and said in Russian, "You stupid fuck, look what you've done." He faced Victor again. "I'm so sorry. And that's such a nice suit, too. I can see you are a man who cares about how he dresses, as I do. I would give you money for a replacement, only I don't carry any quantity of cash, and who has a checkbook these days?"

"There's no need, really," Victor said, thinking it would have drawn less attention to himself if he had backflipped out of Nikolai's way.

"There's every need." The Ukrainian reached into his inside jacket pocket and produced a business card. He handed it to Victor. "I'm afraid I'm in the middle of a crisis at the moment, otherwise I would take you for a new suit, but here's my card. Call me and we can work something out. If you are ever in Moscow, I will have my tailor make you a suit so fine it will make you weep."

Victor took the card. In both Cyrillic script and English, it said: VLADIMIR KASAKOV. There was a phone number and a Moscow office address.

"That's very kind of you, Mr. Kasakov," Victor replied.

"Now, before my employees can do any more damage, you must excuse me."

Victor nodded and headed to the front entrance. He didn't turn around, but he felt eyes watching him the whole time.

Outside it was cold and the doorman looked far too frail to be still doing the job at his age, especially in this weather.

"Taxi, sir?" he said to Victor.

"Yes, thank you."

The doorman raised a thin arm to signal to the passing traffic.

Victor's gaze drifted to the eleven-story building whose ugliness was all too apparent even at over six hundred yards. The assassin had been right to shoot from there. Other buildings were closer, but not as well positioned to see an uninterrupted view of the hotel entrance. Victor would have used it himself, had their roles been reversed. He would have been more careful not to die there, however.

Victor saw his reflection in the hotel's glass doors and noted that he didn't look too dissimilar to the man he'd shot. He wore a charcoal-gray suit with a white shirt and sky-blue tie underneath his black overcoat. Perfect urban camouflage.

His dark hair was short and not styled, his beard trimmed short. He looked like a stockbroker or lawyer, one that kept a smart but unremarkable appearance. He blended into the background, seldom seen, rarely noticed. Unremembered.

In the taxi, he unwrapped a stick of peppermint chewing gum and folded it into his mouth. He'd read that gum made a good substitute for cigarettes but no matter how much he chewed, he wasn't able to inhale any smoke from the stuff.

He had the driver take him to Gara de Nord train station where he purchased a ticket to Constanta and boarded the train seven minutes before it was set to depart. He left his seat six minutes later and walked down two carriages before disembarking five seconds before the doors closed and locked. He left the station by a different exit, climbed into another taxi and told the driver to take him to Herăstrău Park where he walked leisurely through the park before exiting and entering the Charles de Gaulle Plaza. He took a seat in the lobby and read a complimentary magazine while he watched the main entrance.

With no one registering on his threat radar after five minutes, he stood and descended the stairs to the lowest level of the underground parking garage. One of the high-speed elevators then carried him to the top floor. He went back down in a different elevator to the fourth floor and used the stairs to return to the lobby. He left the building by a side entrance.

He walked to the closest subway station and stayed on for thirty minutes, switching trains and doubling back on himself before changing routes and leaving at the University of Bucharest station. After a pleasant walk through the campus, a taxi took him to Elisabeta Boulevard near to Bucharest City Hall and from there he walked the short distance to the entrance of the Cişmigiu Gardens.

The park was quiet and peaceful. He passed few people as he made his way to the circular alley of the Rondul Român where he spent some time looking at its twelve stone busts of famous Romanian writers while he finished his counter-surveillance. His precautions were as essential a part of fulfilling a job as squeezing the trigger. The successful execution of a contract depended on remaining unnoticed and untraced. Nearly anyone could kill another person, but few people could get away with it once, let alone time after time.

For years, Victor had plied his trade with complete anonymity. Working freelance, he'd killed quickly, efficiently, silently. Those who employed him had no idea who he was. No one did. He had lived in near isolation—no friends, no family—no one who could betray him and no one to be used against him. It hadn't lasted, and in hindsight, it was inevitable. He of all people should have known nobody could remain unfound forever.

When Victor was content no one was observing, he left the Rondul Român and walked to the center of the park where a manmade lake was located. He paused on an ornate footbridge, removed the briefcase from within the suitcase, looked around to make sure he was alone, and discreetly dropped the briefcase into the lake. The rifle weighed just less than fifteen pounds and sank straight to the bottom.

Victor left the park via the southeastern exit and caught a bus. He took a seat on the top level, at the back, disembarking after half a dozen stops when he was sitting alone with no other travelers nearby. The suitcase remained on the floor by his seat.

He thought about the man whose life he had saved. When he had received the contract, he'd had no information about the assassin's target, only that he had to survive. Had the incident in the hotel lobby not taken place, Victor would have thought little else about him. But now Victor knew his name, and it was a name he had heard before. Few people in Victor's profession would not have known it. Vladimir Kasakov was one of the biggest arms dealers on the planet, if not the biggest. He was an international fugitive. Normally, Victor cared little about the motives behind his jobs, but he couldn't help but wonder why his CIA employer would be so keen on saving the life of such a man.

It started to rain again and Victor increased his pace to match those of commuters around him. No one paid him any attention. On the surface, he knew he was just like them— flesh and blood, skin and bone—but he also knew that was where the similarities ended.

You know what makes you special? someone had once told him. *People like you, like me, we take that thing inside us others don't have and we make it work for us, or we stand by and let it destroy us.*

And he'd spent his life doing just that, making it work for him. But his carefully maintained existence had fallen apart six months before and in the following maelstrom he'd fantasized about retiring, about trying to make a normal life for himself. That had been then. Now, even if Victor wanted to, there was no chance he could walk away from what he did for a living.

He knew his new employer would retire him permanently if he tried.